VAMPIRES AND VIXENS

LOVE BITES BOOKS 1 AND 2

LAUREN SMITH

THE BITE OF WINTER

LOVE BITES - BOOK 1

THE BITE OF WINTER

CHAPTER 1

So hungry. God, I'd kill to eat.

Zoey Blake gazed longingly through the diner window. Families were nestled in red leather booths, plates of burgers and fries spread out like a feast. The light from the diner beckoned to her, promising warmth and comfort. It was everything she wanted, and everything she couldn't have.

The harsh December wind cut through her thin flannel shirt and whipped her hair hard enough to sting her face. Hunger swelled up inside her like an empty balloon. A moan escaped her lips as she tried and failed to ignore the pain.

A little boy in one of the booths reached with chubby hands to grab his mother's milkshake. He sucked for a long moment on the straw before pulling back, a grin of delight on his face. Zoey could imagine the thick creamy ice cream and the sweet tangy taste of a maraschino cherry.

One of the cooks left the grill and walked toward the entrance, wiping his hands on his greasy apron. When the door swung open, Christmas music exploded into the street. The happy sounds reminded Zoey that Christmas was only a few weeks away. She used to love Christmas: the songs, the presents, the food...her family. She shuddered and buried the painful memories deep inside her.

The cook glanced down the empty street outside the diner and caught sight of her.

"You coming in?" His gruff voice momentarily distracted her from the greasy smell of food.

Zoey gulped and took an instinctive step back, her hands clutching the only real possession she had left in the world. A black leather portfolio. She'd tucked it safely against her chest, the leather barely holding warmth to her body.

"Sorry, I...I can't..." She couldn't say the words. *Can't afford it.*

Even after a year of living on the streets, shame still heated her cheeks. This time, she welcomed it. She was cold all the time, even in the summer. Her jacket had been stolen the winter before, leaving her painfully exposed.

The cook's eyes hardened.

"Then get going. You're scaring off paying customers."

Of course she had to leave. Heaven forbid he toss her some of the burnt burgers or even some moldy buns.

She'd have gladly taken them. Far worse food had ended up in her stomach when she'd been desperate.

With a shaky nod, Zoey backed away from the diner and eased into the shadows where the restaurant's light couldn't penetrate. She just wanted to disappear. No one would miss her. No one would care. Everyone she had a connection with was gone. And it was all her fault.

Unshed tears formed at the corners of her eyes, and a shiver from the cold rattled her spine so hard it hurt. Self-pity was not something she could indulge in. But it was hard to ignore her circumstances when she'd spent the last month calling a ragged sleeping bag under a highway overpass home. Food was harder to come by than a decent place to sleep. The homeless shelter was half a mile away and always filled up so fast they had to turn away most of the people who showed up. They served only two meals a day with small portions since their food bank supplies remained low.

Her stomach rumbled a protest. She had to stop thinking about food.

"Damn it." She put her fist in her mouth, stumbling back into the alleyway next to the diner. The ache inside bent her over, and she wrapped her arms around her waist, hugging herself as she prayed the pain would begin to dull. Finally, it abated, briefly, and she leaned back against the brick wall of the alley, breathing slowly.

A soft scuffling was her only warning.

Zoey's eyes flew open. A man in rags and a heavy

overcoat lurched toward her. A knife glinted in one hand, the blade flashing when it caught the glow from the diner.

"Hands up!" The man's rotten teeth barely showed behind his thick brown beard.

Terror seized Zoey, squeezing her lungs until she couldn't breathe. Her hands shot into the air.

"Wha...what do you want?"

"Your purse. Hand it over!" he rasped, taking one step closer.

Fear hammered against her ribs until she felt nausea and bile push their way up her throat. "I—I don't have one." She still clutched her portfolio in one hand, her fingers stinging in the cold air.

"Give me your fucking money!" His black eyes gleamed in the dim light. He could have been any of the men she'd seen at the shelter earlier today, only they were sad and broken. This man was something else. Something evil lurked in his gaze and mirrored the spark of his blade inches from her face.

"I don't have any. I have nothing...I'm sorry." Her hands shook as she took a tiny step to the side, inching away from him. Her stomach, once so desperate for food, now clenched as she struggled to control her terror.

"Don't *lie* to me! Give me what you're holding!" Flecks of spittle shot from his chapped lips as he lunged for her portfolio.

"No!" She stepped back, dropping her hands to use the portfolio as a shield.

The man held his blade with one hand and snatched at the black leather book with the other. With a cry of panic, Zoey lost her grip and the portfolio fell to the ground. Pages and photographs scattered across the snow.

"You stupid bitch!" The man snarled and dived at her.

Zoey tried to shut her eyes, but instinct kept her lids wide open. Everything slowed down. The knife slipped between her ribs inch by painful inch. He pulled the blade back out, the cold metal sharp against her flesh as he thrust it in again. Her strangled scream was drowned out by a passing bus.

Her soul seemed to coil up tight before shooting out like a firecracker, leaving her body behind. All the work, the pain, the loss of the last two years was over. Every second she'd cried, every second she'd picked herself back up, none of it mattered anymore. Her attacker pulled the blade back out and cursed before he fled into the street.

Zoey crumpled to the ground, one hand over her side. All around her the pieces of her life, the bits she'd held on to were soaking into the soil along with her blood. Hot liquid oozed through her fingers, warming them. Pain lanced through her chest with every breath. The world spun as she slid onto her back. The night sky above was lit with a smattering of faint stars, like a handful of diamonds strewn over black velvet. Her eyes burned with tears. Blood continued to pump between her loosening fingertips as she grew too weak to keep any pressure on her wounds. A tear welled up, thick and heavy, and eased down the side of her face. The trail of moisture chilled beneath the passing breeze.

Ice dug into her shoulder blades, cold and unforgiving. Invisible rocks dropped onto her chest, and a rattling noise escaped her as she fought to breathe. Her toes were numb and her arms too heavy to move. Muted laughter from people passing on the street seemed so far away. Would they see her? Did they hear her scream? Would they save her? The chill stealing over her warned her it was too late.

Too late for everything she'd never had a chance to do. A life unlived, a heart unloved, a soul alone.

Suddenly, the world around her darkened as a shape blotted out the winking stars. Glowing eyes, the color a wintery green, met her own. They pulled at her with the power of a sorcerer's spell. The sound of her favorite winter song, the "Carol of the Bells", began to echo in the air around them.

"Damn." His voice was rich and dark, a luscious baritone that made even her dying body tingle with lethargic awareness. He held one of her sketches, the white paper looked so sharp against the black sky. His eyes moved from her to the paper, some strange emotion she couldn't read flashing in his gaze.

The man looking down at her had the face of an angel,

all angles and lines. His strong jaw, proud nose and bewitching eyes were framed with a halo of black hair from his head as he bent over more to look at her. The epitome of beauty. So handsome that she shivered. She truly was dying, and an angel had come for her soul.

He knelt down next to her. "I can save you. I only need you to trust me. Can you trust me?"

She tried to speak, and although her lips moved, no sound came out. Finally, she managed a jerky nod. Something deep inside her responded to his eyes. They emanated with warmth and the promise of safety shone from their depths. She trusted him.

Her angel did something unexpected. He raised his wrist to his mouth, bit into it and then put it against her mouth. She tasted blood and jerked away from his bleeding skin. A heavy scowl pulled his dark brows down.

"Poor sweetheart, just drink." The Irish lilt to his voice made her feel warm, despite the pain and the chill that threatened to consume her. Something about him, being so close...everything inside her seemed to stir to life in a way she hadn't realized she could.

A hand cupped the back of her head and held her captive while his wrist pressed deeper between her parted lips. Zoey gasped as the blood poured into her mouth and she was forced to swallow. The hand behind her head lightly massaged her scalp, the sensation wonderful and soothing. She relaxed into his gentle touch.

The tang of blood still coated the insides of her mouth when he pulled his wrist away.

"Easy, love, easy. You'll be okay now. I won't let any harm come to you." He cupped her face with his hands, his eyes fixed on hers, capturing her attention. "You will have no memory of tasting my blood. Only that you are safe, you are protected."

"Safe," she whispered. She had no memory to explain the oddly metallic taste in her mouth.

The man stroked her cheeks and nodded to himself before speaking again. "Would you let me take you home and care for you?" His earnest expression was so sharp that Zoey believed it. He wanted to help her.

"Y—yes." It was the only word she got out before she lost control of her body. Her lashes started to fan up and down and then fresh pain hit her like a freight train. She was barely aware of the man picking her up in his arms.

The sky above whirled, and the lights from the stars formed silver circles, like a cosmic Spirograph. She clamped her eyes shut as the man who held her leapt forward. The wind rushed around them, and her long hair whipped around her face but Zoey was lost in the aches surging through her body in tidal waves.

A second, an hour, a month, she wasn't sure when they stopped until she felt them grind to a halt. The pain faded, leaving her sore and bruised. She surrendered to exhaustion, hearing the man speak one last time as she let go.

"I want to keep you, little one. Keep you and never let you go."

Ian Kennedy stared down at the little woman in his arms as he reached his home. She was so light and he knew she should weigh more than she did. A wee waif of a body in ragged clothes. Pity stirred in his chest like a feeble bird with injured wings.

The night was quiet in the small neighborhood where he lived. No one was watching as he slipped the key into the lock of his home and entered. A gray tabby cat lounged on the couch, watching him with silver eyes.

"Lizzy," he greeted softly. The cat let out a soft purr, her tail twitching. She was one of three strays he'd rescued in recent years, much to the frustration of his friend Connor O'Shea.

Carrying the unconscious woman into his bedroom, he eased her down onto the comforter and placed a pillow beneath her head. He grit his teeth when he leaned too close to her and the irresistible scent of blood filled his senses.

But there was more than that. Even dirty and unwashed, the scent of living on the streets didn't repel his senses as they usually did when he crossed paths with the homeless while he searched for hosts to feed from at night. A tingling ache filled his mouth, and with a low curse, he tried to stop the inevitable from happening. But he failed. Twin canine teeth extended down, ready to sink into the flesh of his prey. The flesh of the woman he'd just rescued.

Ian took a reluctant step back. Space, he needed some space or else he might give into his temptation to feed on her. She'd be out for a few hours still. He'd used his innate ability to affect her body's responses to him and gently put her to sleep. It was one of the few benefits of being a vampire.

Vampire. The word still made him cringe, but there was no point in denying what he was. He'd been alive for a hundred and ninety-five years and the older he got, the stronger his abilities seemed to become. Not only could he sway the will of most humans, he also possessed a potent ability to draw his prey to him.

This seemed to be common to all his kind. The glamour, as he liked to call it, was something every vampire possessed to some degree. Something like a pheromone, it drew human prey to them, made their victims susceptible to suggestion, to desire. And with him, it created a false sense of adoration in women. Ian rarely left the house until much later in the night to avoid being around crowds. The glamour often resulted in chaos and strange behavior.

The hollow pit in his stomach reminded him he'd been on the hunt when he'd encountered the young woman being attacked. Feeding was a priority if he was to be around her without succumbing to temptation.

It was obvious she was malnourished and needed care. And more than anything, he wanted to care for her. Too many years had passed since he'd looked upon mortals as something other than...

Shutting his eyes a brief moment, he saw flashing dark eyes, heard a woman's laugh. He'd known great love for a mortal once. Lara. His body had never felt so... human since he'd been turned. But when she'd been taken from him, he'd lost that sense of life and turned back into the predator he was.

Which is why it was so puzzling that in only an instant of seeing that woman attacked tonight, he'd needed to protect her. It was as though in her moments of terror and her dying breaths, she'd called to him—much as Lara had when he'd first met her.

With a regretful sigh at leaving the woman alone, Ian headed back outside, taking only one normal step before his body leapt into motion. The high speed of his travel, yet another one of his abilities, moved almost too fast for human sight to track. Within a minute he was in an alleyway across town, outside the diner where the woman had been wounded. The alley was empty but littered with papers. The papers from a leather portfolio lay inches from a pool of blood.

Ian knelt and began to gather the papers. Each was either a sketch or a photograph, each was captivating. He stood as he collected the binder and the last sketch. It was one of an old man, his face wrinkled, his hands gnarled as old oak tree roots clutching at a blanket as he sat on a park bench. Sadness, regret, loss of memory, all of these were locked deep into the old man's eyes. Whoever had drawn this had captured that, emotions Ian had felt every day since he'd been turned into a monster.

Something inside his chest stung and he gasped. That was odd. He'd never needed to breath before, still didn't, but his body had reacted as though it had. And the little prick of pain in his chest felt familiar, but he couldn't be sure what it was. He thumbed through the other sketches and photographs before he tucked them safely into the black binder.

"We never intervene except to feed," Connor's voice from years ago came back to him. *"The mortals must live out their lives and we cannot intercede."*

But Ian had done just that. Saved the woman from certain death. Why? He'd been moved before in the many years he'd existed like this, but there was something about her, the way she'd protected these pieces of paper as though they were her very life. The way she saw things, the details she evoked, had been a shock to his system. Jerking him out of the seemingly endless night and forcing him beneath a sun, one that didn't burn. There was only warmth here, a craving for something he lost over a hundred years ago.

A woman that made him feel like that? After so long?

That was a woman he had to save, even if only to understand why she affected him like this.

"Connor will bloody kill me when he finds out," Ian muttered to himself. He glanced around. A skinny blonde-haired waitress suddenly exited the diner's backdoor in the alley to throw a large black trash bag into the dumpster. She stilled when she saw him, her eyes first widening, then slowly turning almost slumberous.

The damnable glamour was already at work. He might as well feed while the opportunity presented itself.

"Hello," she said, wiping her hands on her apron and taking a few steps toward him.

Ian tucked the portfolio into his coat and zipped it up to keep the book in place before he started toward the woman.

"Hey there, lassie," he chuckled, hiding the hint of his fangs as they slid out. A wee bite was all he needed.

THE RIVER RAN BLACK, like water over obsidian, rushing away endlessly. Connor O'Shea leaned against the bridge railing watching the water. His fingertips clung to the stone, digging in hard enough that it would have ripped his skin apart if he'd been mortal. But he wasn't mortal, hadn't been for almost two centuries. Hunger beat at his insides, hunger for blood. It never ended, the urge to track and feed, to prey on humans, a constant reminder of what he no longer was.

Inside the pocket of his coat, his cell phone buzzed. He let out a low growl. It was probably Ian. The man never seemed to know when to leave him alone. Once, long ago, they'd been inseparable, as close as brothers. But they hadn't been that way for many years. Something was missing. He knew it. Ever since they'd lost their beloved Lara more than eighty years ago, he'd felt his body, his cursed soul, reverting to its monster state. He was on that slippery slope toward darker urges and he dreaded to contemplate what would happen to him, or worse what he'd do, once he stopped caring about life entirely. The words of Nietzsche regarding staring into the abyss came to mind.

If only I could jump, let the water consume me and swallow me in its depths.

But it wouldn't end things; he'd only wash up on shore somewhere and be that much hungrier.

He shook his head, trying to rid himself of the dark thoughts. In the distance, the city lights twinkled, heightened by a hint of merriness he sensed even from the many miles he was from home. Christmas time. A season he used to love. Now it filled him only with regret, with sorrow and longing...so much longing for a life he'd been robbed of. Being immortal was a curse. Time was frozen, like an old broken clock on a mantelpiece. The tiny metal arms never moved, never let time pass another second forward, and always reminded you that you did not work as you should. You did not belong.

I only want to move forward. So simple a wish, yet he knew it would not be a Christmas wish he'd ever be granted.

Santa doesn't visit vampires. He chuckled, but it was a far from merry sound. *If I saw Santa Claus, I'd likely take a bite out of the jolly old man.*

His phone vibrated again and he pulled it out. Voice-mail. He hated cell phones. The damn things were such a nuisance. All the chiming, the alerts, the notifications. He hit play and put it to his ear. The message was from Ian, garbled and cut out, but the main part of the message was clear. Ian had brought home a woman for Connor to feed on, but for some reason, Ian said the woman liked to be frightened as part of the excitement. Role-play. Bah. It didn't sit well with Connor, but if the woman needed it to enjoy being fed on, well, he'd oblige her.

He stepped away from the bridge and turned his attention toward the city. Time to feed.

CHAPTER 2

Zoey was warm. So warm. When was the last time she hadn't woken up to her own shivers? Weariness bled out of her, leaving only a pleasant sense of quiet, and she wondered if she was dead. There wasn't any other way to explain the sudden change in her physical surroundings. She wasn't in a hospital.

Forcing her eyelids open, it took her some time to adjust. She was lying on a massive, and incredibly soft, feather bed with a thick blanket wrapped warm and snug around her body. Like a human burrito. The thought made her giggle. She had to be dead. This had to be heaven. The last thing she remembered was the bright lights of the diner. Christmas bells ringing. The flash of a knife. Snarled words. Pain. Her heart pounded at an unsteady rhythm, and her breath quickened.

Breath? How was she breathing? And then it all came back. The man with the face of an angel and the voice of a sinner, the one who could tempt her to sell her soul for just one caress. Had he saved her? How?

Zoey's hands started to shake as she remembered blood oozing from the wounds in her chest. Fearful, she tugged the blanket down and lifted her blood-stained shirt up. The skin was clear except for two small pink slashes between her ribs. Zoey pressed her fingertips down on the marks, testing them. They were sore, but they felt like an old injury, not something that would have killed her the night before.

Suddenly remembering she was in a strange place, she looked about the room, half hoping to find the man who'd brought her here. The bed was huge, its frame a dark wood, almost black. Despite the dimness, she could see the walls had lovely black and white photos of Paris and a few other places she thought she recognized. The crisp contrast of the photos was stunning and made her strangely homesick.

Before her life had fallen apart, she'd been studying photography. It had been her dream to live her life behind the lens, capturing moments for people. Weddings, baby showers, children's sporting matches. She wanted to capture life in vibrant colors and a contrast of grays. Nothing would have made her happier than to take photos of the events that marked the milestones in people's lives.

But that was gone, all gone. Her camera was likely still in some pawnshop collecting dust. Food and rent had been a priority, not her future. How long ago had that been? Zoey didn't want to count, but it had to be somewhere around eight months.

She sat up, pushing her hair out of her eyes, and the memories out of her head. Had the handsome guy with the Irish accent brought her here? His whispered words came back to her, the promise to keep her safe and take care of her. She vaguely recalled him asking if he could bring her home, and she'd agreed. She didn't think of herself as a weak person, but after everything she'd been through it was such a relief to think she might have help for the first time in forever.

She did feel safe. Wherever he'd taken her, she knew he wouldn't let harm come to her. It was stupid to trust a stranger, but her gut had told her to, and she'd never ignored her instincts before.

The man who'd helped her had held her tenderly, gently, as though he'd treasured her. Maybe he was like a Good Samaritan, a handsome man who stopped to save a complete stranger. If not that, he surely pitied her, enough to show her some compassion.

She didn't want anyone's pity, but it was better than apathy. She wanted to believe there were still good people out there. After everything that had happened in the last year, she was afraid to hope. But it was almost Christmas. The holidays brought the best out in people. Usually.

If only she could stay in this bed forever, wrapped in the blanket with the peaceful quiet all around her. Too many nights at the underpass had left her nervous and tense while she caught a few hours of sleep. Zoey glanced around the room, checking for a clock, but there wasn't one. The sky was gray through the blinds of the large window next to the bed. It could be evening or early morning, she couldn't tell.

Beside her on the bed lay her black portfolio. She snatched it up, wincing when her sore muscles complained. The sketches and photos were all out of order, but neatly placed back inside. She barely remembered dropping it when the man had attacked her. Her rescuer must have gone back and collected all of the pages. More than a few were dried and wrinkled in places where snow had seeped through. Hugging the portfolio to her chest a moment longer, she set it back down on the bed.

She jumped when someone knocked at the bedroom door.

"Excuse me, love. May I come in?" That beautiful, whisky rough voice. Definitely Irish.

"Uh...yes."

Her hands curled into the blanket and she raised it up to her chin. She felt oddly exposed as the man eased the door open and slid inside. Zoey craned her neck to look up at him. He had to be at least six-three, with black hair long enough to touch the collar of his shirt and a thin layer of stubble. He looked like a pirate off the cover of a romance novel. His white shirtsleeves were rolled up to reveal muscled forearms, and the two top buttons were undone below his throat. She was struck by how large he was. His shoulders alone were massive. She had the sudden urge to touch them, feel the strength of the muscles beneath her palm. Her mouth ran dry as a quickening in her blood made her feel light-headed. He was a stranger; why did she want to suddenly kiss him? It made no sense at all.

"How are you doing?" He came to the bed and raised a hand to her forehead. His skin was cold, shockingly so, and she flinched from the contact. The man's face paled and he pulled back. "Sorry about that."

"It's okay. Just...cold." Even though she didn't want to be cold again, she'd suffer it just to have his hand back on her forehead. The whisper of a secret thrill skated along her skin, and already she missed his touch.

The man turned away and flicked on the lamp on her nightstand. The wash of gold light illuminated her mysterious rescuer. His face was just as beautiful as she'd remembered. Sharp angles and masculine perfection highlighted by dark brows above piercing winter green eyes. Faint lines bracketed his mouth as though he smiled often.

She met his gaze with a shy smile. Men like him never glanced her way, not even out of pity. Ever since she'd lost her home, she'd become almost invisible to the world.

Especially men. A blush flooded her cheeks when she realized how she must look to him. Hair unwashed in thick oily strands, blood staining her flannel shirt and mud-stained jeans.

"Oh God, I must have ruined your bed!" She struggled to get free of the blanket and flopped like a fish over the edge. She braced herself for impact, but his arms shot out and caught her. She was pulled up and trapped against his upper body in a gentle embrace.

"Careful, love." His eyes glittered with mischief. "Now, about your stomach. It's been grumbling for the last several hours. How about I fix it for you?"

Zoey blinked, unsure of what he meant.

He smiled. "I could go out and get something for you to eat?"

"That's really not necessary. I...I should go." But she really wanted him to let her stay. At least for another hour. Long enough for her to preserve some warmth before facing the cold again.

He shook his head. "No. You're not leaving." His voice brooked no argument.

Zoey clamped her lips shut, happy not to argue. It was probably unwise to stay with a stranger, even a handsome one. But she needed a day, at least one day away from the cold. But she couldn't forget his promise— she was safe with him. And as silly as it was, she believed it.

He strode to the door with her still tucked firmly in his

arms. "Let me get you settled on the couch. Unless you'd like to wash first?"

Zoey must have made a noise, something to indicate how desperately she wanted a hot shower, because his chest shook with silent laughter.

"A shower it is, then." He changed directions and headed down another hallway. He released her legs, letting her stand while he opened the bathroom door. A large glass shower stall was in the corner, and an even larger whirlpool tub was next to it.

She started to walk to the tub. "Oh, wow." Maybe she wanted a bath first—a good long soak would be better.

"What's your name?" The man's question distracted her. She spun on her heel, shocked to find him shutting the door, sealing them both in the bathroom.

"Zo..." She swallowed, her mouth suddenly dry. "Zoey Blake."

He extended his hand and she placed her palm in his. "A pleasure to meet you, Zoey. I'm Ian Kennedy. I live here with my friend Connor O'Shea and three cats, Titus, Cleo and Lizzy."

Three cats? And a roommate? Maybe her fallen angel wasn't into women. That would be just her luck. To be rescued by a god among men and find he was more inter-ested in his roommate.

"Thank you for bringing me here, Ian." She hesitated before finally asking what had been nagging at the back of her mind. "I was attacked by a man in that alley. I know

I was hurt pretty badly. What happened? I remember you helping me...but..." She needed him to explain how she'd magically healed from something that should have killed her. The details of that were still fuzzy. The only thing she remembered was her lips on his wrist and feeling safe with him.

"That's an interesting story," he began, but her stomach interrupted. "I'll tell you after you've cleaned up and gotten some food in you." He winked at her.

"But—"

Ian placed a finger over her lips, a quick smile flitting past his face, giving him a boyish charm. It also made her insides hum to life.

"Shower, food, and then we'll talk. Deal?"

She agreed, albeit reluctantly.

"Good." Ian reached for the top button of her shirt. Before she could stop them, her hands shot up, fingers curling around his wrists. She looked up at him from beneath her lashes. Even though his fingers were cold, whenever they brushed her skin an electric shock jolted her more awake. She wanted that jolt, that kick to her system more than she wanted to shower or eat. The blood in her body pumped through her wild and hard enough to rush against her ear drums.

Ian undid the first button of her shirt. Slow and methodical, he proceeded to undo the others.

"I..." His voice was hoarse. "I'll get you something to wear. Go ahead and hop in the shower." He released the edges of her shirt and turned away, exiting the bathroom. He didn't shut the door behind him.

Zoey stared at the open door for several seconds before she came back to herself. A shower! She wanted to strip off her clothes and rush in, but she took her time, enjoying this as much as possible. There was no telling when she'd have the chance to bathe in hot water again. She toed off her black Converse shoes, peeled off her socks, unzipped her ragged jeans and slipped out of her underwear.

Looking over her shoulder at her reflection in the mirror, she flinched. Her body was covered in grime. Weeks of dirt and muck covered her skin. With a shiver of revulsion, she turned back to the shower and reached for the polished chrome knobs. She cranked them hard, hot as they could go and waited until steam curled up from the gray tile floor. She stepped inside, sliding the glass door closed behind her.

The water burned. It felt so good, like heaven. She let the scalding spray wash away the dirt, but she felt something deeper inside being cleaned. The chill in her bones gradually vanished as she rubbed the masculine-scented body wash over her limbs. She couldn't help but think of Ian, rubbing his hands over her body. Once she was squeaky clean, she turned to her hair, lathering it with the shampoo and then the conditioner.

There was a single razor sitting on a shelf on the back wall of the shower. It was a large masculine thing but

Zoey snatched it up anyway. She wanted to look her best for Ian and smooth legs and underarms would help. When she'd finished, she simply stood beneath the spray, soaking further in the heat.

And then she started to cry.

Sobs choked out of her, fat tears leaked out and she rubbed her fists against her closed eyelids, trying to banish them. Exhausted, she leaned forward, resting her head against the marble, eyes closed as she breathed in slow, ragged breaths.

Her body hurt. Her chest expanded as she sucked in air and a twinge of pain came back to her. She touched her smooth unmarred stomach and chest again, trying not to think too hard about how she'd been miraculously healed. The faint pink scars she'd seen a short while ago were only pale pink lines. Relief followed the tears as she regained control of herself. She was safe, warm and clean. It was something to be happy about, even if it didn't last more than a day.

The shower door behind her slid open, a trickle of cold air teased her, making her turn around. Ian stood just outside the shower, his jaw clenched.

Zoey could barely breathe. His gaze raked over her. Heat flooded her face, and she looked away. It had been over a year since she'd been naked in front of a man. She was naturally a little shy, but there was something about the way he looked at her that made her feel vulnerable, a feeling she liked.

Everything about this situation should have freaked her out. Did he want to have sex with her? Did he expect her to sleep with him because he'd saved her and brought her home? If that was what he wanted...she was afraid to tell him no. He held all the power here. He'd given her shelter, a shower, had promised food. Was she going to barter her body for the comforts she'd been deprived of for so many months?

Take a deep breath, she told herself. *I'm in a strange man's house, and he is gazing at my naked body with heated interest.* That should scare the hell out of her, and it did... but it was also exciting. She wanted more. She wanted his hungry gaze on her, his gentle hands exploring her. Someone to care about her, even just a little bit, even just for a little while. As long as he was gentle, kind, and made her feel alive and warm and excited then she wouldn't feel forced.

"Zoey." He caressed her name, yet she could read the concern in those eyes. "I heard crying. Are you okay?"

She slicked her wet hair back from her face, then dropped her arms to curl around her waist.

"I'm fine. I just... I'm sorry." She didn't know why she was apologizing. It didn't seem to matter. He was gazing at her mouth, a look of starvation on his face, one she knew only too well. With slow, measured actions, he stripped out of his clothes until he wore nothing but black boxers.

"Ian?" she whispered, a little anxious as he stepped

inside and slid the door closed again, sealing them together in the intimate, steamy confines of the shower. Even as her mind cautioned her that he was a stranger, her body stirred to life in anticipation in a way she hadn't in a long time.

"Let me kiss you. Just one kiss. I want to remember… It's been so long." Ian dropped his head until his forehead rested against hers. His hands came up to cup her face, his thumbs pressed against her cheeks.

Passion built up inside her like a warm, dark cloud. One that fogged her mind with visions of twining limbs, whispered sighs and sated pleasures. She needed this one kiss too, more than Ian did.

"Okay."

He lifted her chin and put his mouth over hers. It was a spark to tinder, and she went up in flames. A wildfire raged between their lips. More. She had to have more. It was crazy, insane, but she gave in and arched her body into his. His hands moved from her face down to her waist, sliding over slick skin. His palms slid up her back then down to her butt. His thumbs pressed into the flare of the front of her hips, his fingers dug into her lower back, pulling her closer. He feathered his lips, soft and fleeting before she whimpered in frustration. This was no time for teasing. A breathless chuckle escaped Ian as he spun them around to pin her against the marble wall of the shower.

His mouth assaulted hers, taking everything she gave

him and demanding still more. He moaned when his tongue slid between her parted lips, tangling in fierce play. The hot spray of the shower struck Ian's shoulders, thick droplets formed over his skin and Zoey fought the desire to lean forward and lick them away.

At some point, her legs were lifted and parted. Ian's hands grabbed the back of her thighs. He pulled her up until her breasts were level with his mouth. She gasped in shock as his lips settled over one peak, sucking hard on the tender, erect tip. Her legs wrapped around his waist as she clung to him. Zoey's eyes fell shut as bliss began to pulse and throb between her legs, the almost forgotten rhythm wild and frantic. She rubbed herself against him and the massive erection barely hidden by his boxers.

She jerked in his arms when Ian's teeth grazed over her other nipple, pricking the sensitive skin.

She squeaked when he nipped at the underside of her breast. The zing of pain only made her throb harder and her core filled with her wet arousal.

Ian growled. His tongue flitted over one nipple before his mouth moved back up her chest to her neck. He nuzzled the side of her throat, teeth scraping over skin. His soft inhalation of breath was an erotic whisper.

"You smell so good, Zoey, love. I can feel your heat..." His words trailed off into a gruff curse when her stomach rumbled loudly. Ian sighed, resting his cheek against her collarbone.

Finally, he leaned back and let her slide down his body until her feet hit the floor.

Her body wanted to scream in frustration at being denied his touch, his kiss. "Why'd you stop?"

"I'm sorry, Zoey. I took advantage and it was wrong of me." His hands seemed reluctant to part with her waist, but he turned his face away, eyes roving about the bathroom, as though determined to stay away from her. He was panting, apparently struggling to regain control.

His apparent desire to put distance between them, to take back what they'd done, hurt her more than countless days of hunger or cold. What he'd given her had been so wonderful. A glimpse of unbridled passion and a sensual exploration she'd never had the chance for until now. And he'd taken it all away with a well-intended apology.

"Please don't say that. I...I liked it." She couldn't believe she felt comfortable enough admitting it. She followed her brave words with the cowardly action of wrapping her arms around her chest, hiding her breasts. His gaze moved back to her face and she was struck again by the lovely green of his eyes. She'd never seen such a pure color. She'd have happily stared into those eyes forever and never want anything more, except for another kiss. She'd sell her soul and bargain away her heart for a touch of those lips on hers.

"I know. But it was wrong. You don't owe me anything. You're free to stay here until...until we can get you back on your feet. I'll leave something on the counter for you to wear. Don't worry if I'm gone when you get out. Settle on the couch and rest up a bit."

He cupped her chin and leaned down for a kiss, and it was anything but chaste. How could he pack so much erotic promise in one little kiss?

When he stepped back, her body screamed in protest, but she didn't stop him as he slid open the shower door and stepped out. Water pooled around his large feet onto the small bath rug. He reached behind himself and closed the shower door, putting the fogged glass between them as he strode away.

The corners of her mouth pulled up in a smile. Ian. She liked him more than she should and she didn't know him at all. Except that he could kiss like a dream and not just on her mouth. Her cheeks flamed and she stifled a breathless giggle as she remembered the way he'd fit his mouth to her breasts, sucking and tugging on each nipple with hungry insistence. Each pull on her breast sent a trail of fire straight to her clit. The memory had her aching all over again.

Frustrated, she washed between her legs, but it wasn't much use; she stayed aroused as she stepped out of the shower. She toweled off and blinked in shock when she noticed the folded white shirt sitting on the counter. Surely, he brought something else to wear. Why hadn't he brought pants?

Zoey buried her face in her hands, massaged her cheeks and sucked in a deep breath before blowing it out.

She'd practically had sex with Ian in the shower. Maybe her reaction to him gave him the impression she was easy. She was mortified about how her inner moral compass seemed quite happy to ignore all this. Searching the drawers for a comb, she found a black brush instead, and quickly untangled her wet hair.

Clean. Finally clean. It felt so damn wonderful. This time, when she raised her eyes to the mirror, she saw herself. A plain Jane with chestnut hair and brown eyes. But at least it was her, not some homeless, grimy, smelly creature. No one really understood what it was like to lose themselves to a life on the streets. A person lost their identity when they lost their home, work, money, and family. All of it had vanished in a year and it had changed her forever. Yet now she could glimpse Zoey Blake again, even if her face was a little gaunt, her eyes a little sunken. She was still there somewhere.

Zoey picked up the white shirt left on the counter and slid her arms into the sleeves. It had to be one of Ian's. It hung down to her mid-thighs and her hands vanished in the long sleeves. She rolled them up until she could find her wrists. Outside the bathroom, she heard a distant door slam.

"Ian!" Her heart leapt as she ran to the open the bathroom door. Her smile vanished when she stared up into another man's face. Just as attractive, yet the opposite of Ian, with golden hair and dark eyes, looking more innocent. Yet Zoey could tell he was far from that. Something kicked her hard, raw animal desire for this complete stranger... It was just like when she'd first watched Ian cross the bedroom and come to her—an irresistible need to kiss him, to curl her arms around his neck and offer herself to him in every wicked way she desired. Vaguely she realized something was wrong with her, if she was reacting so irrationally to these two strangers.

The man's lips parted, and he snarled, his canines long and menacing, like fangs.

"Such a succulent feast for dinner? Ian shouldn't have..." The man licked his lips and reached for her.

CHAPTER 3

Zoey couldn't even summon a scream. The man was like some kind of Viking warrior with bronzed gold hair and honey brown eyes that promised wicked sins and wild abandon. His lips peeled back in a feral smile that reminded her of those old Bela Lugosi vampire movies. His massive shoulders blocked any exit from the bathroom and his dilated pupils forced her to step back. An unexpected wave of desire swept through her to run her hands up the length of his chest, digging her nails into him while she kissed a path up to his mouth.

"You're not Ian," managed to come out of her mouth, though barely above a croaked whisper.

"Sorry to disappoint. He brought you here for me. I promise once we get started you won't miss him." The man's face, while handsome, was somehow cold and frightening. His eyes stilled her in place like a frightened hare coming face to face with a timber wolf. Even though she was afraid, she still had that ridiculous urge to jump into his arms and beg for a kiss.

What is wrong with me?

"Please don't..." Zoey wasn't sure what she was asking, but anything else she might have said was silenced when the man seized her and jerked her into him. She collided with his broad chest, feeling the hard muscles against her breasts through the thin protection of his shirt and hers.

"Let me kiss you, love. Just say no if you don't want a taste." He licked his lips.

She knew she should deny him, but she wanted that kiss, as stupid and illogical as it was.

She nodded. "Yes."

One large palm moved up to hold her by the back of her neck as he dropped his head, taking her mouth with his. His other moved down her back to shape the curve of her ass. He clenched it tight as he bit her bottom lip and invaded her mouth.

Her body went off like a pail full of Black Cat fireworks. She couldn't contain the moan of pure drugged pleasure and the wild urge to let him do whatever he wished to her. His tongue dueled with hers for dominance, and she quickly, willingly surrendered. When he coaxed her to enter his mouth, her tongue flicked against his fangs.

The fog that flooded her brain when he'd started to kiss her was temporarily penetrated with a beam of clarity, like sunlight streaking through morning mist. He had fangs... She should be afraid that he was...was...what was he? Zoey fisted her hands now trapped against his chest and tried to push him back. She failed. He growled against her lips and then released her. His chest moved with rapid breaths and for some reason that eased her mind, if only for a second.

"You want to be scared? I can scare you." His voice had lost its gruffness. He was all silk and seduction now.

She leaned one hand against the bathroom counter, trying to steady herself. Her legs insisted on buckling after that mind-numbing kiss. "What?"

"Run," he snarled. "Run and hide or I'll rip your pretty little throat out!"

Light gleamed against the stark white of his fangs and Zoey didn't hesitate. She shoved past him and fled the bathroom. Her instincts finally took over and shook off the remnants of that insane arousal he'd spiked her body into moments before. She bolted down the hall toward the front door but he was suddenly there at the far end of the room, arms crossed, blocking the door.

"That's not how this game works, pet. You run, I catch you. Then I feed and we fuck."

Zoey stared at him from across the room as she tried to process his words.

"Feed and..." She couldn't bring herself to say the

other word. It was so coarse, so raw, so...primal. She was torn between fear of what his fangs suggested and desire for what he was offering. Sleeping with him would be beyond anything she'd ever experienced. The riotous shivers rippling through her weren't from terror, but pure lust.

The man cocked one eyebrow and gestured for her to move. "Run. Now."

She didn't understand what was happening, or why he was doing this to her but she didn't want to stick around and find out. It was obvious her body was ready to betray her and encourage her to sleep with both this man and Ian. However, that was not what her brain wanted her to do so she had to escape before he got too close again. That sexy mojo he seemed to ooze that made her unable to think past her libido.

There were other rooms, rooms that had windows. If she could just get to one and get outside, she'd find someone to call for help. Zoey picked the first door she came to and slammed it shut behind her. She flicked the lock into place. She darted over to the window and shoved up against the window sill. It didn't budge. She hissed in frustration, fists smacking against the glass. There wasn't time to bust through the window. Zoey whirled around, hastily scanning the room. Hiding under the bed? Not an option. The closet? Also not an option. She stared at the locked door and her heart leapt into her throat, lodging there as the knob jiggled.

"Come on, pet. Don't make me break the door. It is *my* bedroom after all," the man on the other side teased. He had an Irish accent as well. Was this Ian's friend Connor? She hoped not. Otherwise she'd have to warn Ian his friend was...was a...

"Okay, I'm losing it," she muttered. "He can't be a vampire. That's just ridiculous." Her eyes zeroed in on the still jiggling doorknob.

The man chuckled low from the other side of the door. "Not as ridiculous as you think."

Zoey gasped. The knob suddenly stopped moving, and the lock slowly twisted. She threw herself at the door, hands gripping the lock, fighting to keep it in place. It was a battle she knew she'd lose, even as her fingers screamed against the metal, biting into it as the door pushed inward.

"No!" She dug in her heels, using her body's weight to keep the door shut, but the man simply knocked it open. Zoey stumbled backward and fell against the large bed. The man stood in the doorway, the light from the hall turning him into an ominous silhouette of strength and danger.

"Scared enough?" His question caught her off guard but when he advanced another step, she screamed.

She scrambled backward over the comforter, sinking deep into the downy softness, giving him all the time he needed to pounce. He gripped her ankles and tugged. She fell onto her back as he dragged her toward him. Ian's large white shirt rode up to her hips and she thrashed, fighting for her life. She expected him to force her legs apart and mount her.

He didn't.

Instead, he drew her legs together, his touch tender but firm, winding one arm around her calves and holding her still as he climbed onto the bed next to her. Zoey pushed up on her elbows, breathing hard as he leaned over her. She wasn't sure how long they stared at each other. The room was dark but his eyes seemed to channel what little light there was. The burnt sienna depths ensnared her, held her prisoner. His palm tightened on her calves and then after a moment loosened.

He slid his hand up her outer left thigh under the dress shirt. "I don't like it when you're afraid of me," he whispered. "Ian said to scare you, but...I don't care for it." He seemed to be talking to himself more than her. "The last thing I want is to frighten you or take you against your will." His words cut through the rising fear and instead brought back that insane arousal she didn't understand.

"Tell me now, little one, do you not want me to touch you?"

The hand beneath her shirt moved in slow circles over her hip, then her belly, his fingers drifting closer to her mound. Her entire body surrendered to the violent shaking that rippled through her. The gentle sensuality of his touch thrilled her, and the fear that had mounted in her seemed to ebb away. He didn't want to scare her. Maybe he didn't want to hurt her either.

"I...I don't *not* want you to touch me," she admitted, unable to actually say she wanted him. It was close enough, and the way his eyes glittered, she knew he understood what she meant. She remembered something he'd said earlier. "Scare me? Why would Ian want to scare me?" Where she'd found the strength to speak, she didn't know.

He chuckled, his breath teasing her hair as he brushed his lips over her ear lobe. "Some women like a bit of fear." His teeth grazed her neck. "Heightens their pleasure." His tongue flicked against her skin. "But I don't want you scared, I want you *hot*."

The word came out a soft growl and she was ready to surrender everything to him in that moment. It was wild and insane and she wanted him, was tempted by him. No man had ever made her feel this crazy, except Ian. Ian! She'd lusted after him before and now she was craving this other man's touch. It was madness and she knew it, but she didn't want to fight it any longer.

The man's hand drifted between her thighs, one finger finding her clit and pressing. She arched off the bed right into him.

"There now, see? We don't need fear," the man whispered a second before he licked the shell of her ear. Sharp tingles of violent pleasure electrified her spine and she whimpered.

"You...you're not going to hurt me?" She eased onto her back and he followed her down, his mouth doing wicked things below her ear. His hand between her thighs began to play. His fingers parted the slick folds of her sex and stroked lazy patterns into her burning center. It was so hard to think, to speak, she just wanted him to take her, now, to bring her to a burning explosion so she could forget about everything but him.

"No, pet. I won't hurt you, but you may feel a sting."

His fangs sank into her neck. The pain was unexpected, but the pleasure that followed was even more of a surprise. Her hands found his biceps, and she curled her fingers into his skin as she held on for dear life, riding the building waves of pleasure from the bite and his touch. His mouth worked at her neck, sucking as he drank, but she couldn't find it in herself to care. He'd said he wouldn't hurt her. As foolish as it was, she trusted him. Just like she'd trusted Ian.

The man parted her core with two fingers and thrust them inside in a slow rhythm that gradually built in speed. She circled her hips against his hand, urging him deeper. She needed more.

"Please..." she gasped and wound one hand through his long, dark blond hair.

When he didn't respond, she tugged sharply. He lifted his head. Blood stained his lips a deep red and his tongue flicked out, swiping the blood away. His warm eyes were wreathed in crimson, and his fangs now gleamed lean and dangerous from behind the curve of his sensual lips.

Clarity cleared his gaze and he started moving his hand faster, his fingers pumping harder, deeper. He added a third finger and she screamed. Something detonated inside her, lighting her up like the stars in the winter sky. She imploded, all sense of self vanishing. She was in ecstasy.

A distant crash invaded her cloud of hazy delight and the man leapt off her. Zoey blinked, trying to focus her blurry vision on another, someone standing in the doorway.

"Zoey! Zoey, love, are you hurt?"

Ian.

"I'm uh...I don't know...Ian..." She hesitated, looking at the scowling form of Connor lingering at the edge of the doorway. "He...He's a vampire. That guy is a vampire."

Ian closed his eyes, drew a deep breath.

"I know."

She tensed with apprehension. "You know?"

Ian bit his bottom lip as though embarrassed. She saw the tips of two fangs peek out of Ian's mouth. Her jaw dropped.

"We both are."

CHAPTER 4

Ian was a vampire? They both were? Zoey blinked, her brain short circuiting as she tried to process this information and failed.

"Oh my God. He bit me! Am I going to turn into one?"

Ian was suddenly above her, his hands on her neck, her legs, everywhere as he checked her for injury.

"No, lass, no. You won't become a vampire. That takes more than just a bite to accomplish."

Relief surged through her. She wasn't going to go Bela Lugosi after all.

"Connor, you damned fool. What are you doing biting her?"

Connor, she'd been right to assume it was him, shifted uneasily by the door, his blond hair still wild from her hands running through it.

"You left me a message. Said she was my dinner and I had to scare her."

"What? That's not what I said, you *amadan!*" Ian scooped Zoey up into his arms. She burrowed into him instinctively. The remnants of her climax still rippled through her and his strong arms absorbed her trembling.

"Ian…" Connor growled.

"I said I had a guest and was bringing her dinner. I warned you to be sure *not* to scare her. Bloody hell man, she'll never forgive me. Not after you attacked her."

Ian carried her to the living room and settled her on the leather couch. He grabbed a heavy thick blanket and tucked it around her. Connor followed at a distance, his eyes avoiding Zoey's. That irritated her, not that she could say why exactly.

"Ian, I'm sorry. The message cut out in places. I thought I heard what I heard. I didn't know. It's clear she's your dinner. I didn't realize you were bringing them home again. You usually eat out."

Ian, who had been brushing hair back from Zoey's face, tensed. His eyes caught hers and held them for a time before he spoke to Connor.

"She's not my dinner. She's a woman who's in need of some help. I offered her a place to stay and to get her some food." He pointed to the kitchen countertop, which had several take-out bags from the nearby restaurants.

The scent of the food drifted beneath Zoey's nose. Her mouth watered. Hunger hit her stomach like a physical blow. Food. God, she was ravenous. She'd quite forgotten it when she'd been beneath Connor on his bed.

Her eyes strayed to the kitchen where the food was. It took every ounce of self-control not to run straight at it. Somehow she felt making sudden movements in front of a pair of vampires was a bad idea.

Vampires. She still had to process that, but she could do that later, when her stomach was full.

"Who is she, Ian?"

Ian lifted her up and sat back on the couch with her in his lap. "Her name is Zoey Blake."

It probably should have bothered her that he just moved her about and picked her up without asking. But she liked that he simply took control—and more importantly, that he seemed to enjoy keeping her close. Even with the allure of food so nearby she was reluctant to leave his arms.

Connor's eyes narrowed to slits. "And *why* did you bring Zoey here?"

The air about them seemed to vibrate, like someone had just plucked the strings of a harp and the sound waves still traveled along the air. The hair on Zoey's neck rose and her skin tingled with awareness of the two men and the situation.

"She has nowhere else to go. The lass lost her family, her home. I found her dying in an alley where some whoreson had attacked her." Ian's voice was full of quiet desperation, but tinged with an edge of defiance.

Connor's lips twisted. "So you thought you'd bring her home and play nursemaid? What about your promise to me? No more mortal lovers. Not after what happened to Lara."

Zoey stiffened. Mortal lover? "Who's Lara?" She glanced up at Ian. The movement brushed her lips across the line of his jaw. He tensed, chest and arm muscles hardening. The sudden bulge she felt beneath her had her blushing.

"You test me, love. Be careful." Ian's warm breath stirred the crown of her hair, eliciting small shivers from her. "Connor, she stays. Get used to the idea. She's mine, and I will care for her. You are welcome to help, but do not make me choose between you. I will pick her. We swore once to protect the innocent. Zoey is as innocent as they come."

"Hey! I'm not that innocent." Zoey was no stranger to sex—assuming that's what he meant. There had been a few boys in college before she was forced to drop out, and even if it had been a few years, she still remembered the mechanics of it. Even if she'd been involuntarily celibate lately, she'd still held her share of wicked fantasies, her current one featuring the pair of men both arguing about her.

Connor snorted. "You're as green as the grass near Belfast."

"I'm not sure what that means," Zoey shot back, a tad

uncertain but still riled enough to glower at him. "But I think I'm insulted."

Ian chuckled, but it died once she glared at him with all the fury a woman could muster, which seemed to be enough to make his eyes twinkle despite his lack of a smile. She turned her glower to Connor, hoping to have a better effect.

"Don't argue with me, pet," Connor growled. "I'm liable to turn you over my knee and smack your arse until it's red."

"You're not to touch her." Ian shielded her with his arms, but she wasn't scared. Connor's threat had her body heating, and the promise of his hand on her ass, even in punishment, melted her insides. God, she needed help. This was so wrong. She shouldn't want him to spank her, and it sure as hell shouldn't have aroused her.

Connor turned his back on them and slammed his hands down on the granite kitchen countertop. His head dropped between his hunched shoulders.

"Connor?"

Tension rolled off Connor's back in waves. She couldn't help but remember what happened minutes before when he'd had her on her back. There hadn't been any tension there, only passion. Her surrender, his domination, and a release the likes of which she'd never felt before. Her womb clenched at the memory of his fingers pumping inside her. Then she remembered she was in

Ian's arms. She raised her head and saw his nostrils flaring. Surely he couldn't...*smell* her arousal?

God, I hope not.

"She's helpless, Connor. I refuse to put her back out onto the streets."

Connor turned back to face them. "Another stray, like your cats. But you can't keep her, Ian. She's a human, not a wee animal."

Ian's shoulders stiffened. A low growl emanated from his throat. Zoey's hackles rose, and she realized that Ian was just as dangerous as Connor, although he'd hidden it from her with his outward gentleness.

As the thought filtered through her hungry mind, she felt a sudden stab of anger, and the prickling of tears behind her eyes. Why hadn't she seen it before? She would have, she argued to herself, if she hadn't been so hungry.

Ian didn't look at her with passion—he looked at her with pity. She'd mistaken his intentions in the bathroom earlier when he'd kissed her. Men did that, didn't they? Sleep with women they pitied?

The pain of that thought wracked her insides with an angry sadness that choked her. Zoey was too angry to say a word. Emotions ripped through her and she didn't dare open her mouth; otherwise she'd say a thousand things she'd regret.

Connor looked away. "You should have let nature run its course. We cannot save every mortal we come across."

"Let nature run its course?" Ian's reply was barely comprehensible as it came out in a vicious snarl. "Do you remember when nature ran its course back in Ireland? Our families starved, our people died on the streets, like the very animals I try to save. How dare you hold that against me, against her!"

She couldn't stand to be there a second longer. She had to leave. Zoey shoved at Ian's chest. Whatever was going on between these two, she didn't understand it, and she didn't want to. She was too hurt by Ian's words. A stray? No better than a starving cat on the streets? That's how he saw her? A thing to be pitied, not a person to be loved?

Ian fought her for only a second before he let her go. Somehow, that made everything worse. She bit back a fresh well of tears.

He didn't even care enough to fight to keep her in his arms. It stung—no, it burned—like a knife sliding between her ribs and piercing her heart.

Zoey slid off the couch, her bare feet sinking into the soft thick carpet. She had to tug Ian's white dress shirt down to cover her bare thighs. Both men stared at her, their gazes drawn to her legs.

"Ian. Where are my clothes?" She said it softly, but he heard her.

The confusion on his face would have been endearing at any other time, but the tension in the room was thick enough to smother her.

"Why do you need your clothes?" Ian's face was a mirror image of the brooding Connor on the other side of the room.

"I think I should leave. You both clearly have things you need to discuss, and I don't want to be in the way."

"No!" Ian barked. "Absolutely not."

Zoey flinched, but held her ground. "I'm sorry, I can't stay. I don't want your pity..." Her voice trailed off, face flushing when she realized she'd wanted something else. Him. When her eyes strayed to Connor, something hit her in the gut. As frightening as he was, she had to admit he fascinated her as well. When it had been just the two of them alone in his bed, he'd chosen not to scare her, but instead to overwhelm her with raw passion. She'd been a moth to the fire of his embrace.

She wanted Connor. She wanted Ian. It was insane to want them both, yet she did. They were immortal creatures, vampires. *Vampires.* She still hadn't fully processed this. Eventually she'd have a hell of a headache when she had to accept that fact. But she wasn't going to think about that right now, not when she had to figure out what she was going to do and where she was going to go. She was still homeless. A stray. They didn't want her, they only pitied her.

Zoey raised her chin, trying to think of all of the things she should be proud of, and not let her own self-pity weigh her down. If she left now, she might make it to the shelter before they closed and maybe, just maybe they'd have space for her in the main room, rather than having to go back to the underpass.

A shudder of fear tinged with anxiety shot up her spine. Another horrible night under that concrete bridge… hoping no one would attack her. It had happened before. Hands groping in the darkness, trapping her limbs, fetid breath on her face, rags shoved inside her mouth to prevent her from screaming while an accomplice stole what little food she'd kept for when she needed it. That was what she had to look forward to.

"You can't go, love. Please." Ian's tone was heavy, but his fists were clenched and his taut expression revealed surprising determination.

"I won't be an object of pity, Ian. Besides…" She pointed at Connor. "He doesn't want me here."

A storm cloud hovered over Ian's features as he turned back to his friend. "I don't give a damn what you think, Connor. I'm keeping her. So apologize to the lass. If you won't, I'll take you outside and beat you until you do."

The threat was delivered with no hint of the gentlemanly front Ian had shown her up to now. This was an animal establishing his dominance where a female was concerned. Recognizing this for what it was made Zoey shiver with forbidden desire. She shouldn't like the idea of Ian being possessive, but she did.

In another place and time, Connor's scowl might have made Zoey laugh. He looked like a spoiled child who was being told "no" for the first time. She had a feeling he got his way more often than not when they quarreled. Finally, his expression changed to one of stony defiance.

"Fine. She can stay. For now."

That was all he said. No apology, no negotiation. Just a gruff reply before he stalked from the room.

Zoey winced when he slammed the door to his bedroom. He'd shut her out, but it felt like more than that. Why that mattered, she was too afraid to consider. She didn't want to contemplate that she was crushing on a vampire...make that *two* vampires. She remembered the way he'd pleasured her, the way it felt to be powerless and yet feel so safe with him.

Ian's voice broke through her thoughts. "Zoey."

She raised her eyes and saw him leaning against the side of the couch, his green eyes dark with concern. He closed the distance between them so he could cup her chin with one hand. Sparks tingled from that single point of contact, making her flush with heat.

"I don't pity you. Never think that. But I do want to help, and I need you to stay. Please." There was desperation in his voice that filled his every syllable. It made her feel guilty for denying him something he needed.

She reached up and curled her fingers around his strong wrist. "Why do you need to help me?" She didn't pull his hand away, merely kept hold of him, like a grounding rod to attract the lightning strikes his gentle yet possessive touch seemed to bring.

His thumb traced her lips, his eyelids dropped to half-mast as he gazed at her mouth.

"Connor and I are best friends. We grew up in the same village in Ireland. We watched our friends and loved ones die during the Great Famine over a hundred and fifty years ago. It..." His voice grew hoarse and soft. "It ruined me, ruined us both. We were turned into immortals against our will. I remember...hearing Connor shouting and begging to die. I was too weak to cry out...I screamed in my head, but it didn't stop the pain, or the blood from flowing from that creature's wrist to my mouth. A little blood would have saved me, but the creature drained me and turned me. Made me one of them. I hated that I was helpless."

"You gave me your blood...I remember now." She licked her lips, the memory of that horrible moment came rushing back.

Ian's eyes darkened to sharp slices of jade. "Only enough to heal you from your wounds. I wouldn't have taken the choice of life or immortality away from you the way it had been taken from me."

She could see in his face that this meant something to him. The choice to be what he was. Immortal.

"Thank you for saving me. I didn't really say that before..."

He grinned. "You were in shock, love. And you're welcome. I will admit to selfish reasons though. I wanted to take you home with me."

As sweet as his words were, Zoey couldn't let herself read too much into it, not when she might get her hopes up for something that could never be. She tried to change the subject back to the story of his turning. "What happened after you changed?"

"I was condemned, as was Connor. We both swore we'd never let another creature suffer the way we had, the way our families had. When I found you, it was like I was mortal again, watching my sister starve to death. I had to save you."

Jealous pain cut through Zoey's chest. She didn't want him to think of her as his sister. Not after the way he'd kissed her. A sense of grief flooded through her as she absorbed his words. His sister had starved. Zoey knew how terrible that fate was. But the fact was she couldn't remain here with them.

"Connor's right, Ian. I can't stay here. Not forever."

"So stay awhile. Let me care for you until you can get back on your feet."

It was so tempting. She wanted to say yes, to agree to anything he asked. He was a dream, a wonderful and strange one. Maybe she had died in that alley after all, and the afterlife was nothing more than this, a dream that she'd be teased and tormented with for the rest of eternity.

Promises of a life I'll never live.

"Okay. I'll stay for a while. But once I'm ready to leave, you have to let me go."

Ian nodded soberly and stood. He walked over to the kitchen bar and started opening the bags of take-out sitting there.

"Shall we feed you before it gets cold? I have fried rice, tacos, cheeseburgers and pasta. What would you like?"

She heard the false cheer in his tone. He was hurt, but so was she. At least she could have some food as consolation. She forced a smile.

"Can I have a little bit of everything?"

Genuine warmth twinkled behind his eyes as Ian flashed a grin. "Finally, something I can do."

He grabbed some dishes from the cabinets and started digging food out of the bags.

She suddenly recalled they'd mentioned a woman named Lara. She focused on it rather than her hunger pangs. "Will you tell me about her?"

"Who?" Ian asked.

"Lara. I want to know about her."

Ian blew out a slow breath as he closed the cabinets, his hand on the silver knob, hesitating before he spoke.

"Lara was a dream. More fantasy than reality I think sometimes. I met her in 1923 and fell hard for her. So did Connor. My father would have called her one of the wee folk, a faery. She was wild, free, and so full of life. She made us remember what it was to be human. In a way, it *did* make us more human. You see, vampires sometimes find something akin to a true mate."

"A true mate?" It sounded more like a werewolf thing

from those movies she'd seen. Then again, she had assumed werewolves and vampires didn't exist. She sure wasn't going to ask about werewolves.

Ian turned to study her over his shoulder. "Vampires aren't like other creatures, we don't have mates like they do, but sometimes we find another who makes us feel alive again. We hunger for the joys of living again, we crave things mortals crave. Our hearts may even beat. We aren't human, but we come close."

"How often do you find these true mates?" she asked, fascinated by the thought of vampires somehow becoming more human.

He shrugged. "Connor and I went a century before we met Lara. She touched us both in that way, and neither of us could resist her."

"You both loved the same woman?" Zoey couldn't imagine that scenario ending well. Both of them struck her as possessive and she'd only known them a short time.

"We did. Lara, bless her, didn't seem to mind. She handled the both of us just fine."

Her face heated and her body flushed with interest. "By both you mean…" she couldn't dare finish.

"In bed. At the same time. We weren't jealous of each other, and she liked us both equally. It was an arrangement all three of us enjoyed." He admitted it so simply, as though he truly hadn't minded it at all.

"Are you and Connor...lovers?" She blushed at her brazen question, but she wanted to know.

Ian shook his head. "No," he chuckled. "Lord, no. We are like brothers. Sharing a woman is something we can do and enjoy doing, if the woman wants both of us."

An image came of her stretched out over Ian's body, him filling her, while Connor was behind her, kissing his way down her back, his hands rubbing...

Zoey shook her head. What a dangerous thought. Tempting too.

"Would you ever do that again? Share a woman with Connor?"

Ian froze, still holding the plates. His face was a painting of sadness, grief coloring his eyes and the shape of sorrow twisting his mouth downward.

"If the right woman came along, another true mate, one who would love us both, perhaps. But I would want to keep her, *forever*. I would want to ask her what I never had the chance to ask Lara. That she turn immortal, so Connor and I wouldn't have to lose her. Neither of us can suffer that again."

Whatever spell of melancholy had woven around his features seemed to ease and vanish. Zoey was thankful. She knew just how deep such wounds could be and how they never fully healed.

She digested his words. Change into a vampire? Could she do something like that? Could she be someone's true mate? The odds were against her, since neither man mentioned she was. It made her heart ache and she rubbed at her chest with one hand.

She waited, ignoring the stab of hunger as best she could, while Ian filled a plate for her. When he returned to the couch, he set two plates of food on the black wooden coffee table.

"So do you drink blood from the vein like Connor, or do you drink from bagged blood or something?" It was a valid question. Connor had after all, sank his teeth into her neck and drank when they'd been...well, no need to dwell on that. Vampires only drank blood in the movies and books, right? Then again, she probably shouldn't be accepting horror movies as any type of truth for what real vampires were capable of.

His lips quirked. "I drink from the vein." Ian lifted her legs up on the couch and sat down, placing her legs onto his lap and settling the thick blanket over them both before reaching for their food.

She took hers gratefully, inhaling the heady scents of the most delicious food she'd ever smelled in her life.

"But you're eating food..." She gestured to the small mountain of tacos he had on his plate, while she picked up a cheeseburger on hers and took a hearty bite. The moan that escaped her lips was very unladylike.

Her mother would have given her a "look" if she'd been there. Her mother had always stressed a woman was judged by her manners. A pang of longing shot through her, momentarily killing the hunger. She'd have given anything to have her mother back, even for just a few minutes.

She sent a silent apology to the heavens.

Sorry, Mom, I'm so hungry.

"Good?" Ian's lips twitched as he took a bite of one of his tacos.

"You have no idea. My last meal was from the garbage can outside that diner where you found me."

"Dear God…"

Shame colored her cheeks. But somehow her ability to filter what she said had gone out the window when she'd started eating. It just felt so good to have something so tasty and warm hitting the empty black hole of her stomach.

She flushed an even deeper red and tried to divert his attention. "So, food. You're a vampire but you can eat it?"

He blinked, eyes softening as he let her change the topic of conversation.

"I can eat. My body doesn't need it, but when I'm inspired, I can certainly enjoy food. I thought it would be rude of me not to eat when you do. It has been several years since I've wanted to eat. I'd forgotten how much I like tacos." He chuckled and offered Zoey a fork.

She took the utensil and used it to fill her mouth with fried rice before replying.

"Inspired?"

"Vampires lose their appetites when they lose interest in life. When you live forever, things around you change faster, even though you do not. When you're a mortal you live life at this breakneck pace, racing to fill up your life with memories, emotions, thoughts and sensations. With a vampire, that's all slowed down to a snail's pace. There's no hurry, no rush. You have forever to do as you wish. And so many things lose their appeal over time."

"What about blood? Do you have to kill someone when you feed?" Her heart pounded harder as she waited for an answer.

"No. It depends, of course, on the vampire. Control is really what matters. Some vampires like to kill, but most do not. The risk of discovery by mortals is too high. Connor and I drink enough to leave the host human healthy. We don't kill." The way he said that last part made her feel as if he almost said "anymore."

"So you really live forever? You don't die or turn all Nosferatu and get all creepy?" she asked.

"No. As long as we have blood every now and then, we stay just the way we are."

"Immortality sounds nice."

Zoey didn't miss the grimace on Ian's face. "It's a curse. When you lose urgency, you find you do very little with your life. It becomes tedious and then meaningless. For men like Connor and me, 'tis hard. We were raised to work, to help others. The idle life of immortality doesn't suit us. We're easily bored. You...however, you fascinate me." His eyes had become bright as Chinese jade. "When I was buying food for you, I had to order some for myself. I wanted to taste the food, see if it was as delicious as I remembered. I was inspired by what you would feel and wanted to experience it myself."

Zoey had a feeling there was some deeper meaning to his words, but she couldn't decipher it, and she was too hungry and tired to give it much thought.

"Oh," she replied. She knew she'd have to face this whole "vampires are real" issue later. After she was full.

His rich baritone laugh made her skin tingle with a new awareness of his masculinity. It intruded upon her instinct to eat. How long had it been since she'd been near a handsome man and been able to think of something other than food and finding a warm place for the night? Too long. Now she was on a stranger's couch, her legs over his lap, sharing a meal in an incredibly intimate setting.

"That's all you have to say? Oh?" He echoed her tone and she laughed. His green eyes lit up again with that light that bewitched her. "You find out we are vampires and you don't have anything else you want to ask?"

Zoey was distracted by the muscles of his throat as he took another bite of a taco. Sure, she had plenty she wanted to ask, but right now she was torn between thoughts of food and sex. A ridiculous giggle bubbled up from her lips. She sounded like a guy. Sex and food on the brain.

"What?" Ian asked, eyeing her thoughtfully.

"Nothing." She resumed eating and with a shrug, so did he.

Once she was stuffed to overflowing, she put the plate on the coffee table and settled deeper into Ian's arms. It was all too much. Her stomach wasn't ready for so much real food after months of near starvation. After only a few minutes, the nausea struck. She struggled out of Ian's grasp and ran for the bathroom.

"Zoey?" Ian's voice was close behind as she reached the toilet and fell to her knees over the porcelain bowl. Her stomach clenched, and she retched violently. Zoey's hands shook on the toilet seat as she coughed and spit up. Cool hands settled on her shoulders, pulled her hair back from her face, keeping it out of the way. Even now, Ian was too good to her.

"Breathe through your mouth, rest your head on your arms," Ian coached. His touch was soothing as he rubbed her back. "I've been to enough late nights at pubs to know how this works."

Her stomach roiled again but she swallowed it down and sucked in a quivering breath.

"I'm so sorry...I ate too much. Should have known."

"It's my fault. I should have remembered you wouldn't be able to handle so much. I would have been better off bringing you soup." His lips brushed her temple in soft kisses.

She winced. "You should leave me..." She coughed

again. "I'm not exactly at my best." With a low groan, she spit into the toilet and her stomach twisted again.

His arms wrapped around her and his chin settled on her head. "I'll never leave you, Zoey. Not when you need me the most."

"Why? Why do you care, Ian? I'm nobody to you."

"You're wrong. You mean something to me, love. When I saw you in the alley way, being attacked, I watched you try to protect that book of sketches you have. Against my better judgment, I intervened. When I came over to you, lying there, dying, I saw those sketches and photos all over the ground. You had such vision, you showed such an understanding for life. Someone like that? I couldn't just let them die. And now that I've kissed you," he chuckled, "I think... I might be addicted to your taste." He said the last bit in a teasing tone, but she couldn't help but hope it might be true.

She harrumphed, but managed to smile. "Can I have a glass of water and some mouthwash? I feel better." It was true. Her body seemed to have relaxed after getting rid of the contents of her stomach. Pity. She'd loved eating all of it and now she had an empty stomach again.

Ian let her go and retrieved what she needed. When she was done rinsing her mouth, she sagged back onto the floor and shut her eyes.

She was so tired. Exhaustion was like a heavy wool blanket, weighing her down and surrounding her with warmth.

"Are you ready to sleep?" Ian's question barely made it through her fatigue.

She nodded jerkily, unable to control herself. She wanted to collapse against him and rely on his strength for support. Again she thought she ought to have been bothered by all this. Why was she so willing to let him take control? But for some reason she trusted him. *An Irish vampire. Imagine that.*

"Up you go." He rose from the bathroom floor, Zoey in his arms. She laid her head on his shoulder, loving how perfect it felt and knowing sadly it wouldn't last. It was her last thought as sleep closed in and swept her away.

CHAPTER 5

Ian carried his delicate bundle down the hall toward his bedroom. He had no intention of taking her anywhere else. She belonged to him, even if she didn't know it yet. Zoey needed someone to look after her and provide for her. It was an old-fashioned notion, perhaps, but he was as old-fashioned as it got. It was a man's duty to spoil his woman and give her everything, even if she didn't need it. Zoey was in desperate need of spoiling.

The rags she'd been wearing—he'd thrown them out as soon as she'd stepped into the shower. He'd peeked of course, seen her enjoying herself and slipped back out, leaving one of his shirts for her to wear. He was a man, not a saint.

Scratch that, he was a vampire, not a man.

He'd been a lusty man even before he'd been turned,

as he recalled. The blood lust of a vampire seemed to have heightened his sexual needs and desires. Yet there was a price to it as well. A curse that cut deep.

Because of the glamour, he could never be sure if a woman he was with truly desired him, or was merely responding to *what* he was. It wasn't their fault, they truly believed they felt what they did, only to wake from it like a pleasant dream once he was no longer around.

He just wanted to feel normal, to lust after a woman who truly wanted him back, not worrying about whether it was the vampiric pheromones that lured her into his arms like a docile lamb. When he'd kissed Zoey in the bathroom, it had taken every ounce of control he had not to lay her on the floor and taste every inch of her satiny skin. It had been so long since he'd felt that desperate for a woman in that way.

But she was fragile now. He had to respect her and respect how she must be feeling. Only a cad like Connor would take advantage of her in such a state.

The damned fool.

"I hope you know what you're doing," Connor muttered from the doorway.

Speak of the devil and he appears.

"I do."

Ian saw his friend leaning against the doorframe. His arms were crossed and his brows lowered. Their skittish black cat, Cleo, rubbed against Connor's ankles, purring loudly. She'd taken a shine to Connor and vice versa, not that he would ever let Ian see him return her affections. Ian often heard him talking to the cat in low soothing tones when he believed Ian couldn't hear.

"What if Seamus comes back, Ian? Do you want another death on your hands?" Connor's tone seethed with repressed anger.

Ian froze in front of his bedroom door.

Seamus. The name filled him with dread. Life had a funny way of changing those things that used to seem so certain. Seamus had once been like a brother to him, just as Connor was, but when they'd been turned that all changed. Seamus had rejected the plight of their village, instead choosing to follow in the wake of their sire, stealing lives and indulging in his thirst for blood. He'd turned his back on all the things that had made him human.

Ian and Connor had rejected their sire's cruel lust for pain and death, killing him when they first had the opportunity, and forever making an enemy of their old friend. It had been revenge that led Seamus to slay their beloved Lara, but Ian knew, as well as Connor, that the cold fire in Seamus' heart had not dulled since then. If he found another opportunity to hurt them, he would.

Even knowing that, in his heart Ian was loathe to admit it. "We haven't seen him since 1923. He won't come back. He took Lara. Shouldn't he consider himself avenged?"

Connor's bitter laugh was anything but reassuring.

"You know better than that. Seamus will never stop. He wants us alone and miserable. It gives him purpose." His eyes burned into Ian's with an intensity born of certainty. "You bring the lass into this, and she's as good as dead. Not tonight or tomorrow, but someday."

Ian looked down at Zoey's face. The dark circles under her long lashes filled him with worry. She needed him. He needed her. He wouldn't let Seamus take her away.

"I'm tired of running away. If he learns of her, if he comes here, I'll be ready. He has no right. If you won't stand up to him, I will." Ian walked away, leaving his friend in the hall without another word.

A LARGE SILVER-COATED Bengal cat lay stretched out on Ian's bed.

"Off with you, Titus."

Titus was one of their three strays—Cleo, Titus and Lizzy. Cleo rarely left Connor's room and Lizzy was far too independent to stay in either of their rooms. She preferred to make the living room and kitchen her personal space.

Titus raised his head, his golden eyes unwavering as he stood, stretched and pawed the thick bedspread before he finally pounced off the bed and stalked imperiously from the room. Ian grinned. Titus and Connor didn't get along, probably because they had too much in common.

Finally, Ian was alone with Zoey, exactly what he

wanted. He set her down on the bed and she stirred. He closed the door and turned back to her. All cleaned up, dressed in one of his shirts, she was an erotic fantasy come to life. A small frame, full of muscles and curves in all the right places, though too thin from lack of food, something he'd soon remedy. Her silky hair tumbled around her face and shoulders in waves.

Soon he hoped to be fisting his fingers through it, tugging as he plundered the sweetness of her mouth. He could tell she was innately passionate. He would work to bring her to climax and savor each little shiver and cry of pleasure as he learned the song of her body. She'd beg for his touch when she was ready, and he'd happily give it to her and more, once she was on fire with arousal.

Ian shrugged out of his clothes and tugged on a pair of flannel pajama pants. He didn't feel the cold, of course, but he wanted Zoey to be warm when she slept next to him, as warm as she could be next to a vampire. He paused, considering this. An electric blanket might not be a bad idea.

He pulled back the thick down comforter and slid his arms under Zoey's back and knees, lifting her up and tucking her into the bed. She sighed, buried her face in the pillow and rolled over as he walked around to the other side.

Her dark lashes fanned up as her eyes opened. Her gaze pierced him like a lance. Such innocence, such life, such hope had once been there, yet it was clouded now by countless days of pain and heartache. To have gone from such happiness to such hopelessness...he knew all too well what that was like.

The night after he turned, the world had become shades of red as he fought his thirst for blood. The vampire who had sired him and Connor, Seamus had cruelly sealed them inside their small cottages with their family members. Unable to escape, he had done the unthinkable and fed on his own parents and his sister, tasting their blood and cursing his soul to hell as he did. Only then, when he lay among their bloodless corpses, did his sire set him free.

Connor had endured the same fate, and there was a hollowness in his friend's gaze that hadn't vanished in two centuries. There had been no tears to shed, but his heart had bled all the same as he'd had to leave his life and his slaughtered family behind. Seamus had fared better, but little did they know it was because he'd found a taste for darkness. They'd had to go with the vampire that sired them, but after a few short years, they'd learned how to survive on their own. Only then did they have the chance to kill their sire and escape, while Seamus swore revenge.

As the decades spun faster and faster past them, he and Conner had grown apart. Connor withdrew into himself and his guilt at living on while his family had died. Until Lara. She had been the key that had brought them back together. A true mate to both of them. He and

Connor started enjoying life again, feeling so close to human that it had seemed to be a miracle. Ian's own despair had waned in the burning light of Lara's jubilant life.

But that also ended, as all things must. Seamus had murdered her in cold blood, and they'd been too late to turn her. Her death had forced Ian and Connor apart again. And yet they stuck together. In the end, they had no one else to turn to.

Zoey was still watching him, with eyes that reflected an old soul. A soul that seemed to see right through him.

"Did I fall asleep?" Zoey murmured.

"Only for a few minutes. Go back to sleep."

She blinked, her eyes drifting from his face to his body, over his bare chest and pajamas. He couldn't help it when his body responded and his cock twitched in anticipation. A delicious burn swept across her cheeks, and she pulled the covers up to her chin.

"Are you...are you gonna sleep here too?" There was something so intimate about sleeping next to someone. More intimate than sex. When two bodies occupied a single space, both relaxed and were at their most vulnerable, limbs tangled together, their dreams free to weave together, tying the two people closer than anything else ever could. He knew that for her to sleep next to him would be a sign of trust.

Ian leaned forward, curled his fingers into the

comforter's thick white fabric and peeled it away from his side of the bed.

"I'd like to if you don't mind." He made a show of fluffing a pillow and then met her shy gaze with a steady one of his own, hoping it would reassure her.

"Do vampires sleep?"

"When dawn comes we do. It's hard to wake us. We're very groggy if we don't sleep."

"Oh...so it's close to dawn?" Zoey started to sit up, but Ian leaned over her and placed a palm on her shoulder, urging her back down into the bed.

"Dawn is a few minutes away. Is it okay that I sleep here? Next to you?" He wanted her to say yes, to throw her arms around his neck and cover his face with kisses. It was a foolish dream, to want her to genuinely desire him. But it had been so long since he'd known a woman's touch in affection, not because of the influence of his glamour.

Ian waited as she weighed her options. Emotions danced across her expressive face, giving her feelings away in ways she never realized. Her fear, worry, and concern soon turned to desire and eagerness to be with him. He could read every one of her subtle expressions and each fascinated him. It had been many years since a human had captured his interest like this.

"Ian...about what happened in the bathroom, before you went to get the food—"

"I enjoyed it. A lot. If you aren't ready, then you have

but to say the word. Just let me sleep here, let me hold you so I know you are safe." There weren't words to tell her how much he needed that.

She'd been so close to death. He'd been lucky enough to bring her back. He was just beginning to realize how fortunate he truly was in saving her. She was a puzzling conundrum of sweetness, independence, creativity and compassion. While she'd showered, he'd taken another look at her art and couldn't wait to ask her a thousand questions about why she chose to sketch and photograph things and people the way she had. Her understanding of the world around her, seeing things others never bothered to look at, fascinated him.

Now that he'd talked with her and kissed her, he couldn't imagine the light of her life being snuffed out like a candle. It would be too much like Lara and he couldn't lose Zoey like that. It was a thought that he knew would haunt him for years, knowing she would someday have to die, as all things did, all except creatures like him and Connor. He just didn't want it to be soon, and not while she was with him.

Vulnerability, fear and need all warred in her soft, sad eyes. Their chocolate depths were filled with heart-breaking memories, weighing him down with a single look. What he wouldn't give to inspire those eyes to spark with life and laughter once again. To turn the sadness he'd glimpsed in her portfolio to pictures and sketches of joy, of beauty.

"Why do you care about me being safe?" Her eyes watered. "No one's cared...not since my family died."

A second later, Ian was in the bed, Zoey's body tucked in his arms as he cradled her against him.

"You need someone to care about you, love. I want to be that person. So let me." He used his fingertips to brush the hair back from her face. Her skin was as soft as the petals of a new flower, like velvet beneath his fingertips. Her pulse beat a rapid rhythm in the delicate blue vein in her neck. Out of pure instinct, his fangs began to lengthen. He struggled to fight off a wave of hunger. She wasn't to be bitten, though Connor had already tasted her. The healed puncture wounds on her neck made his anger flare to life again.

"What's the matter?" she asked, an edge of worry in her tone.

"Connor bit you. I don't like seeing you hurt." He touched the skin where she'd been bitten but she didn't flinch. "I should pound him into a bloody pulp for that."

"It doesn't really hurt. I'd say getting knifed was far worse." She was trying to joke, but it was no doubt a mask to hide the memory of her violent attack.

"You've got to stop saying things that break my heart, lass." Ian pulled her even closer. They were pressed together, skin to skin, from chest to toes and it heated his blood in a way he'd forgotten was even possible.

He rubbed his knuckles over her cheek. Her lashes fluttered and she leaned into him. When she looked up at him, disbelief mixed with exhaustion and humor shone in their depths. They were such a lovely shade of brown—light, almost cinnamon red under the lamp light. He'd never seen a shade of brown so warm and animated before. It fascinated him.

"This is crazy. I'm in bed with a vampire who just wants to cuddle."

"Well, I want more than that, but the last thing I wish to do is force you." He stroked her lower lip with the pad of his thumb.

She glanced up at him. "Every time you touch me, I get this wild urge to kiss you." Her admission made her blush.

With a heavy sigh, he tightened his arms around her. "Zoey, there's something I must tell you about me and Connor. About vampires." He prayed she wouldn't turn away, wouldn't run from him after he'd explained things.

"Okay." She dragged the word out, as though attempting to calm herself, but he didn't miss her increased heartbeat.

"Vampires have a magnetic pull to them. Most of us call it a glamour, because with prolonged exposure, a mortal will begin to see things fuzzily, so strong is the desire to be with us. Like clouding your senses. It helps to lure prey to us and make them aroused. Willing. 'Tis hard to tell what's true desire and what is from this pull."

"A magnetic pull?" Zoey asked, brows drawn together as she seemed to puzzle her way through the information.

"Yes. We used to consider it magic, but I think perhaps it is more compared to animal pheromones. It acts on a mortal subconsciously, but powerfully."

"Vampire mojo," she whispered to herself. "I was right."

"Vampire mojo?" Ian almost laughed, but sobered when she answered him with a grave nod.

"I couldn't figure out why I was terrified of Connor chasing me, but the second he was close to me, I just wanted him too much to care about how frightened I was."

Ian stroked a hand along one of her arms, seeking to soothe her. "That's why I was furious with Connor. He took advantage of you, knowing how you would react."

She shook her head. "No, he didn't. I remember him asking me if that's what I wanted, and there was this moment of clarity, like that crazy desire had been lifted, but I still wanted him. Just like I still want you," she added the last in a shy little whisper.

"You want me?" He was too afraid to hope it was true. But how was he to know? Too many years had been wasted in his early years after turning, as he'd tried to figure out whether a mortal woman was truly interested in him, or whether it was the work of the glamour. Aside from Lara, it had always been the glamour, and that realization had always been painful.

"I do, but I'm so afraid that you don't want me back, that it's just my appeal as a walking Happy Meal that draws you in." Her words would have made him laugh, but the fear of rejection in her lovely eyes cut him soul deep.

"You are irresistible, Zoey. If I didn't hear that sweet little heartbeat thumping so madly against my chest, I'd have to question whether or not you might be the one with a glamour."

Her skeptical little scoff had him grin as she wrinkled her nose. "I doubt I'm irresistible."

"You know...a man might call that a challenge." He couldn't help but stare at her lips, drawn to the movement of her tongue slipping out to wet her lips. What would it feel like to have that tongue lick him, or those lips wrap around his cock as she sucked him into oblivion? She would be a natural, with her sensual curiosity. A devious, but shy smile danced across her lips. She was new to this sort of teasing, but he sensed she was enjoying it. She was challenging him, but not outright.

"A man? But not a vampire?" she asked.

Ian's lip's tilted up into a smile. She was brave enough after all.

"Be warned, Zoey. You challenged me." He curled one arm around the back of her neck, pillowing her head as he rolled on top of her. Her knees were locked together, but when he lowered his head and stole her lips, she softened. A few more seconds at the opening of her mouth, and once he'd gained entrance, her legs fell apart. He slid his hips between her knees and groaned as he settled into the cradle of her thighs.

It had been years since he'd allowed himself to truly enjoy a woman's body like this. She was built perfectly, small, compact. He loved spanning his hands over a woman's full thighs as he licked at her center, and he would do this with Zoey before long. Yes, he would thoroughly taste her in every way possible.

He coaxed her lips farther apart to slide his tongue inside. Her startled gasp made it impossible to resist deepening the kiss further. He wanted inside her mouth, inside her. He desired her, wanted to possess every part of her, even her heart...as foolish and dangerous as that was.

Zoey's hands explored his back, shaping the contour of Ian's muscles. He purred like a tiger at her eager touch. She tilted her head back, exposing her throat. He could hear the excited clatter of her heartbeat. He nuzzled her neck, then licked the spot where her pulse beat against her skin, the place where Connor left puncture wounds. The faint taste of dried blood was still there, calling to him like a siren's song. The urge was too hard to fight. He rubbed his hips against hers, grinding against the heated core of her body which was now blissfully bare to him since the shirt had ridden high on her waist.

Ian dropped his head and gripped her neck with his teeth, letting his fangs hold her still. He didn't break the skin, but his need to bite, to mark his prey was overwhelming...

Prey!

No. Zoey wasn't prey. She was his charge. She needed his protection. Ian let his fangs recede as he stared down at her. Her eyes were glazed over with desire. Her lips were swollen from his kisses and all he wished to do was to keep nibbling them like succulent fruit.

"Do you believe me now, Zoey? My sanity is practically in shreds." He pressed his hard shaft against her, both thankful for the shield of his pajamas and disappointed he couldn't slide against her slick sex and feel it against his cock.

The temptation would be too great. He'd sink into her, take the innocence he knew was there and not give her the proper love-making she deserved for their first time together. Sure, she was acting well enough as though she knew what to do, but he knew a sensual innocent when he saw one. Despite his body's needs, it was too soon. She deserved to be seduced, courted, wooed. He would give that to her, even if it killed him. They both deserved to know what lay between them wasn't the result of the glamour, but from true desire. His heart gave another strange little tug and he winced, breathing almost painfully for an instant.

"Why'd you stop?" Her hands rested on his shoulders, her fingertips caressed his neck.

"Because you're tired and need to rest, and I won't be able to stay awake much longer."

Zoey's lips formed the most adorable pout. "But I don't want to stop."

"I know, love, I know. But you're exhausted. There's plenty of time later." He kissed the tip of her nose. "Go to sleep."

She scowled. "No." Her brows drew down in a line and her lips plumped in a deeper pout than before.

He narrowed his eyes and focused, using his power of influence. "Go to sleep, Zoey."

She continued to scowl, but it was lessened by a heavy yawn. Her lashes batted up and down wearily.

"Did you just vampire voodoo me? I'm..." Another yawn broke her words apart. "Can't keep...my..." Her lashes fell and stayed fanned out over her cheeks. Her breathing slowed, as did her heartbeat. Her hands dropped from his neck to her sides.

Ian's body screamed in frustration. He focused on maudlin thoughts of the years when he and Connor had been mortal. It stilled his body's needs and brought him down from the blissful high of kissing Zoey. Kissing her was like looking up at the night sky, seeing endless stars or submerging himself in the ocean, feeling the waves roll past his body. It was powerful, unending, bigger than any one person.

With just one simple brush of his lips on hers, he no longer felt like Ian Kennedy. He wasn't an immortal, wasn't a man, he felt like something more, something greater. It made him want something, something he'd dared not hope for since he'd been turned. He dared not breathe the word. He wasn't ready and neither was she.

Instead he focused on Zoey and her power over him. The way she overwhelmed his senses. He'd never been that aroused, that lost in the moment with any other woman, except with Lara. He forced his mind away from those memories. She was many years gone and Zoey was here. Sweet, vibrant Zoey. It was time to start over, to live his life again. Seamus and Connor be damned. He was going to enjoy this Christmas.

CHAPTER 6

Connor O'Shea lay on his back in bed, glowering at the ceiling. One palm rested on his stomach, the other behind his head, providing a cushion. He was mad enough to punch something, but he wasn't that sort of man. He never let his temper manifest in anything but his words.

His father had used his fists, and Connor swore he'd never be like that. When a woman got his ire up, he tended to seduce, and then fuck her into blissful submission. Zoey wasn't like other women. It wasn't just her body that held him fascinated. It was the way her emotions flitted across her face, so full of expression, of meaning. After nearly two centuries mortals had become faceless, nameless, a means to an end for him. A way to survive. But not so with Zoey. He'd tasted her blood and what he'd seen through the connection, one he hadn't meant to allow, would have knocked him flat if he hadn't been on the bed.

A vampire could connect to their prey while feeding, but as a vampire grew more disciplined they could shut out the connection. He had been too lost in his game of capture and claiming of Zoey that he hadn't been prepared to block out her memories.

They'd rushed through him in wild, brilliant flashes, like summer lightning striking in the distance. *Warmth of a noon day sun upon his skin, the sound of wind chimes tinkling in a faint breeze, the excitement of blowing out birthday candles, a room heavy with the scent of sugar and melting wax.*

A hundred days of light and laughter had embedded themselves into his soul. She'd given him a gift of her life and she'd never known it. A mortal life with mortal blessings. One he could take into the darkness of his own heart. His chest squeezed and he huffed, suddenly short of breath. What a strange sensation. He hadn't ever done that before...except once, long ago with Lara. That had been a time when his body had seemed to revert back to its most human state, *almost* human at any rate. Did that mean...?

No, Lara was my true mate. And Lara is gone. This is fascination, nothing more. An echo of what I lost.

He didn't know what to do about Zoey. She was fiery, passionate, yet she seemed too sweet. He preferred his women wicked, wanton, willing to try anything in bed or out. He doubted Zoey would ever be so bold...

Yet her eyes had darkened with such fire when he'd brought her to climax. Her sheath had been tight, wet and so hot it scorched his fingers. She wasn't a virgin, no, but she was damned close. The right man, or former man, could tempt her to release the wanton woman he'd seen in those eyes.

He'd known right away she hadn't been with a man in quite some time. The look of shock on her face when she'd come—like she'd never felt such a violent outburst of pleasure before—nearly undid him. It would have been heaven to sink into her wet center and feel her walls clench down around him. He'd have taken her slow at first, built up to a blinding, pounding rhythm and have her screaming for more, harder and harder until they both collapsed in exhaustion from ecstasy.

Connor snarled and leapt out of bed. "Fuck!" He stalked out into the hall and into the bathroom. He stepped into the shower and cranked the knob over to cold, praying it would shock him out of his state of need.

The water helped a little, but he was still too aroused over the helpless, little, human female. He needed to stop thinking about her, about the way she felt beneath him, the scent of her skin mixed with the natural scent of her desire. His own skin seemed to glow with a hint of color, a faint hum of warmth despite the icy water sluicing over his skin. Yet another sign of a true mate. *Bloody hell.*

Connor shut off the water and stormed out of the shower, frustrated that he couldn't make his body forget her. He curled a towel around his hips, scowling at the tent that popped up. He stopped in the hall, arrested by the most intriguing aroma. He couldn't remember the last time he'd smelled something that good.

Curious, he padded toward the kitchen, following the scent like a bloodhound. It led to the take-out bags left on the counter. He opened the nearest sack and peered inside. Several small items were wrapped with wax paper. He reached in and retrieved a...taco? He unwrapped it and lifted it to his nose. The spices and the meat smelled good. *Really good.* He'd walked by a taco food truck just the other day and yet the scent there had been dull, a fraction of what he was taking in now. Connor cocked one hip against the bar and then took a huge bite. The taste exploded in his mouth, his taste buds set alive by the rich flavors.

He scarfed down the rest of the tacos and explored the other sacks with growing interest, his stomach still rumbling.

After fifteen minutes he'd downed half the fried rice, cheeseburgers and spaghetti, washing all of this down with three colas. His stomach was fit to burst, but the fullness was fantastic. It had been ages since he'd felt such need or felt so satisfied. How long had it been since he'd eaten human food? It had to have been before the Second World War...right after Lara died.

Connor eyed the empty take-out bags.

The sound of murmurs and sighs from Ian's room reached him. With a sinking feeling, he was facing the simple truth again.

Zoey. It had to be. She'd resurrected his appetite and, from the sounds of it, Ian's sex drive. Connor's as well, as much as he hated to admit it. He'd been as randy as a stoat when he'd gotten her on her back earlier. A frown tugged at his lips. He didn't want this. He didn't want to be reminded of everything he'd lost. Everything they'd both lost. And what they could lose again.

No more true mates, no more mortal lovers. I'm done with them.

Damn that Zoey Blake and her petal soft lips and killer curves. She was going to be the death of both of them.

Ian's room grew quiet. No more sweet murmurs or little sounds of lovemaking. Zoey's light breathing penetrated the silence, but that was all. Connor glanced about the kitchen and the living room, feeling oddly alone. He'd never minded before now how barren their house was, or how not having a woman of his own felt. But now it did. There were no photos except the ones Ian took of places they'd lived, nor items from the old days to remind either him or Ian of the passing years. They'd both thought it best to keep looking forward.

He and Ian had lived here for three years, and in that time they'd never met the neighbors or even spent time making this place a home. They couldn't afford to, not when they had to move every fifteen years so people wouldn't notice they didn't age. Immortality was a stagnant state of existence, yet they were always moving, leaving life after life behind. Zoey's presence in the house added something that he'd sorely missed, and it scared the hell out of him. Life was always followed by death, and he was so bloody tired of death, except, perhaps, his own.

Connor threw out the empty take-out bags. Lizzy bumped against his shin, purring, and he bent down to stroke her. He'd given Ian hell for bringing the cats home at first, but he'd soon learned to tolerate having the animals around. Perhaps he even enjoyed them. It put him into a routine, feeding and caring for them. Although he'd never tell Ian, it was nice to have something alive to touch every now and then. Something that wouldn't end up being his dinner, that is.

He would have preferred to seduce a woman and stroke her instead of a cat, but women were too much trouble, and he'd long since abandoned pursuing them. The only females who received his undivided attention now were Lizzy and Cleo. Titus, the male cat, avoided him and the feeling of distrust was mutual.

The cats were good for Ian too. They seemed to ground him. Give him purpose. Connor hated that he and Ian hadn't spent much time together in the last twenty years and it was putting a strain on their relationship. Even though they lived under the same roof, he and Ian took turns going out to hunt for their meals, avoiding each other as much as possible. It hadn't been on purpose, but now he saw that they'd fallen into a comfortable pattern living as near strangers. They'd once been like brothers, but the years had distanced them and he longed to get that brotherly camaraderie back.

Once again his mind strayed back to Zoey. No doubt she'd be a strain on their relationship too. Ian would want to keep her, like every stray he came across. And Connor would protest. But Zoey was human, not a cat. If she stayed, he'd end up bedding her. It was only natural; she was an attractive woman and he had only the wickedest thoughts of what he'd like to do to her. He was man enough to admit it. If Zoey stayed under his roof, he'd have her on her back, screaming in pleasure before long.

But Ian wanted her too...hence the complication.

They'd been able to share Lara with no jealousy. She'd loved them both and they'd cared only for her happiness. They had feared it would be hard to be with a woman and share her since neither man was attracted to the other, but she had made it easy. She'd been one of a kind.

Connor doubted Zoey would be willing to share a bed with two men, even if their sole intent was to fuck her mindless with pleasure.

A wave of sudden fatigue rushed through his limbs, and Connor knew he'd delayed too long in getting back to his room. Dawn must be minutes away. The exhaustion was numbing. Fighting it off, he stripped his towel and dropped it halfway down the hall. He stumbled into his room just as the heavy metal blinds installed in his windows dropped down, settling him in darkness. Though the daylight would not kill him, it would put him into a heavy sleep and if left too long, it would eventually burn his skin severely. He collapsed onto his bed, letting exhaustion chase him into darkness.

Damn, he wanted to be holding the mysterious sensual Zoey. But she was with Ian...

THE THIN LAYER *of ice on the black asphalt was more treacherous than Zoey realized, until it was too late. She tightened her mitten-covered hands over the steering wheel but her grasp slipped. Tires squealed and the light from her headlights spun out over the cliff's edge.*

Zoey screamed, but it was cut short as the car skidded past the end of the thin metal railing. There was one moment where the world seemed frozen, and then it all dropped away. The pit of her stomach collapsed and seconds later, the screech of metal and the horrible crashing of her world began.

The car rolled over and over. Snow, ice and rocks exploded through the empty space where the windshield had shattered. When the car came to a final stop, Zoey was trapped, her seat belt strangling the life out of her. She couldn't breathe. Her mittens dug into the belt but she couldn't get hold of it to jerk it off. Black dots spotted her vision and white pain seared her body. Even hanging upside down, the vision in her cracked rear view mirror was all too clear.

Her parents were in the back seat. Blood across their faces, their eyes wide and sightless as they looked out past her, seeing only what the dead could see.

"No...please, God, no..."

Zoey woke with a desperate wail of deepest agony. Cold tears dried down her cheeks and wet the pillow below her. Cold arms were wrapped around her body and she felt the shape of a masculine body curled up behind her. For a moment she couldn't remember where she was or who she was with. The icy cold body startled her, as though she'd woken up with a corpse, and she frantically scrambled out of bed. The body in the sheets didn't move and she could barely make out the man's features in the near pitch darkness.

The awful memory of that horrible night was submerged beneath the tide of memories from the last several hours—the sharp sting of the stabbing in the alley, the surprise of Ian's sudden rescue, the burn of his kiss, the ache of her body beneath Connor's. Ian. It was Ian in the bed. Her heart started to beat again at a frantic pace, as though desperate to catch up with itself after being still for several seconds.

Ian's bedroom was so dark that Zoey was hesitant to move at first. She didn't want to stub her toe on a bedpost. Her eyes sought the only source of light, a sliver of gold that crept in from beneath the door to the hallway.

She tugged the edge of Ian's shirt down and shivered. It would be so easy to crawl back into bed with him, but he was so cold. His heart didn't beat. It was not the most comforting or natural thing when she started to think about it.

Zoey didn't want to go back to sleep, not just yet. The dream still lurked in the corners of her mind. The guilt that ate away at her threatened to resurface. Her mouth was dry. A glass of water would be good. There had been too many nights where she hadn't slept well due to dehydration. She eased the door open and slipped into the hall, looking for the kitchen.

The clock on the sleek black oven read 3:45 PM. She'd slept through most of the day? It was such a relief to realize she'd gotten more than a few hours of sleep in one sitting.

After finishing two glasses of water, she set it in the dishwasher. Everything in the cupboards was brand new and seemed to be unused. Zoey wondered if Ian and Connor even owned dishwashing detergent. Probably not.

"Couldn't sleep?"

The husky murmur behind her ear was so soft and unexpected that she let out a squeak of surprise.

She turned and came face to face with Connor's bare chest. He was so tall she had to tip her head back to look him in the eye. She swallowed hard. His face was inscrutable, but the curve of his mouth had distracted her from whatever she'd been about to say. Warm brown eyes, like hot cocoa.

His answering laugh shook her as he pressed close. Something hard dug into her stomach and she jolted in shock.

"Easy, pet. 'Tis just my body making its desires known." He curled one hand around the back of her neck, possessive and dominating yet not harmful. The message was clear. She wasn't to move, to escape until he allowed it.

"You're naked!" Her voice was too shrill and breathless as she took in in the length of his lean, muscled... gloriously bare body. The blush that burst on her cheeks was hot enough that she broke out into a sweat. Rope after rope of corded muscle formed a six-pack of abs; she could feel every smooth hard contour as her breasts pressed against it. Damn, he was too tall, how could they ever...

Zoey shook her head, failing to clear the fog of lust that swamped her. Never in her life had she been so close to losing all sense of control. This had to be what Ian told her about, the glamour, the vampire mojo as she liked to call it. There didn't seem to be a world outside those perfect pectorals and biceps. There was just him. Connor. One hundred percent male. And she was a tiny delicate female by comparison. Knowing that he desired her sent bursts of electricity through her, both weakening her body and strengthening her own desires.

Connor's fingertips stroked her throat, the cool press of his fingers a balm to her fiery, sweat-covered skin. His gaze seemed slumberous as he looked down at her. She was a goner. He'd have his teeth in her neck, and she didn't stand a chance.

"Shall we get you naked too?" The suggestion flowed from his sensual lips with such lazy confidence that Zoey's knees turned to jelly. She would have collapsed onto the floor at his feet, but she stayed upright because his hips jerked forward, digging into hers, keeping her pinned.

"What do you think? Lose the shirt and show me that pretty skin, Zoey..." Her name, so often sounding childish when anyone else said it, sounded positively erotic the way the syllables rolled off his tongue. Her head felt light as she sucked in a harsh, much needed breath.

"Umm..." Nope, there would be no more articulate words from her today. *Cavewoman meet Caveman*, her inner voice giggled wildly.

Her mind blanked as he cupped her ass and lifted her into the air, then set her down onto the counter, bringing her face level to his. His hands cupped her cheeks, keeping her still. There was the barest hint of hesitation in his eyes, and then he took her mouth hard. She had no choice but to open up as he thrust his tongue inside. He seemed determined to devour her, consume her with his frantic play. Her hands found their way to his shoulders, digging her nails into him.

Connor's hands molded around her shoulders, squeezed, then slid down inch by inch along her back, tracing the curve of her spine until he found her hips and tugged hard, dragging her to the edge of the counter. His cock rubbed against her open folds, and she whimpered at the violent need she felt to have him inside her. He rocked, teasing mercilessly, but never giving her what her body screamed for.

"Oh, God, please!" she rasped between deep, drugging kisses.

His hands kneaded her ass, the movement along with his gyrating hips was going to end her... He seemed to sense that she was fraying at the edges and drew his head back, gazing directly at her. His eyes, once brown, were almost black now and wreathed with just a hint of crimson around the pupil that would have scared her if she hadn't been driven insane with sexual need.

His hands moved back up to her shirt at the collar and in one swift move, tore the shirt apart. Buttons went flying as he tossed the clothing away. He growled low as he held her away from him to stare at her exposed breasts. They felt swollen and heavy, the tips peaked and begging for his attention. She was too shy to ask, so she arched her back, offering them to him without words. Conner dropped his head to her neck, nibbling her collarbone with frustrating tenderness, then moving lower.

Zoey hissed as he took the nipple in his mouth. He suckled hard, pulling on the tip, his tongue laving and his teeth scraping over it until she whimpered and moaned. Waves of heat assailed her and she fisted her hands in his dark blond hair. Her eyes clamped shut as cold air teased her breasts. He lifted his mouth away and straightened.

He grabbed her by the waist and carried her over to the couch in the living room, stretching her out beneath him. Before she could react he'd flipped her onto her stomach and covered her body with his. She felt his cock slide between the cleft of her ass as he slid against her from above. His mouth was on her neck, kissing, licking, nibbling. One forearm rested by her shoulder, propping him up enough to prevent him from crushing her. His other hand cupped her breast, squeezed, pinched her nipple and smoothed its way down her waist to the fiery wet heat between her thighs.

She raised her hips up, encouraging him to enter from behind, to take what she freely offered. His next growl sent skittering tingles along her spine as he cupped her between her legs, pressing the heel of his palm on her clit. She pushed against his hand, trying to rub against him, anything to satisfy the need clawing at the insides of her body.

She cried out Connor's name as he slid his thigh between hers, pressing against her bottom, the added pressure sending her over the cliff of self-control. She turned her head over her shoulder, needing his mouth on hers. He complied, briefly dueling with her tongue, feeding her thirst for more of everything, more of him.

"I need...need..." Before she could get out the rest he sunk three fingers deep into her, pushing her open, stretching her to accommodate him. This was beyond anything she'd ever dreamed of, all muscle and strength, passion and sex in one tall, exciting package. He'd fuck her into a coma if she let him, and she wanted to let him. Sleeping with Connor would strip her of her soul. She'd become a mindless wanton creature craving him and only him and the idea was *so* appealing.

Connor didn't waste time as he worked her body to a frenzied climax. He rocked himself against her bottom, mimicking the harried patterns of a wild mating.

Her head flew back, pressing against his shoulder as she came. He continued to work his fingers, refusing to give her time to breathe as he brought ripple after ripple of ecstasy to the surface. Her body quaked, her limbs spasming beneath his body.

Something warm splashed on her lower back and Connor shouted a curse, muffling it somewhat by lightly sinking his teeth into her shoulder, enough so that the sting sent a second smaller orgasm through her already weakened and sated body. The only thing that stung her in that moment was knowing he hadn't been inside her. Was he concerned about pregnancy? Was that even possible with vampires?

Finally, he released her neck, kissing the bruised skin before he sighed and rested his cheek against her.

Connor held her for a long moment, neither of them

thinking or speaking, just his body above hers, keeping her pinned to the couch as they both recovered. She didn't want to move, couldn't move. She wanted to stay here forever. Nothing else had to exist outside this moment. One wondrous moment followed by soft breathing and the gentle journey of coming down from heights of pleasure.

The haze of desire was gone, but in its place was something more, something concrete she could cling to. Not glamour. Whatever had just happened between them, and what she was feeling now, that wasn't because of that. Her thoughts were lucid now, even as tired as she was, and she *still* wanted him, wanted to be in his arms, even just to be held.

Zoey's eyes had almost drifted closed when she felt Connor shift above her and get up. She protested with a lazy "No..."

He returned with a damp dishtowel. Smoothing the towel over her lower back and between her thighs, he wiped her clean. She ought to have been embarrassed, but she was too exhausted to care. He got up again, disappeared through a door just off the kitchen, probably the laundry room. Turning on her side, she watched him as he walked back. He was so beautiful and...still aroused. She dropped her eyes and blushed, all too aware of him and his... She shut her eyes and feigned a yawn.

A cool breeze drifted over her skin and with it she returned to some semblance of reality. She was lying naked on a couch in a house with two men she barely knew, and she'd had sex...well...sort of...with one of them. And she couldn't forget the most ridiculous part of it. They were *vampires*. That part never seemed to get less strange, and yet she questioned so little about it.

"You should go back to Ian's room, lass," Connor said. His voice forced her to look at him again. He was standing there, arms crossed, still completely naked, watching her.

Zoey rubbed her eyelids. Maybe this was all some strange dream. Maybe she was still dying in that alley and this was all some hallucination as her body shut down. The thought made her shiver and not in a good way. But this couldn't be a dream because everything felt too real.

Maybe I should just accept this for what it is. Any woman would kill to be in her place right now with two gorgeous men...er...vampires, interested in her.

It was the second time she'd given in to Connor's seduction. Shame should have weighed her down, but instead there was only a melancholy fatigue. She forced herself to get up and retrieve the torn white shirt from the kitchen floor. She slipped her arms into the oversized sleeves and tugged it back over her body, thankful for even the minimal cover it provided. The buttons were gone, but the shirt was large enough to wrap around her like a robe. Connor stayed still, studying her with his honey-brown eyes, no longer black and the pupils not wreathed with fire anymore. Human eyes. Not the eyes of a predator.

Under the weight of Connor's stare, she dared not raise her own eyes. She fled down the hall back to the sanctuary of Ian's room. She slid back into his arms, glancing at the glowing red numbers of the clock on the nightstand. It was already after four in the afternoon. She'd slept most of the day away, which didn't really matter, given that she was now apparently on a vampire time schedule.

In a few more hours Ian would probably be awake. Why had Connor been up? Was he less affected by the sun than Ian? She'd have to ask one of them later. She was curious enough to risk that. She pulled the thick down comforter higher up on her and the movement woke Ian. He shifted, tightened his hold around her waist, brushed his lips over her cheek in a sweet sleepy kiss and then dozed off again.

Guilt filled her with an extra helping of self-loathing. Twice now she'd been pleasured by one man and run straight into the arms of another... God, was she that easy? There wasn't another way to see it. She despised herself, lusting after two men. One who clearly intended to use her, and one who clearly wanted a relationship. She kept giving herself over to the wrong man. It should have been Ian, the man who'd professed to care about her, that she should have been with. Shouldn't it?

What had happened to make her this way? Was it losing her parents, or was it when her life had crumbled around her and she'd realized she would do anything for food and a warm place to sleep? She'd never sold herself. She'd escaped that fate...so far. Was staying with Ian and Connor the same thing? Did it matter that she hungered for them and the passion their touch inspired in her?

Ian shifted next to her, nuzzled her neck and grazed his teeth along the sensitive skin leading up to her ear. She sighed and stirred restlessly as tingles of fresh arousal burst inside her like a flash-bang. Her body should have been too tired to respond with any interest, but here she was, hungering for Ian.

"You okay?" Ian murmured.

She rolled over to face him, curling into him as he pulled the blankets up to her chin.

"I got thirsty." The half lie fell bitter on her lips.

Ian's nose touched hers, rubbing in an Eskimo kiss that had her blush. She melted when he put his lips to hers. The kiss was fire and honey combined. The need for more was there, but he controlled it, even though he settled a hand on the flare of her hips, pushing the white shirt up past her stomach. The sensation of him being naked there, his hand so close to the apex of her thighs had her quivering all over again. He dug his fingers into her with the barest hint of a bite and she arched into him, capturing his lips as her own need made her lose her grip on her control.

When she broke the kiss, he gave a smile that made his eyes crinkle. "I was thinking, when we get up later, we could go Christmas tree shopping. Connor and I don't have one but since you're here it would be nice to do things properly. You'll stay here with us for Christmas, won't you? I know you want to get back on your feet, but jobs will be scarce until after the holidays."

Zoey's fingertips traced the strong line of his jaw as she considered his offer. She wanted to stay, but should she?

"Do vampires celebrate Christmas?"

"Connor and I do. We're Catholics and haven't been struck by lightning entering a church yet, so I've got to believe we're not creatures of evil. Connor threw a vial of holy water at me once, claimed it was for test purposes, but I knew he was in a foul mood that day. Nothing happened of course. Just got wet." He chuckled.

Zoey pondered that. She hadn't even considered that Ian or Connor might be evil. She knew they were vampires, but neither of them had made her skin crawl like the man who'd attacked her in the alley, who had been all too human. Perhaps vampirism wasn't religious but scientific, like their bodies evolved, or were affected by a virus in the blood of another vampire, rather than anything supernatural. Theories about vampires in popular culture seemed to welcome every possible explanation these days. She wished she knew what the truth was, but it seemed even Ian and Connor didn't know what they really were.

Turning back to their conversation, and Christmas, she grinned hopefully up at him.

"You'd really buy a tree just for me?"

His lips curved in a boyish smile. "Absolutely. Wouldn't be Christmas without one."

"Okay. I'll stay."

"Good. I would hate to have to vampire voodoo you into staying," he teased.

She punched his chest. "No more of that, thank you very much."

"Very well," he sighed. "Go back to sleep, I'll wake you in a few hours when it's evening."

Content enough to agree, she tucked her head under his chin and snuggled closer. His skin was cold, but it warmed where she touched him and falling asleep was all too easy.

She prayed the nightmare wouldn't return.

CHAPTER 7

Connor leaned against the kitchen counter, palms spread on the granite. He was still naked and aroused as hell. The residual guilt he normally felt when finding any level of satisfaction since Lara's death hadn't surfaced. Another sort of guilt did. He'd just taken Zoey—or rather, *almost* taken her—seduced her with her own desire as he'd done to countless others. She'd enjoyed it, of course, but that didn't mean what he'd done had been right, regardless of why he'd done it.

It was the dream. He'd been unable to stand looking into her eyes and seeing the remnants of the nightmare that had woken her up. He'd been there with her through every silent scream, every panicked second of the night that had changed her life.

He hadn't meant to get inside her head. Ian had the

power to influence and manipulate mortals, but Connor's immortal gift was different. One minute Connor had been lost in the darkness of his own dreams, and the next he was caught up in Zoey's mind. Invisible, yet experiencing her fear as she lost control of the car and went over the cliff's edge. He'd felt the impact that had killed her parents, yet she'd somehow survived. He wasn't sure how she'd escaped the car; she'd jerked awake before he could see the rest. He'd woken as well, body shaking as though he'd been hit with a shot of adrenaline.

It had taken every ounce of his self-control not to march into Ian's room and steal the scared little woman away and offer her the comfort she needed. But he'd waited, listening to the padding of her bare feet on the kitchen floor and the creak of the faucet as she got a glass of water. But soon he couldn't resist any longer.

When he ventured into the hall and saw her in the shirt and nothing else, rational thought fled and his libido had taken over. He had to touch her, taste her, tease her, please her. Anything to erase the wounded shadows in her eyes.

He hadn't intended to sate himself as well, but she'd been so deliciously wild in her release that he'd come all over her delectably round backside. It had shamed him as much as it had embarrassed her. He'd cleaned her as best he could, but she'd still turned tail and ran from him. Straight back to Ian.

He cursed and pounded a fist against the granite

counter. The stone cracked. There was no going back to sleep, not while he was on edge like this. He was able to shrug off the daylight easier than Ian and had little trouble staying awake when he had to. In an hour the sun would be low in the sky. He needed to get out, breathe the fresh air, restore his sanity.

Connor went back to his room, pulled his clothes on and stepped back into the hall. There were soft murmurs in Ian's room again. Talk of Christmas trees...

Conner snarled silently. Well, there was only one way he could think of to compete with Ian and his damned romantic side. He could offer Zoey things she needed, practical things, not just trees and nostalgia. A woman needed clothes to stay warm in this weather. And if it so happened that he was able to help her in and out of those clothes...well, he'd show her just what else he could offer once she was flat on her back beneath him.

Connor returned to the kitchen, found his wallet and keys and left the house. His Land Rover was parked in the driveway, a light bit of snow dusting the windows and car roof. The evening sun drooped over the treetops to the west. Lethargy struggled to take hold of him, but he'd always been strong. With enough rest, he could resist its call. It was a pity that a strong cup of coffee wouldn't help, though. His vampiric metabolism didn't allow caffeine or alcohol to affect his body.

Christmas lights adorned the rooftops and lined the sidewalks. Only their house lacked any such merry twinkle. He'd never bothered with lights before, but now he wished he'd had. Perhaps he should.

Connor shook his head and headed for his car. He brushed the snow off the windows and got inside. There was a mall nearby and he could get what he needed there.

The sun's fading UV rays didn't penetrate his Land Rover's tinted windows, and the rush of energy that came from the darkness of his car was a relief. Connor had learned to love the heavy cloak of darkness and the power that came with it. Zoey was like the night, a clear midnight with a bright moon. She enveloped him, energized him, made his every dark desire writhe in the shadows of his heart. She made him long for tangled sheets and sweat-soaked limbs twining in the erotic movements of wild sex.

The images had his body rioting with arousal once again. No. Zoey needed sweetness and soft wooing, the sort of things Ian would give her.

Connor navigated the streets, driving carefully, never more aware of the danger of ice-slickened roads. He couldn't erase Zoey's memory of her car shooting off the edge and crashing in the snow.

Holiday shoppers packed the sidewalks when Connor reached the mall. Parking was hell, but Connor waited until a spot opened. Patience was just one of the few perks of being immortal. A mother passed by his car as he pulled into a spot, towing her three children in a line. They toddled after her in marshmallow-shaped winter coats sporting a rainbow of bright colors. The last little boy, who looked to be about four years old, stopped and stared at Connor from beneath a ski cap and scarf up to his nose. Connor shut his car door, locked it and slid the keys into his pocket, watching the boy with the same interest.

The boy tilted his head back to stare up at Connor.

"Are you a giant?" the boy asked in the way children always did when they noticed something obvious that no adult would ever consider saying out loud.

"I am, and you're quite the wee lad, aren't you?" he replied. He'd had plenty of siblings when he'd been alive and knew to answer a child with an answer akin to what they'd asked. It made them feel more grown up, which was quite important to children.

"Yup!" The boy agreed. "Merry Christmas, Mister!" His muffled exclamation had Connor's lips tug up in a reluctant smile.

"And to you," he echoed. He didn't like to think about his own family, the one he'd had to kill when the need for blood had taken over and he'd been locked inside the house with them. They'd been starving, on the verge of death, but it hadn't mattered. Both he and Ian had murdered their own kin because they hadn't known how to control their bloodlust. But that was the past, a very distant one. He focused on the happy memories, the ones that made him smile—it was that or feel his heart bleed again and again for the rest of his eternal life.

He turned to face the monstrous mall and squared his shoulders. If mothers with children could survive the frenzy, he could as well. Surely it couldn't be as bad as the wars he'd fought in over the last two centuries.

The throngs of people would surely have suffocated him, if he'd needed to breathe. Thankfully he did not. His body still drew breath, out of habit more than anything, but it was unnecessary. Long ago he'd been dumped in Dublin Bay with iron boots on because of a bad debt—it had taken him two days to walk back to shore to find a blacksmith to remove them.

The first stop he made was a department store. A nice-looking woman in her mid-thirties, wearing a nametag that read "Candace" smiled knowingly as he took in the endless clothes racks.

"Overwhelming, isn't it?" Her eyes were warm and her smile genuine.

"A bit." His voice dropped low as he made sure no one else could hear him admit it.

"Who are you shopping for? I can help," Candace offered, a bright smile warning him that he ought to control his effect on her before she gave him her phone number. Connor was ready to refuse but then realized he did need help. He willed himself to be less desirable. It was strange to think that a physical affect like the glamour could be controlled through his will alone, but that was how it worked.

"It's my woman. She needs clothes...underthings... shoes...everything."

"New relationship?" A twinkle of amusement danced in Candace's eyes.

"Very new."

"Well, tell me about her. What does she usually wear? Do you know her size?" Candace led him over to an area with casual clothes.

"She's small...but with curves that could kill a man," he replied without thinking and held out his hands to show Zoey's hip size. Candace's cheeks reddened but she studied his hands and nodded.

"Size eight, perhaps? How short?"

Connor tapped his hand to his chest. "Comes up to here exactly." He'd never forget that, not when she'd tilted her face up to look at him. The wariness and arousal warring with her past pain all there for him to see in such lovely eyes.

"Five-foot-four then?" Candace started pulling out pairs of jeans, checking sizes. She handed him a light and dark pair of jeans, then waved for him to follow her to a sweater rack. "You really should get her proper measurements, but I assume this is meant to be a surprise?"

"Yes."

Over the next hour, Candace helped him gather several pants, tops, a couple of coats, sneakers, boots and even a few strappy heels and a couple of fancy black dresses. Everything a young woman would need. She'd just informed him of their return policy in case the measurements were off when he remembered Zoey needed undergarments.

"What about...underclothes?" he asked Candace.

"Oh! I forgot." She ushered him to the lingerie section.

Connor's eyes nearly bugged out when he'd stared at the lacy thongs and sheer lingerie hanging on the mannequins. There were also flannel and silk pajamas as well as robes and slippers. His eyes kept drifting back to the see-through items.

Since when did women wear such... Christ, the last time he'd been with a woman such lacy, strappy things hadn't been nearly as enticing as these newer more revealing creations.

"Men usually buy the more revealing items, but...if I may give you some advice?"

Candace paused and Connor nodded.

"Keep your girlfriend warm. Buy something thick and soft for her."

Connor admitted the woman had a point. Zoey would look delicious in lingerie, but she'd freeze when she slept.

"Better go with the flannel," he said.

Candace smiled and started gathering a robe, slippers and flannel PJs before turning back to Connor.

"And the...sexy stuff?" She tried to hide a smile. Connor grinned back at her and pointed to the little red see-through garment that had a fringe of white fur on the edges of its short skirt.

"I want that."

"Lovely choice. The Christmas babydoll is always popular this time of year."

Connor could see why. The top part was practically transparent and would cup Zoey's breasts nicely, while the small red bikini bottom would reveal more of her glorious backside—a backside that he still ached to cup and mold and, Lord help him, smack it. *Hard.* She'd made such a sweet little moan when he'd done that last night.

His cock swelled at the thought, pressing against the front of his black wool pants. The damned thing seemed to have a mind of its own, thanks to Zoey.

He let Candace take him back to the checkout station and handed over his credit card. It had been ages since he'd had such a good time. Shopping for his woman had been entertaining. And she would be his woman. He stilled. His woman, but Ian's too. There was no way he could separate his friend from Zoey. They would share, like before with Lara. An old ache, one he so often tried to deny, burned a hole in his chest when he thought of Lara.

"Thank you, Candace. You've been very helpful." He took the three large bags and winked at the shopping store clerk.

"You're very welcome, Mr. O'Shea." She handed him back his card. "Your girlfriend is a very lucky woman. She'll love the things you bought. I promise. *Any* woman would."

Assured by her words, Connor left the store grinning.

The urge to get back home and shower Zoey with these gifts was so strong that he nearly used his preternatural speed to return to his car. The drive home took far too long. His usual patience evaporated long before he pulled into the driveway. The sun was below the horizon now, and the streetlights illuminated the nearby houses. The warmth of their glow mingled with those of the Christmas lights. He was struck by the beauty he'd taken for granted far too long. With a shake of his head, he turned back to the car.

Connor retrieved the shopping bags from the trunk, hurried to the garage door and ducked inside. He kicked the snow off his boots and headed to the living room. He ground to a halt when he saw Zoey curled up on the couch covered in a blanket. Lizzy, the tabby, lounged on Zoey's lap, little white-tipped paws kneading the blanket. Ian was in the kitchen staring at the bare cupboard with a scowl.

"There you are. You didn't answer your phone. We need groceries. Food." Ian's eyes dropped to the bags Connor carried. "But it seems you've been shopping already."

Connor walked over to Zoey and set the bags at her feet.

"I have. For Zoey." He let his voice caress the name as he'd done earlier when she'd melted into his kiss. Her eyes flicked from the bags up to his face.

"Oh... I couldn't... Whatever you bought you have to

take it back." She tucked her feet up under the blanket, as though to get as far away as she could from the bags, like they were filled with poisonous snakes.

The anticipation that had been slowly building in his chest as he waited to see her pleasure died a swift death. His chest tightened and his features reverted to a mask of stone.

"I bought them for you." His tone was harsher than he'd meant it to be.

Her eyes narrowed and a flush of red accented her cheeks. "And I can't accept them. I have no way of repaying you."

Repay him? *Repay him?* What a stupid notion.

"I don't want your money." Again his tone had more of a bite than it should have.

"Oh, I see. You expect me to pay you some *other* way?" Her tart reply made him bare his teeth. His fangs slid down in anger.

"Bloody hell, woman, I would never expect you to... It's Christmas!" He snatched the bags up from the floor and marched off to his room. His pride was wounded, his good intentions sullied by her black assumptions. When he reached his room, he threw the bags down and slammed the door. The wood splintered a little as it crashed into the frame. The anger in him deflated, replaced by the empty pang of disappointment.

I was a fool to think I could show her I care...that I want her as much as Ian does.

He wished he could go back to yesterday, when he'd first laid eyes on her. If only he'd sent her away and never looked back. But she'd stayed and the walls of ice surrounding his heart were nearly melted through. She was a damned ray of sunlight determined to pierce him clear through his soul.

He'd done something nice, and she'd thrown it back in his face. Perhaps she wasn't the sweet, warm-hearted woman he'd believed her to be. Did she mean to play him against Ian? Or worse, she might want only Ian. He didn't want it to be true, he wanted…

Damn. He wanted *her*, just wanted her to like him the way she liked Ian.

But Zoey wasn't Lara. Zoey had rejected him and chosen Ian. There wasn't anything he could do to change that. He and Ian were like brothers, and he wouldn't fight to take a woman who didn't want him. There was only one thing left to do. He'd leave tonight and spend the holidays somewhere else until Zoey left his home.

What if she didn't leave? He couldn't come back if she was still here. His self-control was fraying and he wouldn't last if he had to be around Zoey and not have her. A heavy weight pressed on his chest. He was thankful, however briefly, he wasn't mortal, or else he'd have trouble breathing.

Connor sat on the edge of the bed, propped his elbows on his knees and covered his face with his hands, rubbing his eyes. A sigh of defeat escaped his lips.

CHAPTER 8

"Not that I want to encourage you to choose him over me," Ian said slowly, "but you must believe Connor's intentions were good."

Guilt gnawed at Zoey's insides. She kept making mistakes, such big mistakes when it came to these two men.

"Even if he's just being kind, I can't take these things. I don't want to owe him."

"Zoey." The exasperation in Ian's tone was surprisingly thick. "Twas a gift. You can't owe someone for a gift. You need those clothes. I threw yours out because they were in a sorry state. You might as well take what Connor bought for you."

"You *threw out* my clothes?" She set Lizzy on the couch next to her and tossed the blanket off her body. As she jumped up, the edges of his buttonless shirt fluttered, threatening to fly open. She snatched the shirt ends and wrapped them tight around her. Grudgingly, she realized he had a point. She needed clothes.

Ian walked over to her and cupped her face with his palms.

"It's been thirty years since he's shown any interest in life. I was worried I was losing him, Zoey. He was turning more animal than man. But with you, I see the old Connor, my friend. He's trying to reach out and connect with you. Please let him, for my sake."

Ian's eyes were bright with emotions—love, regret, longing, and determination. He was asking her to share herself, at least a part of herself, with Connor because he loved the man like a brother and would do anything to save him, even share her.

It should have bothered her to think that a man would share her with his friend, but it didn't. She found it wondrous, sweet even, that the two of them would go so far in order to ensure the other's happiness. How many people could say they'd do the same?

Zoey's throat burned. "Okay," she agreed. Not for Ian's sake, but for Connor's. He needed her, more than Ian needed her, at least on some level. The realization that she could help him made her pride regarding his charity irrelevant.

Ian dropped his head and placed a kiss on her lips. "Thank you."

It burned like a well-kept fire by the hearth, a reassurance that he would be there when she returned. The parting of their lips was a tender thing, full of longing. When it ended, the flutter of lashes and the softening of his eyes became only a sweet memory as she turned down the hall and approached Connor's room. She rapped lightly on the door, using her free hand to hold her shirt together.

"Go away!" he bellowed. It would probably have been wise to leave him alone, but she didn't. Instead, she opened the door.

Connor sat on the edge of his bed, elbows propped on his knees, chin resting in one palm. He dropped his hands and stared at her as she entered. The glare on his face would have turned a less determined woman into stone. Zoey knelt at his feet by the shopping bags and looked up at him. A small black cat peeped out from under the large bed, yellow eyes wide and unblinking.

"*Mreow?*"

"Hush, Cleo. I'll make her go away," Connor promised. The cat slunk further back under the bed, vanishing from view. She appeared to be a sweet but timid thing.

Zoey ignored Connor's brusque tone. "Well? Aren't you going to show me what you bought?" Where she summoned the casual curiosity in her tone, she didn't know.

Connor glared at her.

"Fine. I'll just look myself." She reached for the bag closest to her. Connor snatched it from her hands.

"You said you didn't want them," he snapped. "You *rejected* them."

"And now I'm *un*rejecting them." She plucked the bag from his hands and set it down, reaching inside to pull out a pair of brown leather ankle boots and a couple of comfortable-looking jeans.

"You can't just unreject something," Connor growled. He seemed to be under the foolish belief that his side of the argument had merit.

Zoey ignored him and stroked her fingertips over the butter-soft leather boots before raising her gaze to his with admiration.

"These are lovely." She meant it too. They were beautiful boots, and she couldn't wait to wear them. Hopefully, they fit.

Connor leaned forward, tore the boots from her hands and held them aloft.

"A pity you like them now, because you cannot have them. You cannot go around changing your mind."

Zoey rose to her feet and leapt at him to get the boots. "I'm a woman. We're allowed to."

He lifted the boots higher. When she jumped to reach them she fell into his body, knocking them both onto the bed. Connor groaned as she wriggled up him to get at the boots. When she slid back down, a hard bulge in his trousers rubbed against her. She fought off the wave of desire that swept through her with all the danger of a riptide.

"Easy, pet. You'll be the death of me." Connor dropped his head back onto the bed as she got off him, kneeling by the rest of the bags, her new boots clutched to her chest. She dared him with an aggressive stare to come after them again.

"What else did you get me?" She started pulling items out of the rest of the bags.

Connor gave in and watched her, quiet and pensive, his brown eyes dark with turbulent emotions. Zoey held up a bag, offering it to him.

"Would you like to show me what else you bought? I'd like to see. It was really very thoughtful. I'm sorry about what I said earlier. I've been on my own for too long. Everything has a price, usually one I'm not willing to pay. All of this is just so...insane. I mean, I got rescued by vampires who are buying presents. I think I'm allowed to overreact a little, right? Say you forgive me. Please, Connor." She peeped up at him, praying he'd forgive her for acting like a fool. His gesture really had been grand, and she'd been a fool to treat his kindness so suspiciously.

The hardness in Conner's eyes was not the least bit comforting. After a long moment, however, a hint of warmth returned. His eyes became like a fresh pot of brewed coffee, dark and hot.

"I'm sorry, lass, I reacted like a wounded bear. I should have been more understanding." He cleared his throat, then waved at the bags. "I bought a little of everything..." He took the bag she offered, pulling out a classy black cocktail dress that had a low dip in the back that would almost reach her backside if she were to wear it. Understated, yet incredibly sexy, just the way she wished to be when she pictured herself with a normal life. How had he known?

Sometime later, Zoey sat back on her heels, surrounded by a small mountain of clothes. Only one bag remained untouched, a small red bag with fancy tissue paper. Her fingers caught the handles at the same time Connor's did.

"Oh, that's not for you—"

"But..."

"Go on, Connor. Let her open it." From the doorway, Ian peered in, his tone more dangerous and seductive than it had ever been before. A knowing grin crossed his lips. He leaned against the doorjamb, wearing only a pair of faded blue jeans, the top button undone. Something about that, the half-dressed man in front of her, sent shivers through her. These men would surely drive her mad. Her perception of both of them was changing. She should take neither man lightly. Like it or not, she was at their mercy.

"Go on, Zoey, open it," Ian encouraged. His look was almost feline and highly predatory, as though he hungered at the sight of her.

Her hands shook as she removed the tissue and

brushed over something soft and furry. She gripped the item and pulled it out of the sack. It was a babydoll, a thin red piece of lingerie, the hem of the flowing skirt-like top lined with white fur.

"Oh!" Her lips parted with a little gasp.

Connor's face paled, and he tugged at the collar of his black sweater.

"I'll take it back," he muttered and reached for it.

Zoey shook her head and clasped the lingerie to her chest. "No! I like it. I've just never worn something like this...before." The blush that followed her breathless words must have reached the roots of her hair.

"I wouldn't worry. You won't be in it long." Ian's dark promise sent a shiver through her. Zoey didn't know what to say to that. She swallowed and gathered the mountain of clothes and stood.

"Thank you, Connor. These are wonderful." *You are wonderful*, nearly spilled out as well. The last thing she needed was to make a spectacle of herself by revealing how much she liked him. How much she liked them both.

"You're welcome." His gruff reply made her smile for some reason.

"You should shower and change," Ian said. "We can go out when you're done." She nodded and tried to slide past him through the doorway, rubbing against him as she passed. A riot of heat spiked through her when his masculine scent and the barest hint of aftershave drifted beneath her nose. Her body flushed, eager to finish what every one of his kisses had promised her.

Zoey forced herself to flee to the bathroom and escape the temptation Ian presented. She needed time to gather her thoughts and steel herself against the advances the two vampires made against her. She had to be sure her mind was her own. Knowing what she knew now about their glamour, and how it affected her reaction to them, it was easy to doubt what she was feeling. They were sex on a stick to her, but was that actually how she felt? Or just a chemical manipulation of her body reacting to them? The last thing she wanted, the last thing she could afford, was to be swept away by her hormones and getting confused about what was real. If she had time to think with some distance, she might be able to figure out what she really felt about Ian and Connor.

None of the trees in the lot were right. They were all too perfect, too flawless. A Christmas tree ought to have character and be unique. Zoey rubbed her new mittens together and glanced around, looking for her pair of tall Irish vampires. She couldn't help but smile when she spotted them hovering at the back of the lot, shoulders touching as they stared at something she couldn't see. Zoey attempted to sneak up on them, trying not to laugh.

"'Tis the sorriest looking twig I've ever seen," Ian said to Connor.

"More like driftwood than a tree," Connor agreed. "What do you think, Zoey?"

So much for being sneaky. They hadn't even glanced in her direction. Zoey put her hands on their shoulders and gently nudged them apart so she could what they were looking at.

"It's perfect!"

"You must be joking," Connor said.

But she wasn't, and she couldn't stop smiling. Clearly neither of them had ever watched *A Charlie Brown Christmas*. It was the perfect tree. More like a large, five-foot high twig with some misplaced branches.

"Can we get this one?" she pleaded. Ian and Connor's mouths opened slightly.

"Really?" they asked in unison.

"Of course! My father always said that the perfect tree was the one that was unique, different. The saddest looking trees are usually the ones with the most charac-ter." Zoey stepped up to the tree and reached out to touch the nearest branches.

"It looks a bit like Ian's—"

Ian silenced Connor with a light blow to his stomach.

Zoey ignored them as the two vamps tussled like over-grown boys; she looked instead at the tree. The pine needles feathered over the thick wool of her mitten. So many memories of other Christmases, ones that were bittersweet to recall. Her mother at home with chili cooking in the crockpot, while Zoey and her father made the annual trip to the tree lot to find the right tree. God, she'd missed the heavy scent of evergreen.

She bit her bottom lip to stop it from trembling. Her breath caught in her throat. It was all too much, too soon. She turned away and bumped into Ian's chest. His arms curled around her, pulling her into his body. The sobs came, and though quiet, they wracked her body.

"Shhh…" Ian soothed.

"Ah, it means that much to you…" Connor muttered from somewhere behind her. "We'll get the twig… er…tree."

A laugh bubbled in her throat, and she stared up at Ian. Connor was right behind her, so near that she was suddenly, intensely aware of how close all three of them had become. It struck her in that moment that the three of them felt right. She shared the intimate space with them and there was no awkwardness, no competition or concerns. She'd been so worried and ashamed for wanting them both before, but the temptation was too great to resist. Why should she fight something that felt so right?

She wiped her eyes with her sleeve and managed a watery smile.

"My dad and I used to buy the least perfect tree on the lot. It was our tradition." She looked away, shy and a little embarrassed by her reaction. "I wasn't prepared for how sad it made me, to be here without him."

Ian stroked her hair back from her face and brushed a kiss over her forehead.

"Let's make a new tradition then. Connor, get the tree."

Two hours later, Zoey was sitting in a lawn chair in the driveway laughing as Connor and Ian argued about how to rig up the Christmas lights on the roof. The two century-old vampires couldn't agree on traditional lights or icicle lights.

"Zoey, love, tell Connor here that these are more appropriate..." Ian came toward her, holding a string of traditional lights.

Connor growled and tripped Ian as he passed by. Ian face-planted in the snow, only to jump up and leap at his friend like an animal. The two men wrestled like tiger cubs. Zoey wasn't worried; she heard laughing amidst their scuffling.

"Calm down, you two! Go with the icicle lights." Both men stilled. Ian had Connor in a head lock. They both raised their heads, reluctant grins on their faces.

"Fine. Icicles it is. You can make it up to me later, Zoey. But I only accept payments in kisses." Ian winked.

Zoey blushed all the way to her toes. The idea had a

little too much appeal, and she was sure she'd happily get herself deep into debt.

"Let's go inside and warm up," Conner said. "Well, those of us who need to. We'll finish the lights tomorrow." He and Ian stood up and brushed snow off their clothes.

The house was warm and merry. The tree by the window was lit up and covered with shiny balls and various ornaments that the three of them had hung before going outside to put up the Christmas lights. Music drifted through the air along with the scent of nutmeg and gingerbread.

It was everything she loved about the holidays, and even though she missed her parents, being here with Ian and Connor somehow felt just as special. A new memory to add to the old. Never in a thousand years would she have guessed she'd be spending Christmas with two handsome immortals, each determined to seduce her and care for her at the same time. She doubted any other woman would be as lucky as she was tonight.

A naughty idea tiptoed feather light into her mind. She bit her bottom lip to hide the smile it gave her. Was she brave enough to do it? Was she ready? She shot a glance at Ian and Connor. Connor was stretched out, feet propped up over one arm of the couch, hands clasped behind his head, looking relaxed for perhaps the first time as he watched *A Christmas Story* on the TV. Ian was busy in the kitchen putting away the leftovers from their dinner in the fridge.

A stirring of hope filled her chest. She wanted to fit into their world, to be a part of both their lives, and sharing them was one way to start. It had worked with them once before, and did she really mind the idea of having them both? Was that somehow being greedy? Perhaps after having nothing, a little greed wasn't such a bad thing.

With a grin and a touch of nerves, she went to find the red babydoll.

CHAPTER 9

Zoey checked her appearance in the bathroom mirror. Nervousness fluttered inside her with the chaos of a swarm of butterflies trapped inside a net. She could do this. She *wanted* to do this. She just prayed things would work out. Choosing between Ian and Connor was not an option. It was so clear how close these two men had always been, like brothers. Loving one without loving the other would drive a wedge between them and ultimately drive them apart.

Please let them both want me enough to share me. They'd shared Lara, after all. Could they be the same with her? Even if she wasn't a true mate, she wanted to prove to them she could love them both equally, because she did. How it was possible in just a few days she didn't know, but she did.

She loved the way Connor hid his sweetness beneath

a gruff demeanor, and how he never restrained his passion when he was with her. And she loved Ian's tender-hearted smiles and irresistibly seductive kisses. Both had an adorable way of trying to give her everything she wanted and needed, like it was coded in their ancient DNA to care for their woman. It was time she showed them how much they meant to her.

She stepped out of the bathroom and walked down the hall, all too aware of the carpet beneath her bare feet. The two men, *her* two men, stood in the kitchen sipping coffee, studying the small village of gingerbread houses they'd made earlier that evening. Much to her dismay, Ian and Connor had made an elaborate castle with a moat being attacked by a dragon, while she'd opted for a traditional little house that looked pathetically plain next to it.

Connor said something, pointing to her house, and Ian burst into a rich laugh. They seemed so comfortable with each other now, so different from that first night when they were ready to rip each other's throats out. The strain between them was gone, that tension reduced to a bad memory.

Ian was the first to catch sight of her. His coffee mug crashed onto the floor. Connor turned and caught his breath, then grinned.

"It looks so much better on you than the hanger." Even though his words were quiet, they struck her like a shot of warm brandy.

Zoey smoothed her hands over the red babydoll and

tried to will away her self-consciousness. She'd been naked around both of them, had kissed them and done much more with much less on than this piece of lingerie. She wanted to be sexy and wild with them. Maybe it wouldn't matter if she had only a little sexual experience compared to these men who'd lived for two centuries. They'd probably slept with hundreds of beautiful perfect woman in that time. She hoped she could measure up. There was so much passion in her right now she felt ready to burst.

Ian nudged the remnants of the coffee mug aside with the toe of his boot. "Do I get to collect my kisses now?"

"Don't frighten her," Connor whispered as he started to prowl toward her.

Ian also approached, but in a far more casual way. "You're doing a good enough job of that yourself. You're not on a nature documentary, you know. She's not a wildebeest."

For the first time since meeting them, Zoey truly felt like the prey she always knew she was to the vampires. A walking Happy Meal. The hungry looks they gave her were evidence that they'd eat her up if given half the chance. In a good way, of that she had not doubt, but she also knew that she might end up getting bitten again. She had to trust they could control their natures with her in the height of their passion.

Ian reached her first, his palms cupping her shoulders. His skin felt cool against her heated flesh, but not as cool as before. His green eyes were warm and bright, like grass on a summer's day.

"Tell me you won't choose just one of us." Ian's tone was urgent and barely above a growl. "You can handle us both, can't you?" She knew he didn't just mean physically, but emotionally as well.

A second set of hands, Connor's, slid around her hips from behind as they trapped her between their tall, firm bodies. Zoey shut her eyes and nodded, more to herself than either of them.

"Yes. I want to be with you. Both of you." There. She'd said it. Now what was she supposed to do?

She turned to look over her shoulder at Connor. Some silent communication seemed to pass between them.

"My bed or yours?" he asked at last.

"Mine tonight, yours the next." Ian gave Zoey a look so scorching she wondered how she didn't get burned.

"Is that okay with you, Zoey?" Ian cupped her cheek and watched her reaction closely.

"Yes…"

Connor slid his hand around hers, the grip comforting as he led her down the hall, Ian following behind them. Once inside, Connor shut the door and leaned back against it. Zoey looked between the two and wrapped her arms around her waist nervously.

"Look, I don't know how to start this. Will somebody just kiss me?" She felt like an idiot asking like that, but it was what she needed.

Ian's voice became a deep, honeyed rumble. "As you wish."

He grasped her face in his hands and leaned in until his lips touched hers. Every worry, every fear faded away. Ian could do that to her—ease her anxiety and yet still melt her inside with his touch. His lips moved over hers, delicate, teasing, tasting. She responded, lost in the rhythm of their mouths. Ian's tongue sought a playful dance with hers. Zoey moaned with pleasure. A single kiss, long and sensual, was all she needed to come alive. She opened her eyes long enough to see Connor still leaning against the closed doors, arms crossed.

"Show him your passion, Zoey." Connor's whisper betrayed his own hunger to join them. A wicked smile flirted with the edges of his lips.

"Yes, show me, love." Ian forced her back a few steps until she bumped into the bed.

His hips pinned hers against the mattress. He smoothed his hands down her back, over the swell of her backside, the bikini bottom barely a barrier to the cool skin of his palms. Her flesh burned with his erotic touch. He gripped her ass, jerking her up against him so her feet left the ground. She wrapped her arms around his neck, hanging on as he raised her up to set her on the edge of the bed. Ian urged her to crawl back toward the headboard and he followed, coming down over her body. His hands gently pried her shaking knees apart as he settled into the cradle of her thighs.

"You all right?" he whispered before kissing her. It was a soft brush, a little caress of reassurance, and it relaxed her instantly.

"I'm fine. It's just been a few years since I…" She bit her lip and looked in Connor's direction. She saw him push away from the door and step toward her.

"You'll be fine, love. We're here to please you, aren't we, Connor?" Ian kissed the corner of her mouth and then trailed his mouth up to her ear, licking inside.

A sharp pang of lust hit her womb and traveled like lightning up her spine back to her ear. She arched with a hiss as he repeated the erotic licking, and the folds of her sex throbbed with hot desire. Ian continued the wicked torture of her ear, rocking his still clothed body against hers, until she'd dissolved into a puddle of incoherent desire.

Then he relented, just as she was on the verge of coming. He sat back on the bed and removed his sweater, tossing it aside. Zoey gazed up at him, trembling with vulnerability and hunger as he loomed over her, his palms settling into the comforter on either side of her head. She shivered and watched as he slid down her body until his face hovered above her mound. When he hooked his thumbs in her bikini bottoms and tugged them down her legs, she clamped her eyes shut, suddenly shy. What would he think of her? She'd never had a man go down on her before.

"Open your eyes, Zoey." It was Connor's voice next to

her ear. Her lashes fanned up and saw him on the edge of the bed next to her, watching her. His dark eyes glittered, wild and savage.

Ian pulled her legs apart, tapping behind her knees and she bent them without thinking, setting her heels in the bed, allowing Ian to stare down at her. She tore her gaze away from Connor only to see Ian's green eyes flash with a strange sheen of crimson.

"I'm dying to taste you," Ian growled in a voice so low that she felt its vibration more than she heard the words. His palms slid down her inner thighs and she threw her head back against the pillow. Her body convulsed when Ian's thumbs rubbed slow patterns along the skin of her legs, just inches from her core.

Connor now demanded her attention, cupping her cheek and turning her to face him.

"Kiss me," he purred, then stoked her lips with a mind-numbing kiss—the sort that stole a woman's heart and soul. Like a first and last kiss and every one in between. It had a certain magic that could hold a woman frozen in time, bound by a mix of love and passion. Zoey's eyes singed with tears as she tried to return the power of the moment, reflect some of that intensity back to Connor, to show him she felt the same as he did.

She never got the chance, because Ian kissed the top of her mound and nibbled his way down. Her hands flailed as she tried to find his shoulders, his hair, anything to grasp on to as he licked her slit.

Connor swallowed her scream of riotous pleasure as Ian continued to taste her. Something jerked her arms above her head, pinning them firmly out of the way. Zoey forced her eyes open again. Connor had captured her wrists and was keeping her distracted while Ian played between her legs.

Thoughts couldn't form, words wouldn't come, there was only wave after wave of building, aching pleasure as she strained to reach the climax she desperately needed. She was helpless against the two of them, only able to accept whatever they gave her. Years of anxiety had wound her tighter than a cork in a bottle and she was so close to bursting free.

"Please...Ian...let me come. God...just let me come!" she begged, breathless between Connor's kisses.

Ian's breath tickled her inner thigh as he licked and nibbled his way to her knee. She wanted to scream in frustration as the desire inside her continued to be left unfulfilled.

"What do you think, Connor? Should we grant her wish?" He smoothed his hands up and down her thighs, rubbing her sensitive skin, but she needed his mouth back on her clit, or better yet, his cock deep inside her.

"Connor..." she whispered, meeting his eyes with a desperate look.

There was a wildness in his gaze, and she glimpsed the predator he'd tried to hide tonight. He seemed to revel in her echoing need for release. His grip on her wrists tightened and he dropped his head to nip her lower lip. She arched in his arms, and both men chuckled.

"Take her slow, Ian. Make her work for it." His dark voice stirred her senses and made her heady with anticipation.

Ian sat back and Zoey was treated to a fresh view of his chest and the way his muscles flexed as he shrugged out of his jeans. His cock sprang forward and she wanted to stroke the massive length of it.

He came forward again, cupped her ass, lifted her up and then with one hand guided the tip of his shaft into her. Zoey held still, even though she wanted more than anything to squirm in eagerness.

While Ian began to press into her an inch at a time, Connor tore the spaghetti straps of the babydoll's top and ripped open the sheer bodice, baring her breasts. He filled his hand with one, pinching and rolling the beaded nipple between his thumb and forefinger while his mouth settled over the other peak.

Her body flushed, then she screamed as Ian thrust into her. He stretched her to the breaking point and she thought she might die from the sudden mix of pleasure and pain. Ian withdrew, leaving an awful empty feeling in its wake. Seconds later, he was driving back into her, surging deeper. He groaned at the same moment she did when he thrust to the hilt.

"Christ, you're so tight," Ian's accent grew thicker

than she'd ever heard before and it made her inner walls clench around him. A wildness filled her.

"Harder!"

Connor lifted his head, shared a cat-like smile with Ian. "She's been a good lass, give it to her."

And he did. Ian gripped her hips as he took Zoey to the edge at a pounding pace. Connor moved back, his palms cupping her face as he gazed down at her. Zoey looked back and forth between the two. Beneath the hunger, the desire, their eyes were filled with softer emotions, ones she felt as well, and she was mesmerized by it.

Finally it was too much. She surrendered, her back bowing up off the bed as her climax took her. Stars dotted her vision—the white hot intensity of her union with Ian shaking her to the very foundation of her soul as she came. She was barely aware of Ian's own roar of satisfaction. Her fell body limp and sated as she felt Ian withdraw from her.

"Ian?" she asked, trying to keep her eyes open.

"Shhh…" he whispered from somewhere beside her. "Rest a bit."

Even wanting to stay awake, her body craved sleep and she obeyed and immediately slipped into a deep, dreamless sleep.

～

Zoey woke a few hours later to Connor's teasing kisses. Her eyes opened briefly as she returned his kiss, curling her arms around his neck.

"Are you ready for me now?" he asked, his accent thick yet soft, making her body shiver.

"Mmmm," she moaned in answer, kissing him again. The blankets were pulled from her body and he was moving between her thighs, right where she wanted him.

"Zoey, lass," he groaned as he raised her hips, taking him inside her. "Christ, woman!" he hissed and thrust harder, burying himself completely. Once again she was filled to a near breaking point, but it felt wonderful.

"She feels good, doesn't she?" Ian chuckled from the nearby darkness.

Connor's laugh turned to a curse as he sank into her again. Zoey loved having all of him inside her, possessing her in a way she hadn't thought possible. Knowing Ian was watching only made her blood run hotter, her own arousal spike. Connor gripped her knee, pulling it tight to his hip, molding them together.

She thrashed her head against the pillow as he took her, body and soul. "Connor...God...that feels so good..." Both of them had her, all of her. She could only pray they'd be merciful and remember she was just a mortal. She screamed in pleasure. Connor collapsed on top of her, panting against her neck. He licked her skin even as her inner muscles clamped around his cock.

He nibbled her ear. "Hmm. Mind if I have a wee bite?"

She giggled.

Ian shoved Connor's shoulder. "Now, Connor, you greedy bastard, I've not had the chance to taste her yet." Conner rolled dramatically off Zoey and then Ian was pulling her over his body. She rested her chin to his chest, boneless, shutting her eyes. She was vaguely aware of Ian lifting one of her arms to his mouth and nibbled playfully.

"One taste?" he asked. "I want to know you, Zoey. Please let me taste you." She opened one eye and stared at him. "Drinking from you will let me see inside your heart, your mind."

"Will it hurt?" she asked. The last time she'd been bitten it had been when she was beyond aroused, but now she was sated, and more aware of herself. She didn't mind that this would let him see into her. She had nothing to hide from him.

Connor leaned over beside her and kissed her shoulder. It felt so good to lie there with them both, exploring, delighting in their appetites.

"It might sting at first, but if you relax, it will ease."

Zoey wasn't frightened, but the intimacy of giving her blood was something she'd never expected to face.

"Okay." She drew a breath as his fangs slid out and he bit into her wrist. She tensed as the sting sharpened.

Connor touched her cheek. "Relax, pet," he said, turning her face toward him.

Sharing blood with Ian, just as when Connor had tasted her, formed some mystical connection between them. Invisible strings seemed to weave her and Ian together—two souls, nearly merged.

"Tell me something about you, Zoey," said Conner. "Before the accident, what were your plans?"

Zoey rested her face against Connor's cool palm, watching his lips move as he spoke. Ian sucked at her wrist a second longer then licked the wound closed. He stroked her hair, the gentleness of the motion making her feel warm and safe.

She turned and rested her cheek on his chest.

"Before... I wanted to be a photographer. I was good at art, loved to sketch, but what I really loved was taking pictures. I was enrolled in photography classes. After the accident, I had to drop out of art school and sell the house. There were so many expenses. Eventually I even had to pawn my camera..."

Her words died as emotions began to clog her throat. Selling that camera had been like the last bell tolling in a cemetery, reminding her she had to give up her dreams. It was all dead now, every hope she had for that future. She jerked away and started to sit up. Ian rolled, pinning her beneath him on the bed.

"No, lass, you can't shut us out."

"Too late for that," Connor added.

She rubbed at her eyes, wiping away fresh tears. She looked away from them around the room, noticing the lovely pictures on the walls.

"When I first woke up here, I thought I was dead. The room was filled with pictures of places I've never been."

"Ian took those. He likes to snap a picture every now and then. He even set up the camera on timers to get shots during the day that he couldn't manage in person. It's a bit of a passion for him too. We'll take you with us, when we travel next," Connor promised.

Zoey wanted to cry even harder. He made it sound so natural, so *normal* that she'd be with them. But this wasn't going to last forever. How could it?

Ian slid off her so that she was nestled between their bodies. "Er...Zoey. We'd like to talk to you about something."

She forced herself to smile, but it was brittle. She feared the worst. "Yes?"

"What would you say if Connor and I asked you to stay past Christmas? We've grown quite fond of you, and neither of us wishes for you to leave. Now—" He pressed a finger against her lips before she could protest. "We know you've got your pride, and this has nothing to do with charity."

Connor echoed the tender look Ian gave her with a slow caress, rubbing her stomach and tracing the spot where she'd been stabbed. How did he know where to touch her? The scars were all but gone, and had been mere hours after she'd woken up in their home.

It was madness to even consider their offer, but she couldn't resist. She was hopelessly in love with them. Any excuse to stay was worth considering. "I have to support myself, if I stay…"

"What if," Ian said slowly as though trying to carefully convince her of his words. "You return to your classes, get your degree and open a studio? We could be investors. Right?"

"We could," Connor agreed instantly and sat up next to her in bed. "Investments are how we get by these days. We want you to stay."

That surprised her and filled her with a sense of hope. It scared the hell out of her. They wanted her to stay. She wanted to stay. But she had to be sure it was the right thing to do.

"I'll think about it."

"Good." Ian kissed her and soon both men were tucking her beneath the covers as sleep took over. No nightmares could take away the sense of peace and safety these two had given her in that moment.

CHAPTER 10

The cathedral was beautiful. The massive stained glass windows glowed with candlelight from within. Multicolored shadows splashed over the snow below the glass like a frozen kaleidoscope. The gothic spires of the old edifice rose up into the clear midnight sky, majestic and mysterious. A pair of ten-foot tall archangels guarded the entrance, their wings curved around their shoulders, heads bowed as though in mourning.

Zoey held her breath, taking in the old world splendor from across the street.

The last week had passed quickly, too quickly for her. Wrapped up in her new intimate life with Ian and Connor, she'd lost all track of time. Like staring into a snow globe and imagining herself far away from the cares of the world in a tiny house, flakes of snow swirling around her. The past few days had been an endless dream full of delight and wonder. Between the erotic nights spent in the arms of her men and exploring the city without a care, she'd found herself. They'd helped her live again, not just exist.

The church doors opened. Light spilled across the icy walkway, painting the frozen water a rich gold, like the midmorning sun striking a river's surface. Goosebumps rose on Zoey's forearms, and she rubbed them through her thick winter coat. The sight before her humbled and moved her in a way she hadn't felt since before her parents died.

The building was filled with life as the parishioners inside began to sing. The night breeze pulled the notes out into the air around her like an unseen choir of angels. The sounds of elation and love were wondrous. She felt like a child again, as if hearing music for the first time. Then the feeling of something greater stirred inside her bones, demanding to be recognized.

Faith. It had been so long since she'd believed in anything. She'd lost her faith and faith in herself...but no longer. A gasp of joy escaped her in a foggy puff of breath and she laughed.

It was nearly midnight and mass would start soon. She saw Connor and Ian at the back of the parking lot, still talking by the car. They'd join her soon, but it wouldn't hurt to run inside and grab some seats. She checked the street and stepped off the curb to cross. She slipped a few times as she reached the middle. The road was covered in black ice, and she knew full well how dangerous it was. Her clutch purse slipped from her hands, and Zoey knelt to pick it up.

A car turned onto the street, tires whining as it tried to right itself. The driver accelerated and the headlights flashed onto Zoey a second too late. She scrambled awkwardly, trying to gain traction. The driver hit the brakes and the car fishtailed out of control.

The purse fell from her hands as the car struck her.

As though she were in a dream, everything that followed seemed not to be happening to her, but to some other poor soul. She could only stand by and watch.

Bones shattered, organs were crushed, her breath was stolen as she flew fifteen feet away. She slid over the ice like a broken ragdoll and then stopped. Everything went numb except her face. One cheek was pressed against the freezing ice and it burned like fire.

She was facing the church and the bells in the tower above her began to sway. They tolled loud and clear as the midnight hour struck and Christmas Eve turned to Christmas Day. The screams of the people nearby were drowned out beneath the merry clamor of bells. They were all she could hear and she clung to that sound, fighting to stay conscious.

Zoey sought to make sense of the shapes and movement before her. Most were blurry silhouettes against the pale light from the church's entrance. The stone angel on the right was the only thing she could truly see. Everything else was too confusing, too dark. The angel's head was bowed, its gown rippling around its legs, pulled by an ancient wind strong enough to move stone.

Then the massive feathered wings, once shrouded in grief around its body, suddenly flung wide. Diamonds glittered on the wing tips as the stone cracked and splintered. White fire shot through the fracturing stone. It was the most beautiful thing she'd ever seen. The angel shivered, and the stone dust covering it blew away. The explosion of light that followed, bathed Zoey in its fiery heat, and she let go.

"Do you think she'll like it?" Ian asked Connor as they stood by the car. People passed them on the way to mass, laughing and filled with holiday cheer. It used to make him sad to see such joy, but now he was full of happiness as well and the mood of these people was an added blessing.

"You're sure it's the one she pawned?" Connor studied the camera Ian had handed him that they'd hidden in a new camera bag in the back of the car.

"I saw the shop's name when we bonded, and this camera. It's either hers or one just like it." Ian tucked the delicate piece of equipment back into the bag and set it in the backseat, next to the other presents they'd purchased that evening.

Ian hadn't told Zoey yet about the bridge between their minds. It was something he planned to tell her soon. From the moment he touched her a week ago, he'd known she was his true mate, and Connor's. She belonged to him and Connor just as Lara had. It made one wonder if there was in fact such a thing as reincarnation. They were fortunate to have been given a second chance at finding someone who would bring them close to being human again.

He wasn't sure if she'd been aware of the subtle changes: their human appetites, their warmer skin, the occasional need to breathe. It had been happening to both him and Connor, just as they remembered what it had been like with Lara. A wondrous sense of life. Zoey was the woman he wished to build his future on. She was his salvation.

"She'll love it." Connor gave a boyish grin as he turned toward the church. "We'd best get inside before mass starts."

"Try not to vamp out this time. It always causes a panic." Ian shook his head, laughing.

Connor smirked. "You do that one time for a laugh and get branded for life. I thought the good Father would have enjoyed a livening up of the Christmas mass." He'd flashed a bit of fang and fiery eye just for fun back in the

1840s. It had not been well received by the presiding priest.

"We almost *were* branded. And staked."

"Come on. Father Callahan was the most boring priest in Irish history. We saved those people from dying of boredom."

"And had to move to America as a result."

The sound of screeching tires interrupted their conversation.

Ian's instincts died. He was rooted to the spot, watching helplessly as a car spun out of control and hit someone standing in the middle of the street. A woman. He heard the impact crush her body and the shocked, pained exhalation as she fell to the ground.

A last breath, one he'd heard so often in his nightmares of late. A sound that would follow him forever into the shadows of the valley of death.

"Zoey!" Connor's voice was distant, as though it were underwater.

Zoey? That couldn't be Zoey, not her. Not her.

They ran to the body. The body. She was barely more than that. Her soul was leeching away. Blood dripped from her lips onto the icy road. Her eyes were half-closed. Life still glimmered in their luminous depths, gazing at something he couldn't see. He followed her line of sight and saw only a large stone angel in the churchyard, flakes of snow swirling around its bowed head and wings.

Connor was on his knees, checking her injuries. The

crowd around them were calling for help and dialing 911. When Connor raised his head and met Ian's eyes, they spoke without words.

She's nearly gone. Not long now.

It had happened once before, watching the life leave the woman they'd loved. They'd been unable to stop it then. Lara had slipped away. There one minute and gone in the next, final breath. Life was such a delicate thing, so many ways it could end. Each breath, each beat of a human heart was a gift, one so often taken for granted.

Connor's voice broke. "Ian, I *cannot* do this again."

Ian's chest seized as he saw Connor's face. He was fully human in that instant. They both were. Grief, loss and love were not for immortal hearts, or so he'd believed. After eighty years, he'd thought he'd never be able to feel this way again. Zoey had changed them, brought them back their humanity. Ian would be damned if he let her slip away.

"Grab Zoey. Let's get her home!" Ian shouted.

They had no time, not if they were going to save her. Connor picked Zoey up in his arms and headed straight for home, moving like lightning, leaving a bewildered crowd behind him.

CONNOR BURST into his room and laid Zoey on his bed, barely breathing. She looked so beautiful, even as she lingered so close to death. Ian appeared in the doorway a moment later, face pale.

"We'll turn her." It was not a question.

Connor nodded. At first he'd meant to protest, but looking at her now he was in total agreement with Ian. They had to save her. They bit their wrists and took turns giving her their blood.

If they succeeded she might hate them, but they had to take that chance. So long as Zoey was alive, or at least as alive as one of their kind could ever be, he could never regret the decision. Maybe someday she'd forgive them. After several long minutes, they stopped and waited. Her body shuddered, one last breath released so softly that Connor barely heard it.

"Zoey..." Pain flooded from his breaking heart.

"Were we too late?" Shock carved lines in Ian's face as he knelt by the bed.

"We can't be... She can't... not again. She *can't* go now."

Even as much as he wanted to believe he could deny fate, Connor knew that mysterious forces in the vast universe sometimes took control. Perhaps the angels had wanted Zoey, and they'd come to claim her. How could he, an immortal cursed to live on blood, argue his right to keep her? He didn't deserve her, and neither did Ian. Maybe they were monsters after all. Monsters didn't get happy endings.

Ian dropped his head into his hands, shaking with

silent sobs. They'd failed. Connor sat down next to the still body. His chest quaked as he struggled to draw breath, as though he was dying along with her. Of all the times he'd longed for death, had stared into the obsidian waters of the river night, it was nothing compared to now, except perhaps when he'd seen Seamus standing over Lara's dead body. It had happened again, the thing that made his dead heart stir to life in his chest was gone.

"Oh lass, you always were too good for the likes of us." Connor stroked her hair back from her face, his eyes burning with tears he couldn't shed.

His eyes closed and she was still there, haunting him. He could see her brilliant smile, the one that lit her face with a strange and wondrous magic. Connor's hands clenched. He could almost feel her small hand in his, his fingers lacing with hers as though she'd been made for him. The memory was strong, and it broke his heart all over again. Without Zoey he was nothing...

Just one more moment, holding her in his arms, if he could only have her back. Long enough to tell her everything in his heart.

THE HOUSE WAS QUIET. Zoey's parents were cuddled up on the couch, the TV screen showing *It's a Wonderful Life*. Zoey sat by the fire, a blanket around her as she watched her parents talk softly to each other. Her father smiled and her mother laughed, whispering something in his ear.

Her father turned, confusion crossed his face as he saw her.

"Zoey, what are you doing here?"

"It's Christmas," she replied with a bright smile and got up.

Her mother's eyes shone with a bittersweet shimmer. "Go back, Zoey."

The words stung. She belonged here, didn't she? With them. Something pulled at her stomach, a cramping pain that made her double over.

She raised her head. "Dad...I want to stay with you..."

Her father shook his head sadly. They were her family, her life, why did they not want her here?

"We are always with you, sweetheart. Never forget that. But you can't stay. Your place is back there, with them."

Them? "No...Dad please..." Tears sparked in her eyes, and she rubbed her fists against them.

"Zoey, you've lived so long with your suffering. It's time to accept the joy of the life you've been given. Our chapter is ended. That book is on the shelf. But you still have a story to live, one all your own."

Her parents came over, kneeling on either side of her and hugged her tight. That feeling of closeness burned into her heart and mind, like the last kiss given by a lover, or the final wave from a departing friend. Sorrow and grief shared space in her heart with the memories of better, brighter days. Her mother stroked the hair back from her face.

"We love you, wherever you go, whatever you do. We are with you. Now go. Live the life destiny has given you."

The sharp pain struck her stomach again, and her parents faded into a gentle mist that rose up from the ground.

A SPARK SKITTERED through Connor's fingers where they'd touched Zoey's cheek. His eyes flew open as the spark whipped through his hand where it had contact with her skin. It was a spark he recognized. Of life, after a fashion.

"Zoey?" Hope fluttered within him like a dove with newly mended wings. The pulsing of Zoey's flesh grew sharper and stronger as that immortal spark took hold of her.

They'd done it.

"Christ, Ian, she's going to make it!" Connor nearly whooped with joy. Ian lifted his tear strained face and reached for Zoey's limp hand by the edge of the bed.

"We did it!"

Everything would be all right now. As long as she could forgive them...

"We did it."

"Zoey..." The voice she heard was raw with pain. She knew that voice, yet she didn't know it.

"Zoey, we love you. You cannot leave us. Do you hear me, woman?" Another voice growled.

"Find your way back, I can't lose you," the first voice whispered.

Cool fingers stroked her flesh and the sensation was startling, amazing, like an electric surge to her system. A flash of violent pain shuddered through her and she let out a cry. Her body seized. She couldn't stop the rolling waves of pain. Bones snapped into place, flesh, tissue seemed to pull back together. Every second was pure agony and she couldn't do anything but shout and writhe. Tears and sobs came without control.

"Zoey, let it go. Let it all out."

She surrendered, letting the emotions and the physical pain spiral through her. After several seconds it faded and she was still—utterly still except for an occasional tremble. Her eyes fluttered open as she took in the scene around her.

She was lying in Connor's bed. Connor. She knew him, loved him. And Ian. She loved him too. Her two great loves sat on either side of her, their eyes wide with worry, tension stretching their mouths into tight lines.

"Thank God." Ian's tone was full of reverence and relief.

Zoey tried to move, her body was limp and sore, as though she'd been beaten all over.

"What happened?" she asked, her voice cracking with pain. Her vision sharpened, the fabric of the comforter beneath her fingertips whispered under her skin, the feeling so strong, so...sensual. Her body was different. It felt alien in so many ways and yet right.

"You died," Connor answered bluntly, eyes dark as tree bark in winter.

Ian shot him a baleful glare. "Tact, Connor." He turned back to Zoey. "Do you remember the car hitting you?"

The memory returned with shocking clarity—the sudden impact and breaking of her body...and then it all was muddled after that.

"Connor and I...we turned you." Ian looked away and cleared his throat. "We couldn't lose you, Zoey. We'd been through that once before. A world without you was a world we couldn't live in. I hope you can forgive us. We made the choice without you, and I'd vowed I'd never do that. But you're ours, a true mate, just like I told you about. You remember?"

She stared up at them, amazed at this new brighter sight she had. Vampire vision? Connor took her face in his hands, stroking her cheeks with his thumbs. The sensation was a thousand times stronger, more arousing and enticing than she could ever imagine—as though she could feel every cell of her skin as he brushed his fingers over it. Her eyes tracked his as he studied her seriously.

"You can hate us," said Connor. "But know that we love you and we chose to keep you here. You were meant to be ours, not to sleep in the company of angels."

His words struck something bittersweet inside her. A strange dream of an angel with wings of diamonds and fire... She blinked away fresh tears. Her father's voice echoed in her mind. *"Your place is back there, with them."*

When had he said that? She couldn't seem to recall. Funny, she felt as though she was missing something, but whatever it was, it didn't matter anymore. She flung her arms around Connor's neck, covering his face with kisses. Then she turned and opened her arms to Ian. He scooped her up, pulling her toward him as he took her mouth hungrily, his lips trembling beneath hers. When they pulled apart, she was laughing.

Ian's brows rose. "Well, that certainly was not the reaction we expected."

Connor chuckled darkly. "It certainly wasn't the way I acted when I was turned."

"Me neither. Then again, our sire had not exactly been the welcoming sort." Ian nuzzled her cheek, his long lashes tickled her newly sensitive skin.

Zoey pulled back and looked at them both. "Is it hard? Being a vampire?"

"It won't be easy. At first you'll fight hunger for blood every day, but we can help you. We'll teach you everything you need to know. How to feed and not kill. How to control the glamour."

"And I can stay..." She was afraid to ask more clearly what she wanted to know.

"With us. Forever." Ian stroked her back soothingly.

"That's all I've ever wanted," she whispered. "The only present I could have hoped for."

Ian winked at her. "Better than the flannel PJs?"

"The PJs are a close second."

She leaned into Ian and Connor hugged her from behind, the embrace warming her body and her soul. She wasn't alone, and she'd never be alone again.

A new chapter had opened for her, and she couldn't wait to see how this new life would unfold.

Thanks for reading *The Bite of Winter*. I hope you enjoyed it! *His Little Vixen*, Seamus's story is next! To see how a sexy Irish vampire get all twisted over a sassy female fox shifter turn the page to start reading!

HIS LITTLE VIXEN

LOVE BITES - BOOK 2

PROLOGUE

IRELAND · 1849

Seamus Gallagher leaned weakly against the wood frame of the narrow bed where his little sister lay, trying to convince her to take a piece of bread.

"Take it, little one."

She was only twelve, and the sight of her starving was breaking his heart. The farmhouse around them was eerily silent; the once boisterous sounds of their other family members were no more.

"No... Seamus...," Kayleigh protested. Her soft, birdlike voice, the voice of a child, now matched her emaciated body. He brushed back the reddish-gold hair from her forehead, now dewed with sweat as her small body fought its losing battle for life.

"Yes. You need it more than I do. *Please.*" He pressed the loaf of bread into her tiny hands. He couldn't lose her to the famine. Kayleigh was all he had left. He could survive anything if he could only get her to eat.

Her eyes were half-closed as she pushed the bread away.

"No... Kayleigh, you must eat." His vision was blurring, and he blinked as he tried to clear it. Breaking off a bit of bread, he lifted it to the child's lips. She chewed on the bread, but there was so little light left in her blue eyes.

Seamus's cracked lips stung as he attempted to swallowed. Kayleigh needed water, and he had none to fill her aching, empty belly. He had no strength to walk outside to the well anymore. His own stomach burned with hunger, but he ignored it as best he could. Kayleigh was all that mattered. He could... He could...

The thoughts seemed to drift on an empty breeze. His head lolled against the bed, his fingers loosely curled around Kayleigh's small wrist.

The door opened, and moonlight slowly filled the tiny room of his family's little cottage.

"Well now, my dear one..." The silken voice crept in from the darkness, growing like gloom upon his mind. It was the angel of death, come to take them both away.

Seamus resigned himself to the coming darkness. He only hoped Kayleigh's suffering ceased before his.

"Help...," he whispered to the voice. "Help her, please." He tried to glimpse the face that accompanied such a beautiful voice, but the shadows collected like vast cobwebs in the dark corners of the bedroom, making it impossible to see.

"The child?" The voice turned almost sweet. "You want the child to be saved. Not you?"

"Yes… Anything for Kayleigh." He struggled to squint in the dimness to see who had come into his home. Out of the darkness, the speaker emerged, and his heart skittered in his chest.

A tall raven-haired woman peered down at him. She wore a bell-shaped gown of watered silk, the color of a frost-covered lake. Her bodice glinted with jewels that dazzled his weary eyes. He'd never seen such a lovely woman or such a lovely gown in all his life. He'd worked the land, slept many a night amidst the sheep and cattle. Wherever this woman came from, it was a world he'd never belong to.

She came closer. Her white-gloved hands lifted her skirts, and Seamus caught a glimpse of her dainty black boots and a slender pair of ankles. But it was her face that stole his breath away.

"You are an angel," he gasped. There was no other explanation. The beautiful winged brows, violet eyes, and the flushed red Cupid's bow lips were any man's dream of a perfect woman.

"Angel? No, I am far from an angel, but you are sweet to think so." The woman sat on the edge of Kayleigh's bed, and Seamus was struck with the guilt that such a clean, fancy woman would be sitting in the dusty, filthy home he had been too tired to clean while searching for food for his sister.

"How old are you?" the woman asked him. She cupped a gloved hand under his chin.

"Twenty-five, my lady," he whispered. His vision was blurring again, and he feared he would not be able to stay awake much longer.

"And your name?" She smoothed a hand down her skirts, studying him as though they might be sharing tea on a fine afternoon rather than in the ruins of his family home just after midnight.

"Seamus Gallagher."

"Seamus... I have a bargain to make with you."

He dared not speak—he was too afraid this was all some starvation-borne delusion. Perhaps he lay dead on the floor already.

"Give yourself to me—heart, body, and soul—and your little sister's life will be returned to her."

He looked from the woman to the child dying in his bed. "I don't understand."

"Of course you don't, but you will soon enough. Now..." The woman's sweet tone turned even more soft. Each word was coated in the sweetest of sugar. "Now, do you agree? You, in exchange for the child?"

There was no hesitation. He would do anything for Kayleigh.

"Yes. Me for her." The words rasped from his parched lips.

The woman's violet eyes darkened. Her pupils expanded, and the purple irises began to churn into a deep ruby red. She removed one of her gloves and then put her wrist to her lips. He watched in horror as she sank sharp little teeth into her own flesh. Blood dripped down her wrist as she then pressed her arm to Kayleigh's mouth.

"Drink, child, but only a little taste," the angelic voice crooned. Kayleigh's eyes were closed, but one of her small hands twitched and then lifted to grip the woman's wrist. The hushed, sucking sounds made Seamus's stomach roil. His sister was drinking blood.

"What are you doing to her? Stop." He tried to drag the woman's arm away. Without looking, she grabbed him by his throat, holding him still while Kayleigh continued to drink.

"That's enough now." She removed her wrist from Kayleigh's lips, then handed her the forgotten loaf of bread. Only then did the woman release her hold on Seamus's throat.

Seamus exhaled, and the aching in his ribs robbed him of much of his remaining strength. "She won't eat."

"She will now." The woman pointed a delicate finger at his sister. "Watch."

He looked to his sister's form and gasped. The light of life was bright again in the child's eyes, and her pale cheeks blossomed with fresh color. The darkened circles under her eyes vanished. Kayleigh raised the bread to her lips and nibbled on it.

"Kayleigh." Seamus's heart burst with relief. "Are you all right?"

Kayleigh nodded, her eyes drifting between him and the woman.

"As you see, the child is better. Now, you must give me what I promised."

Seamus lifted his head, tearing his focus away from his sister.

"I..." He swallowed, dust gathering in his dry throat. "Do what you will." He could not find the energy to care about himself, not any longer.

The woman slid off the bed to kneel in front of him, not caring whether her skirts became dirty on the floor.

She removed her other glove and cupped his face in her cold hands.

"You are quite beautiful, even so close to death. How beautiful will you be once I have given you immortality?"

Her eyes swept over his face, boldly assessing him. He had felt handsome once, before the crops failed and the famine set in. But that was over a year ago. Now he felt ancient and bone-weary. A second later, his mind registered what she'd said about immortality.

"What?"

She smiled, her Cupid's bow lips parting as she leaned in to kiss him. He closed his eyes, now firmly convinced that he was dreaming or dying. But she didn't kiss him. Her mouth brushed against his throat, and her slender hands, so cool to the touch, parted the neckcloth he wore and tore his shirt open. Her nails dug into his chest as she pushed him flat on the floor.

"What are you doing?" he asked.

She crawled up his body, her skirts pooling around her and the crinoline petticoats bending against his body. "I'm taking what's mine," she purred. She rubbed herself against him like a contented cat. Then, without warning, she sank her teeth into his throat.

Seamus shouted in pain and tried to pry her off him, but he was too weak, and she was far too strong. His head spun as she sucked on his neck. He kicked his legs and clawed at her tiny shoulders, but she didn't move. A few minutes later, he was gasping for breath, struggling to stay awake.

"Almost there, my dear one," she whispered in his ear. Then he felt her skin against his mouth and warm, salty blood slipping between his lips. He tried to resist and spit the blood back up.

"Drink," she ordered.

Seamus's eyes burned with tears as he gave in. He couldn't fight anymore. He stared up at her, helpless, watching his own blood drip from her mouth down to her chin. Her eyes were red, glowing with a feral, animal hunger. She was beautiful and deadly, and she was killing him. He felt his body dying around him. Dying and changing, like a rocky shore being eroded by the ocean over centuries.

As the seconds stretched into minutes, the acidic taste changed and it turned almost sweet, like rich wine. A hunger he'd never had before in all his life took hold of him, demanding he drink, that he satisfy his needs. He was strengthened by the taste and clutched her wrist to his mouth, drawing on her vein.

"Just a little more," she cautioned, then struck him hard when he refused to release her arm. "*Enough.*"

He relaxed back on the ground, and then it happened. A moment later, his breathing just *stopped*. It felt like he was holding his breath underwater. There was pain, *so much pain*. The woman slid off him, licking her lips. He saw blood, *his* blood, still coating her petal-soft mouth.

"You taste divine, my darling Seamus." A gleam of primal joy lit her face in a way that should have frightened him, only he had nothing left to be frightened of.

Seamus closed his eyes. His lungs felt as though they had turned to ash, and that was when he knew he was well and truly dead.

Several eternal minutes later, his body began to pound as waves of heat and cold moved through him. Then he heard it. The slow build of sounds—Kayleigh's breathing, a distant cry of a fox deep in the wood, and the silence where his own heart should have been beating—filled his ears.

"Open your eyes," the woman said. "Open your eyes and *see* me, Seamus."

He did as the woman commanded. It was impossible not to obey. The compulsion was so strong that his eyes bolted open and he gasped, though not from any need to breathe. As he looked about, everything was sharper, clearer, deeper. He could see the very motes of dust dancing in the moonlight.

"What did you do to me?" Seamus asked. His voice was his, yet it wasn't. There was an added silkiness to it, even richer than his voice from before the famine, before the starvation had begun a slow ravage of his body.

"What did I do?" The woman's voice drew his focus from the changing world around him. She looked even more beautiful than before, and her voice sounded like a choir of angels.

"Yes, what did you do?"

"I gave you what all men dream of, Seamus. I gave you immortality." She rose gracefully and held out her hand to him. "But immortality has a price. You belong to me now. You're mine, now and forever."

He placed his hand in hers as he got to his feet. But his body moved too fast, and he collided with her. She caught him, laughing, the sound like bells.

"Come with me. Let me show you the world. It all belongs to you now." She tried to drag him toward the door. He nearly went with her, but the slow, steady sound of a beating heart drew his focus back to the bed. Kayleigh was still there, needing him to take care of her. How could he have forgotten? His death and now rebirth had almost robbed him of his only family, burying his memories of who and what he once was in a bath of blood. But he dug deep, seeking those memories out, protecting them.

"Wait. My sister…" He stepped toward the bed. "She has no one else."

The woman rolled her eyes. "Bring the child if you wish."

Seamus lifted Kayleigh into his arms and carried her outside the cottage and into the night, following their mysterious savior.

"Everything is going to be all right now, love," he whispered in his sister's ear. She stirred and snuggled into his chest. She smelled beyond tempting, and the beating of her heart was a loud but comforting sound that kept the strange new thirst inside him at bay.

Whatever happened now, he would protect Kayleigh and care for her. Even if that meant obeying the beautiful angel.

And though she had mastery over his body and soul, he knew she held no power over his heart.

CHAPTER 1

Sadie Harris groaned as the flight information on the big screen in the airport gate area changed from *Delayed* to *Canceled*.

"Oh God, you can't be serious."

The word *Canceled* flashed in red over and over, as if taunting her. A pit formed in her stomach as she glanced around at the other few passengers in the tiny regional airport, sitting in those dark-green thin leather chairs of the waiting area, watching for their plane to arrive. Now they began to realize it was never going to come.

"Shit, shit, shit..." She grabbed her carry-on luggage and her purse, following the other beleaguered passengers, who all headed for the gate desk. The female attendant stationed there offered a wan smile that didn't promise any help as the passengers all jockeyed for a place in line. By some miracle, Sadie was first in line and stepped up to speak to the attendant.

"Yes?"

"Hi, I just saw flight 208 is canceled. Can I get rebooked on the next available flight to Galveston?"

"Let me check." The attendant pursed her lips as she clicked through screen after screen, and then she shook her head. "Looks like it will be a week before we have a seat open."

"A *week*?" Sadie's heart plummeted, and the pit in her stomach grew bigger. She didn't have a week. Her heat cycle was a day away, maybe less.

Sadie was a shifter, a fox shifter specifically, and when her heat cycles came, she had to get out of town fast. Her scent would become irresistible to any other shifters nearby, and if the Yampa Valley werewolves caught her at home during a heat cycle... She shuddered at the horrific thought.

"I'm so sorry. Do you still want to book a flight?" the attendant asked.

"No, thanks." She turned away from the desk and headed for the exit. Once outside, she pulled the hood of her sweatshirt up over her head and shuffled past the other few cars parked in the airport parking lot. *Dammit.* What the hell was she going to do now?

When she got to her car in the parking lot, she called home. She and her grandmother Vera shared a cozy stone cottage at the edge of the Yampa Valley pack's territory.

For as long as Sadie could remember, she had lived in that house. She'd been only two when a nest of vampires had killed her parents. Sadie had spent the day with her grandmother, and when night fell and they hadn't returned, they soon figured out what had happened. Ever since, her grandmother had raised Sadie with a set of rules to survive as a shifter. And the most important rule? *When your heat comes on, leave town.*

Vera finally answered the phone. "Sadie? Is your flight on time?"

"They canceled my flight, and the next one isn't for a week." She held her breath, wondering how upset her grandmother would be and trying to figure out what to do.

"*What?* Oh God, Sadie. Don't come home. Just drive to Denver, you understand? Get to the city and rent a high-rise hotel room. Stay there until the heat passes."

"Okay, I can do that." Sadie drew in a deep breath, trying to ignore the slow building of heat beneath her skin. In a day or so, the need to mate would be so strong that she would jump the first male she saw. But a human was better than a werewolf. No werewolf would be sweet and gentle. They would use and abuse her and probably kill her when they were done. She had seen the body of another shifter once, a female who hadn't been lucky enough to escape the wide-ranging Yampa pack's territory when her heat cycle hit.

Years ago, Vera had brokered an uneasy peace with

the pack. It was amazing what holding a shotgun to the balls of an alpha werewolf could accomplish in the way of diplomacy. One thing the pack had agreed on was staying away from Sadie, but when the heat came on, the scent was irresistible, and the pack couldn't be expected to steer clear of her. Her grandmother's age had protected her, but at twenty-four, Sadie was a prime target when the scent of her need was thick in the air. She and Vera both knew the werewolf pack risk the peace settlement to come after her.

"Call me when you get to Denver, sweetie. Be safe." Her grandmother's normally tranquil voice was tremulous.

"I will. I promise." She started the engine and ended the call before she left the parking lot. She had a lot of ground to cover if she was going to reach Denver. She could get a hotel room, slap on a "Do Not Disturb" sign, shift into her fox form, and wait out the heat if she didn't find a human male she liked. But if the heat got to her before then...

Don't think about it, she reminded herself. *Just drive.*

But her gas icon flashed a warning on her dashboard. Shit, she couldn't make it to Denver without fuel. She pulled into a gas station and started it filling up. Then she went inside the convenience store to buy some water. As she walked along the aisles, she realized she wasn't alone. A man stood right behind her; his face was reflected in the refrigerator glass. She tried to keep calm as she faced Cyrus, one of the werewolves of the Yampa pack.

"Hello, Sadie, where are you off to?" Cyrus asked, his voice always a little too smooth.

She'd had run-ins with the Yampa pack before, and they'd teased her a lot, usually in a mean-spirited way, but they didn't generally scare her except when she went into heat.

"I'm headed to the airport, got a plane to catch. Traveling for work."

"I thought you wrote online articles," Cyrus said, one russet brow arching. He leaned against the wall fridge so she couldn't get past him. Then he slowly inhaled. She winced.

"I'm...traveling for research on this one. Can't write about something unless you visit it, you know?" She turned to walk away, hating to give him her back and feeling exposed, but she had to get out of there.

"You smell real good today. New perfume?" He sniffed her again, leaning in close, and this time she realized the clerk at the counter was watching them.

"Yeah, great herbal shampoo, actually. You should try it," she lied. "Well, it was nice seeing you, Cyrus, but I have to go or I'll miss my flight." She all but sprinted to the counter, slapped down five bucks, and ran for her car. As she got in, she saw Cyrus standing just outside the store, watching her. Then he slowly pulled out his cell phone and made a call. Her stomach knotted in terror. Did he know she was close? Could he smell it?

Sadie floored the gas pedal once she hit the highway, trying to put the miles between her and Cyrus.

She was halfway to Denver when the heat rolled in like a tidal wave. She swerved into the nearest public rest stop and scrambled out of the car into the woods. Once she was far enough away not to be seen, she fell to her knees and welcomed the transformation. Her bones and muscles shifted and contorted, and her body shrank until she was a furry red bundle trapped beneath the weight of her jeans and sweatshirt. The vixen inside her was now on the outside. The creature was now in control.

Sadie clawed out from the pile of clothes and crouched low, sniffing the air. Her ears twitched this way and that as she listened to all the sounds around her. A mole was burrowing deep beneath the roots of a tree. Several rabbits stopped nibbling plants as they sensed a predator was among them.

The vixen was hungry, but the need for a mate was stronger. She threw back her head and let out a shrieking cry. The sound echoed off the trees around her, but the cry went unanswered. Male foxes, not shifters, refused to answer. They heard the slightly off pitch to her calls and knew she was not like them.

A hawk landed in the branches above her. Sadie's keen eyes studied its sharp beak and dangerous talons. Her focus took in the micro movements of the hawk's eyes as he tilted his head, studying her back. A moment of mutual respect passed between them. Both were predators, but neither would attack the other. Not today.

Sadie padded deeper into the woods on her glossy black paws. The vixen knew the woods well and headed straight for a stream, where she bent to lap up fresh cold water from its edge. Tiny fish shimmered just beneath the surface, catching her attention. She abandoned her other concerns for the moment and pounced on the minnows, batting them out of the water and onto the rocks, where she ate a light meal, filling the hole in her belly.

The skies began to darken above as a fall thunderstorm crested the nearest mountains. Sadie started to head back to the car, but the heat struck her again, more powerful this time, driving her deeper into the woods, once more calling for a mate that did not exist at least not here.

The low sound of a wolf's howl echoed off the trees from several miles away. Her fur bristled, and panic sent shivers through her.

The Yampa werewolves had heard her. The hunt had begun.

Sadie dashed deeper into the woods, heart pounding as she struggled to take control over the vixen. As a shifter, she was both fully human and fully fox, two entities sharing one body that could change.

The Yampa pack were much the same, only wolves not foxes. And while they weren't the hybrid man-animals that were depicted in movies, other bits of lore were right on the money. At the full moon, the wolf took over completely, making them far more animal and far more dangerous.

The pack alpha, Ulrich, was a cruel bastard. Sadie had met other werewolves over the years. Most were noble men and women. But not this pack, and definitely not Ulrich. She had begged her grandmother to move a hundred times, but Vera refused to abandon her family's home, despite the danger the pack presented. She was there first, after all.

A fresh howl split the air, and Sadie picked up her pace, trying to make it back to her car. The vixen didn't want to shift back to human form, because they both knew the danger. If the pack caught her as a woman, she would be violated over and over until it killed her. If they caught her as a fox, she would be ripped to pieces. But that was at least a quick death. Sadie caught the scent of humans and food on the breeze. The rest stop wasn't far if she could just—

A howl came from somewhere ahead of her.

No, no, no. They had found her car. She couldn't go back there now. She changed direction and ran, trying to leave the smallest tracks possible. It was going to be dark soon. The longer she was out here, the more likely they would run her to ground. Another series of howls came from all around. She sprinted harder, faster, away from the calls, knowing she wouldn't make it far at this pace.

Sadie evaded them for almost half an hour, but her paws began to ache and her senses were overwhelmed with the mixture of scents all around her. Some were natural, some unnatural. She reached a field and skidded to a stop at the sight of an electric fence. Her ears pricked at the faint electrical humming that was too high for humans to hear. She turned to go back into the woods but froze. Wolves were on the wind. Their sharp, dark, musky scent was impossible to ignore, and it came from all around her...except the direction of the fence.

Her animal instincts kicked in. She lowered her body to the ground, ears laid flat as she crept along, hoping to find an opening in the fence. She crossed a fallen tree, leapt above the safety of the grass, exposing herself for a brief instant. In that moment, she saw the wolves.

Ulrich, the alpha, was pure black with yellow eyes. His reddish-brown beta, Cyrus, was headed in her direction, and the silver-gray omega, Dracen, was moving away slightly. They all froze when she leapt above the grass. Then they started to run as one, a trio of unholy howls chasing her down the fence line. She panted and clawed at the earth. It didn't matter what tracks she left behind now.

The crush of underbrush behind her was her only warning. Dracen, the quickest of the pack, tackled her. His jaws clamped down on her neck as they rolled over and over until they came to a stop in a jumbled cluster of fur and limbs. Sadie scrambled, clawing at him in desperation, but he pinned her down by the throat. He didn't do anything except keep her pinned, however. He was waiting for Ulrich. Ulrich was the real monster. Cyrus was just as vicious, but Dracen was less so. He was almost reasonable.

The vixen wanted to scream, to cry for help, but Sadie seized control. Any prey-like sound would only get her neck snapped that much faster. The other two came into view. Ulrich growled softly, his eyes glowing as he licked his snout in eagerness.

Dracen gave her throat a squeeze, his teeth sinking in as a warning that she should stay still. Sadie went limp, her body sagging as she tried to feign defeat. It took every ounce of her own willpower not to let even one muscle twitch because Dracen would feel it.

Ulrich and Cyrus returned to human form, standing before her and Dracen fully naked.

"Well, well, well, little Sadie didn't get far enough away this time. A little vixen in heat. Can't say we've ever had the pleasure of fucking one of those before." Ulrich snickered. Cyrus nodded as they both eyed her hungrily. The vixen growled, wanting to sink her jaws deep into Ulrich's flesh.

"Dracen, change back and we'll take her to the compound."

Ulrich stepped toward them as Dracen loosened his hold on her and started to change. Sadie acted fast. If there was one thing she had an advantage on over wolves, it was her agility. She jerked out of Dracen's loosened grip and shot straight toward the barbed electric fence.

The barbs cut her, but it was the thousands of volts of electricity that she really felt. The breath rushed out of her, and she hit the ground a dozen feet from the fence. It felt like someone had punched her so hard that her heart had exploded.

"Get that bitch!" Ulrich bellowed.

She almost smiled. The fence was too high to jump, and the spaces between the wires had been barely big enough for her to get through. Sadie tried to clear her body of the fiery heat pulsing through her in agonizing waves. Shifters could heal most wounds quickly, but the surge of electricity had left her jittery and weak. She managed to stand, but she still shook violently from her nose down to her tail.

Can't stop. Have to keep going.

She moved through the farmland pasture, but her run was little more than a trot. The others would find a way around the fence soon enough, but with luck she could find some kind of shelter first. A copse of trees ahead gave her a flicker of hope. She could climb high and rest out of reach. But as Sadie reached the base of the first tree, she knew she wouldn't make it. She gave a half-hearted jump, but her claws scraped at the bark, finding no purchase.

Exhausted and hurting, she moved on, trudging through the forest for what felt like hours. The last rays of sunlight slipped beneath the horizon, and darkness claimed the world. The breeze carried the distant howls of the angry Yampa pack toward her. But they soon turned to cries of triumph. They had found a way around the fence.

Can't stop. Must keep going.

She pressed on and glimpsed a stretch of asphalt through the woods.

A road! If she got onto it, she might find her way back to the rest stop and get to her car. But that was a big *if*. Her paws hit the highway, dragging with every step as she started to cross. A sudden roar deafened her, and she turned, blinking into the bright lights of a vehicle speeding around the bend, bearing down on her. Screeching metal blended with her own terrified scream before she collapsed and darkness swallowed her.

CHAPTER 2

Seamus Gallagher gunned the engine of his motorcycle as he sped down the curving highways of rural Colorado. His helmet's black visor kept most of the fading sunlight from his face with its UV protection. The rest of his outfit—biker boots, motorcycle jacket, leather gloves, and jeans—protected the rest.

Sunlight was not his friend. It didn't turn him to ash like in those silly movies, and he sure as hell didn't sparkle like in those teenage romance books. What a load of bullshit. Still, he couldn't deny he had read all of them. Twice.

Vampires, *real* ones, got drowsy in the daylight and fell into a coma-like slumber. Even being indoors while the sun was out made most vampires catatonic. But Seamus was tough. Cassandra had made him that way. Ever since she had turned him, she had used him, trained him, and pushed him to his limits. He'd learned to power through sunlight so long as he didn't have too long of a direct exposure to it.

Cassandra had wanted him to be a perfect, ruthless killer, but he had failed her. She hadn't been able to break him of his hold on life and his love for his family and friends. So out of spite, she had done the unthinkable. In the 1920s, she had murdered Lara, the mortal lover of his closest friends, Ian and Connor, two other vampires Cassandra had turned during the famine. Unlike him, Ian and Connor held no special place in Cassandra's black heart. They were simply pawns in her war amongst the other vampire covens. When they'd outlived their usefulness, she'd let them go.

But not me. No, she kept me chained to her side.

But when he'd gotten free of her and went to live with Ian and Connor, Cassandra had gotten her revenge. Hurt him by hurting those he loved. Seamus didn't want to think about the horror he'd felt that night when he had found the poor woman dying, but flashes of memory still hit him. A gold-fringed flapper dress. Dark hair cut in a fashionable bob. She'd smelled like freshly cut roses and summer sunlight.

He had cradled Lara in his arms, trying to make her last moments peaceful. That was how Ian and Connor had found him, clutching the woman they'd both loved, and they'd assumed the worst. That *he*, not Cassandra, had killed their human lover. It was exactly what she had wanted, to deprive him of those who'd become blood brothers to him.

He had lost his friends and his home that night. He'd boarded a ship to America and never looked back. Yet Cassandra still looked for him. He'd heard the rumors as he moved from coven to coven over the years, but he always faded into the shadows before she could catch him.

Colorado was the perfect place to hide. Cassandra loved big cities with parties and rich prey. Her avarice had only grown over the centuries. But coming here? Here there were green mountains, cerulean skies, and white aspens that moved like ghosts in the hills and the valleys. It was a place of peace, a place of rest, something Seamus was convinced Cassandra would avoid like the plague.

He leaned his bike around the sharp bend, the beam of his headlights illuminating the road. A flash of red in front of him gave him only a moment to react. He slammed the brakes and ended up sliding his bike in a rapid skid along the asphalt. For a split second he thought he might stay upright, but then the bike gave way and he hit the highway hard, rolling a dozen feet from his bike, which screeched to a stop on its side.

He lay on his stomach, panting, not from the need to breathe but out of a deep instinct that had never fully gone away. The part of him that remembered what it was like to be human.

"Fuck," he groaned. Definitely a rib or two was

broken. He would need to feed if he wanted to heal up in a reasonable amount of time.

A whimper escaped him as he tried to move. *Wait, no.* That sound hadn't come from him. He pulled his helmet off and checked the road. Something dark and reddish-gold lay beneath his overturned bike.

Seamus got to his feet and went to his bike, ignoring the dizzy spell that hit him. He lifted it up, standing it on its kickstand. And then he saw it, the crumpled furry heap. He had hit an animal.

"Shit." He crouched down by the animal. "Sorry, little guy. I really am." He examined the creature closer. It writhed and whined softly.

A fox. A tiny one. Golden eyes gleamed, and its black-tipped muzzle twitched as it gazed up at him.

A howl in the distance sent chills down Seamus's spine. Fucking werewolves. He knew a pack was nearby. He'd picked up their scents all over the place between Denver and Steamboat Springs.

"They hunting you?" he asked the little fox and reached out to pat the creature's head. But when the fox nodded, *nodded* at him, he knew something else was going on.

"What the hell?"

More howling, closer now, made him forget about the fox's penetrating stare. Without thinking, he picked up the injured creature and tucked it against his chest, half zipping up his jacket to hold the fox inside. Then he got his motorcycle upright and revved the engine.

A pair of yellow eyes in the dark woods followed him as he started down the road. He raised his middle finger at the wolf, laughing at the howl of rage that followed. No fox stew tonight for those furry assholes.

Half an hour later, he pulled into the parking lot of an expensive resort. He usually stayed off the grid, even in small towns, but he knew his latest alias as Seamus Green wasn't on Cassandra's radar yet. This little paradise in the mountains would be the last place she would expect to find him. She had tried to turn him into an elegant society vampire, one who preyed on rich and influential ladies in ballrooms, but he'd lived and died a poor Irish farmer. The call of the land was in his bones.

He parked his bike and checked on his furry passenger. He wasn't going to set it free here, not until he was sure of its condition. He would sneak it into the condo, keep it comfortable, and call a vet first thing in the morning.

Seamus walked up to the doors and swiped a keycard that flashed his name to the reception desk. The girl working there buzzed him inside. He'd had the foresight to have his room keys and passcard delivered to his last residence a few nights ago so he wouldn't have to waste time checking in during the day. The resort catered to people who were private in nature, which was perfect for a vampire who needed to keep a low profile.

The woman at the reception desk beamed at him, her smile inviting him to take more than her blood. "Evening, Mr. Green! We've been expecting you! We've had your luggage delivered. If you need anything else, just call the front desk. I'm Heather."

"Evening, Heather. Thank you." He smiled back at her before he turned to the elevators. He wouldn't mind sinking his teeth into her later, for just a light snack to heal his injuries. But first he had to get the little passenger in his coat settled.

He took the elevator up to the third floor and found his room. The fox made a soft noise. Seamus stroked its head as it peeked out of his jacket.

"Hush, buddy, just a second." He pulled his key out of his pocket and unlocked the door. The suite was impressive. A massive kitchen and a large dining room and living room made up much of the space. Beyond that was a master bedroom with a huge bathroom. He might not care for the big city, but that didn't mean he didn't enjoy certain luxuries.

The decor was mountain rustic, with rough-hewn tables, dark rich wood, and leather furniture with brass accents. For the first time in weeks it felt like he could relax. He had shipped his luggage and clothes ahead of him since he traveled on his motorcycle. He didn't have much, but what he did have mattered. He checked the boxes sitting just inside the door before he headed into the kitchen and unzipped his jacket. He laid a dish towel on the counter, and with as much gentleness as he could manage, he set the fox down on it.

The creature lay on its side, breathing shallowly. It looked like hell. Bloody scratches along its sides drew a frown from Seamus. They didn't look like injuries from his bike, but rather from claw marks. It must have been through one hell of a fight.

He wet a cloth with some warm water and dabbed at one of the deeper slashes. The fox hissed and snapped at him, but it fell weakly back onto its side.

Seamus cleaned the wounds with warm water and soap, careful to keep his hands out of its reach. By the time he was done, the creature had given up trying to defend itself. Its tail swished once, and he noticed he'd been wrong in one of his initial assumptions.

"Well now, you're not a buddy at all. You're a little vixen, aren't you?" He chuckled, and the fox's tongue darted out, licking her nose. "Well, lass, try not to move too much. If you make it through the night, I'll take you to the vet tomorrow, okay?"

The exhausted little fox closed her eyes, and he relaxed. He realized then he needed to move her. He didn't want her to jump off the counter and hurt herself in the middle of the night.

"I'm going to pick you up now. Don't bite me. I'm just trying to help you find a place to sleep."

She nuzzled the towel and huffed softly. He carefully lifted her up, bundling her when she didn't attack him. He cradled her against his chest and headed into the bedroom. He chose a spot on the floor between two comfortable buffalo-plaid chairs. He set her down on one chair, then grabbed the heavy warm throw blanket off the end of the bed and made a small nest out of it. He slid the fox into the nest and tucked her into the blankets so only her head peeked out. Then he tossed the bloody towel into the laundry sink.

The vixen remained still in her nest, but her eyes were half-open. Her ears twitched whenever he moved about the room, but she didn't try to flee or hide. He stripped his jacket off, followed by the rest of his clothes, before pulling the covers back on the bed. He didn't normally sleep at night, but after the fall on the road, his body needed time to repair and rest. He would find that little receptionist in a few hours and feed enough to recover without raising suspicions.

He folded his arms under his head and closed his eyes. Outside, the breeze moved through the aspens and the pines, creating a steady hushing sound that made him think of a rapid river back home in Ireland.

A sharp pain of longing for home tightened his chest. His family, his *whole life* had been there before the famine had stolen it all. All but Kayleigh. She had lived to be one hundred and three, a mother to seven, grandmother to twenty-three, and great-grandmother to forty-eight. She was Seamus's true legacy, the only good thing he had ever done in his life. Cassandra had not taken Kayleigh's life, no matter how many times she had threatened to. It was not out of kindness, however. She simply knew that crossing that line would lose her any chance of forcing Seamus's loyalty. If she'd killed Kayleigh, she'd have had to kill them both.

But Cassandra had killed people to try to keep him in line. She'd killed Lara and turned his best friends against him. Now, after all these years, Ian and Connor weren't that far away. They lived a mere three hours from Denver, and that was no accident. He hoped to find a way to make amends for what Cassandra had done to them. By now it was possible that they even knew the truth of what had happened that night, but even if they did, they no doubt held him equally responsible.

He reached for his cell phone and dialed the number the private investigator had emailed him. It rang twice before Ian answered.

"Hello?" Ian asked.

Seamus opened his mouth to speak, but no words came out.

"Hello?"

He ended the call. Was he really so stupid as to think he could just call them up and talk it out? But it wasn't as if a face-to-face encounter would work out any better. They would kill him on sight.

"Fuck," he muttered and closed his eyes, trying to rest. He had to stop thinking about the past. Only heartbreak would be found there.

CHAPTER 3

Sadie yawned and moved a bit, kneading her black paws in the blankets the man had given her. She was so tired, but she couldn't get comfortable. Despite her injuries, her heat was still strong. She'd have to find a way to get through it here or find a new safe place to ride it out where Ulrich and his pack couldn't get to her. She sniffed the air around her, and her vixen wanted to cuddle in delight and comfort at the new smells.

When the man had tucked her inside his coat, she had been surrounded by the most divine masculine scent. Pine mixed with a hint of mint and musk. It called to her, lulled her into a trance like no other scent ever had, even during her heat. She had almost whimpered with pleasure as she had burrowed against his chest.

Lifting her nose out of the nest of blankets, she

inhaled the scent coming from the nearby bed. She needed more of it, more of him. If she could just get close to him, maybe she could fall asleep easier and heal.

She clawed her way out of the blankets and sniffed the air. Her ears twitched back and forth before she leapt onto the bed. Her body ached as she padded across the large bed toward the man. Being so close to him soothed her somehow. He made her feel safe, and right now she needed that.

When the man didn't stir, she crept closer, carefully placing her dainty paws on the bed. When he didn't move, she walked right up to his body and sniffed him. He smelled good, so damn good. Human males didn't usually smell like this. His scent was stronger, more potent and almost hypnotic. Something about that bothered her, niggling at the back of her mind, warning her that most humans didn't smell like this. But her vixen was too tired to listen to her human side.

She settled down against his side and laid her head on his chest. She dozed for maybe an hour before the heat began to build again beneath her skin. Sadie whimpered, trying to fight the change that was coming, but she was too weak. Like many shifters, her body changed between its two forms during heat, trying to find the form that was most comfortable while she went through her mating cycle. Her body reshaped itself, bones and muscles contorting and elongating until she lay naked and human.

The man beside her jolted out of bed just in time to see her fox tail wag once before shifting back into her human form and disappearing.

"What the—?"

Sadie gasped and fell out of the bed, trying to conceal her nakedness with a bedsheet as her human sensibilities returned to her. She closed her eyes, waiting for him to scream, but there was only silence. She lifted her head and peered over the top of the bed at him. He stood there in his boxers, staring back at her.

Damn, he was gorgeous. Her fox hadn't been interested in his looks, only his smell. But her human eyes drank in the sight of him. All that corded, lean muscle, a six-pack for abs that made her mouth water. His face was a work of art. He had a raw, rugged beauty only certain men had—mostly models—with a chiseled jaw, and a sensual mouth. His eyes promised that if he started flirting, a girl would beg him to take her to bed. His dark-red hair was long and ruffled, carefree rather than styled.

"You're a shifter. I should have known a normal fox wouldn't have survived getting hit by my bike," he grumbled in the most seductive Irish accent she'd ever heard.

"You know what I am?" Her voice came out slightly rough from disuse over the last day. Shock coursed through her. How could a human know what a shifter was? Yes, there were some humans who knew about them, but the average person? Definitely not. Which meant he wasn't an average person.

"Yes, I was too distracted, or I would've clued in earlier. I smelled the wolves but didn't smell you. Then again, their stink was overpowering."

"You smelled them, how...?" Her stomach sank. There were only a few possibilities she knew of, and none of them were good.

The man smiled, and she saw something that cooled her heat faster than ice water. Fangs gleamed where his canine teeth should have been.

"Vampire!" she gasped. Terror and rage warred inside her. Flashes of memory came back, ones she would never forget.

Her parents' bodies drained of blood, the heavy scent of decayed earth, rotten blood, and fear clinging to the scene. She'd clutched her grandmother's neck and stared at the bloodied bodies, her innocence of the world forever shattered. Vampires loved to drink shifter blood. It gave them a high. Vampires were known to get addicted to it.

The vampire lifted his hands in front of his chest. "Easy."

Sadie stayed in a protective crouch. Something about this wasn't right. Why didn't he smell like those other vampires? She couldn't run because she was naked and too tired to shift. And even if she could, where would she go? Her body was still cut up and bruised. The scent of her blood filled the air, and she saw his eyes turn from blue to a glowing red.

"Don't come any closer," she growled, the deep sound resonating throughout the room.

The man's eyes narrowed. "Look, I didn't know what you were, okay? I've got no quarrel with you, and I don't plan on making you a snack, but you shouldn't leave. Those wolves are still after you—I can smell them. They came into the city. It's not safe for you to leave this apartment."

"It's not like I'm safe in here either." She grabbed the blanket nearest her and wrapped it around her like a cloak. The bed separating them, despite its large size, didn't put nearly enough distance between them.

"Look, I understand you have no reason to trust me, but you can. I don't feed on shifters." His shoulders dropped as he lowered his hands a little, the gesture slightly comforting because he looked less tense, less ready to pounce on her.

Sadie stared hard at the man. "Why not? You know what our blood does to your kind."

"I do. But I'm not like most vampires. I don't give in to my instincts. Not fully. I remember that you are people, like us. It's not right to hunt you down and drain you just for some quick high."

Sadie's animal instincts could usually find a false note in someone's tone when they lied to her. All she heard from this man, this *vampire*, was truth.

"Why should I believe you? Your kind killed my parents. You can't control yourselves any more than those werewolves out there." She wasn't sure why she blurted that out. She always kept that part of her past private, even with the other shifters she'd run into over the years.

"For the record, I don't kill my dinner." He scowled, crossing his arms. "Morals aside, it's sloppy and bad manners."

"So, you admit you want to eat me?" she shot back.

He growled softly in frustration and rolled his eyes. The sound did something to the vixen inside her. The hostility she felt suddenly stilled as a wild flutter of excitement coursed through her. The heat, which had vanished, was coming back because he had triggered it. This cycle had to be particularly bad if a vampire was turning her on.

"I need to leave," she gasped. "I need to go—" She took two steps before she crumpled against the bed. Her body ached with need, to burrow into the arms of a strong, protective male and lose herself to the instinct to mate. "Dammit."

"What's the matter?" The vampire took a step closer. Sadie wished she could have growled at him, but she didn't have the strength.

"Heat... Mating heat...," she muttered, breathless.

"What can I do? I can help." The vampire came around and crouched down beside her next to the bed.

"I..." Her voice thickened with shame. "I need skin-to-skin contact."

"What does that mean exactly?" he asked. "I don't want to misunderstand you."

"Touch me. Hold me until the need passes. It comes and goes, but physical contact helps."

"Okay, I can do that...if you'll let me." His gaze burned into hers. "I swear I won't hurt you. I swear on the lives of my living family. That vow matters to me. I would not break it."

She half laughed, half sniffled. "I don't have much choice."

He held out his hands. "May I?"

Sadie nodded. The vampire gently grasped her body and lifted her up onto the bed. He pulled her into his arms. He wasn't warm, like her, but his cool body felt good against her burning skin. Their faces were mere inches apart on a pillow.

He shifted her so their bodies fully pressed together. "This okay?" She shivered as her naked body touched his.

"Yeah." Sadie closed her eyes and moved closer, tucking her head under his chin.

"What's your name?" His deep rumbling voice had a soft purr to it.

"Sadie Harris. You?"

"Seamus Gallagher."

She nuzzled his throat, taking in that delicious scent. The scent of the woods and something dark and male came off his skin. Maybe it was the heat, or maybe it was something to do with him being a vampire.

"So… Sadie, how does this heat work? I don't know much about fox shifters in heat."

She could listen to that gorgeous accent all day. Again she found herself wondering if it was vampire glamour or if it was just him.

"It's different for every shifter species. For foxes, like me, it happens every six months. I was trying to leave town because the Yampa Valley pack would rape me, probably even *kill* me if they had the chance."

"Those were the wolves chasing you?"

"Yeah." Sadie inhaled deeply. "My grandmother and I live at the edge of their territory. My grandmother's relatively safe at her age, but not me."

"You feeling any better now?" he asked. "Is the urge calming at all?"

"Yeah, sorry. It's hard to get comfortable when I'm like this. Usually I just…" She stopped that train of thought short.

"What?"

"Normally, I go somewhere fun on vacation for a week. I always know when the heat will hit. I was headed for a cruise today, but my heat set in early."

Seamus tightened his hold on her. "And what happens when you are on these vacations? Are you sick like this?"

"No. I usually grab the nearest attractive human and, well…"

"Have your way with him?" he answered for her.

"Yeah. The sex calms me. It eases the heat." She couldn't help but chuckle at the thought of some of those encounters. "And the men certainly don't mind. Hell, most of them leave with their egos wildly inflated."

"*Oh...*" The single syllable held so much weight and tension that she could have been burned by the sudden flare of heat between them.

"What? No offer to take me?" she quipped.

"No, my ego is just the right size. If you want me, you're welcome to ask."

"That doesn't *sound* like a vampire."

He shot her a meaningful look. "I may be a vampire, but I'm still a gentleman. I don't take anything unless it's clearly offered."

Sadie digested this for a long moment. "So...are you a young vamp, or an old one?"

"Young, I suppose." His tone was full of patient amusement as though he was used to the question. "I was turned in 1849."

"That's not young! You're old." She drew back to look up at his face.

Seamus quirked a dark gold-red brow. "I've met vampires dating back to the Roman Empire. I suppose I'm not young, maybe middle-aged."

Sadie's nose wrinkled. "I still don't get why you aren't trying to take a bite out of me."

His gaze grew distant. "I learned a long time ago to control my hunger, even when I was desperate. I had a sister once, a mortal. The last thing I wanted was to harm her. I learned that control out of the necessity to protect her." He slid a palm up and down Sadie's back as he talked. The caress was soothing, and she had to admit she liked it. She wriggled closer, bumping against his thighs.

"As much as I am enjoying this, I will need to feed soon. The fall I took off my bike broke a few ribs. I was going to go downstairs before this happened."

A stab of panic hit Sadie at the thought of him leaving, but also of him staying to feed on her. "Okay, will you come back after?" she asked.

"Of course. It is my home, after all. My *new* home for now, anyway." His chuckle made her feel dizzy in a delightful sort of way. Damn, that heat had really messed her up. Her grandmother would be furious if she ever found out that Sadie had cuddled up to a vampire because of it.

"Okay, go. I'll just stay here, if that's all right. As soon as I've got this heat under control, I'll be on my way."

Seamus brushed the backs of his fingers over her cheek. "You don't have to go. Those wolves are still out there somewhere. There's a spare bedroom here. Stay at least until they give up and go home."

She eyed him levelly. "Why are you being so nice to me? Shifters and vampires don't get along."

"Who says that?" he asked, his eyes soft as he stared down at her.

"Everyone."

"Well, *everyone* is wrong." He slipped out of the bed, and she immediately missed the feel of his body beside hers.

"You're strange for a vampire. You're not like the others." She shuddered as dark memories tried to claw their way to the surface.

"Given most of the vampires I've known, that sounds like a good thing."

Sadie cocked her head a little, baffled by him and her reaction to him. "It is, I think."

She was sure that any other vampire would try to feed on her, but Seamus was different. His scent, his touch, it calmed the wild terror within her, as well as the instincts that screamed both desire and danger. None of that made sense.

She'd been close to a vampire once before during her heat. The vampire had chased her onto a train platform, and she had boarded the train seconds before the doors closed. He had missed her by mere inches. She hadn't forgotten the stench on that one. He had smelled like old dirt, rotting things, and deep despair. How was it that Seamus didn't smell like that?

The door clicked closed as Seamus left, and Sadie collapsed onto the bed, trying to calm her racing heart. After a moment she collected herself and went in search of the bathroom. She found a massive shower with seven heads aiming in all different directions and a large bench at the back.

"Holy crap. *That* should do the trick." She grinned as she turned on the shower and steam filled the room. She dropped the bedsheet and stepped inside.

She moaned in delight as the hot water hit her. Dried blood and dirt washed away, leaving stinging open wounds. They would soon heal if she was able to rest. She would feel even better if she actually had sex, but she was not asking Mr. Sexy Fangs to help her out in that department. Ignoring the fact that he was a bloodsucking fiend, he was definitely panty-melting hot. He was exactly the kind of guy she would have dragged into the nearest bedroom during her heat. Hell, she would have jumped him out of heat as well. With that slightly long hair just past his ears, all red waves of silk, and those soft blue-bonnet-colored eyes, and that toned, muscled body...

Sadie moved her hand down her body, pretending it was him touching her. There was nothing wrong with pretending, and she really did want to fantasize about how it would feel to be taken by him. That was the beautiful thing about daydreams—they could be whatever she wanted, and no one would know, no one would judge her for them.

She shut her eyes and imagined him coming back into the room, stalking her like she was prey. The thought set all her senses on fire, charged her with sexual energy. A female shifter's true mate had to prove his worth, his strength. To hunt down his mate, to claim her, and do so gently so as to earn her trust as well as provide her with exquisite pleasure. It was a fine line between danger and desire.

She had slept with regular humans during her heat cycles, but none of them had ever excited her the way Seamus did. Just *thinking* about him pinning her down and sinking into her body was more arousing than any of the times she'd let a human male into her bed. Would it be so bad to let Seamus...?

No! That was insane. She could not even think such a thing. Despite his gentlemanly claims, he could still lose control and feed on her—and when that rush hit, he might accidentally drain her. It was a risk she couldn't take. She needed to find a way to calm the heat. She needed a human male as soon as she healed. She would find another place to stay. Then she could...

A lone howl from somewhere outside made the glass in the sliding door leading to the balcony quiver.

Ulrich. He was near. Waiting for her.

Sadie shuddered as she stepped out of the shower and dried off. Her heat and desire temporarily faded as fear consumed her. She returned to Seamus's bed and curled up into a ball, pulling the comforter over herself. Seamus's alpine scent was the only thing that seemed to calm her as a second howl came, closer this time.

CHAPTER 4

Seamus stepped out of the elevator and spotted his prey. The human scent seemed lackluster compared to the enticing fox shifter he'd just left upstairs.

He still couldn't believe this was happening to him. A shifter in heat. In his room. As if he didn't have enough to worry about trying to reunite with Ian and Connor, now he had werewolves and foxes thrown in. With a sigh, he focused on his current need: blood.

Heather, the sweet receptionist he'd met earlier, was behind the desk looking at a large aquarium that held two large box turtles. She was dropping pellets into the water at the top of the tank and talking softly to the turtles. Before coming across Sadie, Heather would have held his full attention and been exactly the thing he wanted at this moment. Now she was just a passable food source compared to the mouthwatering creature in his bed.

"Heather," Seamus greeted.

"Oh!" The girl turned to face him, her hand to her heart. "Mr. Green. You startled me. What can I do for you?" She tugged her short black polo shirt down over her khaki pants. The resort logo was embroidered in gold thread on her left breast. She couldn't have been more than twenty, with wheat-colored hair and brown eyes. Pretty by anyone's standards. But his initial interest in her had faded. After holding his little vixen upstairs and smelling her need, Heather wasn't remotely interesting.

He leaned against the counter casually. "Lovely turtles."

Heather blushed. "Yeah, they're sweet." She stared at him with innocent eyes, and he could hear her heartbeat race even from five feet away.

"So, what can I do for you?" she repeated.

"Well, I'm a bit hungry." He wet his lips and began to let his vampiric glamour work on her. A vampire's glamour could do many things, including make a vampire appear more attractive, and it would also allow him to apply a bit of compulsion to make humans do what he wished.

"Hungry?" Heather echoed. "For what?"

"For you." He waved her closer, and she stepped into his space.

"Me?"

"Yes. Are there cameras here?"

"Only in the lobby," she replied, her eyes now a little glassy. "But not in the closet behind the elevators."

"That will do." He took her hand and led her to the closet past the bank of elevators and flipped on the light. There was just enough space for them to squeeze into this closet next to each other. He closed the door and cupped the girl's face.

"This won't hurt, I assure you."

Heather nodded, her face a little dreamy and her eyes slightly blank.

Seamus brushed her hair from her neck and slid an arm around her back, pulling her to him. Then he lowered his face to her neck. His mouth watered as the thirst took over. His fangs extended down, and the tips throbbed in anticipation as he could hear the beat of her heart.

Heather gasped as he sank his teeth into her throat. Blood filled his mouth as he pulled on the vein he struck. His body burned with pleasure as he drank deeply. When the *thump-thump* of the girl's heart weakened by just a few beats, he pulled away and rasped his tongue over the puncture marks, sealing the wounds closed. Then he cupped her face, examining her eyes in the dimly lit broom closet.

"Thank you, Heather. You helped me find what I needed." He continued to use his compulsion on her. Then he picked up one of the spare shampoo bottles.

Heather blinked in surprise. "I did?"

"Yes, you definitely did. I was out of shampoo."

She brightened with a smile. "Oh right, of course! Please let me know if you need anything else."

"I will. Thank you, Heather."

He opened the closet door and ushered her out ahead of him. She wandered back to the reception desk and sat down, her head starting to clear. The buzzer for after-hours entry sounded and caused the front desk phone to ring. Heather answered whoever was waiting outside.

Seamus cleaned the last traces of blood off his lips before he stepped into the hall by the elevators. He glanced at Heather to check that she was okay. She was smiling at a brown-haired man she had just let inside the lobby. Color suffused her cheeks as she flirted with the man.

She was fine. Seamus had taken just enough blood to heal his injuries, and to help him resist Sadie's allure. He wanted to keep his word. He didn't want to feed on her, but he hadn't told her how damn good she smelled, good enough to tempt him to take a bite if he wasn't careful.

The nearest elevator chimed, and he stepped inside. Just as they started to close, the brown-haired man from the front desk stepped into view, his back to Seamus.

An acrid, foul scent hit Seamus's nose. His nostrils flared, and he recoiled just as the doors closed.

Werewolf!

Terror seized Seamus. They knew Sadie was here, and they were going after her. He didn't stop to think about why that mattered, why he cared so much about a vixen shifter he didn't even know. He would have intervened to save any human or creature, but risking his own life, which he fully admitted he was prepared to do for Sadie, that was something different.

He stared at the digital floor numbers changing on the elevator panel, his hands curled into fists. The second the door opened, he sprinted for his room and rammed the keycard so hard into the electric lock he almost broke it.

"Fuck!" He barreled inside his apartment and slammed the door behind him, bolting the lock.

His eyes swept the main room. One advantage a vampire had over shifters was speed. He could move faster than them, and process what he saw faster too. No windows were open. They were on the fourth floor. No one could climb up here. He rushed toward his bedroom and darted inside.

"Sadie, wake up," he hissed as he dug through the box of clothes he'd carried into his room. He found a black T-shirt that he knew, given his size and height compared to her tiny frame, would reach down to her knees.

"What's the matter?" She bolted awake, pulling the covers up around her body.

"Put this on. Now. A werewolf got into the building." He tossed the shirt at her and headed to the balcony. The tall windows opened onto a sizable deck. Moonlight lit up the courtyard below as he stared through the thick glass.

"Seamus, if one is here, he'll smell me. I have to leave."

"They could be trying to flush you out. How many wolves are in the Yampa pack?"

"Three. It's a small pack," Sadie said. "An alpha, beta, and omega. The alpha, Ulrich, is the most dangerous one—"

"Wrong," he interrupted her. "The most dangerous pack member is the omega."

Sadie joined him at the window. "No, that's not true."

Seamus tried to ignore the delicious scent of the woman as she stood beside him. "An omega acts friendly, sweet, biddable. On the *outside*. There's always a moment when the omega can turn alpha, and you'll never see it coming. They will always be more dangerous. Point is, all three of them are dangerous."

"Trust me, I know that. They've been jerks to me for the last five years," she snapped. She crossed her arms over her chest. "So what's your plan?" While some might have seen it as a brave, defiant posture, he saw it for what it was. She was hugging herself. The sickly-sweet scent of her fear, mixed with her natural aroma and her arousal, didn't lie. The combination made his cock go hard in his jeans. *Great.* That was the last thing he needed if he had to fight a werewolf pack on his own.

He dragged a hand through his hair and cursed under his breath. "I need to think..."

"I don't think we have a lot of time for that," Sadie muttered.

Someone rang the doorbell.

Seamus growled, "Stay here. Don't make a sound." He headed for the door and spoke through it.

"Who is it?"

"Deliveryman. Got a package for you."

"Yeah, you have the wrong place." Seamus knew full well this little game wouldn't be played very long.

"It says it's for unit 402. Come on, man, just open the door."

Seamus gritted his teeth. He would open the fucking door all right. Open it and rip the wolf's heart out of his chest if he didn't walk away. Last thing Seamus needed was a war with the local werewolf pack, even if they were a small one, but he wasn't about to hand Sadie over to them.

He unlocked the door and opened it just wide enough for his face to appear. He stared at the werewolf.

"If you want to keep your heart, *dog*, walk away now." He flashed his teeth and let the man see his fangs.

The werewolf grinned. "Sounds good to me, bloodsucker. I was just a distraction anyway."

Distraction? "Sadie! Get—" His shout was drowned out by an explosion of glass and Sadie's sudden scream.

Two of the hulking wolves must have scaled the condo building's walls and burst into his bedroom through the windows. Glass covered the floor as one of the two werewolves transformed back into a man.

Seamus lunged toward them, but the werewolf at the door pushed through and wrapped a meaty arm around his neck. A vampire might be stronger, but this wolf knew how to use weight and leverage like a pro. Raw strength meant nothing from this position. Seamus fell to his knees as the man behind him choked him into darkness. Although he didn't need air to breathe, if he didn't have blood flowing to his brain, he would pass out.

"Nighty-night, bloodsucker." The werewolf laughed.

Blackness crept into his vision, but Seamus wasn't afraid. He had danced this line before, had tasted the edge of nothing both as a mortal and as a vampire. His body slumped to the ground, and he gripped the faint shred of consciousness the way Cassandra had trained him to. It would give his body time to regain its strength.

"Where is she?" someone growled. "I smell her everywhere. I heard her scream. So where the fuck is she?"

"She has to be here. He called her name," another male replied, the one who'd choked him into that edge of darkness.

"Tear this place apart. Find her."

One of the wolves kicked Seamus hard in the ribs. "And the vamp?"

"Shoot him, but don't kill him. He has boxes with the London Blood Society seal on them. The last thing we need is that coven coming after us. But we need to send a message about sticking your nose where it don't belong."

Good old LBS, Seamus thought hazily. He'd belonged to the society for the last decade or so. He liked to connect with other vampires who valued human lives, who lived by a code of conduct designed to protect humans. It was one of the things Cassandra hated about him. Part of the society's ethos was to keep humans safe from paranormal creatures. They'd even partnered with human organizations like the Brotherhood of the Blood Moon. The alpha wasn't wrong about potential reprisals. Membership in the LBS had its privileges.

Seamus heard the slide of a pistol being pulled back. Pain exploded in his back as shots rang out, but he didn't move, didn't twitch. Blood pooled beneath him. He would have to feed again soon or risk passing out completely.

"She's not here. She must have escaped. Search the halls and down in the courtyard. Be quick. Someone's called the cops by now," the alpha ordered.

Sounds of booted feet moved past him, as well as the click of nails as a wolf walked away. Then heavy smothering silence.

Seamus pushed himself up onto one arm, pain lancing through him. His vision sharpened in the darkness. He inhaled slowly, sifting through the scents in the apartment. Fetid rotting smells of werewolves, his own scent, and buried beneath it all was Sadie's irresistible aroma.

"Sadie." He whispered her name as he struggled to his knees. He needed blood fast, or he wouldn't last long. If he passed out here and the cops found him... Well, it was safe to say things would get far more complicated for him.

Something moved on one of the tall shelves in the living room. He tensed, but the object dropped to the ground and pranced toward him.

The vixen. Somehow she had changed back into a fox and scaled the shelves to hide.

"Stupid wolves," Seamus groaned and fell flat on his face.

SADIE STARED at the vampire who had saved her life. He had given her just enough time to hide, and it had cost him. She moved close, nuzzling his face with the tip of her nose. The human part of Sadie was torn between leaving him here—he was a bloodsucking fiend, after all—or trying to find a way to help him. But the vixen? She *demanded* that they help him. Her inner fox seemed to trust Seamus in ways Sadie could not begin to understand.

Reluctantly, the vixen surrendered control to Sadie, who shifted back into her human form. She retrieved the black T-shirt from the floor where she had abandoned it and knelt by Seamus.

"Hey... You need to get up. I want to help you, but I don't know what to do." She rolled him onto his back and gasped when she saw the dark blood staining his body.

"Oh God." She covered her mouth.

"Blood…" Seamus breathed the word so softly she almost didn't hear it.

Oh no. Oh no, no, no. She couldn't feed a vampire.

"Please…" He reached for her wrist, his hold gentle, or perhaps just weak.

"Seamus, I don't think—" His hold on her wrist dropped, and she gasped and clutched his shoulders. "Seamus?" He didn't respond. "Look, I don't know how to…" Her heart raced as she placed her wrist to his mouth. After a moment his lips parted and he bared his fangs, even though his eyes were still closed. He bit down.

She yelped and tried to pull away on instinct, but he gripped her wrist and held fast like a man, or *vampire*, possessed. He sucked on her wrist, and the pain faded into a dull ache. Soon her head was dizzy, and she slumped down onto the floor beside him. She worried for a moment that he might lose control and drain her dry.

His eyes were open now. The bright blue was gone, replaced by fiery red. He sucked on her wrist a few more seconds and then let go. His tongue dragged over her skin where he had punctured it, and she whimpered in fresh pain. But to her surprise, the wound healed before her eyes.

"Seamus, are you okay?" Sadie asked. The world was still spinning around her.

"Yes… Thank you." He rolled onto his side to look at

her in dazed wonder. "Your blood... It tastes like sunshine."

"That must be because I'm a shifter," she murmured.

"No... It's something more. A shifter rush makes everything spin, and it makes everything feel fuzzy. But not your blood." He licked his lips and moved toward her again. Sadie jerked away.

Seamus blinked, and the red irises began to give way to blue. He fell onto his back and heaved a deep sigh.

"We can't stay here. They'll be back."

Sadie examined her wrist where he had bitten her. There were only two small, quickly fading red marks left over now. *Amazing.*

"So what's the plan?"

"I just took three bullets to the back. Give me a minute to think and heal." He twisted a little, and when he sat up, she saw three bullets drop from his healing back to the floor, making soft rapping sounds. He stood, stripped out of his shirt, and tossed it to the floor.

"I need my phone."

"Your phone? Why? Who are you going to call?"

"A couple of guys who want me dead."

"What? Why?" Sadie scrambled to her feet, trying to avoid the broken glass around her.

"It's a long story, but they're close enough they might be able to help."

"So you're going to call some guys who want you dead...to help?"

"That's the idea."

~

Cassandra stood on the balcony of the penthouse suite overlooking the city of Chicago. Behind her, a man lay dying on the floor.

"Help me," the man begged. Cassandra ignored him. He was like all humans, inconsequential. Humans had something precious, yet they wasted it, squandered so freely what she craved. The light, the laughter, the pleasure, the feeling of a heartbeat, the taste of food and the feel of…everything. She'd stopped feeling long ago. There was no pity left in her heart for mortals, not when her jealousy of them and their foolishness nearly choked her. She despised mortals.

She looked down at the man. "You have been given the gift of death, and now you shall embrace it." She spoke softly to the man just as the light in his eyes began to fade.

"Madam?" She turned at the familiar voice of her second-in-command.

"Yes, Victor?" She ignored the dying man and turned to Victor in the doorway of the suite. He was tall, dark-haired, with coal-black eyes. Handsome. But he lacked the fire that her last second had.

Seamus had been one of a kind. There had been a slight roughness to him, a feral edge, yet he retained a soft heart, one she had done everything to destroy and harden. The thought of that beauty existing in the world either as mortal or immortal had caused her a physical pain. She'd wanted to possess it, possess him, and then destroy him for the way he made her feel.

But she had failed. He remained almost as pure as the day she'd turned him. And that had filled her with a strange and almost wild longing. He alone had made her remember what it meant to be human. To shed tears, to smile and laugh with joy. For a brief time, she'd forgotten that she'd distracted herself with games of power and politics, and for once, she'd basked in the glow of Seamus's life. Even as a vampire, he'd never fully given up on his mortality. He'd clung to it, and it had clung back in a way she'd never seen before in an immortal.

A vampire had to be cold to survive, and yet somehow, Seamus had managed to avoid becoming like her. Quite the opposite—she'd started to weaken when he was with her. She took fewer lives because she couldn't bear his disapproving scowl. Maybe, given time, she could have stopped killing altogether. But Seamus hadn't given her a chance. He'd betrayed her and fought his way free, breaking past the compulsion of her control as his maker and escaped.

Cassandra had been hunting him ever since.

"What news do you have?" she asked Victor.

"Colorado Springs. A man fitting Gallagher's description."

"Are you sure?" She stepped over the now dead human and left the balcony. Victor held up a cell phone. She glimpsed a man straddling a motorcycle at a rest stop. The red hair, all wind tousled, made Cassandra's body quicken with excitement.

Yes, that was her Seamus. The years had been kind to him. He still looked as delicious as ever. During his long absence from her coven, her bed had not gone empty, but she could return him to his place at her side. He would share her bed again, and all would be as it should.

After a suitable punishment, of course.

"Where is he now?"

Victor shook his head. "We aren't sure. We have scouts fanning out around Colorado Springs and the surrounding areas. It's difficult because Gallagher can travel in daylight. Most of our scouts cannot."

Cassandra swept her dark tresses over her shoulder, plaiting them into a braid, a habit she'd had since she had been mortal.

"Keep me informed as to his whereabouts. I want him."

"Yes, madam." Victor's focus swept to the dead man. "Shall I dispose of him?"

"*It*," she corrected, "and yes." The thing was only a husk now. An empty one. No longer even human, no longer a concern.

She moved into her private room and threw herself onto the bed, glaring up at the ceiling. There was nothing exciting about the world anymore. It was dull, her life painted in gray tones that left no spark, no joy. Only Seamus had given her world color, and she would do anything to get him back.

CHAPTER 5

"Are you going to explain why these guys who want you dead are going to help us?" Sadie asked. She had pulled his large black T-shirt down over her thighs and was curled up in the passenger seat of the pickup he had just rented under his alias. He'd hastily loaded his motorcycle into the back and all of his belongings in boxes. Then he had snuck his scantily clad vixen past the slightly compelled receptionist and into the waiting truck. They didn't have much time. He could tell by their scent that the wolves had left the immediate area, but they'd be back when they didn't find any new trace of Sadie.

"Soon enough." Seamus drove through the darkened streets of the sleepy ski resort town until he found a Walmart. Then he sized her up for a moment as he parked the car.

"Stay here. Don't run off," he commanded.

Sadie's nose wrinkled in an adorable way. "I don't need to stay with you. Hell, I probably should've rented a car of my own." This last was muttered to herself rather than to him.

He gently captured her chin and held her gaze.

"Stay here." He used his compulsion on her, but only the slightest bit. He needed her to be safe, and right now he couldn't risk her doing something foolish out of a sense of pride or bravado.

But there was more to it than that. After he'd tasted her blood, something inside him had changed. He'd healed from his wounds far faster than normal. Sadie's blood was just as he'd said. Liquid sunshine. It had hit his system like a bolt of lightning, but rather than hurt him, it had helped him.

Part of him wondered if he was addicted to her blood, if this was something that would slowly drive him mad with hunger and put her life at risk. He knew he should probably let her go before he did something bad, but he physically couldn't walk away from her. Seamus was not about to let her shift into an adorable vixen and slip into the night and vanish on him.

Sadie's hazel eyes turned a bit glassy. She nodded. "I'll stay."

"Good." He exited the truck and headed into the store.

Half an hour later, he rolled out of the Walmart with a cart of clothes, shoes, and food. It was difficult to remember that he was traveling with a mortal. But he'd grabbed some stuff he hoped she would find appetizing. His own appetite usually stayed on blood. Vampires could eat regular food—it just didn't have the allure that blood held for them. But as he'd browsed the food aisles, his nose had twitched and his mouth had watered a little. It had been a long time since he'd been even remotely interested in food. Blood was simply far less messy for a vampire.

He loaded most of the bags in the back and then got into the driver's seat. He passed Sadie a bag containing packages of premade food. She dug through it as he started the truck.

"Junk food?" She lifted a box of Hostess cupcakes out of the plastic bag.

Seamus shrugged. "It seemed appetizing."

She laughed and opened the box, removed a cupcake from a plastic package, and took a bite. "God, I haven't eaten one of these in years. They go straight to my thighs." She licked her lips but missed a dash of white cream.

Unable to resist, Seamus leaned over and wiped the cream off her lip with his thumb and licked it. A sweet, sugary taste exploded on his tongue. How was that possible?

"Hand me one." He held out a palm as they hit the highway.

"What?" Sadie stared at him.

"I want one." He wiggled his fingers at her. She slowly handed him a cupcake, a confused expression on her face.

"Vampires eat food?" She watched him rip the plastic wrapper off and take a bite of the cupcake.

He almost moaned at the decadent taste. Perhaps he had simply not had human food for so long that the sheer novelty had become overwhelming. "We do. Although, over the years our appetites fade as our interest in mortal life fades."

"Well, it seems to have perked up again." Sadie shifted in the seat, clearly uncomfortable. "How did you become a vampire? I mean, did you choose it or..." She trailed off.

"Not exactly," he hedged. It was a little hard to talk about his life before. There had been so much pain and heartache when he had been mortal.

"Not exactly?" she echoed.

He didn't want to answer her, but it seemed she wasn't about to let him ignore the question. And the more he thought about it, the more he felt a desire to tell her. It made sense. Right now he needed her to trust him. Their continued safety depended on it.

"My family died in a famine. All that was left was my sister Kayleigh and me. I had managed to steal a loaf of bread, but she didn't have the energy to eat. I was almost dead myself when..."

"When...?"

"A vampire named Cassandra found us. She offered to save my sister, if I gave myself to her. I didn't fully understand what she meant by that. But I needed to save Kayleigh, so I agreed."

He rubbed his hands on the steering wheel as he spoke. Seamus focused on the dark skies and endless road ahead of them as he tried to keep the memories of that night distant. The soft strains of music on the radio and the trees on the sides of the highway whipping by kept him grounded in the moment.

"Cassandra was building a coven at the time, and she liked having strong, dashing men as her soldiers. She turned two of my best friends, Ian and Connor, as well, but I was her *favorite*." Seamus uttered the word with a growl.

"I'm guessing being her favorite wasn't a good thing?"

How could he explain the way he'd felt when she'd feed until the heart of her prey gave out and their limp body slumped to the ground? She'd lick her lips and stare at him, challenging him to defy her, to call her a monster, to give her a reason to put him in his place.

He'd learned, though, that he could stare back, show his compassion for the victim, and she would find herself hesitating before a kill. Sometimes she even spared the poor soul. She resented herself when she was with him, yet she still craved him, because he'd become her conscience, the angel on her shoulder willing her to fight the dark thirst inside her. But he had no interest in spending his eternal life fighting that losing battle.

He sighed. "No. It wasn't. She likes to have one male

above the others to share her bed and follow her commands. I held that position until Kayleigh died of old age and her children and grandchildren had all died. Her great-grandchildren are safe from Cassandra; their lineage is too scattered to be used against me."

"Wait, she didn't turn Kayleigh?" Sadie asked.

"It's never wise to turn children. They don't physically age, but their minds do, and they become trapped in their childlike bodies. It drives them to madness. Even the worst of my kind know better than to make that mistake. So Kayleigh remained mortal. Even when she came of age and Cassandra offered, I said no. Life is precious. I would not have robbed her of it for anything. So Kayleigh was safe, except when Cassandra thought I was resisting her too much. But Cassandra knew that if she ever harmed Kayleigh, I would break my compulsion to obey and I would kill her."

Sadie stilled in the middle of rummaging around in the bags of food. "Compulsion to obey? Is that, like, the thing where they go, 'Looook into my eyes...'" She said the last bit with her arm bent over the lower part of her face as though she had an invisible cape and was trying to imitate Bela Lugosi.

"You don't know much about vampires, do you?"

"Just stuff from the movies, but they never seem to agree on the lore. The Yampa pack keeps most covens away. It's one of the reasons my grandmother and I have stayed, even with the risks my heat brings, the pack's protection helped us. Even lone vamps don't spend too much time near pack territory, and after my family..." She stopped, her breath suddenly short. "After they were killed by vampires, my grandmother would never let me near one. I've had a few close calls when I was traveling, but it's not like I took a vamp out to dinner and he told me his life story."

"Your parents were really killed by vampires?" he asked quietly.

She had shouted that at him when she'd realized what he was, but in all the chaos that followed, it had slipped his mind until now.

"Yeah." She set the bags of food down on the floor of the truck and wrapped her arms around herself.

"No wonder I scared you." He shifted his body so that he faced her. "Look, I get you don't trust vampires, I wouldn't either in your situation, but you can trust me. Have you ever heard of the London Blood Society?"

"Only whispers." Sadie's eyes seemed to glow in the dim light. A shifter trait, no doubt.

"Well, they're the good guys. Some of the best vampires—and by that I mean the ones who value mortal lives—run the LBS. I'm a member. Vampires like Cassandra don't belong to the LBS. Hell, they're scared of them. They're sort of like the watchdogs for humanity. They see humanity as a precious thing, not something to be scorned or harvested."

"But I heard they were some kind of alliance against the shifters," Sadie said.

Seamus shook his head. "It started that way, but things changed. The LBS now has treaties with major shifter packs all over the world. We're about protecting life, *all* life."

Sadie studied him, still hesitant. "So the London Blood Society are like the vampire Boy Scouts?"

Seamus chuckled. "And Girl Scouts."

"Okay... So they protect shifters like me?"

"Yes, *we* do. That's why I promised you I wouldn't feed on you."

Sadie smirked. "Except that you did."

"Well, those were exceptional circumstances, and you *did* offer."

"I know, I'm just—" Sadie suddenly bent double, clutching her abdomen. "*Shit.*"

"What's wrong?" Seamus could smell the hunger of her body spike, and she looked uncomfortable, even in pain.

"The heat," she whispered. "It's back."

"What can I do?" he asked as he pulled the truck over to the side of the road.

There were no signs of other cars coming down the highway, so they likely wouldn't be bothered if she needed to change into a fox again. Maybe she just needed ten minutes of alone time out in the woods.

"I need to..." She moved across the seat to straddle his

lap and bury her face against his throat. Her nose trailed up his skin, making his fangs extend in response. Unsure where to put his hands, he settled them on her waist, and he noticed that the T-shirt he'd given her rode high up on her body when his fingers touched bare skin halfway down around her bottom.

"Jesus," he muttered.

She snuggled closer, rubbing herself against him. "God, I love your accent." She tested his control on every level, as a man and a vampire.

"Sadie," he warned as she nipped his neck playfully.

"Hmm?" She giggled.

"I'll hold you, but I can't... Look, you aren't yourself, so I... I can't..." But she didn't stop with her play. It was like she was drunk and not herself at all.

"Oh, I'm still me, just a more fun version." She looked at him and tapped her lips in a flirty way. "This is the *instinctive* me." She leaned in and kissed him. The heat of her mouth sent wild bolts of excitement through him, and dark hungers reared up inside his mind.

Pin her down, hold her wrists, take her neck... Drink.

He shook his head, trying to break the kiss. The old Seamus wanted to take what she was clearly offering, but he couldn't. He wasn't that vampire anymore. That vampire had belonged to Cassandra, and he had died the day Cassandra murdered Ian and Connor's lover and framed him for it. Still, he was afraid of what would happen if he tasted Sadie's blood again.

"Sadie, please," he almost begged, but then she nipped his neck. "You can't do that. I'll bite back. It's...instinct."

"So?" she whispered. "Trust your instincts." She sank her teeth into his neck, harder this time. Her human teeth wouldn't break his skin, but she would leave a mark. White-hot desire exploded through him, and with a growl, he shoved her flat on the truck seat and pinned her down.

He sank his teeth into her neck. The sweetest blood he'd ever tasted hit his tongue like ambrosia. It tasted like the sun, with a gentle burning on his skin, like when he used to lay in a field as a mortal, staring at the clouds, unafraid, for hours.

He drank deeply, drawing her essence into his body, taking in the glorious feeling, and then... Then he was swept away on a tide of memories, only they were not his own.

As a tiny child, Sadie clutched her grandmother, her chubby arms curled around the woman's neck as the scent of blood filled the air.

"Oh no...no...," the woman cried out in a broken sob.

Sadie tried to look, but her grandmother covered her face by burying Sadie's head against her neck.

"Don't look, baby. Don't look."

"Mommy?" Sadie whispered.

"Mommy's gone, baby. So is daddy. It's just you and me now." Her grandmother turned to leave the woods. Sadie

rebelliously raised her head, needing to see what had scared her grandma so much.

Her parents' car was abandoned by the side of the road. Two bodies lay on the ground by the woods. The man had been brutalized, with bites and blood all over him, and the woman... She was half-naked and pale as death. Sadie wasn't sure what she was seeing. She only knew that what lay in the forest was a horror unlike anything she'd ever seen. The dark-spotted bark of the ghostly white aspens all around them seemed like a forest of black eyes, watching Sadie. It filled her with fear. A fear that would haunt her dreams for years to come.

Seamus jerked back from Sadie and sat up in the truck seat, panting. Her blood moved through him, rolling in slow warm waves, filling him with pleasure. But those memories were like a black stain inside him. It ruined the purity of her blood by the echoing pain, loss, and confusion her memories had left behind.

He looked to Sadie. She lay still beneath him, her hands on his hips, but that lust he'd seen was gone. Her hold was relaxed, almost hesitant.

"What... What was that?" she asked in a frightened voice.

"What did you see?" He feared he'd forced her to relive her worst memories again.

"I saw you. I *was* you. You were starving, trying to feed your sister... But then the vampire came... Oh, Seamus." She sat up and threw her arms around his neck, hugging him. She wasn't hot anymore. Her heat had passed for the moment.

"I'm sorry," he muttered, holding her tight to him. "I didn't know you would see that when I bit you." He didn't dare tell her what he had seen. She was only just now starting to trust him. Something deep within him demanded he earn her trust and not let her go.

"No... I'm sorry. I made you bite me. I hate how the heat makes me wild. It really is me, though. I'm no different, just less inhibited. Most men wouldn't mind."

"Most men weren't born in the last age of chivalry," Seamus said with a wry chuckle.

"Chivalry, eh?" She looked down at their bodies. She was straddling him again, and his hands were cupping her bare ass. He reluctantly took his hands from her delectable bottom, and she giggled.

"Sorry. It's a natural place for a man's hands to go." Lord, this woman had a way of making him as flustered as a boy with his first maid.

"Oh, I'm not complaining. I just like this side of you, the less controlled Seamus."

He quirked a brow at her. "The less controlled version pinned you down and bit you." He didn't add that he would have fucked her hard if it hadn't been for her painful memories.

"Do your victims...? I mean, do people always see your memories when you bite them?"

"Never. I don't know what that was." He'd certainly

never heard of it before with other vampires feeding on shifters. And that scared the shit out of him. After almost a hundred and seventy years, very little scared a vampire. But this? This was beyond what he was comfortable with.

Sadie combed her fingers through her hair, and they sat there in the dark of the truck for a minute before Seamus cleared his throat and started the truck again.

They rode in silence for an hour before he spotted a motel up the highway a bit. He didn't want Sadie's scent to be easy to track if the pack had come this far after them, but he couldn't keep driving to Denver tonight. Sadie needed to sleep; she had barely rested before the attack in the condo, and this truck was no substitute for a warm bed. He hadn't missed the bruises and cuts on her body. She was still injured. He'd made sure to buy a first aid kit while inside the Walmart.

He stopped the truck in the parking lot and nodded to Sadie. "Stay here. I'll get us a room." Then he went into the motel lobby and spoke to the clerk.

"One room, two queen beds." He pulled out his wallet and waited for the older man to hand him a room key and tell him the price. Then he slipped the man an extra hundred.

"Never saw you," the man replied without even blinking. He pocketed the cash and went back to watching the small TV on his desk.

"Much appreciated."

Seamus returned to the truck and took Sadie to their

room. He unlocked it and stepped inside first, checking to make sure it was empty. Then he waved her inside. She scrambled out of the truck, pulling down the T-shirt over her naked body and then ducked inside the room. Seamus left her to get settled while he brought the Walmart bags in from the truck.

When he finished hauling their supplies inside, Sadie sat down on the bed and dug through the bags of clothes, sorting them out. She held up a pair of black lace panties, dangling them from one finger. She tilted her head at him. "Seriously?"

"Er... I wasn't sure what you might like. There are others in there," he assured her. "Including, er, what do they call them on TV? Granny panties? But I feared that might also send the wrong message."

"Yeah, real no-win scenario, isn't it?" Sadie's lips twitched into a half smile. "You probably get away with murder when you use that Irish accent on girls, don't you?"

He smiled back. "Actually, I do, lass." He made sure his accent was extra heavy when he spoke that time. It earned a little chuckle from her.

"Yeah, I thought so." She pulled out a long plaid button-up shirt. "Pajamas?"

"Yes, they looked rather comfortable on the mannequin. I thought you might like them."

"I do. You didn't get—oh!" She gasped in delight when she found the bag of hair care products and facial cleaners. "Okay, these are *amazing*. All sins are forgiven. Thank you." She leapt off the bed and rushed into the bathroom, closing the door behind her. He listened to her hum while she turned on the water and climbed into the shower. It took quite a bit of self-control to keep his mind from thinking of joining her in there.

Instead, he pulled out his phone and typed in the number to Ian's cell phone. There was no avoiding it now. He needed their help. The Yampa pack might come all the way to Denver, and he couldn't let them get to Sadie.

His hand trembled as he dialed the number. Ian answered after two rings.

"Look, whoever the hell this is, I'm blocking you if you don't quit calling."

Seamus mustered his courage and finally spoke. "Ian, it's me. I need your help." The silence was too long on the other end.

"Seamus?" Ian's tone began as shock, then soon shifted to anger. "How did you find me?"

"A private detective." He didn't want to lie to his old friend. The truth was the only way he was ever going to get Ian to trust him again.

"You come anywhere near us, and Connor and I will rip you to pieces and set your body on fire."

"Please, Ian. I know you have no reason to trust me, but I'm begging you. I need your help."

"Whatever you think you can get from us, the answer is *no*."

Seamus closed his eyes, trying to find the right words to make his friend see reason and listen.

"On my sister's grave, Ian. I swear to you, I did not take Lara's life."

"You, Cassandra, or by her command, it makes no difference. You're just as much to blame."

"Give me one minute to explain. Then if you want to hang up, I'll never call again."

There was another long silence before Ian spoke. "Just a minute. Connor can't know I'm talking to you. He wouldn't give you one second, let alone one minute."

The sound of a door closing followed Ian's words. Seamus figured he must be slipping outside to go unheard.

"You have five minutes. Start talking."

"I didn't kill Lara. Cassandra lured me there. I was breaking away from her. You remember how much she compelled me to obey her."

"She compelled us all," Ian conceded.

"You and Conner were able to escape, but I wasn't. I was done with her games, her boredom, her bloodlust. She knew I would kill her if she ever touched my family, but turning you and Conner against me? It was only too easy for her once she found you. She left me a letter that she was going to kill Lara, and even told me where she was going to be. I was too late to stop her. I caught Lara in my arms, barely alive, too late for me to save her. That's how you and Connor found me."

Ian was silent a long moment. "If that's really the truth, if that's really what happened, why didn't you tell us?"

"I was holding your beloved woman in my arms, covered in her blood. You knew that I was still Cassandra's thrall. You wouldn't have believed me, not after the fight we had before you and Connor broke free of Cassandra."

"I regret that," Ian replied. "We left you behind. We shouldn't have."

Seamus rubbed his eyelids with his thumb and forefinger.

"No, you were right to go." Seamus sighed. "You needed to escape her, and I wasn't strong enough to do so. Not then."

"So what's this about, Seamus? You've been silent all these years. What's changed now? Why call us?"

"Cassandra thought dividing us would tighten her hold over me, because I had no one left to turn to. But instead it was enough for me to break her bond. I've been trying to stay under the radar ever since, keeping to places where she wouldn't look for me."

"Okay. And?" Ian's tone remained unconvinced.

"Yesterday I got involved with a shifter."

"Wolf?"

"Fox. I hit her with my motorcycle. She's okay, but I've gotten between her and a vicious pack of werewolves. We need a safe place to hide."

"You and the shifter? You never tangled with shifters before."

"I didn't exactly plan this."

"Why not let the shifter fend for herself? You don't owe her anything."

Seamus squeezed his cell phone hard. The idea of leaving Sadie alone infuriated him. He'd never abandon someone in need of protection, especially a female.

"It's not about owing anyone anything. She needs help. She's also in heat. Those wolves will tear her to pieces after they force themselves on her. I can't let those mangy bastards do that." He drew in a breath. "Say you'll help us."

"So you want to just come and hide out with us? That's it?"

"You make me sound like a damn coward," Seamus growled.

"The problem is, those wolves may not stop coming after her. You can't stay with the shifter forever."

He was right. Sadie was going to be on her own at some point, and she said she lived at the edge of pack territory. Those wolves would come after her hard, and he had only made the situation worse. At some point the hunt had stopped being a game to them and had become about making a point. Sooner or later, they were going to rip her apart.

"Will you let us come, then?" Seamus asked Ian.

"Yes, but you get to face Connor if he hasn't calmed down after I break the news."

"Warning taken."

Ian cleared his throat. "Oh, unless your private detective told you, we aren't alone anymore."

Seamus was surprised, but not unhappy, that his friends had found love again. "You mean...?"

"Her name is Zoey. She's different from Lara, but we love her just as much. We never thought we'd be blessed with a second mate." His voice roughened. "We didn't make the same decision as we did with Lara."

"Zoey's not mortal?"

"Not anymore. We almost lost her, but we were able to turn her. She's happy with us. *We're* happy." Ian's joy was effusive.

Seamus smiled. "I'm glad to hear that, Ian. I regret Lara's death every day and despise myself for not getting there in time to save her."

"Now that we know the truth, you can bet Cassandra will pay."

"Ian, *no.* You need to stay clear of her. She's too powerful."

Ian laughed. "Things change. She may have been powerful a hundred and seventy years ago, but the London Blood Society won't stand for her violence, not anymore."

"Be careful, Ian," Seamus said.

The sound of the shower stopping told him Sadie was

done. "Ian, I need to go. You've got my number. Send me your address, and I'll text you when we're close. We need to rest tonight but will be headed your way tomorrow."

"We'll be waiting," Ian replied. "Be safe, Seamus. You can't turn your back on a wolf pack."

"I know. Thanks." He hung up and checked the doors and windows, not that those would hold a vampire, let alone an angry pack of wolves. He would stay awake while Sadie slept, but it was going to be a long night.

CHAPTER 6

Sadie stepped out of the shower with a heavy sigh. She could have stayed under that spray of hot water all night. The last day had been hard on her body. Red scratches still lined her stomach and shoulders, and bruises circled her throat. She looked like hell. There was an awful sense of exhaustion that extended to her very soul. Everything had gotten messed up so fast. Ulrich and the others would be completely obsessed with catching her now. They weren't like other werewolves. Most packs had the occasional asshole, but overall werewolves weren't bad. Ulrich, however, was cruel, and Cyrus fed off his mean spirit. Dracen...well, he just seemed to go along with everything, which meant he wouldn't help her if she got captured.

She should have left earlier. All of this could have been avoided. She could afford to take time off. Her job as an online journalist was flexible, and she worked wherever she happened to be. Sadie cringed as she realized that she had left her laptop in her car, abandoned at the public rest stop. She was going to have to call her grandmother and a towing company.

"Sadie? You all right?" Seamus's voice came through the closed door. She shivered in delight and attraction at that Irish accent. What was it about him that made her insane with lust? Other than the whole heat thing, of course. But right now, just knowing he was on the other side of the door made her so hungry. Hungry in a way she had never been with a human male during her heat.

Was it his lean, tall form, or the way his broad shoulders tapered to a narrow waist that she wanted to wrap her legs around and squeeze? Maybe it was those baby blue eyes that melted her from the inside out, or the way his mouth curved as he flashed her a boyish grin that promised passionate nights that would completely devastate her.

God, I've got it bad for Mr. Sexy Fangs.

Back in the truck, she had been so overwhelmed by her heat that she had climbed the vampire like a tree. He'd tried to warn her about his instincts, and he'd been right. She had pushed him too far, and he had bitten her.

Yet he hadn't killed her. He'd stopped. Even when he'd been badly wounded and could easily have drained her out of a sense of self-preservation, he hadn't. It was something worth remembering. He really was one of the good ones.

Then there had been this flash of images in her mind, a blur of voices. She'd seen Seamus starving, felt the pangs of hunger as though they had been her own, watching with despair as a young bedridden girl lingered on the verge of death. She'd looked as though one strong breeze could blow her through an invisible curtain where she would perish in a land beyond breath, beyond life.

Then the vampire had appeared. An angelic creature with jet-black hair and blue eyes, offering salvation. Seamus hadn't known what he was agreeing to. He hadn't chosen this life—he'd only wanted to save his sister.

"Sadie?" The doorknob turned, and she snatched the nearest towel up to cover herself just as Seamus's face peeked through the door. "You alright, lass?" His concerned stare swept over her, and she forced herself to relax.

"Sorry! I'm fine, I swear," she gasped. "I was lost in thought."

Seamus looked her over again, more slowly this time. His eyes narrowed.

"You're hurt." He pushed the door wide open, his broad shoulders filling the doorway and making Sadie step back as her instincts warned her about being cornered. Yet an undercurrent of excitement ran beneath her skin. There was something tantalizing about being trapped in a small space by a male her body desired.

"I'm okay, really." She tried to adjust the towel around her body, but Seamus stepped closer, towering over her. Flutters of arousal stirred in her belly, and she clenched her thighs. He tilted her chin back, examining her neck.

"From the wolves?" he asked. His finger tentatively touched the mark on her throat where Dracen had held her down.

"Some." Her throat felt dry as he trailed his finger along the marks on her skin, she shivered at his touch. "The omega had me by the neck. The other marks were from my escape." The vixen warned her he was too close, too much. She tried to push his hand away, but all she did was brush her fingers over his. She raised her eyes to meet his, and he was frowning slightly.

"How did you escape?" He pushed back the towel at her hip, exposing the red scratches that still glared angrily on her skin.

"A small hole in a barbed electric fence." She shied away from his touch, not because she didn't want it, but because it felt too good. The heat cycle still pulsed within her, calling for her to take a male to bed. If she wasn't careful, she would take this vampire, and things were complicated enough as it was.

"I bought some medical supplies. Let me tend to your injuries."

"No, that's okay." She needed him to give her time to regain her control.

"Please, I need to care for you." There was a desperation in his voice that puzzled her. He cupped her chin, the pad of his thumb stroking her lips. "Vampires have instincts too. I don't like seeing a female hurt, especially someone I view as under my protection."

"Okay. Just...try not to turn me on, okay?" She shouldn't have agreed to it, but she had a feeling he would get his way no matter what. His hand dropped from her chin and grasped her wrist gently. As he moved back, the cool air from the hotel room's AC hit her skin, cooling her down. Yet wherever he touched her, she burned.

Seamus led her out of the bathroom and nudged her toward the nearest bed. The backs of her knees hit the bed, and she fell onto her bottom, still clutching the towel. He retrieved a first aid kit and set it on the bed beside her. She watched him take out several antiseptic wipes and a few bandages.

"I will heal," she murmured as he approached her with his tools.

"I know, but it's a good idea to attend to the open scratches. You can still get an infection."

He wasn't wrong. Shifters like her had strong healing abilities, but they weren't impervious to infection. Given the way her wounds felt so raw, she was glad to have him treat them.

He tended to her injuries, and there was nothing for her to do but watch him while he worked. The slight scruff on his jaw, that playful mouth, the eyes that rseemed to gaze into the past nearly two centuries. He was a mystery to her.

Seamus pushed her towel aside, just enough to get at the gash on her hip. His long fingers dabbed gently at the wound with a wipe. She stiffened as the cloth moved across the inflamed area, though the softness of his touch was like butterfly wings against her damaged skin. She saw the concentration on his face as he leaned back to grab the antibacterial gel and methodically applied it to her flesh. A sudden lump grew in her throat as his fingers drew back, replaced by a square cotton bandage, sealed with the firm but soft touch of his whole hand. She imagined those hands gripping her, leaving red marks on her back and thighs and shoulders as he rode her to heights of ecstasy...

Done with this side, Seamus indicated for her to move the towel to the other. As if in a trance, she did so, turning the part in the towel to her other hip. He averted his eyes to avoid seeing anything he was not supposed to. Still the gentleman, despite everything. Then he started all over again on the other side, with deft fingers and a light touch that left pockets of heat in the air between them.

Would it be so bad to try to transfer that scent from his skin to hers? To mark herself with his aroma so that the scent of him blinded her against her worries? Seamus's attention shifted to her throat, and she wondered if he wanted to drink her blood again. Part of her hoped so.

"Does it hurt?" His voice had a whiskey roughness to it that made her blood hum.

"Not so much. It did before, but Dracen, well, he's not cruel. Not like the others. He's never been mean to me before."

"He's the omega? I told you, don't be fooled by their behavior."

"I know, but still."

"You know them by name, huh? How often do you cross paths?"

"The pack and I sort of steer clear of each other most of the time. I shift frequently at home, but I don't stray much in the woods when I know they're out. This was the first time we've ever really had an issue. If my heat hadn't come early, I would have been fine. But my flight was canceled, and then things got out of control."

Seamus spoke through slightly gritted teeth. "You're acting like this was your fault, that you made the wolves act like murderous animals. It's not your fault. Your scent is irresistible only because they've chosen to embrace their animal selves, rather than learn to control it. 'It's in our nature.' I've heard that more than once to justify or excuse such behavior. Not just from shifters, but vampires as well. It's no excuse. They had no right to chase you and threaten you."

"I know." She always hated feeling like her heat cycle was her fault. It would have been nice not to have to flee her home twice a year.

"Any other wounds I should know about?" Seamus's eyes swept over her. She saw the possessive hunger buried beneath that calm vampiric gaze.

"No, I'm okay. Seriously." She shifted on the bed, heat building between her thighs as she tried to ignore it. His nostrils flared, but he said nothing as he packed up the kit and handed her a bag of clothes. She accepted it and retreated to the bathroom again, locking the door behind her. Just in case.

She changed into a comfortable pair of underwear, a T-shirt, and boxers. When she came out, Seamus was standing by the window. He'd peeled the curtains back an inch and was watching the parking lot. He cut a handsome figure silhouetted against the lights from the parking lot. The black shirt he wore clung to his body like a second skin, and his jeans fit snugly. She couldn't help but stare at that ass of his.

"I called my friends while you were in the shower," he said, still watching outside.

"The ones who want to kill you?" she asked, still clinging to that detail. The man, or vampire, sure knew how to leave her hanging in suspense with a good story.

"Yeah. We got things sorted. Hopefully."

"Are you going to tell me what happened?"

He glanced back, a smirk on his lips. "Curious as a fox?"

"That's cats. It's *clever* as a fox."

"Uh-huh." Normally she hated cockiness in a guy, but

he made it work for him. She wanted him to look at her like that just before he went down on her and... Sadie jerked her thoughts away from sex with Seamus yet again.

"Come on, you have to tell me. I'm headed into this mess with you. I should know the back story, right? If only so I can tell your friends, 'Don't hurt me, I'm not with him,' when they decide to rip you limb from limb."

He abandoned his position at the window and stretched out on the bed closest to the door. "Your undying loyalty is noted."

Sadie smirked. "Hey, you're the undead one here, not me."

Seamus folded his hands behind his head. It was a picture of relaxed masculinity that made her all too aware of his physicality. There were just some men who could lie down on a bed like that and make a girl want to purr and cuddle up next to them. But she wasn't going to do that. She was going to stay on her bed and control herself.

"When I bit you, you said you saw me back when I was mortal. When I agreed to be changed. That you saw Cassandra, the vampire who turned me?"

Sadie nodded and pulled back the covers of her own bed and crawled beneath them. He turned off all the lights except the one by the bed. Yellow light reflected off his eyes, giving them a strange glow.

"Not long after she turned me, she found my two closest friends and turned them too. They were starving, like I was. Our entire village was wiped out in a matter of weeks."

"That's horrible," Sadie whispered.

"Aye, it was," Seamus agreed. "There's nothing worse than an empty belly. It drives a man to madness. Can make him do unspeakable things. I didn't even believe Cassandra was real, even after she had turned me into a monster."

Sadie almost told him he wasn't a monster, but he was. She had called him a monster herself. Yet he had protected her, risked his life for hers, and was caring for her. Monsters didn't do that.

"Ian and Connor were like my brothers. Cassandra learned of this and turned them, hoping it would secure my loyalty to her. She wanted an army to protect her, but my bond with Ian and Connor went deeper than she realized. When Ian and Conner broke free of her grip, she feared I would soon join them. So she decided to sever our bond. She killed the woman Ian and Connor loved and framed me for her death."

"Wait, you said *woman*, as in one? Was it some kind of love triangle thing?"

Seamus chuckled. "Ian and Connor shared everything, including the woman they loved. They have no attraction to one another, but they are happiest when they both pleasure a woman together. It is a bit unusual, I admit, but love is love, isn't it?"

"Well, yeah," Sadie agreed. "Still, it sounds complicated." She was fascinated by the idea of a woman having two men in her bed, but it didn't exactly appeal to her. Foxes could be jealous lovers, but once they had a mate, they wanted no other for the rest of their lives.

"I was too late to save her. Ian and Connor found me holding their woman in my arms. If they hadn't been lost to grief, they would've tried to kill me, I have no doubt. So for the last hundred years, Cassandra has left me without my strongest allies."

"Why?" Sadie watched him as he stared at the ceiling. His profile was attractive, the sensual mouth, the square jaw, the scruff of a barely there beard starting to show. There was a playfulness, a definite sexiness to his expressions, especially his blue eyes, that made her wonder if he used to smile and flirt often before he'd been reborn in blood.

"She wanted me back under control. That is all she's ever desired." He said it so simply, yet she sensed there were many layers to the statements.

"So you called Ian and Connor?"

"Just Ian. Connor would have hung up the second he knew who was calling."

"So Ian's the reasonable one?"

"He's the softer lines to Connor's hard edges. Win Connor's trust, and he'll die for you. Lose it and you've put a target on your back."

"Great, he's a grudge-holding vampire." Sadie yawned and stretched. "So these guys are close to here?"

"In Denver."

"How close are we?"

"Just an hour or so away. They can help even the odds if the wolves come after you again. I'm a good fighter, but three werewolves is a bit much for me to handle. Especially this close to the full moon."

They were quiet a moment before Sadie jerked up in bed suddenly. Seamus jolted in response, wondering if she'd heard something.

"I need to call my grandmother. I forgot. She's probably got the police looking for me. My cell is still in my car."

Seamus tossed her a sleek black smartphone. "Use mine."

She dialed her grandmother's number. After three rings, she answered. "Hello?"

"Grandma, it's me."

"Oh, honey child, where have you been? I've been calling and calling."

"I'm sorry, a lot has happened." Sadie played with the hem of her baggy T-shirt.

"Are you okay?" Vera demanded. "I heard the pack howling a few hours ago. They sounded angry."

"They are."

She told her grandmother everything, right down to sharing a room with Seamus.

Vera's voice softened to a whisper. "He's in the room with you right now?"

"Yes," she replied.

"Are you okay? Is it safe to talk? Is he drinking from you? He can use his compulsion on you, you know."

Seamus stared at Sadie and then, without a word, left the motel room.

"He's gone, Grandma. He stepped outside."

"You think he could hear me?" Vera asked.

"Probably."

"Good. Now's your chance. Steal his keys and run."

Sadie almost rolled her eyes. "It's not like that, Grandma. He's not like what we've experienced with other vampires. He's different."

"I'm sure he is. But I don't care what kind of Boy Scout troop he's part of, you're a shifter in heat. Sooner or later, he's going to jump you and suck you. You need to get out of there now."

"Grandma, you have to trust me. I almost *died* twice today. Seamus is the only reason I'm alive, and he got shot several times for his trouble. I owe him." How could she make her understand that Seamus was in control of his instincts, that there was something about him that made her want to trust him with everything, even her life.

"I'm sure he'll find a way to collect on that debt at some point. Let me talk to the bloodsucker."

"Grandma..."

"Don't you *Grandma* me. He needs to hear what I have to say. Put him on now." Vera used that tone of voice that warned Sadie if she didn't do as she was told, Vera would get in her car and drive to wherever they were to have it out with him in person. She had a knack for getting what she wanted.

Sadie got out of the bed. Unsure of where Seamus had gone, she cracked the door open a few inches and called his name. He appeared as if out of thin air, his face against the door, making her jump and clutch at her chest. She had known vamps could move fast, but not *that* fast.

"Jesus, you scared me!" she gasped.

His lips cured in a small smile. "Sorry, lass. It's easier to be myself when I'm around you. I keep forgetting to act human."

She understood that feeling. It was such a relief not to have to hide her heat or what she was, especially when she needed to shift into her fox form in front of him.

"My grandma wants to talk with you." She handed him the cell phone. "And I apologize in advance for whatever she is about to say."

Seamus grinned as he put the phone to his ear. "Noted. This is Seamus Gallagher, ma'am. I am at your service."

Sadie strained to hear the conversation. Her hearing was good, just not vampire good.

"Listen up, bloodsucker. I am sure you've convinced my granddaughter that you're some kind of hero, but I know your kind."

Seamus frowned. "My kind, huh? You know, your granddaughter used the same term when we first met."

Sadie's face flushed, as she realized exactly how that must have sounded. But she hadn't meant it like *that*. Had she?

"Don't play word games with me. There's no such thing as a good vampire."

Seamus met Sadie's embarrassed gaze as he responded. "I understand your concerns, ma'am. I'm certainly no hero. But I was born in an age where men were raised to have a code of honor. I hit Sadie with my motorcycle while she was escaping those werewolves. I owed it to her to help. Then those wolves wrecked my condo and shot me. Now it's personal, for me and for them. I'm not going to let them have what they want. That means Sadie is safe in my care. Those wolves can go to hell."

There was a long silence. Sadie tried to ignore the smothering sense of disappointment at the thought that she was merely a duty to Seamus. But that was for the best. There definitely shouldn't be anything more to this thing between them.

"So you're going to make the Yampa Valley pack pay for hurting my granddaughter?" Vera asked, her voice full of steel.

"Oh yes," Seamus assured her.

"Fine. But don't you touch or bite my baby. You understand?"

Seamus's gaze moved over Sadie's body in a bold,

sensual caress that left her feeling invisible hands touching her in hot, secret places.

"She's still in heat. I can't make any promises if she needs me."

"Put Sadie back on the phone," Vera demanded instantly.

Seamus handed the phone to her.

"Grandma?" Sadie expected what came next.

"Do not let him touch you, you hear? Shifters don't survive sex with vampires. They can't control themselves. Not forever. Sooner or later he will take too much, get too lost in your blood and you'll be gone. I won't lose you, not like that. I buried my son and daughter-in-law. I will not bury you too." The quivering note in Vera's voice tugged at Sadie's heart.

"It will be okay, Grandma, I promise."

"Call me or text me tomorrow."

"I will. Oh! I had to leave my car on the road off exit 6, half an hour outside Steamboat. Could you get it for me? It's at the old public rest stop."

"Sure, hon. I love you."

"Love you too, Gran." Sadie hung up and handed the phone back to Seamus.

"Fierce woman," Seamus noted, amusement coloring the two words.

Sadie chuckled. "You have no idea. Seriously."

"What happened to your parents?" Seamus asked. His

blue eyes fixed on hers, and she sat down by the bed. "I mean, the details, if you are willing."

"They were coming home from a night out. My grandmother was watching me. When they didn't come home, Grandma put me in the car and we drove out to find them. She found their car only two miles from the house. The smell of vampires was everywhere. They had drained my parents and brutalized their bodies. My grandmother tried to hide it from me, but I saw. It's still in there." She tapped her temple. "Locked inside my skull like a dark phantom. I can't shake the memory."

She couldn't tell him that it had left her afraid to really live her life. She took her annual vacations, usually cruises to sunny places. Places where she was confident there would be no vampires. Completely controlled, risk-free environments.

Seamus cupped her chin, lifting her face up as he peered down at her.

"You're truly afraid of vampires."

She swallowed and nodded.

"Do you fear me?"

"I..." She could feel that need again, the heat whispering beneath her skin to take him, to satisfy her urges. "Sometimes. But it's not like what I feel around other vampires."

"Did you know fear has a scent? For me it's sweet, like cotton candy, or perhaps apple pie. It's different with every person." He stroked her throat now, his eyes burning into a red haze in the blue irises.

"What does mine smell like?" She retreated, hitting the wall beside the bed. He followed her, in a subtle stalking way that sent her pulse skittering.

"You? Like fresh-baked chocolate chip cookies, which have never appealed to me until this moment." His blue eyes continued to cede to that deep crimson glow that warned her he was more vampire than man at that moment.

"You..." She wasn't sure what she planned to say. The thought escaped her as a wave of need made her double over.

Seamus caught her, then pinned her to the wall with his body. The press of him against her calmed and excited her all at once. His hands roamed over her, pushing at the hem of her shirt so he could get his fingers against the bare skin of her lower back. Their eyes locked as he sought her permission to touch, to do more.

"Yes." It was all she needed to say. She pulled his mouth down to hers almost violently. She didn't have to be careful with him—he wasn't mortal. She couldn't hurt him if things got rough. And she wanted things to get rough.

Seamus hissed against her lips as she raked her nails down his back over his shirt. The urge to mark him, to show the world he belonged to her, it was scary and made no sense and was oh so *right*. Her vixen was acting in ways she had never acted before with a male. He fisted a hand into her damp hair, coiling it around his fingers, and pulled her head back in a dominant hold that made her vixen cry out in delight.

This was what she had craved for the last day. This violent passion, this man who could give her whatever she needed. She nipped his bottom lip, avoiding his fangs.

"Bed. Now," she growled.

He picked her up, cupping her ass as he carried her to the bed. He set her down, removed his shirt, and caged her beneath him as he covered her with kisses. He pulled at her shirt, dragging it off her body. His eyes were fully red now as he gazed at her bare breasts. She arched her back invitingly, and he bent down to nuzzle them. The rough scrape of his stubble awakened her nerve endings, and her nipples pebbled. He licked his tongue over one taut peak and cupped the other, brushing the pad of his thumb over it. She squirmed as the sensations over-whelmed her.

"Seamus. Take me now." She could barely be more articulate than that. All of her energy was focused on him and what he could give her.

"You're not...yourself." There was still a shred of control left to him.

She gripped his throat, squeezing as her vixen growled. "I am. Hormones don't change me, only how I assert what I want. Now fuck me, dammit."

Her gentleman vampire stared at her a second longer

before his eyes narrowed. He sat back and moved off the bed. Before she could protest, he gripped her boxers and yanked them off, leaving her fully exposed.

"You want me?" he asked, his Irish accent melting her insides. She nodded.

He pounced on her, rolling her onto her stomach beneath him. Then he pulled her hips up in the air, and she wriggled her ass. She heard the zipper on his jeans, felt the tip of his shaft nudge at her entrance. Then he gripped her hips and thrust deep. Something happened... Something inside of her shifted, like tectonic plates beneath the earth's surface. As Seamus filled her, there was no end to her, no beginning to him. They simply *were*. Part beast, part human, part vampire, one person.

This wasn't simply sex, not in that moment, maybe not ever again. Her vixen came closer to the surface than ever before. Her nails turned to claws as she shredded the sheets. The vampire behind her claimed her, thrusting hard and deep, his powerful hold over her body gentle yet harsh in his passion. The headboard rattled against the wall, and a scream escaped her lips as a climax unlike any before hit her.

Her vision blacked out. A universe of color burst behind her closed eyelids, and she collapsed on the bed. Seamus roared behind her in a sound of pure pleasure, which made her exhausted vixen writhe for more of him. He thrust once more against her bottom, then stayed buried deep within her. She glanced over her shoulder at him. He looked so human then, as though the true art of lovemaking belonged only to humankind and not to the undead. He leaned over her, his chest to her back. Sweat-slicked and hot, he tangled one hand in her hair and pulled her head back, exposing her throat. He angled her face so he could kiss her slowly, passionately. He kissed along her jaw and down to her neck. Then he bit down on her throat.

Something settled deep into a place within her as his fangs penetrated her. His cock twitched inside her, and a fresh but softer orgasm washed over her. He pumped his hips a little, drawing out a soft aftershock in her body as he took her blood. The vixen inside her stilled, a sense of infinite calm taking over.

Peace. Oneness. Mate. The words came from deep inside her animal side, and rolled over in her head as she saw images that accompanied the words.

A field, sunlight shimmering over golden grass. The sounds of birds in the breeze rippling through the aspens in a gentle hush. Across the field, a second fox, a male, with handsome red fur and bright blue eyes.

Mate.

Sadie's head felt light as Seamus rasped his tongue along the bite mark he had made on her neck. He collapsed on the bed beside her, their bodies still fused together.

"I saw you in a field," he murmured as he brushed her hair back from her neck and curled his body around hers. Even though his skin was cool, it felt warmer than usual.

"You saw me?"

He withdrew from her body and pulled the covers back so they could climb underneath. When she faced him, he nuzzled her cheek and inhaled the scent of her hair.

"I saw you as a fox in a golden field. You were beautiful."

She tried to understand what he was saying. Was it possible for him to see her vixen's thoughts?

"How could you see me? I was in my fox's thoughts. She was looking at another fox. She…"

"She was looking at me," he said, still sounding baffled. "I was the other fox. I could tell from the height of the grass, the tip of my nose, the pads of my feet."

"But… How?"

Seamus cupped the back of her neck. "Because we are destined to be mates?"

The world dropped away from beneath her. Was such a thing possible? Surely it couldn't be.

How could she be mated to a vampire?

CHAPTER 7

"We can't be mates," Sadie whispered, as though afraid someone would overhear.

Seamus chuckled. He found her more and more adorable with each passing second. Even lying here beside him, fidgeting as she tried to define what had just happened between them, he *adored* her. His feelings for her were so intense, so strong and sudden that he knew he should be questioning his sanity. He didn't know her at all, yet he did...somehow. When he'd seen the vixen in the field, it was as if he'd caught a glimpse of her soul in a way no other person ever would. She was stunning, brave beyond measure, and perfect for him. He saw that truth plainly now and saw no reason to deny how he was starting to feel about her.

"Why not?" He trailed his fingertip down her nose and pictured the vixen in his mind again. Such a beautiful fox. When he'd first saved her, it had been different. She'd been just an animal. But now? She was so much *more*. More of all the things he'd forgotten long ago, the things that he used to dream about. She was life. She was breath. When he drank her blood, he saw memories that showed him who she was. A child who'd grown up lonely, a young woman who wrote about a life she'd been raised to fear actually living. Yet here she was in a hotel room with a vampire. And she wasn't afraid of him. Not anymore.

"Shifters can't mate with vampires." She stated it as if she were reminding him the sky was blue and the grass was green.

He couldn't resist grinning. "Then what were we doing for the last half hour?" He burned the vision of her in the gold field into his memory. Such peace had filled him and a sense of oneness with everything around him. There was no doubt in his mind that they were connected. What strange miracle had happened between them was unknowable, but also undeniable.

Sadie frowned. "That's not what I meant. I mean...we can't be *bonded*, you know?"

She was wrong. They were bonded. Sadie had been right about hormones and instincts. In that moment he had ceased to be burdened with all those other mortal and vampire concerns. He had simply been another, deeper, *truer* Seamus. He swore his heart had drummed a wild erratic beat. That shouldn't have been possible, yet that had been what it felt like.

He cuddled her close to him, pulling the covers up, and her body arched into his, fitting like a spoon. He leaned over her and pressed a kiss to her shoulder. "Who says?" He chuckled at the little wrinkles forming between her perfect dark brows as she stared at him as though he were an idiot.

"*Everyone*," she exclaimed. "Everyone says vampires can't be mates to anyone except other vampires. You guys are the undead." Her face turned as red as a ripe cherry.

Seamus burst out laughing. "Seriously? You have to stop listening to *everyone*." It was the second time she had let rumors define her understanding of their world since he'd met her. He had been around a lot longer than her and knew that life was infinitely more complex than she imagined. There were very few absolutes in it.

"And we aren't *the undead*," he added a comically macabre tone at the end.

"You died. You don't have a heartbeat." She pointed this out with an adorable pout.

"That's not entirely true. I thought for years you were right, that vampires were the undead. But that's not the truth. When we change, it's simply that. A change. Our hearts don't beat, not exactly, but blood still moves through our bodies, and our hearts make a different rhythm. Here." He placed one of her palms to his chest above his heart. "Close your eyes and focus on the sensation."

She closed her eyes and was silent a long time. Then

her eyes flew open. "It's like an ocean. I could feel the blood moving through you, but it's not exactly a pulse. More like a running river."

"Exactly. Not dead, but alive in a different way."

Sadie's eyes met his, and her lips parted. "That can't be possible. You can't be mated to me. *We* can't be. It's nuts." She shook her head again as though that alone would make it untrue.

He chuckled. "*Ouch.*" For some reason, her protests amused him. Perhaps it was because he knew what he'd seen, what he'd felt, and didn't question it. It was like trying to believe the sun wouldn't rise, when he was staring straight into its fiery rays.

"It's not personal. It's just...*mated?* How could I ever have children? There's got to be a biology issue there. And I've never heard of a vampire baby before, have you?"

Seamus frowned. "No, not that I've ever been aware of." The realization filled him with unbearable sadness. It was one of the many mortal things he'd sacrificed when he'd been turned, yet he'd never really considered it a drawback. But now, holding Sadie in his arms and thinking he'd never have a chance to share the miracle of bringing life into the world cast a shadow over his heart.

"And even if I could, what if *they* couldn't have children? What if they gained that trait from your vampire side? It seems like a failure of my survival instincts to choose a vampire." She was rambling now. "Oh God, when my grandma finds out..."

"She will understand in time."

"Ha! You don't know Vera. She's going to *freak*."

He had noted Vera's bravado on the phone, and he suspected she would be just as bold in person. But he was a charmer, and becoming a vampire hadn't changed that. If anything, it had enhanced that skill.

"What are you thinking?" Sadie demanded, arching a brow in suspicion.

"I was thinking that if I wooed one vixen, another shouldn't be a problem."

His reluctant mate scoffed. "I might be a sucker for those baby-blue eyes of yours, but not Vera. She'll eat you alive."

"Challenge accepted." He rolled her beneath him and teased her lips with his before claiming them in a kiss. He felt good, *really* good. This was no high from her blood. That was different. He had sampled a shifter or two over the last two centuries, and drinking from them had left him wired and on the edge of an uncontrollable euphoria. Sadie's blood moved through him like a sweet, dark wine that relaxed him, yet left him feeling whole. The ever-present hunger for blood wasn't there. He felt...satiated.

He continued to kiss Sadie, their tongues playing together, and he smiled against her mouth.

"Okay, between those baby blues and your wicked mouth, I'm going to have real trouble saying no to anything, aren't I?"

Seamus smiled down at her. "I'm so glad I hit you with my motorcycle."

"*I'm* not. That hurt like a bitch." She smiled back. "But the sex sure helped make up for it."

"Oh? Perhaps we should go again?" He nudged her thighs apart and fell into the cradle of them.

"That sounds like a good idea. Just to be safe, you know."

Seamus made love to her slowly this time, taking his time, kissing every inch of her face, neck, and breasts tenderly. Then he captured her hands and pinned them on either side of her head. She growled softly, but there was no threat behind it; rather, he heard her pleasure. His mate liked a bit of this kind of play. He could certainly give her that. She rolled her hips beneath him, and he nipped at her collarbone in warning.

"Stay still, or I'll tie you to the bed and take my time."

The scent of her arousal filled the air as her eyes closed and she panted beneath him. *Note to self: buy leather cuffs as soon as possible.*

Long after they were finished, when Sadie had slipped into sleep, he held her close, marveling at the way the night had taken a turn.

A mate. He was mated. He would have to tell Ian. He kissed Sadie's shoulder, slipped out of bed, and retrieved his phone from the pocket of his jeans on the floor.

Seamus: Things have become more complicated. I just mated the shifter.

He stared at the screen, waiting.

Ian: You mean a bond? Is that even possible?

Seamus: It is. I've heard of it happening once or twice before. But they soon disappear...or are disappeared, if you know what I mean. Some vampires and shifters like purity in their races.

Ian: Wow. Okay. We'll be waiting. I'm going to break the news to Connor.

Seamus: Good luck. Don't let him kill me when we show up.

Ian: I'll do my best. Can't make any promises.

Seamus set his phone on the nightstand and climbed back into bed to hold his mate. But he didn't sleep. He lay listening to the sounds outside the hotel to see if any howls were being carried upon the wind.

IAN KENNEDY HUNG up the phone and watched his best friend, Connor O'Shea, prepare dinner with Zoey Blake, the mate they shared. Pasta boiled in the large silver pot. Connor sang softly, and Zoey gazed up at him with adoration as she handed him ingredients. The three of them had been together for six months now, and each day was better than the last. His mortal appetites had returned, as had Connor's, a clear sign of finding a mate. Vampires mated rarely, but when they did, it was a deep and intense bond. A bond that when broken could drive a vampire to madness. He and Connor had suffered it once before, but fate had given them a second chance with Zoey.

Zoey turned toward him. "Everything okay?"

He slipped his phone into his pocket. "What? Oh… Yeah." At his uncomfortable response, Connor stopped what he was doing.

"You're lying. What's up?"

"You're going to freak out, and I don't want you to. Finish dinner and then we'll talk."

Connor's eyes narrowed. He turned the stove off and moved the drained pasta to a cool burner. He tossed a towel flat over his shoulder and crossed his arms over his chest.

"Talk."

Zoey poured a cup of sauce over the pasta and stirred it in, pretending to give the two their privacy. When Zoey had come into their lives, homeless, starved, and mortally wounded, they had both fallen hard for her. But Connor had vowed never to love again, not after Lara had been killed. Zoey had saved them in more ways than she would ever know.

"Seamus found us."

Connor's eyes narrowed. "Where is he?"

"An hour or two away."

Connor grabbed Zoey by the wrist. "So he's finally heard about Zoey, eh? The bastard. We have to get her to safety. Now."

"Connor. Wait." Ian stepped in front of him and pried Zoey from his grip.

"Are you mad? He's on his way," Connor snarled.

"I know," Ian whispered. "I *know*. But it's not what you think. Just hear me out, Connor, please."

The thunderous expression on Connor's face lightened as Zoey moved next to him and pressed a kiss to his throat. "Just listen, that's all he's asking."

Connor fisted a hand in Zoey's long dark-brown hair, and the touch seemed to soothe him a little. "Fine."

Ian's shoulders dropped as some of the tension coiling inside him eased. "Seamus needs our help."

"Oh, that's rich," Connor snorted bitterly. "The murderer needs help?"

"I don't think he's a murderer. I don't think he killed Lara."

Zoey gasped. "Wait, you mean, *the Seamus*?" She paled. "The one who used to be your friend?"

"Exactly," Connor replied darkly. "*That* bastard."

"He said it was Cassandra. She killed Lara and lured him to our home. She wanted us to find him holding her on the brink of death."

"Cassandra." Connor spoke the name with disgust. "Why would she do that?"

"You know why," Ian said.

Conner frowned. "Damn. Of course. How could I not see it? *Cassandra*."

"Wait," Zoey cut in. "Who's Cassandra?"

"The vampire who turned us," Ian explained. "You remember how it felt when we turned you to save your life?"

Zoey's eyes widened, and she nodded. "There was an undeniable urge to be close to you, to…" Her face blushed. "To obey you."

Ian nodded. "That's the maker's compulsion. It can fade over time unless constantly reinforced. A blind obedience can be forged if the maker starves the vampire and feeds them only the maker's blood. Cassandra used to do that to vampires who didn't come to heel like the trained dogs she wanted."

"She sounds terrible." Zoey curled an arm around Conner's back, giving him a squeeze. It made Ian's chest tighten with joy. He and Connor had always shared their women; it made them both feel fulfilled when they could love a woman together.

"She was terrible. Very terrible. Like many older vampires, she was born in a time when women were powerless, and so power was all that mattered. She did what she had to do to survive. She became lethal and powerful and, to men, irresistible."

Zoey's eyes met Ian's. "Oh?"

"She prefers male vampires for her covens. There's less competition that way." Ian sighed. "She's never felt safe in all her four hundred years. It was during the great famine that she turned Seamus, then later Connor and me. But Seamus was always her favorite. Whenever he was around her, she became more..." He struggled for words.

"Human," Connor supplied. "She was capable of horrible acts of violence, but Seamus softened her."

Zoey looked between them. "But Seamus didn't like Cassandra, I take it?"

"No. She was beautiful, but cold. Hollow. Seamus clung to his humanity, even more than we did. He wanted out. He wanted us out too."

"He did get us free. He faked our deaths during the Great War. Our coven was fighting the Germans. It seemed even Cassandra had a problem with the kaiser." Connor chuckled. "We were holed up in a fortified town in France called Verdun. The Germans bombed us for ten straight hours. We fought alongside French forces, and when the bombing hit close to our coven's camp, Seamus told everyone we had died. He bought us time to escape. If she thought we were dead, she wouldn't be able to find us and force compulsion on us."

"What about Seamus?" Zoey asked.

"He stayed in Verdun, fighting with the French. He can move and fight in sunlight as long as his face and skin are covered. He would fight at dawn and dusk like our Celtic ancestors. The Germans called him *Meister des Todes*," Ian said. "Master of death."

"I can imagine," said Zoey.

Ian pulled Zoey into his arms and nuzzled her neck. "Rumors began to fly through the German ranks that the devil himself was fighting against them. By autumn, British and Russian forces were launching counterattacks that drew the Germans' focus away from Verdun. Connor and I were still in France, but we were joining another coven at the time, a group called the London Blood Society."

"Wait." Zoey pulled back to look up at him. "You haven't mentioned them before."

"We've kept our distance of late. Right now we consider ourselves semi-retired."

"But who are they?"

"They were founded two centuries ago by vampires who don't want to hurt humans. They want to find a better way to coexist with humans, and to help protect them. They have over five hundred members worldwide." Connor now came up behind Zoey, sandwiching her between them.

"Hold on now. Are you two trying to distract me?"

"Perhaps," Ian and Connor said in unison.

She giggled but soon turned serious again. "So wait, let's get back to Seamus. Why is he here now, and why does he need help?"

Connor looked at Ian expectantly.

"He's found a mate…" Ian hesitated. "A shifter."

Connor's mouth dropped open in shock. "But that's not…"

"Possible? It is, it's just incredibly rare," Ian replied.

"How rare?" Zoey asked.

"Like one in a million." Ian brushed his fingers over Zoey's face. "A pack of werewolves apparently want a piece of his mate, and he needs our help to protect her."

"We're going to help, aren't we?" Zoey demanded as she looked between them.

"That's what we need to discuss."

Conner's face darkened. "Zoey, love, pack a bag. *Now*."

"Now hold on," she protested. "We can't just leave."

"We can," Connor snapped. "If that idiot is bringing a shifter pack to us, then we're going to fight them at our cabin in the woods. I don't want those furry assholes wrecking our neighborhood. So go pack."

"Oh." Zoey blushed and slid past them.

When they were alone, Connor turned to Ian. "Tell me we can trust him. Tell me this won't be a big fucking mistake."

"We can trust him. You know my instincts are never wrong."

"You better hope not, because I *will* take Zoey to safety if this goes sideways."

"She still has her newborn strength. She'd be an asset in a battle," Ian reminded him.

"I can't believe you'd risk her like that."

"She's tough, Connor, and it's the twenty-first century. The three of us are a family, and we all have equal roles. Zoey will fight with us if she chooses to. I won't make her, but I won't try to stop her, either."

"Fine," Connor growled. "But if shit hits the fan, I'm getting her out of there."

"Agreed." Ian glanced around the kitchen. "Now, how about dinner? Then we can pack and head to the cabin."

"Zoey!" They called her name together, and she came running, a streak of color and laughter on her face as she rushed into their arms.

Ian closed his eyes and held her close. She was the real reason why he would help Seamus. If the shifter really was Seamus's mate, he deserved to have a happy life with her. To have the kind of happiness he'd found. He wasn't going to let some fleabags ruin that.

CHAPTER 8

The heat came again at dawn, and Sadie rolled onto her side, reaching for her mate. *Mate...* Her legs were tangled in the sheets, and the driving hunger pushed her toward him on instinct, seeking what only he could give her.

"Seamus," she whispered.

His cool, hard body covered hers, his mouth moving over hers hungrily before he lowered his head to scrape his fangs against her throat.

"Bite me," she encouraged. Her vixen was growing closer and closer to him, sensing his moods and needs. She wasn't sure what was considered normal for being mated to a vampire, but she liked that their awareness of one another seemed to grow with each passing hour.

"Not now. You're still healing," he moaned against her neck.

"And you haven't fed," she countered, then suddenly started giggling.

He lifted his head to look down at her, and she reached up, running her fingers through his dark-red hair.

"What's so funny, love?" he asked.

"Me... Us... *This*." She giggled again. "I'm worried about feeding a vampire. You're worried about not draining me. That's so crazy, you don't even know." She hoped it didn't upset him, but if she was honest, she was still in shock about the whole situation.

"Feeding a vampire is funny?" He was trying to look at her seriously, and failing. He bit his lip, and his fangs peeked out. It should have turned her *off*, not *on*.

"Bite me already," she growled and nipped his arm, sinking her teeth into his skin hard enough to draw blood. He hissed in restrained pleasure and thrust into her body, filling her hard and fast, then lowered his head to her neck and bit her. Pleasure rolled through her like sweet molasses, and the feel of his hips pumping against hers and the sharing of blood exploded like ecstasy inside her head.

Her eyes rolled back in her head, and she surrendered to the rush of blinding light and then... She was pulled toward a tunnel of light and gasped as she hit the ground somewhere else.

A shrill scream overhead sent her diving toward the ground. Sunlight was fading as men and women shouted for help in French. Sadie was trapped—no, not trapped—dwelling inside somebody else's mind. Seamus's.

"Seamus!" a man yelled. "We have to hold the line!" The man wore a military uniform, an old one. World War I? Sadie wasn't sure. They were hunkered down behind a stone wall that had been turned into a deep trench. Men were crouched, clutching rifles. A few were shaking with terror as the shells kept coming. The thunder of enemy fire sounded like the drums of an ancient war god.

Sadie felt Seamus's fear for himself and the men around him. He saluted the man who'd called to him and straightened his shoulders.

"Evacuate the north wall. I'll hold the line." This was like that moment when she'd seen him first turned into a vampire. She wasn't just seeing his memories. She was living *them.*

"Men, to me!" Seamus roared. He lifted his rifle up, and the row of men alongside him did the same. Then they lifted their heads over the barricade all over the stone wall, the village behind them in chaos. Shadows in the distance could be seen advancing.

"Fire!" Seamus bellowed, and the crack of guns firing was drowned out by a fresh scream of mortar shells coming from the German lines a short distance away.

"We cannot let Verdun fall!" Seamus shouted. "Hold the line! Hold!"

The screams of men and gunfire faded into blackness, and Sadie became aware of her own body once more.

Seamus lay still on top of her, his pupils ringed with a ruby-red fire that slowly faded.

"What...was that?" she finally managed to ask.

"What did you see?"

"A village was being shelled. You said something about not letting Verdun fall?"

Seamus's expression softened. He withdrew from her, yet didn't pull away as she cuddled up against him in the bed.

"That was a long time ago. Two or three lifetimes, in fact," he admitted.

"What was it? What battle?" Sadie wished she had paid more attention in history class.

"Verdun. The longest battle of the First World War. My coven—Cassandra's, I mean—were helping the French fight. We didn't want the Germans rolling in. It was one of the few times in history where shifters and vampires fought on the same side. If there was one thing we agreed on then, it was that no single country should rule all of Europe."

"Wow, I didn't know you'd fought back then," Sadie said. "Shifters don't live as long as vampires. It's sometimes hard for us to carry stories like that forward in time, because we have to keep so much a secret. It's kind of amazing that you lived it and can tell people about it." She rested her chin on his chest. His strong hands flexed and settled on her hips beneath the sheets.

His gaze was distant, a hundred years back in the

past. "That was one of the few times supernatural creatures cared about the wars of men. I stood shoulder to shoulder with brave men and women who fought for their lives and their homes. We all knew the Germans wanted to capture the Meuse Heights. It offered a defensive position that would give them a place to fire on the town of Verdun. But they didn't count on the spirit of the French. Cassandra is half French, you see, and she brought us to the front lines to defend her home. Ian and Connor were there with me. It was the last time I saw them for about ten years."

Sadie could hear the regret in his voice. "What happened?"

"I faked their deaths. They escaped Cassandra's coven in the chaos of the battle. When she finally caught up to them a decade later, well, I told you what happened next."

"Can I just say, I really hate this Cassandra woman."

"I know. She's not a good person, but…" Seamus looked at her, his blue eyes deep and pure, no splinters of any other colors fracturing the blue irises. "She comes from a different time. I'm not excusing her, but four hundred years ago, women were property, like cattle or bags of grain. She killed her own maker just a few months after being turned and battled her way into a position of power. Even though I hate her, I admire the strength it took to do that."

Sadie traced patterns on his chest as she tried to

imagine how limiting, how suffocating life was for a woman back then. She couldn't disagree.

"Still, she chose to keep doing it. She could have changed," Sadie finally said.

Seamus chuckled. "Easier said than done." His fingers played a tactile melody on her spine. Despite the serious nature of their discussion, she and her vixen were utterly content.

"What's that supposed to mean?" She placed a kiss to his chest, and he ran his fingers through her hair in a way that made her sigh.

"Vampires *endure*, they do not *evolve*. No matter how much I want to fit in with the people living today, there's a part of me that still behaves like that man who was starving back in the 1840s. I still want to protect those weaker than myself, still want to be a gentleman. When I see the world today, the smartphones filled with silly apps people use instead of talking to one another, it leaves me confused, lost even. I mean... What the hell is so great about Angry Birds or Candy Crush? Why put dog ears on a photo of yourself? I grew up in a time where everyone was struggling between life and death, and now I have to listen to people complain that their mocha lattes don't have enough foam?" He shook his head, a rueful smile on his lips. "I sound like a grumpy old man, don't I?"

Sadie pinched her thumb and forefinger together. "A teeny bit. But I envy you, believe it or not. You've led an amazing life. It makes me feel, well, inconsequential. I haven't fought in any wars, haven't saved any lives. Hell, the most exciting thing I've done is travel on cruise ships."

He cupped her face, his thumb stroking her bottom lip. "The people of my era fought wars so you wouldn't have to."

"But I still don't feel like I've *lived*, you know?"

Her vampire chuckled. "You want to know what I saw when I drank your blood?"

"You saw something again?" She was embarrassed and delighted to know the exchange went both ways a second time.

"I saw you running down a sandy beach, waving a kayak paddle at a bunch of seagulls that were attacking a nest of hatching baby sea turtles." Seamus's soft gaze made her entire body flood with warmth. "You helped those hatchlings reach the sea. You saved lives, and you didn't even think twice."

"Seagulls aren't exactly like taking on the German army."

"No, but every creature holds a place in this world's delicate balance. Those turtles needed to reach the ocean. Those tiny lives matter just as much as yours and mine do."

Sadie stared at him, her heart stilling in her chest as she realized then that she was falling in love with him. It was inevitable. He was too good, too pure hearted, which went against everything she thought she knew about vampires, but perhaps he was right. The world wasn't as black-and-white as she had always assumed.

"You want to shower again before we hit the road? I need to call my friends."

"Sure. Could we get some real food first? Something not sealed in a plastic package with a suspiciously long shelf life?"

Seamus smiled. "You don't want Hostess cupcakes for breakfast?"

"Definitely not. For dessert tonight? Sure. But right now I'd love some eggs and bacon."

"Very well. I suspect I could use something like that myself. It's been too long since I've hungered for more than blood."

Sadie quickly showered and dressed before returning to him. Her heat was waning for now, her hunger abated in a way that it had never been before. It had to be Seamus and the fact that, impossible as it was, he was her mate. The need to shift constantly to find comfort while in heat had faded until it was just a whisper in her mind.

"How are you feeling?" Seamus gripped her waist and peered down at her, his blue eyes always so serious. She wanted to see him laugh.

"Better. Way better. The other times I slept with men during my heat, it was only a temporary satisfaction. With you... It's like you're everything I need." She mentally smacked herself for confessing something like this to him so soon, but it had slipped out, and she couldn't take it back.

"I'm honored to hear that." He dug his fingers into her hips, the hold possessive, just the way she liked to be held.

"Is it different for you?"

"It is. Vampires desire blood above all else, but over time we can regain other hungers, like sex, love, the need for companionship. It's been a long time since sex has meant something above satisfying a primal urge tied to feeding." The rich blue of his eyes was like the lapis lazuli necklace her grandmother wore all the time.

"You are my mate, Sadie. As crazy as it is, my instincts toward you don't involve feeding. I just want you in my arms. It's like an ache when I don't have you close. When a vampire mates, it bonds our soul and heart, just as deeply as a shifter does."

As much as she loved hearing that, she was still worried about the fact that she had mated a vampire, a species so far from her own he might as well be an alien.

Seamus handed her his cell phone. "Call your grandmother. Tell her we are headed to the outskirts of Denver. We'll need to get to my friends' home and hunker down. I'm fairly certain the wolves aren't done with us yet."

"Us?" she questioned as she accepted the phone.

Seamus stroked the bridge of her nose with his index finger. "If they want you, they'll have to go through me."

His words made her heart catch in her throat. She

stared at him, this vampire who was willing to stand beside her, claim her as his mate and defend her life. It was the sort of thing any woman could love a man for.

He leaned in to kiss her. "Call Vera. I'll load up the truck."

Sadie saw the stray bright gold light coming in through the window of their hotel room.

"But the sunlight! Don't you need protection?"

"I'll be fine," he promised. "I just need covering, clothing and a helmet." He pulled on black leather gloves and donned his motorcycle jacket. Then he put on his helmet.

"What happens if the light touches you? You don't turn to ash?"

Seamus snorted and removed his black bike helmet, tucking it under one arm, and then he pulled a glove off one hand and walked toward the thick beam of sunlight.

"Seamus, wait, I don't need to see!" She rushed to stop him as he opened the door a couple of feet.

"Just watch, and then shut the door afterward." He waved his hand through the sunlight, and his expression turned grim. The longer he stood there, the more confused he became. He then stepped into the light, the sun casting its rays over his red hair, making it glow.

"This can't be possible."

"What's not possible?" she asked.

"This." He gestured at himself standing in full daylight, his head and hand exposed. "I should be falling into a deep slumber. I don't even feel sleepy." His gaze drifted from the sunlight to her face again. "Your blood... It has to be your blood."

Sadie reflexively put a hand to her throat. "My blood?"

"Yes. I thought you tasted different. I thought you tasted like..."

"Liquid sunlight," she said quietly.

Seamus raised his face to the sunlight and closed his eyes. A look of bliss transformed his features. Suddenly that bliss was within her as well, glowing like a distant star, growing brighter and brighter inside her until she wanted to spin in circles and dance. She was feeling *his* feelings—an undeniable mark of true mates.

"After almost two hundred years, I'm feeling sunlight on my face," he said, half to himself. He opened his eyes again and looked toward her, holding out a hand and beckoning her over. She stepped into his arms, feeling the sun warm her skin too.

He kissed her forehead and held her close. "You've given me a precious gift." Her senses focused on the steady rush of blood beneath his skin, and it was comforting, like listening to ocean waves on the shore.

"Have you ever heard of this happening before?" she asked.

"Never. Drinking from a shifter wouldn't normally do this. It has to be because we are mated."

They stood in the sunshine for a time, just taking in

this precious moment. Seamus then set his helmet and gloves aside with a grin.

"Guess I won't need these for a while. I'll pack up. Call your grandmother." Sadie watched him from the window as he stepped outside, smiling like a fool as the sun kissed his hair and face. She dialed her grandmother, dreading the conversation she was about to have.

"Sadie?" Vera answered after the first ring. "Are you all right?"

"Yes. I'm feeling a lot better."

"Good. Has the vampire behaved himself?"

Sadie bit her lip. "Grandma, something happened last night."

The silence on the line was telling.

"Grandma?"

"Tell me you didn't feed him."

Sadie groaned. The truth was infinitely more complicated than that. "I shared my blood with him. Willingly."

Her grandmother hissed on the phone, but Sadie continued to talk.

"I think... No, I know."

"Know what?"

"He's my mate."

Vera's horrified reply was largely incoherent except for the last word. "How?"

She cleared her throat, a flush of mortification heating her face. "We were making love, and something happened. Something wonderful. I saw him in my mind, as a fox. He was with me, in my head." *And in my heart,* she silently added.

"That's not possible," Vera insisted. "I didn't think it would happen again."

Again? "What do you mean?"

"I..." Vera's voice cracked. "This really isn't something I should tell you over the phone."

"Grandma, please."

Vera sighed. "I was mated once, a lifetime ago. It was not your grandfather. He came later, after Christopher."

"Christopher?"

"My mate. My vampire," Vera whispered, and her voice broke with emotion.

CHAPTER 9

"You mated a vampire before you married my grandfather?" Sadie's hand shook as she waited for her grandmother to explain the bombshell she had just dropped. All this time she'd feared vampires because of what her grandmother had told her about them. But the truth was, there were good vampires out there, ones who could be mates to shifters. She wanted to be angry, wanted to shout at her grandmother, but instead she felt like she was caught in a swirling eddy of a vast river, being pulled under by confusion.

"I was eighteen, and deep into my heat. Christopher was passing through town and caught my scent. He pursued me into the forest. When he caught me, I changed back to human and, well... My fox wanted him as bad as I did. We mated in a wild frenzy—"

Did she just say that? "Oh geez, *Grandma*..."

"—and he took my blood. I knew instantly he was my mate. It made no sense, but somehow it happened. But he couldn't stay with me. It wasn't safe. The vampire who made him would have killed me, and him. So when my heat had passed, we said our goodbyes..." Her voice broke a little, but she continued. "I watched him walk away, into the brightest sunlight I had ever seen, and I couldn't go with him. Have you seen your vampire in the sunlight?"

"Yes. He wasn't affected by it. Is that part of the mating?"

"It is," her grandmother confirmed.

Sadie held her breath, her throat so tight she wanted to cry. "How..." She choked a little. "How did you have the strength to let him go?"

Her grandmother's breath sounded shaky, as though the memory pained her.

"I let him go because it was the only way to save him, and he knew leaving me was the only way to protect me. What we discovered about vampires who drink from shifter mates was valuable information, a secret that had to be kept at all costs. Many shifters and vampires don't believe that our kinds should mix. Many cross-race pairs go into hiding. Others are...killed."

"I can't let Seamus go, Grandma. He's my mate. I'm falling in love with him."

Vera chuckled. "I'm not thrilled he's a vampire—they bring so much trouble—but maybe your boy is right.

Things are different today. Things are changing. Maybe there's hope for you two. I'm glad you found a mate. It's a gift many shifters go their whole lives never finding."

"You should have seen him in the sunlight this morning. It was beautiful. *He* was beautiful." Sadie glanced out the window. Seamus was still loading up the truck. "But I hate that I've put him in danger. The wolves are getting close again. We're leaving the motel. Seamus doesn't want us to stay in one place for long."

"His instincts are good, then. You need to keep moving, and you must be careful. The Yampa pack is out for blood. Ulrich came here last night. The idiot tried to scare me. He wanted to know if you had returned home. Cyrus and Dracen weren't with him. My guess is they are still out scouting the region for you."

"Oh my God! Are you okay?"

"I'm fine, sweetie. I unloaded a round of buckshot into his furry ass. His cronies will be pulling the pieces out with tweezers for a long time. That will slow him down from getting back on the hunt too fast."

"Thank you, Grandma. But you should leave. I don't want you to be there if he comes back. I can't let them hurt you."

Vera snickered. "Don't you worry about me. This old fox still has a few tricks up her sleeve. Now, what are you two planning to do?"

"Seamus has two vampire friends nearby on the outskirts of Denver who said they will help us."

"You have to be careful. Promise me. Your mate will protect you, but it's possible his friends might not have the same strength and control, especially if you are still in heat." Vera's grave warning made Sadie's stomach clench. She hadn't considered that. They might not see her the same way Seamus did, or even if they did, they might lack his control. It might put her in even greater danger.

"I will, Grandma."

"Take care of your mate." Her grandmother sighed. "If he's anything like my Christopher, he'll try to do something silly and noble."

Sadie bit her lip, fighting back the urge to cry. "I will." The wistful longing in Vera's voice revealed just how much of her broken heart she'd been nursing all these years and what a toll that must have taken. Sadie wished she had told her all this years ago, so she could have helped her, talked to her, done something to ease the pain. But perhaps the pain of losing one's mate was too great to share, even with a loved one. Sadie resolved not to let Seamus make some kind of pointless noble sacrifice in her name. She wasn't going to let him do anything that would break both their hearts.

Once in the truck, they drove to a diner for breakfast. She laughed as he ordered half the menu.

"You'd think you'd never had pancakes before." She took a bite of her omelet while Seamus, in a typical male fashion, plowed through his plate with gusto.

"I haven't," he said after swallowing a mouthful.

"Wait, that's not true. I had them during Victoria's Diamond Jubilee. But it was just for appearances. I never actually tasted them."

"That's tragic." Sadie couldn't help but smile as she watched him enjoy food for the first time in well over a century.

"So, is there anything else you can tell me about these guys we're meeting? I don't feel comfortable going blind into a nest of vampires."

"It's a coven, not a nest. People use the term *nest* when they want to make us sound like vermin."

"Oh..." Sadie swallowed a lump of shame. "Sorry."

"It's okay." He smiled at her. "You've got a whole wide world out there to learn about."

"That's true I guess. I didn't realize there was so much I didn't know," she said as she pushed her empty plate away. "So tell me about your friends."

"Ian and Connor were my friends since we were boys. Ian is more rational, more understanding. Connor is fierce and defensive. It's hard to get close to him until he trusts you."

As much as Sadie found that interesting, she was still worried about what had gone wrong between these two vampires and Seamus.

"So have you had a chance to call your friends and clear things up?"

"I haven't had the time talk to them that much, just to briefly explain to Ian about Lara."

"That's the one Cassandra killed?"

He nodded solemnly. "But I talked to Ian on the phone last night. He's ready to believe my side of the story now. It's just a matter of convincing Connor. He might still rip my head off." Seamus laughed, but Sadie felt suddenly sick.

"Maybe we shouldn't go to them."

He leaned slightly over the table. "It will be okay. I promise. Ian and Connor have a new mate. Knowing Connor, he'll be more protective of her, but if Zoey is as sweet as Ian says, she should soften Connor up." Seamus set down a hundred dollars on the table to cover their bill, and then he held a hand to her. Sadie placed her hand in his.

"It's going to be okay. Trust me."

FOUR HOURS LATER, after she and Seamus had spent time leaving false trails all over the nearby region, Sadie sat on the edge of her seat, nervous as hell. Seamus turned their truck onto an old country road toward a distant cabin by a lovely lake. Mountains climbed high in the distance, and the forest around the property was thick and dark with an abundance of pine trees.

Sadie peered ahead at the cabin in the distance. "Why are they all the way out here? I thought you said they live in the city."

"They do. But they didn't want any bystanders getting hurt if we end up having to fight the Yampa pack."

"Oh. Good thinking." Sadie's eyes fixed on the dying light as the sun began to set behind the mountains. There would still be daylight for another hour, but the shadows were already swallowing much of the landscape.

The door to the cabin opened as they rolled up, and a trio of figures stepped onto the porch. Sadie had gotten used to Seamus and knew she had to rethink what she'd believed about vampires, but knowing she was about to face three more of them was still intimidating.

"You okay? I can hear your heart racing." Seamus parked the truck twenty feet from the porch and touched her cheek; then his fingers brushed over the pulse point of a vein on her throat.

"Just feeling a little outnumbered, but they're our only hope, right?"

"At this point, yes. Stay behind me. Their mate was only recently turned. New vampires have twice the strength of their makers for a year or so, and her lust for blood will be far stronger. If you stay behind me, I can protect you if Ian and Conner need to hold her back."

"You're not helping my anxiety," Sadie muttered.

Seamus got out first and came around to let her out. He acted casual, but his tall, muscled body was a little too close to her as he attempted to shield her from the three vampires until they were half a dozen feet from the porch.

"Ian," Seamus greeted with a nod.

A dark-haired vampire with green eyes nodded back. "Seamus, glad you made it."

"Thank you." Seamus's head moved to face the other male vampire. He had golden hair and dark eyes.

"Hello, Connor."

Connor bristled slightly. "You're here on probation. I'm not convinced you weren't more involved in Lara's death than you're letting on."

"Understood," Seamus replied, but through their mate bond, Sadie could tell that Connor's distrust pained Seamus.

"This is Zoey." Ian put an arm around the petite brunette between the two of them. They were all so beautiful, just like Seamus. Seamus had explained it earlier—when a vampire was created, all the traits that made a person interesting were enhanced. It was a vampire's way of being the perfect predator. Everything about vampires was meant to draw their prey in.

"Hi," Zoey said shyly. "Nice to meet you." She smiled, and a tiny hint of fangs peeked out past her lips as she gave a little wave.

"This is Sadie, my mate." Seamus moved a few inches to the right to let the others have a better view.

"Hi." Sadie waved back. Her heart was still pounding, and she knew all of them could hear it. It must have sounded like a dinner bell.

"You want to come in? We were hoping to have you for dinner."

Everyone stopped and looked at Zoey.

"Er... I mean... I just made dinner," she hedged quickly.

Seamus chuckled. "Thank you, Zoey. We'd like that."

Zoey offered her a warm, open smile. She had a kind face, one that drew people in. Sadie knew she very much wanted to be friends with her, but she wasn't sure she could eat what vampires ate for dinner.

"I'm not sure I could drink blood. I mean, I've had some of Seamus's, but only during" She abruptly stopped herself. Foreplay wasn't exactly polite dinner conversation. "It's not blood, Sadie. Zoey is newly turned, so she still likes food. Ian and Connor are likely eating human food again as well, I assume." Seamus looked to his two friends.

"Yes, that's right. Does a meaty lasagna sound good?" Ian asked with the same warmth and politeness as Zoey.

Sadie's mouth watered at the thought. "Sounds fabulous."

"Come inside and I'll show you your room." Zoey waved her forward. "We can talk while the boys kiss and make up."

Connor shot Zoey a dark look, but his lips twitched. "You'd better make that up to me later, sweetness."

Zoey giggled. "I might." She winked at Connor and blew a kiss to Ian. "Come on, Sadie."

Sadie hesitated and looked at Seamus. He'd just warned her about what might happen with her.

"Don't worry, she's safe," said Ian. "Zoey has remarkable control."

Zoey's face lit up. "They tell me I somehow skipped the whole bloodlust stage."

"Go on then, Sadie," Seamus encouraged. "Trust has to begin somewhere. I'll be right behind you." Sadie leaned in to kiss his cheek and followed Zoey inside. Even if it was masquerading as a lovely rustic cabin in the woods, she was still entering a vampire lair.

SEAMUS DIDN'T MOVE until his mate was inside the house. His ears were trained on the sounds coming from inside, which were that of small talk, not sounds of distress.

"Your mate does seem to have control of her instincts," Seamus admitted, hoping to break the sudden tension between him, Ian, and Connor.

"She is exceptional," Ian mused, offering a shared smile with Connor.

Seamus met their gazes when they both looked back to him. "I'm happy for you both."

"So...," Ian began.

Connor cut in. "You really mated a shifter? What is she? Wolf, cougar, bear?"

"Er... A fox, actually," Seamus said, not sure why he was embarrassed.

Connor threw his head back and roared with laughter. "You mated a bloody *vixen*? That's priceless."

"Mock her at your own risk!" Seamus growled. "She's my mate."

When Connor wiped tears of laughter from his eyes, Seamus lunged at him. Connor caught him, and they tumbled to the floor of the porch, wrestling and punching each other. Ian tried to break things up, only to become an active participant himself. And just like that, things were normal again. They were young men from a farm in Ireland, tussling like lads were meant to.

Finally, Ian, Connor, and Seamus all fell apart on the ground, spent. Seamus laughed and then winced at the soreness of his jaw. He looked at his two friends. There were a thousand things he wanted to say to them, but his throat felt constricted. He swallowed hard and finally spoke.

"Thank you for helping us. Thank you for believing me."

"If what you told Ian is true, then I'm sorry," said Conner. "We owe you our lives after Verdun, and we failed to help you in return. We assumed the worst, and I know my stubbornness didn't help any." Connor held out a hand to him as he stood up. "Brothers?"

Seamus took his hand, and Connor pulled him up. "Brothers," Seamus agreed.

Ian looked between them, grinning smugly, as if he had expected this to happen all along.

"So, tell us about the werewolves," Connor said as the three of them went inside the cabin. Sadie and Zoey were already settled on the couch, coffee mugs in hand. The dark scent of homemade hot chocolate wafted from their cups. They were deep in a conversation of their own, so Seamus, Ian, and Connor headed to the kitchen.

"Sadie and her grandmother live in Steamboat Springs, on the edge of the Yampa Valley pack's territory. There's just three wolves, an alpha named Ulrich, his beta is Cyrus, and then there's an omega named Dracen."

"Just three?" Connor grinned. "Should be easy."

"I thought so, but they have skill. Two scaled my condo to the fourth floor and shattered the window while the third distracted me. They shot me three times. The only reason I'm not dead is because they saw my boxes from the London Blood Society."

"Hang on, when did *you* join the LBS?" Ian asked.

"A few years back. I asked to have my membership kept quiet."

"Oh...," Ian replied. "Well, I'm glad you did. They're a good lot."

"They are."

"So, back to the wolves," Connor reminded Seamus.

Seamus went through what had happened, omitting the details about his and Sadie's mating and explaining how they'd gotten away. His friends followed his every word.

"Sadie spoke to her grandmother this morning. The

alpha wolf returned to Sadie's home she shares with her grandmother and tried to find out where we were. He got buckshot in the ass for his troubles."

Connor snorted. "Sounds like one hell of a grandmother."

Ian raised an eyebrow. "Tell me you didn't leave them a big red sign that says you came here."

Seamus rolled his eyes. "We're not idiots. We drove through quite a few towns, leaving her scent in as many places as possible—that's what took us so long to get here."

Ian nodded in satisfaction. "That will buy us some time, at least."

Seamus ran his fingers through his hair as he glanced at Zoey and Sadie in the living room. "They'll see through that trick eventually. We need a plan to deal with these furry assholes."

Ian and Connor shared a look.

"Sounds like we need to make a few traps before dinner," said Ian.

Seamus nodded. "It's a good idea."

"Ladies, you start on dinner. Us men are headed out to build some booby traps." Connor grinned deviously.

"Wait, what?" Zoey sat up and looked over the back of the couch at them.

"Boo-bee traps." Connor drawled out the word *booby* into two long syllables, as if speaking to someone who'd never heard the word before.

Zoey rolled her eyes. "Yes, I heard that, but why?"

"Best way to deal with wolves," Ian said. "A couple of pits with spikes, netting, maybe even some trip wires and a couple of grenades—you know, the usual."

"Grenades? Where are you going to get those?" Zoey asked.

"We already have them, love." Ian grinned. "In the garage under the fishing tackle box."

Zoey gasped. "You were hiding freaking *grenades* under the tackle box?"

"Easy, sweetheart," Connor crooned. "We'll be back soon." Connor glanced at Seamus and Ian. "Ready?"

"Definitely." Seamus followed his friends out into the darkness.

"GRENADES? FREAKING *GRENADES*?" Zoey hissed. "I love those Irish idiots, but that's insane. I drop boxes all over the place in that garage. I could have blown myself to kingdom come." She looked at Sadie. "Is Seamus as moronic as those two?"

Sadie laughed. "I honestly don't know. I've only been with Seamus for a couple of days."

"But you're his mate?" Zoey's fangs peeked out as she sipped her cocoa again. When she noticed Sadie staring, she smiled sheepishly. "Sorry, I'm still new. Most vampires can retract their fangs until they need to bite.

But when I'm around humans and shifters, I still have a bit of a fang issue. You smell *really* good. Sorry."

Sadie laughed. "It's okay. As long as you don't go for my throat, we're good."

"No problem. I drank before you arrived. Ian and Connor keep bags of blood in the fridge in the garage."

"Next to the grenades?"

"Probably. Lord, those two. I do love them, though." Zoey's face turned dreamy. Sadie knew exactly how she felt.

"It's weird to be so attached to Seamus. I mean, we barely know each other, but I can't imagine my life without him. Considering he hit me with his motorcycle, and how I feel about vampires, these feelings shouldn't be possible."

Zoey's brows rose. "Do you hate vampires?"

"It's complicated. A group of vampires killed my parents when I was a little kid. So I have serious trust issues when it comes to vampires."

"I can't say I blame you." Zoey reached out and placed a hand on hers, squeezing gently.

"Thanks. It's not easy being a shifter, especially a small one. Bears, wolves, cougars—they all have stronger bodies, but foxes? We have only our wits. It's made me nervous and cautious most of my life. I mean... I write online articles and only travel a couple of times a year. I relied on the Yampa pack's presence to scare off vampires for so many years that I forgot to actually live my life."

The moment she said it aloud, tears pricked at her eyes. She had never really faced that fact about herself until now.

Zoey set her cup down on the table. "Can I give you a hug, Sadie?"

Sadie wiped at her eyes. "Yeah, I think I could use one."

Zoey wrapped her in a tight hold for such a petite woman. "You will be living your life from now on, once our boys deal with those wolves. You have a mate, and the world is your oyster, so crack it open, girl."

"I'm so glad I got to meet you." Sadie chuckled, still wiping her eyes.

Zoey grinned. "Same."

Just then the door opened, and the boys stepped inside. All three were dusty, with leaves clinging to their clothes and hair.

"Done!" Ian announced. "We set traps all over the property."

"That was fast," Sadie replied.

Seamus came over to her and ruffled a dirty hand in her hair, making her squeal. "We're vampires, love. Moving fast is in our nature."

"Oh, right." It was going to take some getting used to being around a group of vampires.

"So, the traps are set? Good. We can finally eat!" Zoey pointed at the dining table in the adjacent room. "We weren't about to start without you."

It was quite a comical thing to see vampires chowing down on lasagna, of all things. Before Seamus had mentioned it, she hadn't known eating food was possible for vampires.

Seamus sat down beside her and slipped a hand underneath the table to touch her thigh. Just like that, her body began to sing at his caress. Forget dinner, forget the coming war with the wolves—she wanted Seamus now.

"Better eat up. Seems like these two need a room." Connor chortled. Zoey kicked him under the table, and he muttered an apology.

"Conner's right. She's still in her heat cycle," Seamus explained.

Sadie's face felt like it was on fire, and she looked down at her half-eaten lasagna. She wasn't used to talking so openly of her heat.

"Don't tease her," Zoey warned Ian and Connor.

"We weren't," Ian vowed.

Then, without warning, a sudden howl cut through the night. It was close. *Way* too close. Sadie's entire body seized with fear. Panic clenched her belly with an invisible hand and twisted, filling her with pain. The Yampa Valley wolves were coming for her.

CHAPTER 10

Dracen watched his alpha and beta prowl toward the light of the distant cabin. The wind whistled through the trees, raising the fur on the back of his neck. He dug his paws into the ground and sniffed. There were more scents than just those of Sadie and her vampire here. There were others, and they weren't human. He cried out softly, trying to catch his alpha's attention. But he knew Ulrich, that dick, would probably just ignore him.

He'd never fully belonged to the Yampa pack. He had been outcast from his own pack, the Elder wolves of northern Montana, and had sought refuge in Colorado as a teen. Ulrich had recently killed two dissenting were-wolves in his pack, and had an opening for an omega. Dracen could never let Ulrich know that he had been born an alpha. Most alphas were born, but on rare occasions an omega could rise to challenge for the position. Dracen, while not a true omega, had played the part of one for years to hide his natural desire to lead. Thankfully, Ulrich was so detestable that he could barely have a real pack. It was almost unheard of to have just three wolves in a pack. Most packs had between ten and fifty werewolves. But Ulrich's small pack kept Dracen calm and his natural alpha tendencies hidden.

If Ulrich ever discovered that he was truly an alpha, though, Ulrich would challenge him, and they would fight to the death, which wasn't something Dracen wanted. He'd been cast out of his pack for having a soft heart, and now it would get him killed if he wasn't careful.

"Ulrich?" Dracen reached out through their mental path link.

"What?" Ulrich snapped.

"Danger. I scent three other vampires," Dracen warned. *"They've been all over these woods. We need to be careful."*

"They're just fucking vamps. Do you know how many of them I've killed?" Ulrich prowled over to him, baring his teeth as he made his point. Then he and Cyrus trotted off into the woods ahead of him.

The trees around them rippled with the night breeze, and Dracen growled again. *More* vampires were scented on the wind. Unlike the ones at the cabin, these vampires held an aroma of decaying earth, stale blood, and evil.

Evil had a strong smell. Dracen was all too familiar

with it thanks to Ulrich, but the vampires closing in were far more evil than him.

"More vampires!" he warned. A second later, a black outline blotted out the moon as it swooped down and pinned him to the ground, a silver blade pressed against his furry throat. His body ached in pain, and he whined softly, signaling his surrender. He looked up into the face of a truly beautiful woman, a vampire.

"Quiet, dog. Summon your alpha," a feminine voice said seductively.

"Ulrich, come back! A vampire has me pinned."

Ulrich and Cyrus came running back, but they skidded to a stop as more figures materialized around them. They were surrounded by at least a dozen vampires.

"It's a trap," Ulrich growled.

"Transform, alpha." The female vampire pointed at Ulrich and slightly eased her hold on Dracen's body.

Ulrich transformed into a tall naked man and stepped toward her.

"So, the coward called an army to protect him, eh? I have soldiers of my own. This was supposed to be a hunt, but if it's a war you're looking for, I can oblige," he spat.

The woman made a soft tsking sound. "That's no way to greet an ally."

"Ally? Since when have we ever allied with vampires?"

"Since now." The woman released Dracen. He carefully backed up, his hackles raised. All the vampires around him were tall, powerfully built males. All except for the female before him. He'd never seen a coven like this before. Most were formed of fairly equal numbers. This...this was like a female general with an army.

"What's your interest in the fox?" Ulrich demanded.

"Fox?" The woman's laugh sounded like a beautiful church bell, yet there was a hint of something off, something wrong about her. "None whatsoever."

"You don't want the fox?" Cyrus asked after he changed into his human form.

"No," the woman repeated. She swept her jet-black hair over her shoulder and slid her silver blade back into her long blue brocade coat.

Ulrich crossed his arms over his chest. "So what *do* you want?"

"The red-haired vampire, alive. That's what I want. The others, you can do with them whatever you please."

Dracen looked between his alpha and the female vampire. Ulrich was thinking it over as he sized up the female.

"We want the fox alive," Ulrich said.

"As you wish. I honestly do not care. Now, are you willing to work together? Otherwise, you're welcome to fend for yourselves against their booby traps."

Ulrich glanced behind him toward the distant cabin. "Traps?" The house lights flickered as the leaves partially blocked a clear line of sight. Then the lights went dark. The vampires in the cabin knew they were here.

"Oh yes. You see, I turned three of the vampires in that cabin. I trained them. They aren't easy targets."

Ulrich snorted. "We've killed plenty of vampires."

"Not like these you haven't. They're specialists." The woman's voice deepened, and the chill in her words made Dracen ill, as though he sensed how dangerous she was on a cellular level, dangerous beyond their imagining.

"Fine. We work together." Ulrich silently ordered Cyrus and Dracen to comply.

Dracen, still in his wolf form, bowed his head in agreement, but deep down he was making other plans. He had never liked Ulrich, had only joined the pack to avoid being a lone wolf, but perhaps it was too late for that. He'd stood by and let Ulrich and Cyrus do terrible, cruel things, things that haunted him and tore him apart. He was done standing by, done pretending that he was okay with it. He was already damned for being a bystander to their cruelty over the years, but now he was going to intervene and do the right thing for the first time in a decade. Tonight, he was going to betray his alpha, shed his omega position, and if he was lucky, he was going to save that fox shifter from a terrible fate headed her way on dark wings.

"THE HOWLING STOPPED," Seamus noted.

Zoey looked around at the others, uncertain. "Is that good or bad?"

Seamus stood by the window facing the road, and a gun loaded with silver bullets rested against his palm. He parted the curtain slightly and stared out into the darkness. They had killed the lights in the cabin just a few seconds ago to help his night vision. He saw trees, endless rows of them, but then one of the trees moved a little differently than the others, and he knew their situation had worsened.

"Ian, Connor, it's not just wolves. There's something else out there."

"Vampires?" Ian whispered from the kitchen. He'd pulled out several guns and a couple of long Bowie knives and machetes.

"Afraid so."

Connor handed Zoey a gun and grimaced. "That's not at all comforting."

Sadie sat on the sofa, her hands clenched into the cushions. Waves of fear rolled off her. Seamus wished he could keep her calm, keep her scent under control. It would be hard enough to protect her from the wolves. Now they would be facing vampires too, ones who would find the smell of fear an overpowering temptation.

"Do you have your motorcycle in the garage?" Ian asked Seamus.

"It's in the back of my truck. Why?"

"I have an idea. They want Sadie, right?" Ian moved

through the living room to join Seamus at his vantage point by the window.

"The wolves do. Who knows why the vampires are here?"

"Exactly. They might have different goals. We need to divide them. Take Zoey. With her newborn strength, she can help take out several of the vampires in a fight, and she will be at far less risk than if you took Sadie. We'll have her dress in Sadie's clothes to confuse her scent. Have her sit on the back of your motorcycle, and you two can ride into the woods. Lead the wolves through the traps. Connor and I will hunker down here and protect Sadie."

Seamus balked at the idea. He was never going to agree to separate from his mate. "Why don't one of you take Zoey?"

"That won't work. It must be you. They won't expect you and Sadie to separate. If you make a run for it, they'll expect you to take her with you," Ian insisted.

"He's right, Seamus." Sadie got up from the couch just as a fresh howl, closer to the cabin now, made them all flinch. She joined him and Ian at the window.

"You want me to leave you?" Seamus growled at her.

"No. But you are thinking with emotions. You need to think with your head."

"I'm thinking with my *heart*," he said and caught her chin, tilting her face toward him. "I've lived so long not knowing love. You can't expect me to abandon it so easily."

Her hazel eyes were almost a dark brown in the dim light. "Then let's be smart about this," she said. But even as she spoke, he felt her reluctance to part with him. "Do as Ian says. Take Zoey. You know your friends will protect me."

"Aye, with our lives," Ian promised.

"But..." Seamus's next argument died before it began. He knew they were right. It was something he would have suggested if he hadn't been the one forced to be separated from his mate. "But what about Zoey?"

"We trust you with our mate; you can trust us with yours." Connor tucked a gun into the waistband of his jeans at his lower back.

"But has she ever fought before?"

"What she lacks in skill she'll make up for in raw strength," Conner reminded him.

"I'll be fine." Zoey chuckled, but the sound held a hint of nerves to it that she couldn't easily hide.

Seamus looked down at Sadie and then pulled her into his arms, hugging her tight. "Fate brought us together and bound our hearts," he whispered in her ear. "I won't let it take you away from me." He gave her one more squeeze and stepped back.

"Be safe," Sadie whispered. She wiped at her eyes before she held out a hand to Connor. "Give me one of those."

Connor attempted to hand her a Glock.

"No, that one." She pointed to an AR-15. "Grandma taught me how to shoot a rifle."

"She's going to be fine," Ian said with a chuckle.

Zoey held out her hand. "Okay, give me your hoodie." Sadie removed her sweatshirt, and Zoey swapped with her. As they did, their scents became mixed, but for now the clothing was dominant. Maybe this could work.

"Let's go." Seamus led Zoey to the garage. He grabbed his motorcycle keys, lifted the bike out of the back of his truck, and swung a leg over his bike. Zoey climbed on behind him, one arm wrapped tightly around his waist, her other hand holding and concealing her gun.

"Can you shoot while I drive?" he asked.

"I think so." She tightened her ponytail and pulled the hood of her sweatshirt up tightly around her face. The ruse would only last so long, they both knew it, but if they could take out the wolves either by guns or traps, that was all they needed to do.

Seamus glanced at her over his shoulder. "Ready?"

Zoey tightened her grip around his waist. "Yeah."

He gunned the engine as Ian opened the garage door from the cabin doorway. The door rose, and Seamus hit the gas. A howl sounded from their left as they shot out into the night, and a wolf, a black one, sprinted toward them. Seamus swerved the bike, steering it just as Zoey turned to open fire. Seamus didn't look back; he rode through the fallen leaves, heading toward the first trip wire. He heard the angry howls and saw a vampire's shadow flash by out of the corner of his eye. He swerved right past the two trees with the grenade trip wires. A few seconds later, the vampire ran straight through it. There was a deafening explosion, the force of which rattled the motorcycle so hard he almost lost control of it.

"Hang on!" he warned Zoey. She shifted behind him and fired again. He swept his bike in an arc, hearing the wolf coming after them. The stake pit wasn't far—

He cursed and turned the bike toward a different trap. Someone had found their stake pit and unburied it.

"What's wrong?" Zoey shouted.

"They're onto us. They've found some of the traps already." But hopefully not all of them. He knew of another trip wire and aimed for it, changing course just before they would've collided with a tree, but nothing happened. The wolf leapt over the wire and kept coming.

"He's almost on us!" Zoey shouted in his ear, taking another shot.

Seamus turned to look, and he almost paid for it with his life. Something hit him in the stomach, and he and Zoey were knocked off the bike. It skidded along the forest floor on its side, the engine sputtering as it slid into a bush. Seamus struggled to move, his body hurting like hell.

He stared up at a piece of thick rope that fell away from two trees they had just driven through. Two dark figures stepped out from their hidden spots. Vampires.

"Zoey... Run..." He tried to shout, but it was too late. One of the men jerked Zoey to her feet and pulled her hood back from her face. The black wolf caught up to them and stared at Zoey for a moment, then shook his head at the vampires holding her.

One vampire asked as he leaned in to sniff Zoey, "Not the fox?" She cowered away from him.

The black wolf snarled and snapped his teeth. The vampires who held Zoey turned to Seamus.

Seamus got to his feet just as the wolf lunged at him. He dodged to the side and punched the vampire nearest him. At the same moment, Zoey's meek demeanor vanished, and she attacked the other vamp, sinking her teeth into his neck to rip his throat. The black wolf dove at him again, sinking his jaws into Seamus's arm. He hit the ground hard, the wolf on top of him. Gunfire erupted in the distance, and with the smell of gunpowder came another smell that froze the blood in Seamus's veins.

Cassandra.

"Sadie!" he bellowed, but the wolf pinned him down, and he couldn't get free. He screamed her name again, hoping she might hear the terror in his voice. His mate was under attack from something far worse than any wolf.

"ONE OF THE grenade trip wires blew," Connor said as he and Ian moved to a defensive position near the couch.

They had boarded up most of the windows and overturned the couch facing the last big window. It was meant to be a choke point. It would draw them in, and the three of them would shoot anyone who breached the window.

Sadie put a hand to her stomach. She felt sick. She held the AR-15, using the top of the couch to steady her aim. Ian and Connor crouched down on either side of her.

Ian nodded toward the darkness. "They're coming." Sadie didn't have the same night vision the vampires did, but she did have something else. She let the vixen shift to the surface just enough for her human eyes to change. Earth's magnetic field suddenly became visible as darker shadows pointing north and south, and the sounds coming from ahead lined up with the shadows, helping her pinpoint the exact location of the predators headed her way.

"Got you...," she said. The front window shattered as she shot at the first wolf running toward them. The russet-colored beast hit the ground and lay still. That was Cyrus. Sadie exhaled in relief, until she heard gunshots from the woods, aimed at them.

"Fire back!" Ian shouted.

Something tore through her arm, grazing her one of her biceps, but she kept firing, aiming for the muzzle flashes. The exchange of fire seemed to last forever.

When silence finally settled over them, Sadie glanced

around at the cabin. The walls were riddled with bullets, and the furniture was destroyed. The home was devastated.

"Shit!" Ian cursed as he sniffed the air and then looked at Connor over her head with pure fear.

"What's the matter?"

"Eight vampires are coming. And two wolves. Sadie, shift and run to the lake. Swim across and don't come back, do you understand?"

"No." She shook her head violently, but Connor grabbed her uninjured arm and spun her to face him.

"You will shift and swim across the lake. You will head to Denver and hide. You will not come back." His voice deepened into a seductive, coercive tone that made it impossible for her to refuse.

She crawled away, shifting and escaping her clothes as she did so. She ran toward the back door that faced the lake and escaped out the dog door in the kitchen and into the night. A breeze made her hackles rise as she looked back over her shoulder at the house.

You will not come back... Connor's command echoed with a deep, sonorous sound inside her head the way a voice carried in a cavern.

She raced to the edge of the water and stopped just at the shore where the water lapped at her front paws. Hesitating only a moment, she plunged into the cold lake, swimming through the water. The full moon illuminated the lake and the ripples her passage created. Unable to stop, the vixen retrieved memories, playing them for her over and over as she swam toward safety.

Seamus's fingers brushing over her cheek, a soft unguarded smile hovering around his lips.

"You've given me the greatest gift."

A golden field, a vixen spotting a male fox at the edge of the field, and that sense of oneness, of peace.

Our mate. A mate we love.

Our mate... Left behind to die.

Her vixen threw her head back and cried as she reached the middle of the lake.

You will not come back...

CHAPTER 11

Seamus was shoved to his knees outside the cabin, alongside Zoey. A number of vampires came out of the cabin, dragging Ian and Connor outside and then kicking the backs of their knees, sending them sprawling into the dirt. Seamus didn't move, didn't speak, as the smell of ancient blood and death carried upon the wind. One he knew all too well. He tried to clear his mind as the one person he feared emerged from the woods.

Cassandra looked lovely. She always looked lovely. But just because the moon is beautiful doesn't mean it's not a cold and inhospitable place. She wore a dark-blue brocade coat that reached her knees, and her long dark hair flowed freely down her shoulders. Even after a hundred and seventy years his body still responded to hers, recognizing the vampire who had created him. But his heart wasn't hers, nor was his soul. They would never be hers. Those belonged to Sadie now.

"Seamus, my darling." She walked past her coven soldiers, past the two wolves who watched warily, and stopped in front of him. There was no sign of Sadie, no sign she had been killed or captured. The wolves would have been long gone if that had been the case. It was the only positive thing he could cling to now.

Misery stung him. He knew what Cassandra would do to him. Whenever a soldier escaped her or showed any signs of resistance, assuming she didn't kill him outright, she reinforced her maker bond in the ancient way of sharing her blood. Although *sharing* wasn't exactly true. *Forcing* was more accurate. A gray light of gloom cast a shadow over his heart. This was the end. After this, there would be no more chances to escape. Cassandra wouldn't give him even the slightest bit of freedom.

But at least Sadie wasn't here. She might be safe. His heart told him she was. He could feel her somewhere close, alive, unhurt. That was his hope now. If he had to suffer this slavery to Cassandra for the rest of eternity, at least he'd know his mate was safe.

"I've missed you, Seamus." Cassandra touched his cheek, her elegant fingers hesitant as they caressed his skin. Her power was electric, seeping into his body at the point of their contact. Even after all these years, he could still feel her pull. The older a vampire was, the stronger that magnetism became.

"You may speak," she said, and the invisible binding around his tongue eased. He hadn't even been aware that she'd stopped him from speaking until that moment.

"Cassandra." He uttered her name and nothing more.

She brightened, like a delighted child who had just remembered it was her birthday. "I knew it was *you*. That getting you back would make the gray go away."

Seamus's eyes dropped to the ground. *The gray*. It was what she called the sensation when a vampire began to fade. Fade away into dust, into the past, into death. She had always feared the gray edges of her world. Too old and too afraid to change. A vampire who did not learn to endure, did not survive. Seamus knew he had been her only source of survival for the last century. But he didn't love her, didn't care about her. She was a merciless killer, and he couldn't feel any compassion for her, not anymore.

There was only one way to end this. He would go back to her, surrender himself to Cassandra in the hopes she would spare his friends.

"Cassandra, I beg mercy of you," he said quietly.

"Mercy? For them?" She looked around at her other captives.

"I will do whatever you wish, if you give my friends their freedom."

She smiled. "You're in no position to bargain. You forget, my dear one, that I can bring you back within my control." She nodded at the vampires who stood behind him. They jerked Seamus to his feet, and one vampire grabbed Seamus's hair, yanking his head sideways to expose his throat. Cassandra came over and struck like lightning, her fangs sinking in. He gritted his teeth against the searing pain of her violent bite.

Her nails dug into his chest as she drank deeply, sucking on his vein, draining him of strength and power. He groaned, his body seizing as he nearly collapsed. But Cassandra held him up like a rag doll.

Then she pulled free of his neck and licked her blood-stained lips. Her cold but beautiful eyes narrowed. There was a brief flash of fear in her ruby-ringed eyes before she glared at him.

"You're mated?" she whispered. "How? How did you do it?" She slashed at his chest, causing him to howl in pain.

"You belong to *me*, not some shifter bitch." She looked at her soldiers. "Find the fox. Bring her to me."

She slashed her wrist and shoved it against his mouth, forcing him to drink. Her blood, once a sweet ambrosia, now tasted rotten, vile... He started to heave, but one of the vampires covered his mouth, holding it firm. She then did the same to Ian and Connor, drinking from them and feeding them her blood. A few moments later they stood mute, trapped by her will. Seamus stared between them and Zoey, terrified of what Cassandra would do to her.

"Should I let them keep their pet?" she asked Seamus. "What would you do for me if I spared her?" Cassandra walked toward Zoey and stroked her dark-brown hair, the caress both tender and menacing at the same time.

"Anything," Seamus whispered, knowing she was likely only toying with him, but he had to try. "Please... Cassandra." He had made a vow to protect Zoey as he would his own mate. If that meant selling his soul, he would do it. Her blood was already moving through him, demanding his obedience to her will, whatever it might be. He tried to fight her control, but her compulsion rolled through him like a dark tide, washing away his resistance inch by inch.

"*Anything* is an awfully big word. You and I shall discuss that later. But for now, I will spare her." She waved Zoey away. One of the vampires bound her hands behind her back, and they left her mercifully alone for now.

Seamus's gaze drifted into the woods by the cabin. Two yellow eyes flashed in the dark, and his blood pounded in his veins. Even as Cassandra's control overcame his free will, he could still sense her, his mate.

Run! He wanted to scream, but he couldn't warn her for fear of alerting the others to her presence. The yellow eyes bobbed as the fox slunk closer, still half-hidden beneath the gloom.

Ulrich, the black wolf, turned his head and sniffed. The fox froze, waiting for Ulrich to turn back to Cassandra and the others, and then she began to move forward again. Then, out of nowhere, one of the vampires swooped in and grabbed her off the ground by the back of her neck. She cried out as the vampire carried her small body toward Cassandra. Seamus took a single step toward her.

"Stop," Cassandra commanded. He was trapped in place as though his feet were rooted to the ground.

Cassandra took Sadie by the scruff of her neck and looked toward the wolves.

"Did I not promise you the fox? Well, I did not promise her to *both* of you. Why don't you fight each other for it?" Cassandra nodded at Ulrich and the omega Sadie called Dracen. Dracen bowed his head and, ever the omega, stepped back. Ulrich growled and licked his chops as he took a few steps toward Cassandra. As a result, he never saw the attack coming.

Dracen sank his teeth into Ulrich's throat as he dragged the alpha down so fast and hard that the sound of his neck snapping echoed in the silence that followed. Panting, the silver-gray wolf turned to Sadie, who went still in Cassandra's hold.

"Well done, wolf," Cassandra said, then tossed the fox at him. Sadie hit the ground, and Dracen grabbed her by the neck, holding her immobilized as he turned toward Seamus. He stared at Seamus a long moment, then trotted into the dark forest, carrying his prey.

Seamus felt a knife in his chest as he defied the order from his maker and tried to take another step. Everything inside him was dying. For the first time in his life, he felt what Cassandra meant about *the gray*. It crept in at the corners of his vision, and a strange numbness bled into his limbs.

"Seamus, forget the fox. That union was unholy. Vampires should not mate with shifters. Whatever that was, it was an abomination." She came up to him, cupped his face, and kissed him. He felt nothing, *less* than nothing, but she clearly did.

"You are mine. This is all that matters now. Just me." She turned her focus to the vampire behind her. "Victor, call the airport, have my jet prepared." She trailed her hand down Seamus's chest. "We're going home."

SADIE HUNG limp in Dracen's jaws, her mind too cluttered by chaotic thoughts to make much sense. Seamus. He hadn't been able to help, and it wasn't just because he had been outnumbered. Cassandra had done something to him, got him back under her control. The look of terror in his eyes would haunt her until the day she died. She accepted her fate. She couldn't escape Dracen, and even if she did, what then? There was no hope other than for a quick end.

Dracen stopped at the back door of the cabin and lowered her to the ground, releasing her. She collapsed on shaky paws and looked up at him. The wolf stared back, no licking of his jaws, no hungry expression. He almost looked...concerned?

That made no sense.

Dracen changed to human form, kneeling naked before her.

"Listen, you have to go. Get out of here. That vampire is too strong. She has your mate, and she will never let him go."

The vixen retreated inside her head as she shifted as well. She cowered, covering her nakedness as best she could as she stared at Dracen.

"Why did you kill Ulrich?" It didn't make sense. Dracen had killed his own alpha.

He looked away from her. "I never belonged to Ulrich's pack, not really. I was an exile, and he was one of the few wolves who would take me in. I hated who I had to be while I was with his pack." He dragged his fingers through his dark hair. "I was never like this—ugly, cruel, vicious. Watching you and your mate tonight...it reminded me of who I used to be. A wolf who gave a shit. I was never truly an omega, not in my old pack. I was alpha born."

"You were?" Sadie stared at him.

"I was." Dracen's stare grew hard as he lifted his chin. "I know that vampire is your mate, but you can't stay. Cassandra will kill you. If you care anything for him, don't make him watch you die." Dracen stood and started to walk away.

"Dracen?" she whispered. He looked back over his shoulder. "Where are you going?"

"Home. There's nothing for me here. If I survive the trip home, I'll go back to my pack and win my place as alpha."

"Seamus said you were the most dangerous of the pack. I guess he was right."

Dracen gave a half smile. "Sounds like a smart vamp." He shifted back and sprinted into the woods, heading north.

Sadie trembled, her body slowly starting to chill in a way that told her that her heat had finally stopped. Her scent was changing back to normal, and she wouldn't have that strong heat smell alerting the world to her presence. It was the only good thing she had going for her, and it gave her an idea.

She picked her way barefoot back into the cabin, moving softer than a mouse in the woods when it knew the owls were hunting. She found some jeans and a shirt and put on a pair of hiking boots, then grabbed one of Conner's abandoned machetes. Facing a coven of vampires on her own was not something she should even be attempting, but she had to rescue her mate and her new friends.

Exiting through the rear of the house, she moved over the grass silently, keeping downwind, listening to the voices of the vampires. She came around the corner of the cabin and stilled. Seamus was on his knees, blood smeared over his chest where his shirt had been clawed at. There was an open wound on his neck and a frightening hollowness to his face. He was broken, a man who'd lost his mate and his free will.

"I'm here," she wanted to scream, but she kept silent.

Cassandra stalked back and forth, lecturing Seamus. Snippets of her words reached Sadie's ears.

"Mine, you understand... mistake last time... too generous... do what you are told..."

Sadie held back a growl. There were two vampires nearest her, and she knew if she acted fast, she could take them out, but she needed help with the others. Drawing in a shaky breath, Sadie sprinted from the shadows and into the moonlight straight at the nearest two vampires. She sliced one's head clean off with a machete and stabbed the other in the heart. The second vampire she stabbed moved too fast, and he caught her arm that held the machete and nearly broke it as he twisted the blade free of her hold.

"Seamus! Help!" she screamed.

There was a moment of rebelliousness in Seamus's eyes before Cassandra leaned down to speak in his ear. Whatever she said blanked his features completely. He stood and came slowly toward her.

"It's okay, Sadie, you're safe now." His voice was hypnotic, sweet, but there was something off about it. She felt his compulsion at play. He approached her slowly and embraced her. Confused, she hugged him back, hoping he would whisper his secret plan to escape the vampires, but her eyes fixed on Cassandra, whose evil grin widened. Sadie realized the mistake she'd made and shoved at her mate, trying to get away, but he held her tighter, squeezing until her ribs ached.

"It will all be okay," Seamus said, and sank his teeth deep into her throat. Sadie cried out in pain, clawing at him, but he didn't stop drinking.

"Seamus!" Zoey cried out. "Stop! You'll kill her."

Cassandra laughed. "That's the point." She came to Seamus and put a hand on his shoulder. "Stop. For now."

He growled softly, like a wolf guarding his kill, but then he lifted his fanged mouth away from Sadie's neck. Dizzy, she swayed and would have fallen if Seamus hadn't been holding on to her. This bite was so different from his previous ones. This was savage, primal, the bite of a killer. The Seamus she knew would never hurt her. But as she stared up at his face now, she wasn't sure if she saw that man there anymore.

"Let go of her," Cassandra commanded.

Sadie stumbled and fell to her knees, dizziness sweeping through her.

"Now, here's what we're going to do. I wish to play a little game," Cassandra said in a saccharine-sweet voice. "You're a fox, so it's only natural we have a fox hunt. Right, boys?" The rest of her coven laughed, the sound grating upon Sadie's ears. She wanted to scream, to claw

Cassandra's eyes out, but she held her breath, willing the wooziness to fade.

"I shall give you a fifteen-minute head start. And then Seamus here will hunt you down and drain you dry. No more mate, no more attachment. He will fully belong to me."

Sadie fought her instincts to strike out at the vampire. She knew it would only result in injury, an injury she couldn't risk if she had any chance to escape.

"You may start running in three...two...one." Cassandra waved a hand toward the forest.

Sadie got to her feet and, without looking back, ran. She didn't change, didn't let the vixen control her. This was not a time for blind, instinctive panic. She did use her fox instincts, though. She left false trails of blood, brushing against plants and trees that had stronger scents than her own, then doubling back and changing direction. After a few of these, she found a tall pine and started to climb. If there was one thing a fox knew, it was that climbing solved most of life's predator problems. She focused on strategies, trying not to dwell on the fact that her own mate was going to hunt her.

A sudden rush of sounds and a blur of movement below stopped her breath.

Seamus.

Sadie stared down at the forest floor below. It was like peering through a muddy pond, as the moonlight could only pass through certain parts of the foliage. She clung to the branches, too terrified to move. Was he gone? The blur had passed through below and vanished. She wondered if she should climb back down, but foxes knew when they were still in danger, like a sixth sense. It raised the fine hairs on the back of her neck. And they were all up.

Seamus appeared again at the base of the tree, his hair looking russet in the filtered moonlight. When he peered upward, Sadie wanted to close her eyes and pretend he couldn't see her.

He stared straight at her and bared his teeth. "Found you." He jumped, catching the lowest branch and hoisting himself up in a powerful leap. There was no way out. She was going to die at the hands of a vampire, just like her parents. And it was worse because he was the vampire she loved. He didn't stop leaping until he was at the base of the limb she'd scooted out on. It was her last stratagem: if Seamus dared to follow her out on the branch, it would snap and they would both fall.

"I'll make it quick and painless, little fox." Seamus's voice softened, a seductive sweetness in his tone that sounded almost teasing. "Come, little vixen." He curled his fingers in invitation. She saw death in his eyes, *her* death.

"Seamus, it's me. Sadie. Your mate. Please don't do this—"

Crack!

The branch holding her broke as she moved too far out on the limb, and she tumbled down. Pain knifed through her as she hit two branches before landing on her stomach on the ground. The wind rushed out of her, and she couldn't make a sound. She curled her fingers into the grass beneath her and fought back the pain slicing through her body.

Seamus descended more gracefully, the faint rasp of clothes brushing against branches as he dropped to the ground in a predatory crouch.

Cassandra stepped out from behind the base of a nearby tree. "Finish her." She must have followed Seamus so as to see him finish his kill. To make sure he was loyal... which meant she wasn't completely sure he was.

"Seamus, no," Sadie gasped." You aren't a killer."

"Oh, but he is," Cassandra purred. "He's the perfect killer. That's what I've trained him to be since I first turned him. That's why I adore him." She smiled at Sadie. "Not even a mate's love can change that."

A mate's love. The words held such power, but Sadie was too exhausted, too in pain to see how her love for him could help.

I've fallen for you, Seamus. Somewhere in the last few days, you've become my world. And I can't lose you.

A tear rolled down her cheek as she rolled onto her back and gazed up at the full moon. Seamus leaned over her and pulled her up to her feet.

"Seamus. Don't. I love you," she whispered, holding his gaze. That ruby-red gleam in his eyes was more frightening now because of the cold emptiness behind them.

"I don't want your love," Seamus growled. "I'm not some fox in a field of gold." Just for a moment, she thought she saw a glint in his empty eyes.

Field of gold? Why say that? She remembered what they'd shared in the hotel, that mix of blood and passion that had bound them together, sealing the mate bond.

"One last kiss?" she begged. If he was going to kill her, she needed one last memory of him, one not tainted by evil. And if luck was with her, it might deliver a miracle.

His eyes lowered to her lips, but his dark red-gold lashes fanned down as his cold expression softened but a moment.

Cassandra chuckled. "Your sentimentality is adorably pathetic. Very well." She looked to Seamus. "You may kiss her."

Sadie shivered as Seamus bent his head and kissed her. His lips were soft, infinitely tender as they covered hers. It was a kiss of compassion, a kiss of dark devotion, of quiet, sweet death. His tongue sought entrance to her mouth, and she bit his lip, drawing the taste of his blood into her mouth. He growled in pleasure, not anger. He sank his fangs into his own lip and drew more blood from the deeper cut.

She had once hated the taste of blood. Now she savored it, because it was his. He kissed her again as she drank, and she began to feel better, her wounds mending, her body reviving. His blood was saving her, giving her back her life.

"Do you trust me, love?" his silken voice murmured in her head, though it had been blocked before by Cassandra's control.

"Yes."

"Trust me, my vixen. Trust that I love you."

Seamus pulled back and looked down at her, his red irises glowing in the gloom.

"You've had your kiss," Cassandra said, and looked to Seamus. "Kill her. Now."

"My pleasure," Seamus replied, a dangerous smile on his lips as his fangs sank deep into Sadie's neck.

CHAPTER 12

Seamus sank his teeth into Sadie's neck, and the compulsion to obey Cassandra's command was almost overpowering. But there was a thread of resistance in him that grew stronger every second. He closed his eyes, feeling her blood fill his veins and his own blood still within her, keeping her alive as he drained her.

Trust me, he'd said. Because he had a plan. He only prayed it would work, or else he would lose his mate, the woman he had come to love in just a few days. A sweet madness she'd become to him, and he could not lose her.

Thump...thump...thump. Sadie's heart slowed down, almost to a terrifying stop as he released her body, hating that he had to drop her at his feet as though she didn't matter, even though in truth she was the *only* thing that did.

She hit the ground, limp, her eyes closed, her face

pale. If not for his blood inside her, she would be dead. Seamus fought to repress a shudder.

"Reward me," he growled at Cassandra, trying to sound hungry and aroused, the way he knew she liked him to be.

She smiled. "You truly are back, my darling Seamus." She beckoned him closer, and he came to her, taking her into his arms and violently kissing her. He moved them both backward to pin her against the tree, unleashing his seductive skills. He raised a hand above them, gripping a branch as though trying to hold himself back from his passion.

"I missed you." Cassandra nipped his ear. "Missed you so much. Why did you leave me? I felt myself fading away. The nightmares..." She trembled and moved closer to him. Seamus hardened his heart against the woman who had suffered so much, the woman who, despite her evil acts, had saved his sister Kayleigh all those years ago.

In one quick move, he snapped the branch off above their heads and drove the broken, jagged edge straight into Cassandra's chest.

The makeshift stake sank deep into her chest, impaling her. She screamed, but the sound withered as she fell limp in his arms.

"No... I can't die... I can't..."

He kept his hold on her, not letting her escape her fate. "I'm sorry, Cassandra. For a hundred years I wanted you to see the world the way I did. I wanted you to see life as something precious."

"Precious...," she scoffed, but her voice was raspy. "Those fools...squander their gift. They don't deserve it."

Seamus shook his head. She still didn't understand what a precious gift life was.

"I...hated them. I hated them because they...had life and all I had was...power. In life it was all I wanted...and when I had it...it meant nothing." She turned her pale face toward him, her porcelain skin beginning to crack. "I loved you...you know."

"I know." His throat constricted as he watched that love in her fading ruby-tinged eyes.

"I loved you because with you I felt...alive. Like there was hope... But it was... different this time..."

"Different?"

"My hold on you was weak. I knew... I knew this would happen... I think... I think I wanted it to. I'm tired, Seamus...so tired." She tried to lift a hand to his face, but it fell limp onto her chest.

"You can rest now."

Cassandra's face held an expression he'd never seen before. Peace.

"Maybe... I can." Her last words were raspy and were carried away on the wind as her body slowly broke and turned to ash. Seamus gasped. His heart seized as the weight of Cassandra's compulsion expired. Then he spun and fell to his knees next to Sadie. He bit his wrist and placed it against her cold, pale lips.

"Drink, love. Please…," he encouraged as his blood dripped between her parted lips. Nothing happened. Perhaps he hadn't given her enough of his before? He cradled her in his arms, tears leaking from his eyes. Agony gripped his throat, strangling him as he buried his face in Sadie's neck. He had thought this would work. That she would be all right. That she would survive.

A faint blossom of heat filled her face. Surprised, he pulled back. A pale-rose color had warmed her ashen face. He touched her skin with shaky fingers and felt the blood starting to move within her again. His blood had awakened her. Her chest suddenly heaved as she sucked in a gasping breath.

"Sadie!"

"Seamus?" His whispered name sounded like the heavens were singing.

"Oh God, you scared me," he cried in her ear before he covered her face with soft kisses.

"I had the most terrible dream…that you drank my soul away." She nuzzled him as he held her on his lap, never wanting to let her go.

"It was a bad dream, that's all. It's over now." He stood, cradling her in his arms like a child as he took her back to the cabin. Ian, Connor, and Zoey were all waiting for them.

"What the bloody hell happened?" Connor asked. "Cassandra's soldiers all just ran off."

"She's dead," Seamus said as he took Sadie inside. Ian followed and tipped the couch back onto its feet so Seamus could set Sadie down on it. Bullets had riddled the leather sofa, and stuffing fluffed out of various holes. But at least Sadie could lie on something soft.

"Cassandra's dead?" Ian asked, his worried gaze touching on Connor and Zoey as they both came inside the wrecked cabin.

"Yes." He didn't elaborate, however.

"Is Sadie okay?" Connor asked.

Seamus sat down on the couch and put Sadie's head in his lap so he could stroke her hair. "Barely. I almost had to kill her to earn Cassandra's trust."

"Fuck," Connor muttered.

Ian's shoulders dropped. "I can't believe it's over. I never thought any of us could stand up to her and live. But now... It feels like a weight has been lifted."

Seamus only half listened to his friends and Zoey talk as they started to tidy up the cabin. The sound was a comforting background hum. Right now, all that mattered was the woman he still held, his mate. He listened to her steady heartbeat, relieved she wasn't a vampire. He hadn't turned her; he'd just saved her life. And he was glad, so damned glad.

"Seamus?" Sadie said drowsily.

"Hmm?"

"I'm a little hungry."

"What would you like?" He was so relieved to hear her say that.

"A cheeseburger, a big one..." She paused and giggled a little. "Fries, and a chocolate shake."

He brushed his fingers over her lips and smiled. "Consider it done." He would have given her the world if she had asked.

"Does that mean we're going out to eat?" Zoey asked hopefully, holding up a bullet-punctured pot in the kitchen. "Because dinner is ruined."

"Looks like." Connor chuckled. "I don't want to be anywhere near here until spring." He plucked at his blood-soaked shirt. "I'm going to burn my clothes and put on some fresh ones."

"Good idea." Ian sighed heavily as he glanced around the cabin. "No point in staying here tonight. We ought to drive back to Denver now that it's safe."

"Seamus, do you need some blood? We have bagged stuff in the fridge." Ian opened the door and pulled out a red bag that bore the London Blood Society's insignia.

"I could use it. Cassandra took too much of my blood. I'm still hungry." He'd tried to ignore how good his mate's blood smelled. He wouldn't be drinking from her for a few weeks at least, not until she was fully healed and feeling better.

Seamus continued to hold Sadie while Ian brought him a bag. He bit the top off and started drinking fast.

Soon he was feeling more clearheaded. The mix of Cassandra's blood and his mate's blood had left him feeling disoriented, but that was now dissipating.

He only left Sadie's side to change his clothes and returned to find Zoey had helped Sadie out of her bloody shirt. A first aid kit sat on Zoey's lap while she dabbed at a bloody scrape on Sadie's arm. Sadie was sitting up now and stared down at the cut with exhausted bemusement.

"Could have been worse," she said.

"Did I do that to you?" Seamus didn't fully remember everything that had happened before he turned on his maker. He remembered frightening flashes of him chasing Sadie, biting her, *hurting* her.

"No, that was a bullet from one of the vampires when I was inside the cabin." Sadie pulled her fresh shirt on over her newly bandaged arm, and Zoey gave her a gentle hug.

"I'm so glad you're okay." She glanced at Ian and Connor. "So glad we're *all* okay."

"Hell of a night. Wolves *and* vampires," Ian said grimly.

Connor winked at Sadie. "And a vixen."

"Can we get those cheeseburgers now?" Her face lit up hopefully as she looked to Seamus. He simply held open his arms, and she moved straight into his embrace. The second he embraced her, his heart gave another wild beat. He stilled.

"My heart...," he whispered in shock.

"Hmm?" Sadie nuzzled his throat.

"It's..." His heart gave another rapid *thump-thump*. Sadie pulled away to stare at him, a question on her face. Dumbfounded, he nodded. He hadn't heard it beat in a hundred and seventy-three years.

"We have to call my grandmother." Sadie's hazel eyes were dark and serious, so much so that it worried him.

"Why?"

"She was once mated to a vampire. She might know something about this—"

Crash!

Everyone jumped as Zoey cursed and stepped back from the kitchen with a pair of glasses she'd been washing. She'd dropped them accidentally at the mention of the mating.

"Did you just say Vera was mated to a vampire?" Seamus asked.

"It's a long story, she only told me this morning before we got here. I didn't want to tell you until we were safe from the Yampa pack."

"Change of plans," Seamus said. "Dinner is in Steamboat. We'll grab burgers on the way." He looked down at Sadie in amazement. Being Sadie's mate was changing him from the inside out. Tonight, he would find out why.

Sadie had eaten two drive-through cheeseburgers before she called her grandmother to tell her she was coming home. Then she'd fallen fast asleep in Seamus's arms in the back seat of Ian and Connor's Range Rover while Ian drove. Connor and Zoey followed behind in Seamus's rental truck with his motorcycle in the back. They arrived at Steamboat around three in the morning, which seemed to be just fine for the vampires, but Sadie was exhausted as she stumbled out of the SUV. Her grandmother rushed down the front steps of their house but halted as she saw she was facing a small coven of vampires.

"Sadie, who are they?" She nodded at the rather intimidating group. Ian and Connor looked far too serious with their black outfits and somber gazes.

"This is Seamus." Sadie hugged Seamus, and he gave her a shy, boyish grin. "And these are his friends, Ian and Connor, and their mate, Zoey. They all saved my life tonight."

Vera studied all of them for a time and then nodded. "Very well. Come on in, all of you."

Sadie and Seamus entered the house, with the others following behind. In a few minutes, coffee was brewing and Vera was passing out freshly made caramel coffee cake.

"Newly mated?" Vera asked Ian and Connor as they dug into their big slices of the cake.

"Yes, ma'am," Ian replied. Connor, the devil, simply grinned at Vera. Sadie expected her grandmother to be flustered by his cheekiness. Instead she sighed and patted the side of his face. "You remind me of Christopher."

With everyone seen to, Vera plopped down in her overstuffed armchair by the fire and faced the group. "So, I'm supposing Sadie told you about my mate."

"She did," Seamus confirmed. "She said that he could stand out in the sun like me after he drank your blood."

"Yes. And your heartbeat will come back at times." Vera suddenly smiled. "And you have the ability to change."

"Change?" Ian and Connor said in unison.

"Into a fox."

Connor chortled. "Brilliant. Bloody brilliant." He didn't stop until Zoey elbowed him in the stomach and he choked on his coffee cake.

"Christopher and I discovered all this during that one week we had together. It was incredible, but we thought it was a one-in-a-million pairing. It's why I never told you, Sadie. If vampires knew about it, they would want extra powers, and they would be searching for their mates among us, and not all of them would be good like my Christopher or like you, Seamus. There were also many who believed a mating between two supernatural races was unnatural and should be stopped. Many cross-breed mated pairs were murdered over the centuries. Sadie's mating to Seamus must be kept a secret. I won't have her life put at risk." She fixed the vampires with a stern gaze.

"Understood," Ian replied. "We won't tell anyone. But I'm curious—what is your mate's full name?"

"Christopher Holt," she said. "He was passing through. He said he could never come back, that his master was a vengeful creature. He couldn't escape her."

"Holt?" Seamus shared a look with his friends. "Excuse me." He stood and exited the room, leaving Sadie and Vera baffled.

"Did I say something wrong?" Vera asked.

"No, it's just that... We know him. He was part of Cassandra's coven. He was assigned to her holdings in New York City for the last ten years. He'll be free now that she's dead. I bet he'll want to come back here for you."

Vera's face lit with excitement for an instant, but then just as quickly it wilted. "He won't wish to see me. I'm too old." She touched the fine wrinkles around her eyes and mouth.

"You're his mate," Connor told her. "He'll want you no matter what, with all his heart."

Sadie reached out and took her grandmother's hand, giving it a squeeze. Seamus returned to the room, and all eyes turned to him.

"I caught him headed to JFK to board a plane. He's coming back for you, Vera. The moment Cassandra died, her control died with her."

Vera covered her mouth with her hands, her eyes now sparkling with tears.

"Excuse me." She fled the room.

Sadie lunged after her, but Seamus caught her by the waist and pulled her onto his lap. "Let her go. She needs time to adjust."

"I hope she'll be okay."

"She will be. I only talked to him briefly, but Chris said he has been researching vampire and shifter matings for the last sixty years. He said if she drinks his blood weekly, she'll start to de-age. She'll eventually look like she's in her midtwenties."

"What?" Sadie gasped.

Seamus grinned. "It's the vampire's gift. You give us sunlight and shifting. We give you youthful immortality."

"Wow," Zoey muttered. "That's incredible."

"Life is incredible, isn't it?" Ian murmured as he held Zoey in his embrace. Connor stood on the other side of Zoey, slipping a hand around her waist.

Sadie, still overwhelmed with everything, was ready to faint on her feet. "We have plenty of spare rooms. Why don't you all rest for the day?"

"That sounds good. Chris will be here in the early evening." Seamus rose from the couch and carried Sadie to her bedroom.

"How do you know which is mine?" she asked as he lowered her to the plush comforter.

"Your scent, my love." He pulled back the covers and gently stripped off her clothes. Then he did the same with his own. She thought she would be too tired, but the moment his naked body settled in beside her, she couldn't stop herself. Her heat was over, but her fox still needed to reaffirm her mate was alive and well. She licked his shoulder before playfully biting him. He groaned in delight and nuzzled her temple before feathering kisses over her cheek to her ear.

They spent an hour kissing, stroking, and learning one another in ways they hadn't had time to before. His mouth on hers was magic. He sipped from her lips as though she were a rare wine, and she basked in the taste of him and the feel of his hard body against hers as he pinned her to the mattress. By the time he entered her, she was almost frantic, despite her exhaustion.

They shared a moan as their bodies joined, fusing like two metals in a smithy's forge. She lightly dug her nails into his back as he claimed her, relishing the pleasure as her heart, body, and soul became as one with his. He gazed down at her in that boyish way of his that tugged at her heart and made her fall even deeper in love with him.

"You're mine now, my little vixen," he murmured. "Forever and always." She laughed and closed her eyes as her body burst with ecstasy.

Hours later, as dawn crested the horizon, she allowed the vixen to take over and shifted in her bed, becoming a small red fox. Seamus sensed her change, and he reached into the sunshine to touch her red fur. She arched her back into his touch. A moment later, his eyes widened as his own body began to shift, contorting and changing until a handsome male fox stood on the mattress beside her. His tail stood up, its white tip twitching as his ears swiveled. Sadie pounced on him, yipping in excitement as they rolled on the bed. She playfully kicked him off her and tackled him, biting his neck and ears until he was comfortable playing back with her.

She leapt off the bed and jumped out the open window of the bedroom. He followed her as she trotted into the forest. She threw back her head and let out a call for him. Seamus stared at her a moment, then responded with his own. Her heart jumped in pure joy. She had her mate at long last. She ran through the trees, hopping over gnarled roots and ducking beneath bushes as he followed behind until they reached the stream. They played in the shallows, feasting on the minnows and lapping at the crisp water before they settled down together on the banks of the river in the bright morning sun.

The foxes shared images in their heads, their connection growing deeper as the minutes passed. For the first time in her life, Sadie understood what true happiness was. It wasn't because she was mated. It was because for the first time, she loved who she was. Being a shifter was no longer a solitary burden to conceal from others—it was a blessing. A joyous gift to share and revel in. To know oneself and embrace oneself, *that* was love. She nuzzled Seamus's ear, and he rubbed his cheek against hers.

I am yours, Seamus. Your little vixen. Now and always.

~

***Several hours** later*

Sadie and Seamus stood on the porch, watching the black SUV with dark tinted windows come to a stop in front of the house. Vera stood beside Sadie, her hands trembling.

"Oh God...," she whispered. "Oh God, I'm not ready. He won't want me."

Sadie put an arm around her grandmother's shoulders. "He will. I know it."

A tall, dark-haired man stepped out of the car. Just like Seamus, Ian, and Connor, he had that otherworldly appeal that seemed to come with all vampires. He shut the door and gazed at Vera a long moment, his eyes focused only on her.

"Vera?"

"Chris?"

Seamus pulled Sadie back a bit, giving her grandmother room as the handsome vampire walked toward them.

"My God," Christopher murmured. "You're more beautiful than the day I met you." He moved up the steps and reached for Vera's wrinkled face, cupping it. Tears streamed down her cheeks.

"You always were an old liar," Vera said, openly starting to cry. "You can't want me, not like this."

Sadie clutched Seamus's arm, even more desperate to have someone to hold on to.

"But I do. You have been my everything from the day we met, and I've never stopped missing you, *loving* you." He tilted Vera's face up and kissed her. Vera was stiff for only a moment before she melted into Christopher's arms.

Sadie wiped away her tears and buried her face in Seamus's chest. Her grandmother had suffered so much, lost her husband, her son and daughter-in-law, a life with a mate. Now she would have a second chance.

"Will he tell her? About the de-aging?" she asked Seamus as he led her back inside so Vera had a moment alone with her mate.

"He will, once she has adjusted. It might take a day for her to calm down."

Ian, Connor, and Zoey were waiting for them inside.

"How's Chris?" Ian asked.

"Good, I suppose. He didn't say a word to me. He and Vera are catching up." Seamus chuckled. "So, where are you three headed to now?"

"Denver." Conner frowned a little, as if hesitant as to what he would say next. "You know, you could join us. Plenty of homes are for sale in our neighborhood."

"Oh yes!" Zoey almost jumped in joy. "Sadie, please consider it! It would be nice to have a girls' night out while the boys watch football."

Sadie grinned. "That would be nice. But I need to

make sure my grandmother and Christopher work out before I could leave."

Sadie looked toward the front door. She could make out Vera and Christopher whispering to each other through the shadows cast by their silhouettes against the screen door.

Seamus leaned down to kiss Sadie's cheek. "Have I told you I love you?" he whispered in her ear. He caught one of her hands and linked their fingers.

She squeezed his hand. "Yes, but don't let that stop you from saying it again."

"I love you."

Inside, her vixen was dancing. Was it possible to feel such joy and not perish from it? She was certain life could never be more wonderful or perfect than it was right now. Who knew a shifter and a vampire could fall in love?

But wasn't that just it, though? With love, *anything* was possible.

It had been ten years since Dracen had left his pack in Montana, and there was no telling what he would find when he returned.

He spent two days traveling alongside the highways, staying out of sight of cars as he headed home in wolf form. He'd wanted to take Ulrich's truck, but Ulrich had hidden the keys, and Dracen couldn't find them. So he'd decided to travel in the form he'd always been more comfortable with anyway. He'd spent more time in wolf skin than human skin in the last ten years, and he preferred to have his wolf senses on their highest alert while he headed back toward potentially dangerous territory.

For the entire journey, he worried what might have become of the pack that had once belonged to his father. Would the other young wolves who'd been like brothers to him still be there, or had they been rooted out? Would they support him if he challenged for position as alpha? He didn't know. But it was time to find out. He'd been hiding long enough.

Dracen hit the outskirts of Livingston, Montana, just as dusk fell. Farmers and ranchers around here were quick to pull a shotgun when they saw a wolf or a coyote, so he kept away from open fields until he reached the city. He scented the air, sniffing for food among the various smells. He'd survived on wild rabbits on his way, but he was hungry for human food now. Before he'd left Colorado, he'd taken his wallet, using an old werewolf travel trick of putting it in a harness with elastic straps around his chest that adjusted as he shifted between man and wolf.

Dracen paused, hiding by a dumpster in an alley, watching the cars drive up and down the street, debating what to do next.

A woman exited a bakery across the street. She was petite, with enticing curves and long blonde hair that tumbled down her shoulders. She carried a bag of...he sniffed the air.

Doughnuts! Score!

He was craving a good glazed doughnut or bear claw. He followed the woman carrying the heavenly smelling doughnut bag to her car. There was a chance he might scare her into throwing doughnuts at him. He crossed the street, using the shadows to conceal himself as he followed her into the parking lot. She stopped next to her car and fumbled with her keys. They fell to the ground in a loud clatter.

"Shit." She bent over to grab the keys. As a result, she never saw the man coming at her from behind.

He wore a black ski mask and held a gun. Instinctively, Dracen growled and leapt out of the darkness, sinking his teeth into the man's arm and knocking him to the ground. The woman screamed and fell against the side of her car, clutching her purse. Her eyes were wide with terror as Dracen and the man struggled.

A shot rang out.

Pain hit Dracen like a train as a bullet tore through him. He yelped but didn't let go. He gave the man's arm a vicious shake, digging his teeth as deep as he could.

"Let go of me, you piece of shit!" the man bellowed. He smacked Dracen in the head with the butt of the pistol. The pain dazed Dracen, and he released the man's arm. The man scrambled to his feet and turned to the woman. She held up her phone, already having called someone.

The attacker cursed and vanished into the shadows. Dracen hobbled toward the woman, wanting to see that she was all right. Then he'd slip away and find a place to recover.

"Oh my God," the woman whimpered. "You saved me. You beautiful creature." She held out a hand to him, hesitant but hopeful, the way humans always did when trying to befriend dogs. But he wasn't a dog, he was a werewolf. Not that he wanted to hurt her—he wasn't a wild animal like Ulrich and Cyrus. But once she realized he wasn't some stray dog, she'd freak out.

Dracen knew he should leave, and fast, but found that he couldn't. He was transfixed as he got a good look at the woman's face. Honey-blonde hair, dark-brown eyes, and lips that looked ripe for a man's kiss. These were not features he normally paid attention to while he was a wolf. But there was something about her eyes, a fuzziness, almost blank, but not quite. And then he realized when she squinted hard at him.

She is blind...or close to it.

Fascinated, he hobbled closer, whining softly as he fought off a wave of pain and bumped his nose into her hand and accepted the gentle pat she gave him. Her hand shook, so he held very still, despite the pain. But her scent soothed him like nothing he'd ever encountered before.

"Oh, you poor thing. You're hurt." The woman patted him again and then scratched behind his ears. He would've wagged his tail, but the world around him began to spin. He toppled into her lap as everything went dark.

THANK you so much for reading *His Little Vixen*! I hope you enjoyed Sadie and Seamus's story! If you're excited to read Dracen's story called *Pack Rules*...

be sure to sign up for my newsletter: https://lauren smithbooks.com/free-books-and-newsletter/

And follow me on Bookbub to get an instant release day alert: https://www.bookbub.com/authors/lauren-smith

Turn *the page to read an excerpt from my book Grigori: A Royal Dragon Romance, set in the same universe as The Love Bites series, turn the page! You won't want to miss a sexy Russian Dragonshifter seducing an American professor who's seeking proof that dragons exist.*

"H*ere there be dragons.*"

—Note on a map from the Age of Exploration, regarding
Terra Incognito.

Blue and silver scales whispered against grass as the giant beast crawled across the field toward Madelyn Haynes. Rain lashed her skin and lightning laced the skies. Smoke billowed from the beast's nostrils, and his amber eyes narrowed to dangerous slits as it crept closer. There was no escaping. The creature had finally found her and would destroy her. It had already killed tonight and would kill again. Ash infused the air, the scent of smoke choking her. Fear and rage filled her, drowning her with the overwhelming sensations until she was torn between two instincts: fight or flight. Her skin tingled, the feeling building until it felt like she was on fire.

A man was shouting . . . *"Run!"*

The beast turned away from her, searching for the person who'd cried out a warning but it was no use. The creature would kill her too once it found her.

There was no way she would survive. She was going to die . . .

"No!" The word was a silent scream upon her lips as she tried to run.

Boom!

Madelyn jolted upright, her mouth open in a strangled shout. The covers of her bed were wrapped around her legs, and she kicked out trying to free herself. Panting, she clutched her head as a dull throbbing ache beat behind her temples. She breathed in and out, focusing on each breath and the tranquility it gave her before the headache subsided and her heart stopped pounding against her ribs.

Then she turned on the light by the bed in her small hotel room and reached for her sketch pad and pencil. Using pillows to prop herself up she flicked to a fresh page and began to draw. The lines came easily, as they always did when she had the nightmares of the beast. It left such a vivid image in her mind that she had no trouble bringing it to life on the page. As the sketch began to develop, she knew what she would see. A serpentine creature with an elegant snout, two large wings and a long tail that could snap back and forth like a whip.

A dragon.

For as long as she could remember, whenever it rained, she dreamed of that same dragon. Rain, scales, lightning, and a crashing sonic boom that rattled her awake.

Madelyn studied tonight's dragon. It was blue and silver with a deep sapphire underbelly. The webbing of its wings was a fainter, almost icy blue. It had a large, almost lizard-like frill that fanned up around its head like a lion's mane which was that same glacial blue as its wings. It was an eerily beautiful creature with fierce eyes and sharp talons and was in a predatory crouch as though ready to hunt her down. Madelyn's hand trembled as she set the pencil down and stared at the dragon. A part of her had hoped that leaving the United States—and changing her surroundings—would make her feel less trapped, less hunted. But the nightmares had followed her.

She was still being hunted.

She'd come all the way to Russia to save her career. As a professor in medieval mythology, she had been reading and researching dragons for the last five years. But lately she'd become convinced, as insane as it sounded, that dragons might have been real at some point in history. She was hoping to prove that some remnants of dinosaurs had remained alive into the time of humans, and that could explain the unique collection of global mythology around dragons. How else could dragon myths around the world have such eerie similarities? Something told her there was a kernel of truth to each myth she'd come across, but she had to find a way to prove it.

Or else I'm fired.

Ellwood University had given her a three-month sabbatical to either pursue her theory and prove it, or drop it and attempt to tie her research to more traditional projects. Madelyn had collected her meager savings and rented this hotel room by the month in the Tverskaya district of Moscow.

Outside her window she could see the distance lights of the city and hear the low steady hum of traffic. Moscow was so different from her small town of Shelby, Michigan. Instead of a Russian concrete jungle and tangle of complex cityscapes and police sirens at night, the Midwestern air was filled with the hum of crickets and the throaty songs of frogs in the ponds. Some nights the breeze from Lake Michigan would slip through the windows and soothe her as she slept. Even the winters in Michigan felt pure, clean, not like the dark, dirty snow-covered streets of post-soviet Moscow.

With a shiver of longing for home, Madelyn set the sketchbook aside and glanced at the clock. It was 6 AM. There was little point in staying in bed for another hour. She had to visit the Russian State Library and a few small antiquarian bookstores which could take up most of the day. She'd been here one week and had settled into a routine. *Sleep. Research. Eat. Research. Home. Sleep.*

She had come to Moscow alone and was hesitant about going out on her own after dark. She spent most of her evenings cuddled up in the armchair by her bed, reading. It was certainly safer than going out. Madelyn needed to feel safe. She feared the unknown, and what might be around the corner.

A therapist had once diagnosed her airily with a generalized fear of the unknown, citing trauma from her parents' deaths. She had been two years old, too young to remember the details though she'd been with them when they'd died. Too young to know her own name or where she came from. Neither of her parents had IDs when the police found her in the wrecked car that had rolled into a ditch during a storm. Her name, "Madelyn", had come from the name stitched onto her baby blanket. Her adoptive parents, the Haynes's, had wanted her to keep that name.

Thoughts of her birth parents always made Madelyn sad and oddly helpless. She wished she could have done something to save them from the car crash. She knew that there was nothing a baby could have done, but it didn't erase the helplessness. For a long moment, Madelyn watched the rain outside and rubbed one hand absently on her chest where her heart ached. And then, she did what she'd always done. She buried the memories and the pain and turned her thoughts to her research. It was the best distraction. There was nothing like wandering through the stacks of a library and letting the musty scent of ancient books overwhelm her. It was one of the reasons she'd been drawn to history when she was in college. Surrounding herself with the past, she knew what had happened, and couldn't be shocked or surprised . . . was comforting.

Madelyn crawled out of bed and stripped out of her clothes before she jumped into the small shower, cringing as she expected the icy blast of the spray. There was only so much hot water before it turned cold she couldn't stand a cold shower in October in Russia.

Two hours later, she was dressed and had filled her backpack with notebooks and other research related materials. When she stepped out on the street in front of her hotel, her nose twitched as it picked up the harsh scents of the city. People bustled past her in a frenzied haste to reach their jobs, and for a strange moment Madelyn felt rooted in place as humanity flowed around her. An eerie sense of being watched made the tiny hairs on the back of her neck raise up.

Of course she was being watched. This city was home to millions of people; someone would always be looking at her no matter what. The uneasy sensation inside her didn't disappear, even when she hailed a cab and headed for the Russian State Library.

The State Library was a beautiful architectural cross between Soviet era design and classical design, which called back the days of the Czars. The smell of musty texts and recently cleaned marble steps were a welcome mix of aromas that always calmed Madelyn.

She walked up the white stairs to the upper decks of the library, her eyes dancing from the blue marble columns to the endless shelves.

17.5 million books were here . . . Her heart sped up at the sheer thought of having a world of infinite stories at her fingertips. But she wasn't here to see their vast array of novels. She was here for one book. A heavily guarded tome that required supervision whenever it was handled.

She kept walking and left the modern rooms behind before reaching a wing of the library that housed antiquarian collections. One of the collection areas was a beautiful two-story room with gleaming walnut bookcases illuminated by hanging golden globes of light. A slightly domed ceiling was painted with scenes of Greek mythology, the gods on Olympus displaying their power and might.

A security guard stood at the back of the room by a small reception desk and he waved her over. He greeted her with a warm smile and spoke something in Russian which she thought sounded like hello. She was still listening to her Russian audiotapes and hadn't picked it up as quickly as she'd hoped.

"Good morning," she greeted back. He was different than the guard from yesterday.

"Ahh, English, I help you?" he asked in with a heavy Russian accent.

Madelyn smiled. She'd been relieved to discover that many of the guards were fluent in English to a degree. She knew enough of modern Russian to get by but her specialty was the rare dialect East Old Slavic which she used to read older Russian primary resources.

"I'd like to check this book out please." She retrieved a small piece of paper with the name of the edition in English and Russian and its location on the shelves. The guard read the card and then his brown eyes looked from it to her face, studying her.

"This volume? You are sure?" he asked, his voice was oddly hushed and his face drained of color. He stroked his security badge on his chest with one finger as though he'd done it a thousand times when nervous. He glanced around the room, which was almost entirely empty save for another researcher, an elderly man, who was buried in a stack of what looked to be medieval texts. The man glanced up at them, squinted, and pushed his glasses up his nose before returning to his work. The guard stared at the man for a long moment before he turned his focus back to Madelyn.

"Please, miss, I could get many other books for you, but this one . . . Are you sure?" It was the second time he'd asked that question, and it made her skin prickle.

"Yes. That one." Madelyn assured him. Why was he so protective of this one? This entire room was filled with ancient texts that with proper care could be viewed by researchers. The guard sighed slowly, his face turning red as he nodded to himself and muttered in Russian.

Now she was feeling really anxious. She'd checked out several tomes yesterday but hadn't discovered this particular text until she was pouring over the ancient collection of card catalogues that looked as though they'd been written half a century before. There on the yellowed paper of the cards, in ink that was turning brown, she'd read the name of the volume *My Year With Dragons*. The library had been about to close and she only had time to scribble down the book's information before a guard politely escorted her out of antiquarian collection area. Surely today this guard would let her check it out . . . it was just a book after all.

The guard stared at the card again and then nodded. "*Dah*, okay, we get you this one. Sit, please." He pointed to a small research table near one of the vast glass windows. Then he took a card and walked over to the shelves on the opposite side of the room.

While he retrieved the book, Madelyn set out her notebook and pens with shaking hands before she donned a pair of library approved white gloves to handle the books safely. Why was the guard so hesitant to give it to her? From the text's description in the card catalogue that she'd be able to translate, it was a memoir of an English man who had spent time in Russia. There was no political or social discourse in it that could prompt a

Russian security officer to be concerned . . . But he had been. The man had looked ill at the thought of fetching that tome.

She peeped at the guard from the corner of her eye. He unlocked a glass case on one of the shelves, his head cocked to the side as he squinted at the titles on the spines. Then he used his index finger to gently tug a shorter leather-bound edition free of the case. Once he had it in his hands, he didn't immediately come over to her. For several seconds he stood there, holding the book and staring at her. His lips were pressed tight in a grimace as he finally walked over to her.

"Please be careful. This is special book." He held out the leather bound tome and Madelyn accepted it. Her skin tingled again as she felt the smooth leather in her palms but she hid her reaction. The guard nodded at her again and then walked back to his station.

Madelyn's skin continued to tingle as she lifted the leather tome to get a closer look. The cover was made of thick leather, bare of any titles or identifying marks except the initials *J.B.* in the bottom right corner. Madelyn smoothed her fingertips over the initials and opened the front cover. The title was written on the front page in pen and ink. Not in typeface.

My Year With Dragons—A personal collection of observations about my time spent with the Barinov family, by James Barrow. Dated 1821.

Madelyn whispered the words. It was written in

English, and James Barrow could be English or American. She held the text in one hand and made a note in her notebook before she turned to the next page.

Her heart stuttered to a stop in her chest.

Three pencil sketches depicted the faces of three different men. Names were scrawled beneath each intimate portrait.

Mikhail, Rurik and Grigori. The Barinov Brothers.

The first man, Mikhail, seemed more brooding, his hair dark and his eyes almost black. He seemed worried, but he was attractive and even the shadows that haunted his eyes were enchanting. In the second drawing, the man named Rurik had dark hair and mischievous eyes, with a playful, charming grin on his lips that outshone the white scar drawn from above his right eyebrow down to his cheek as though he'd been slashed. He looked like a bit of a troublemaker but the thought made her smile.

Her eyes lingered longest over the sketch of the man named Grigori. Something about him stilled her, like the moment she stood outside on the first snowfall of winter. There was a strange whispering at the back of her mind, a collection of hushed voices that she couldn't seem to hear clearly enough to understand. She was fascinated by the man's handsome face, the pale hair and light eyes. There was a melancholy beauty to his lips, and an almost rueful smile barely hinted in the drawing—as though he had sat still long enough to assist the artist but as soon as he was able, he'd move again.

While all three men were intriguing, it was Grigori that Madelyn's eyes came back to over and over. Something about his face . . . Like a half-remembered dream. Deep inside her, there was a stirring, as though a part of her she never knew existed had awoken. The voices didn't stop that whispering and Madelyn couldn't help but wonder if she was going mad. Between the dreams at night and now this . . . She drew a deep breath in and let it out, slow and measured, calming herself.

Stay focused on the research.

"Grigori," she test his name upon her lips, finding she liked the way it sounded, the syllables strong and yet soft.

She wanted this sketch. The compulsion to possess his likeness was too strong. She glanced about the room and saw the guard was on his phone, texting and not looking her way. Sneaking her cell phone out, she flicked on the camera and snapped a hasty picture of each of the brothers before she put it back in her purse. Hands trembling, she turned the page again, forcing herself to look totally calm and not like she'd been taking photographs of a protected manuscript.

The next page was a diary entry dated March 16, 1821.

"Dragons are real . . ." The first words of the entry made her body shiver and a sudden chill shot down her spine. She forced herself to keep reading and couldn't help but wonder what James Barrow meant. Dragons weren't real, at least not in the fire and brimstone sense. She was convinced that some extinct reptile species were

behind the legends, but there was no such thing as *real* dragons.

"I met the Barinov brothers in Moscow and learned they were not mortal men . . . they were possessed of strange abilities. The touch of fire, the breath of smoke, the eyes that glowed . . ."

What the hell? Madelyn reread the last few sentences. What was Barrow saying? She'd expected the volume to recount tales of large serpents or lizards that Barrow must have encountered on his journey. As a naturalist, he would have been out in the field exploring different species of animals, and he could have easily glimpsed an ancient breed of reptile that looked dragon-like. The Komodo dragon was a modern example of what many rural cultures still believed were the descendants of drag-ons. It was part of her theory for her research. But Barrow wasn't talking about Komodos or any other type of reptile. He was discussing men . . . Men who had powers. Perhaps the word dragon was simply a metaphor Barrow was using?

She glanced down the page and saw a smaller drawing of a man's hand and what looked like an elabo-rate ring. When Madelyn peered at it more closely, she recognized the style. The metal of the ring had been formed into the shape of a serpent biting its own tail, the symbol for eternity or the cycle of renewal. An *ouroboros*. Another dragon connection, but still not the type of dragon she was searching for.

Rather than read the rest of the journal entry, she turned the next several pages and paused when she came across a full page sketch. The drawing of a sleek, serpentine beast perched on a rock outcropping overlooking the sea made her breath catch as much as Grigori's portrait had. The beast sat back on its haunches and its large wings were flared wide, the clawed tips arching outward as though it was ready to fly. A barb-tipped tail curled around its legs. It was both a beautiful beast and a creature of nightmares, with gleaming teeth ready to snap. Reptilian slitted eyes stared straight ahead at her. The beast in her dreams came rushing back, the hiss of smoke escaping the nostrils, the puffs of breath as he prepared to spew fire, the lashing tail . . .

Beneath the sketch was one word. *"Grigori."*

But the sketch was of a man, not a dragon . . . Was this one of the men with supposed powers?

Whatever this journal was, it was clearly the workings of a man prone to flights of fancy and not a real naturalist. Disappointment made her heart drop to her feet and her shoulders slump. She'd been so hopeful to find a book that could show an anthropological connection to the dinosaurs or explain the worldwide dragon mythology. But this journal was not the answer.

Even though she wanted to keep reading, it wasn't a good idea. Many a good scholar who lost their way down a strange research rabbit hole had to find their way back to good solid research. She refused to let this one odd little book stump her. Better to put it back and move on. Still . . . she wanted just a few more photographs of the book; it couldn't hurt to read it over as long as she didn't use it for her research.

She surreptitiously took pictures of the next twenty pages before she hid her cellphone back in her backpack. Closing the book, she started at the leather surface, wishing she didn't have to give it back. Indecision flitted through her, but there was no real choice. It wasn't hers, and she couldn't keep it. With a sigh, she rose from her research table and walked back over to the security station and held the book out the guard.

"Finished?" he asked, his eyes fixing on the book rather than her as though he was anxious to snatch it out of her hands.

"Yes, it wasn't what I was looking for." She almost didn't let go when he tried to pull the book away from her. Finally the leather journal slipped through her fingers.

"Thank you," she said to the guard. With a heavy heart, she returned to her study station and collected her notebooks and papers before removing her gloves and tucking them back in her bag. Each step away from Barrow's mysterious journal left her feeling cold and distanced in a way that made little sense. A soft feminine voice, like the hum of a murmur from a dream teased her mind.

He has the answers but you're too afraid to see . . .

Madelyn shook off the thought. The notes in Barrow's journal were impossible to believe. He clearly didn't know what he was talking about. He was rambling on about men with powerful abilities and drawing beasts more suited to a role-playing fantasy computer game than he was about creatures that tied to real mythology.

She would have to start back at the catalog again, but she had no energy to hunch over the little metal filing cabinets squinting at poorly scribbled titles and book descriptions the rest of the day.

Maybe I could take a day off. Wander around the library a bit and explore.

The architecture was beautiful and she hadn't really had a chance to examine it before. As she exited the antiquarian room she glanced back one last time. The security guard was holding the journal, and he was speaking into his cell phone. He was also staring right at *her*.

That sense of being watched and being talked about was too strong this time to ignore. The guard said something into the phone and rather than put the book back on its shelf, he set it down and put a hand on his gun holster at his hip.

"Miss, please come back," he said, taking a meaningful step in her direction. "My superior wishes to speak to you. You cannot leave."

"He does? Why?" she asked, her muscles tensing and her hands tightening on her bag.

"The book you chose, he has questions . . ." The guard

said, his gaze darting around her as though expecting someone to come and help him. "Sit down, now." His tone was more forceful than before.

Madelyn knew she should stay put, talk to him . . . but her instincts suddenly roared to life and the only thought that flashed through her head was *run . . . run fast*. Body shaking, she stumbled on trembling legs to flee.

She shoved open the door and sprinted down the hall, hitting the top of the long set of stairs at a brisk run. Everything around her seemed to blur, and her heart was pounding hard enough to explode from her chest. Covering the steps in seconds, she forced herself to slow when she realized people were staring at her. That was the last thing she needed, people seeing a panicked woman fleeing a Russian library like a crazy person. It was a conspiracy theory in the making.

Her breath was labored and her body was shaking with a surge of adrenaline as she tried to walk calmly out of the library. The crowded streets were a blessing as she melted into the flow of people. She only looked back once and caught a glimpse of the security guard from the collections room. He stood at the top of the Russian State Library steps, his gaze scanning the crowd. He was still on his cell phone, talking rapidly.

Lowering herself by hunching over, Madelyn slipped down a side street to catch her breath. What the hell just happened? Sure, she'd snuck a few pictures of a text, but why would he chase her? She hadn't seen any rules about no photography in that section of the library. Why had the guard chased her?

What about James Barrow's book was so dangerous that men would look for her?

Grigori's face and the body of the fierce dragon like beast flashed across her mind. *What have I stumbled onto?*

Want to know what happens next? Grab it HERE!

CHAPTER

TWO

"Peace, Kent! Come not between the dragon and his wrath."

—William Shakespeare, *The Tragedy of King Lear*

Grigori Barinov stood in front of the floor-to-ceiling windows in his executive office, staring out over the city of Moscow. Body alert, every muscle rigid, the expensive gray wool suit he wore felt tight as he shifted. Below him, people were passing on the streets. A flash of silver caught his attention. It was the wink of a diamond earring dangling from a well-dressed woman's ear. With eyes that were ten times as powerful as a mortal's, he scanned the streets, absorbing every detail.

Searching . . .

For the last few days, his senses had picked up on

something in his city. A creature he didn't recognize. It made him restless. Moscow was filled with supernatural beings—werewolves, vampires, shifters of all kinds, and magically gifted humans were all present—but none of them fired up his instincts. No, he'd never felt this before in his life, but he knew in his gut what it was. An enemy was in his city, a creature that posed a threat to him. As a dragonshifter, few creatures in this world could give him pause and put him on his guard. He only wished he knew what sort of beast it was so he could hunt it down and remove the threat.

The sapphire dragon tattoo on his forearm itched, but he didn't scratch it. He knew the dragon inside of him was trying to warn him to stay on his guard. The phone on his desk buzzed and his personal assistant, Alexis spoke.

"Mr. Barinov, you have a call from the Russian State Library."

Every muscle in his body tensed. There was only one reason anyone from the Russian State Library would be calling him. That damn book by James Barrow. He'd been too softhearted and Barrow had been so earnest. He'd gone against his better judgment and allowed the Englishman to spend a year studying him and his brothers. And he'd been paying for it for the last 200 years. He'd been lucky Barrow's heirs had sent him the journal. Thankfully, it had never been sent to a publisher; Barrow had kept his word about his writings remaining a secret.

I should've burned it. But he hadn't been able to.

Barrow had become a friend and Grigori hadn't wanted to destroy the memory. There was also something fascinating about reading an insightful human's observations about him and his brothers.

He couldn't leave it at his office or his home in the country. His enemies had frequently broken into both places more than once, searching for anything they could use against him. He'd thought he'd be clever and tuck it away in a library amid other obscure texts that no one ever looked at in a guarded collection. It had been safe all these years, hiding in plain sight. Until now.

"Mr. Barinov?" Alexis queried again.

"Put the call through." He turned away from the window and walked over to his mahogany desk just as the phone rang.

He answered. "Yes?"

"Mr. Barinov, my name is Yuri. I'm a guard for antiquarian book room at the Russian State Library." A man spoke, his voice hushed and anxious.

"Yes." Grigori waited, his patience on a razor's edge.

"When I first took over security for this room I was given strict and confidential instructions to call you if anyone ever came asking about a certain title in the collection. Someone checked out the *Barrow* book, Mr. Barinov."

Grigori closed his eyes, holding his breath for a moment. "And?"

"I followed protocol. She did not leave the library with

the book. But . . ." The guard hesitated. "She was taking pictures. I have no instructions regarding pictures." The phone cracked as Grigori's temper flared.

"Pictures?"

"Yes. She was using her phone." The guard's voice wavered as though he sensed Grigori's building rage.

Pictures. Fuck, if any evidence of his existence was discovered and exposed in the world of mortals it would put a target on his back and that of his two brothers. The magical world knew of his family, the last three brothers in ancient bloodline of Russian Imperial Dragon shifters, but the rest of the world didn't know . . . *Couldn't know.*

"Can you detain her until I arrive?" he asked the guard.

"But she's leaving now—"

"Stop her!" Grigori barked. The other end of the phone was full of panting, the flapping of rubber soled shoes on marble, a muffled shout for someone to stop. Grigori tried to picture the library in his mind, wondering why the guard couldn't catch up with this woman. Finally the footsteps stopped, and Grigori heard the sounds of streets of the city muted beneath the guard's gasping for breath.

"She ran—I couldn't catch her before she left the library. She's gone. But I have the book."

Grigori sighed. "I will come to collect it. When I do, I want every detail you have about this woman. Her name, where she's from, *everything.*"

"Yes, Mr. Barinov," the guard replied, still breathless.

Grigori slammed the phone down and cursed. His hand was white-hot from his temper and he'd left burn marks on his expensive new phone. With a growl, he pressed the intercom button

"Alexis, please have someone replace my phone in the office. This one met with an unfortunate accident."

A second later his receptionist opened the door, leaning against it to look at him in concern. His dragon perked up beneath his skin at the sight of the woman's killer legs. She was staring at him, the perpetually hungry look in her eyes always an open invitation to share her bed, but he'd never once been tempted. Sure, he'd noticed, and his instincts, so close to the surface, never let him ignore a beautiful woman. But things had changed over the last hundred years. His skin didn't prickle with awareness and excitement. His dragon didn't growl with arousal the way it had in his youth.

No one had truly tempted him enough in a long time to let his bestial urges run free. Had he been in a better mood a smile would have curved his lips. As a younger dragon, he would have bedded several succulent mortals in a day, breaking bed frames as he gripped the wood to keep from harming the females while he fucked them into oblivion. Now his bed was empty of companions, but he wouldn't sleep with just any woman. Not anymore.

"Another accident Mr. Barinov?" Alexis purred as she approached his desk.

"Yes, please order me a replacement."

"Of course." She held out a hand and he handed over the destroyed phone.

Her expensive perfume rolled off her in thick waves. The decayed floral aromas made his nose twitch even as she walked out of his office and closed the door behind her. He never liked perfumes. A woman's natural scent was a heady thing and shouldn't be ruined with perfumes.

He could almost hear his younger brother, Rurik, teasing him. *"As if you know anything about women anymore. You haven't had a woman in over a decade, brother. . ."*

It was true. He found women less and less appealing these last few centuries. His urge to mate, to find the one female in the world that was truly his, had started to drive him mad with frustration. When a dragon reached a certain age, they stopped running wild and craved the closeness of a long-term companion. Most dragons never found their true mates and settled to simply breed with other dragons for the sake of children and to cure loneliness.

His gaze dropped to a framed photo on his desk. It was one of the few of his parents in existence, from thirty years ago, just a few years before they died.

If I could be as lucky as them and find a true mate . . .

No mere woman would suit him. It had to be the right one, one chosen for him by destiny. He would know her by her addictive scent that would send his pulse racing and his blood pounding. If he kissed her, he would catch glimpses of her memories and she would see his. A bond would form the longer they spent together, making them inseparable.

I want that more than anything . . .

He was not going to be tempted by Alexis or any other woman. They would only pale in comparison to a woman who would truly belong to him. He wanted a woman of his own, one to share his heart and soul with. Despite being alive for almost three thousand years, he still hadn't found the one woman that was meant to be his.

The sad fact was he couldn't wait any longer. His once great family, the Barinovs, had included almost a thousand dragons.

Now we are only three. We are a dying breed.

The loneliness he was facing was slowly killing him, an immortal creature. The idea was almost laughable but it was true. A longing for a true mate had haunted him to the point that he was dreaming about her and waking up in the dark, his arms aching for a woman who was never there. He might never find the woman destiny had made for him. It was time to settle, and find a dragoness who could bare him children and continue the line, even if it meant he'd never know true love and completion.

"Mr. Barinov, is there anything else I can do for you?" Alexis asked, her suggestive tone telling him in no uncertain terms that she was offering herself to him if he was interested, which again, he wasn't. She wasn't his type. He liked his women with soft curves, a little petite with sunny smiles and warm hearts. He hadn't met a woman like that in Russian in over a hundred years . . . He was tired of Alexis throwing herself at him when he continually turned her down.

"No." He almost growled the word. Frustration slithered beneath his skin making him irritable enough to snap at her.

Alexis blinked, her face pale as a sheet as she backed out of the room. Smart woman. Dragons tempers were nasty things and it was best to stay clear when a dragon was fuming.

He pulled out his cell phone and dialed one of the few numbers he called with any frequency.

"Grigori? What's up?" His younger brother answered, his voice half-laughing as though he'd been chuckling when he'd answered the phone. The thought made Grigori's temper deflate somewhat as affection for Rurik swelled in his chest.

"Rurik, we have a situation."

"What is it? The Drakor family again?" His brother's tone turned gruff and serious.

Grigori stroked his chin as he replied. "No. They are abiding by our current treaty and staying to the eastern half of Russia." It was true enough. The Drakors were notorious for their egos, and if they had been causing trouble in his territory, he would have heard about it.

Rurik blew out disappointed breath. "I miss the battles. What I wouldn't give for the Drakors to put one foot on our soil . . ."

"You battle dragons," Grigori was torn between groaning and laughing. "Always wanting to start a fight." He loved his little brother, but he was the first to jump without looking—which often put their family in tense situations when it came to matters of diplomacy with other dragons.

Rurik was the family warrior, the one best suited for battle and to wage single combat against other dragons when territorial disputes arose. The Drakors were the other Russian Imperial breed of shifters that vied for dominance of Russia against his family. The Barinovs and Drakors had been enemies for centuries.

"So if it's not the Drakors, what's the matter?"

"Remember James Barrow?" Grigori turned back to his window once again, searching in vain for the creature he sensed but could not see.

"Of course. The Englishman who visited us in the Fire Hills. He was always drawing and scribbling away in that leather journal."

"Yes. A woman was taking pictures of his journal today at the Russian State Library."

"Fuck. That can't be good . . ."

"My thoughts exactly," Grigori affirmed. The journal was almost a handbook on dragons—their powers, their weaknesses—and it had dozens of pictures of the three of them specifically. They might as well have put a neon sign above his building saying *"Real Dragons Inside!"*

"Do you think she believes what he wrote down about us is true?"

"I have no idea, but no reason she has could be a good one. I'm going to the Library to collect the book now and learn everything I can about the woman who took the pictures. I want you to help me track her down."

"Meet me at the club once you have the book." Rurik hung up and Grigori slipped his phone back into the pocket of his trousers before he turned away from the window.

As he left his office, he ignored Alexis's hopeful wave and he took the elevator down to the first floor. Barinov Industries, the family company he created a hundred years ago, had withstood wars, famine, and the many regime changes of Russian governments over the years.

He was not going to let one woman with a cell phone camera destroy his empire. For the last eighty years especially, Grigori had suffered the charade of "retiring" every thirty years and leaving the company to his son, also named Grigori. He'd spend the next few decades pretending to age, dying his hair silver and having new passports and forged birth certificates. The intricate lies he laid in place to keep the company going had cost him time and energy. He would not let his work be ruined by some overly curious human female.

His car was pulled out in front with his driver ready to take him anywhere he wished.

"The Russian State Library," he ordered as he settled in the black leather seat of the sedan.

"Yes, Mr. Barinov." The driver pulled out in traffic and began to head towards the library.

Grigori barely looked at the passing scenery of Moscow, his entire being focused on this mystery woman. Why was she researching dragons, and how had she found out about Barrow's journal? She shouldn't have even been allowed to take it off the shelf. Grigori acquainted himself with the new library director and informed him that should anyone ask for the book he must be called immediately and they were not to check it out. The guard had clearly failed in his duties and Grigori would make sure the library director would have him fired.

The time had come to take Barrow's book home and destroy it once and for all. While he had fond memories of Barrow, the details and personal histories of him and his brothers must be protected and that meant burning the book to ash. And dealing with this woman.

The only mortals who knew of his existence, aside from the ones in service to his family, were supernatural hunters. Namely the international organization called the Brotherhood of the Blood Moon. Pesky creatures, hunters. They rarely came into dragon guarded territories; it was simply too dangerous. Maybe this woman was a hunter, or they had hired her to find and retrieve any info she could on his family. If that was the case, he had a very nice dungeon she could rot away in for the next fifty years.

"Here we are, Mr. Barinov."

Grigori climbed out and told the driver to wait for him. Then he quickly ascended the stairs and entered the library. The guard, Yuri, was waiting for him at the security desk.

"Mr. Barinov?" Yuri held out the faded leather bound journal and Grigori took it.

The leather was warm to the touch and he lifted it to his nose, inhaling. A lingering scent teased his nostrils, the feminine aroma inviting and enticing. For a long second Grigori simply drank in the rich smell . . . it was *pure*. The pheromone sweet, like ripe dragon fruit. He had not smelled something like that in some years. The woman was a *virgin* of childbearing age.

Must have her . . . Need to find her.

His body went rigid as the scent continued to plague and torture his nose with irresistible sweetness. If there was one thing besides a true mate that a dragon couldn't deny himself, it was a virgin. A growl began to rumble at the back of his throat as he pictured himself finding this woman and curling his arms around her and breathing in her scent before he seduced her.

The old Grigori, the wild beast he thought had vanished this last century, was roaring back to life. His dragon was pacing inside him, ready to be unleashed. He wanted to sink his teeth into this woman's neck and hold her still while he thrust into her over and over until she screamed with pleasure.

"Mr. Barinov?" Yuri interrupted the sudden lust and hunger in Grigori's thoughts.

"Who is she?" he demanded in a low growl.

Yuri swallowed hard and held out a photograph, a print of a security camera photo of a woman.

"She is American. Her name is Madelyn Haynes. She's a professor at an American university."

Grigori stared down at the colored photo. It was slightly blurry, but he could tell that the woman had long strawberry blond hair and soft features. An ordinary woman, yet there was something about her face that he found fascinating. The lush curve of her lips, a slightly upturned nose and eyes framed by dark lashes. He lived in a city where beauty was praised and often the only way to survive. This woman would not have been considered pretty by such standards, but Grigori liked her full curves and romantic features more than he did the harsh, bony runway models that populated the Russian nightclubs.

Yes, she would be quite a delight to lock away in his dungeon.

He turned away from the security booth and exited the library. Back inside his car, he texted Madelyn's information to his brother. Within a few minutes Rurik sent the address for a hotel near the Red Square. He texted

Rurik to meet him at the woman's hotel. He had a plan to trap their cunning little virgin and he was not going to let her escape.

ALEXIS PETROV SLIPPED into the ladies restroom close to her office in Barinov Industries. Flipping the lock on the door so no one else could come in, she checked beneath the stalls to make sure she was alone. This was one of the few places she could make a call without being seen on surveillance videos. She dialed a number on the screen, hit call and waited, her heart pounding.

"Drakor here." The deep, growling voice sent shivers through her.

Dimitri Drakor was a veritable god, much like her own boss Grigori Barinov, but Drakor had promised her things Barinov never would.

Sex and power.

It had been too tempting to agree to spy on her boss the moment Drakor had taken her to his bed and promised her the world. All she had to do was tell him what Barinov was up to. It was her boss's fault—if only he hadn't ignored her! She was a former model and she knew she was gorgeous.

How can he ignore me? Me? I walked runways in Milan and Moscow! Resentment prickled her beneath her skin and she scowled.

"Barinov just left his office. He received a call from the Russian State Library."

Drakor breathed softly on the other end of the line before replying.

"Do you know what he was going there for?"

Alexis flinched. "No. Only that the moment he hung up, he left. That means it's important, right?"

"Yes, perhaps," Drakor mused. "Call me immediately with any more news." Then the phone connection went dead.

Alexis stared at her reflection the mirror for a long moment, her eyes haunted and her face suddenly showing her age. All of the parties, the drugs, the nights with powerful men who never called the next day had been a waste. She was past her prime.

Desperation drives us all. She forced a false smile on her lips, unlocked the bathroom door and stepped outside. She needed to be ready for when Mr. Barinov returned.

"I do not care what comes after; I have seen dragons on the wind of morning."

—Ursula K. Le Guin

No one followed me.

Madelyn sighed in relief as she peered around the corner of the next street and watched the tourists mingling by the entrance to the Red Square. After two hours of dodging through streets and ducking into shop doorways, trying to look too interested in cheap touristy knick-knacks, she was fairly certain the guard from the library hadn't come after her. Her heart was still beating hard, but the panicked quick breaths had slowed.

"You're fine, everything's fine," she whispered. She smiled at an old man who pointed at some Lenin-shaped figurines, and she politely shook her head and walked away from his shop.

A young man selling food from a cart on the street caught her eye. She dug her travel wallet out and bought a bottle of water and a meat and cheese pie called a *pirozhki*. Her stomach grumbled as she took the pie and inhaled the tasty aroma. She'd been so focused on running she hadn't realized how hungry she was. As she ate, she kept her gaze alert for the guard, even though she was fairly certain he hadn't followed her. Even if he could find out her name from the library system, she hadn't had to supply any other information. The hotel would be a safe zone.

I hope . . .

Madelyn licked her fingertips as she finished the last bite of her *pirozhki*. She crumpled the wrapper of her pie and tossed it in trashcan before she sipped the last of her bottle of water. Then she followed the crowd across a busy street to her hotel. She was still a bit on edge, but if she got into her room, she'd feel more secure.

The hotel was a bit shabby on the outside, with a grey stoned façade. The faux glass windows of the lobby were slightly fogged with age, but she had a budget to live on and couldn't afford anything more expensive. She wasn't sure how long she'd need to stay in Moscow for her Russian dragon research. She would have been lying if she hadn't glanced at some of the more beautiful five star hotels when she'd been making her travel plans. They had taken her breath away with underground pools and fancy suites with endless amenities. It had been fun to dream about them, but she could never stay at a place like that, even for one night—no matter how incredible it would be to live like a princess in a king-sized bed and look out across the city from a deluxe room's balcony.

She pushed the doors to the lobby open and stepped inside. A faint tingling started beneath her skin, the fine hairs rising on her neck and arms in response. The air around her felt charged with energy, like the moment before a storm broke out. Madelyn paused, trying to assess the feeling inside her body as it responded to the sudden change in the air . . . A queer pulsing sensation began to build inside her, and a headache started to beat against her temples. She'd been fine just moments ago . . . Was her fear from earlier just now getting to her and her body was crashing from the adrenaline high she'd been on?

Maybe I just need to go take a quick nap in the room and take some Tylenol.

A man in blue jeans and a dark gray T-shirt was leaning against the wall by the elevators, his head down as he texted on his phone. Was he waiting for an elevator? He hadn't pressed the button . . . Madelyn tried not to look directly at him, as some men viewed it as an invitation. Her backpack was still full with pamphlets her mother had sent her about how to travel safely in Russian alone.

She couldn't help noting his muscled arms and the general attractiveness of his body. When she joined him at the elevator, she glanced down at her shoes, staring at the scuffed black boots peeking out from her own jeans.

A little flush heated her cheeks as she realized how boring she must have looked. Not that she wanted this man's attention. She didn't, but she'd been all too aware in the last week how unremarkable she was. So many women here wore bright sexy clothes or sleek business suits. She didn't fit into either group with her jeans and a cream colored Cashmere sweater. Not to mention she was a bit on the curvy side and Russian women her age were rarely curvy. They all seemed to be rail thin and ready for the runways and catwalks.

The metal elevator doors swished apart. She and the man both entered the tiny metal cubicle and she hit the button for the fourth floor. He continued to text and didn't hit a button.

Maybe we are on the same floor?

The second the doors slid closed her headache got worse. It was like two invisible spikes were being driven into her temples. She leaned against the side of the door farthest from the man, struggling to breathe. It was as though something inside was trying to claw to the surface.

What is happening to me? Fear clouded her rational thoughts. *Am I sick?* Was there something in her water from the vendor? Had she been drugged?

The man lifted his head a few inches, the fall of his brown hair still shadowing most of his features from view. The door opened to her floor and she stared at him. Was this his floor too? He still hadn't pushed a button for a different floor.

Something was wrong. She swallowed and tried to stay calm.

"Excuse me," the man waved her to go. "Please, go first," he said. His voice low and soft with a musical accent.

"Thank you." She took two shaky steps into the corridor before she realized that something was off. He knew she spoke English? How—she turned around to see him getting out of the elevator behind her.

Oh God . . . was he following her? She'd been warned before going to Russia that human trafficking was a risk and she had to be careful. She struggled to find her key, cursing as she walked to her door and trying not to look too panicked. Shooting another glance behind her, she saw the man was walking the opposite way down the hall.

She exhaled and sighed in relief against the door just as her hands closed around her keys. But she was still shaking and her legs were unsteady. The invisible knot of tension inside her was thrumming hard now, and every fiber of her being was on edge. That old instinct to run was whispering at her.

The key stuck in the lock and she had to jiggle the keys

two times before the deadbolt slide back and she was able to get inside. The apartment was dark. Hadn't she left the curtains open? *I know I did . . .*

The door clicked shut behind her and she set her backpack down on small desk. She took a moment to catch her breath, and let the last few seconds of fear subside. She was safe inside her hotel.

I just need to chill. Everything is fine.

Seconds later, the light next to her bed switched on. A man sat in the chair by her bedside table and lowered his hand from the lamp back to the arm rest.

Madelyn jumped, clutching her purse to her chest. Her throat worked but no sounds out. There was a man in her room. *Oh God . . .*

The light washed over his pale gold hair and the three-piece gray wool suit he wore. Her eyes tracked up his expensive shoes to the beautiful, masculine hands resting on the chair's arms. A thick gold ring wound around the little finger of the man's right hand. She squinted at it and then her heart leapt into her throat. The ring was molded into the shape of a serpent biting its own tail. It looked exactly like the ring in James Barrow's book . . .

"Ms. Haynes, we need to talk." The man spoke, his rich accented voice pouring over her like cognac.

She lifted her gaze to the man's face and her heart stopped beating.

It was him.

The man from Barrow's book.

Grigori Barinov. The melancholic look of an ancient king whose time of ruling had long since passed into the mists, like a Russian King Arthur. With blue eyes and blond hair, he was not what one expected of a Russian man. Most of the men she'd seen in Moscow had dark hair and dark eyes. Strength and virility rolled off him in waves with a dominant air of calm and control that came from years of mastering oneself. Something about that made her shiver deep inside.

"Who are you?" she whispered, her voice catching. Had she passed out in the elevator? Was she dreaming? There was no way this was happening.

He couldn't be Grigori Barinov. Grigori was a man who had lived and breathed and died over two hundred years ago. There was no way he could be sitting in her hotel room looking like an intimidating fantasy. She wasn't sure if it was a fantasy born of secret desires or a nightmare. He had broken into her hotel room whoever he was and that wasn't a good thing.

The man reached up to remove the leather bound book from his jacket. *Barrow's journal.*

"I believe you already know who I am." As he spoke his blue eyes seem to turn to yellow, then to red and then they glowed white hot.

"But . . . You . . . It's not . . ." She couldn't wrap her mind around what he was trying to tell her. It was insane. It wasn't possible.

"Possible?" His full, kissable lips curved into a slow cold smile that sent fresh shivers through her.

"How . . ." she struggled for words, picturing the massive dragon perched on the edge of a cliff by a sea.

Her skin was almost on fire now, the pain making her want to scream but she didn't dare move or speak.

"'How' is not a question I will answer, at least not here." He rose from the chair and she stumbled back a step. He was too tall, at least six foot four. So much taller than her own five foot five. His height made her feel too small, too vulnerable. He could easily overpower her if she couldn't find a way to get out of here . . .

His perfectly cut suit molded to his muscled form like a second skin and his throat above his collar was sunkissed. How could he be even slightly tan in the middle of a Russian October?

"Look, I don't want any trouble." She backed up another step, glancing around. She needed to find her phone. It had some international minutes . . . but she had no clue how to call the Russian police. Never in life had she felt so foolish than she did in that moment. Why hadn't she learned how to contact the police? Would it even matter? A panicked despair battled with her determination to survive.

"We are past that, Ms. Haynes. You're a liability now."

A liability? "But I don't even know what was in that book that even matters—" She swallowed hard and took another step, praying she could get to the door, but then she'd have to beat him to the stairs, because the elevator was out of the question.

"Unfortunately *everything* in that book matters. You must come with me," he said, taking another step.

Madelyn tensed, her hand searching for the doorknob behind her. When she found it, she wrapped her fingers around it and turned. The door opened with her body weight against it. Rather than fall into the open hallway, she bumped into something warm and hard.

"Going somewhere, *malen'kiy tsvetok?*" someone said from behind her.

"Ahh!" She screeched but the man behind her grabbed her around the waist with one arm and covered her mouth with his other hand.

"Little flower?" Grigori asked the man behind her.

"She smells sweet," he replied gruffly.

Madelyn screamed against his hand but the sound was muffled. She kicked out her legs, knocking Grigori back a few steps. He clutched his chest and sucked in a breath, then lifted his head, scowling at her. She thrashed in the second man's arms, but there was no getting free. Blood roared in her ears. Grigori's eyes were blazing and he licked his lips before he spoke to the man behind her.

"Do you have her or not?" Grigori growled.

The man holding her tightened his grip and dragged her away from Grigori. How could he be a man from the past?

Grigori's eyes were back to blue, a pure, unfaceted

color that glowed like a lake reflecting the summer sky. Madelyn stared into the blue depths and her limbs became too heavy to move.

"That's it, little one, let go," Grigori breathed, never taking his eyes off her. The hand around her mouth disappeared and yet she didn't scream or cry out. She was lost in his mesmerizing gaze.

"Let your mind go . . ." Grigori's voice wrapped around her, and she suddenly was falling through space and time. As her eyes closed she saw a distant horizon, a memory so old she never knew she had it . . .

The grass was as soft as velvet as she toddled over toward her parents. They were sitting beneath a tall redwood tree. Her father had his back to the tree with his legs spread so her mother could lay back against him in the cradle of his body.

"She's growing so fast," her father said, smiling, but a tinge of sadness colored his gray eyes.

"Not too fast." Her mother held out her arms to Madelyn. "Madelyn, come here."

Her legs wobbled as she walked over the spongy grass. When she reached her mother, the feeling of being warm and safe made her sigh and nuzzle her face in the crook of her mother's neck. Her father circled his arms around them both, holding them in an unbreakable trinity.

"Why can't we stay here?" her mother asked wistfully.

"It's too dangerous. We must keep moving."

Madelyn didn't fully understand the words, not as a child.

She'd only known that they'd meant leaving the sunny fields and ancient redwoods.

"I wish she didn't have to grow up on the run like us." Her mother's voice was soft with quiet grief.

"I know, honey, I know. Maybe someday she won't live in fear as we do."

The memory started to fade and Madelyn sank deeper and deeper into a dreamless sleep, Grigori's face following her into the depths.

"Give her to me." Grigori held out his arms and his brother handed him the unconscious woman. The feel of her completely in his control, made him relax as they left the hotel room. From the moment he'd picked up her scent on Barrow's book earlier that afternoon, he'd been possessed of a wild need to find her. It hadn't helped that once they found her, his brother had been the one to grab and hold onto her. His dragon had hissed softly inside his head.

"How was she able to stay awake for so long?" Rurik asked. "You used to be able to knock out mortals in mere seconds. That took nearly two minutes." He stroked his chin thoughtfully as he eyed the woman in Grigori's arms.

The uneasy thought struck him too. A dragon shifter's gaze could mesmerize and short-circuit a human's mind and knock them out. But the little American woman had simply looked dazed at first. It had taken too long to affect her.

"Something isn't right about her," Rurik muttered as they entered the elevator and rode it down to the lobby. "She makes my skin crawl whenever I get too close. But she smells divine and I just keep thinking about how much I want to take her to my bed . . ." He leaned over and inhaled her scent deeply.

Grigori almost growled at his brother. This was *his* woman, and he had no intention of sharing her. Rurik was a charmer who never slept with the same woman twice. He had no right to bed this singular beauty and move on.

"What you're smelling is her purity."

"Her what?" Rurik crossed his arms, scowling in open confusion.

It was easy to forget sometimes his younger brother was so young compared to him. There were things Rurik didn't know about their other halves, the dragons within.

"She's a virgin. You've probably never been around one of childbearing age. They put off the most enticing sent. It's irresistible . . . to some." He didn't want his brother to know just how intoxicating the scent was to him. Just a hint of it clinging to Barrow's book had captivated him. Now that he held the female in his arms, her aroma enveloping him completely, he was addicted to it.

"A virgin?" Rurik practically choked on the word.

Before either of them could speak, the elevator doors chimed and slid open. They walked through the empty lobby and headed for the sleek black sedan parked outside. Rurik and the driver helped him get Madelyn inside. Only a few people in the streets dared to stare as they left. Most humans knew when to avert their gazes when in the presence of dragons. Some instincts were still strong in them, and they sensed that Grigori and Rurik were not to be trifled with.

The entire ride to Grigori's apartment building he held Madelyn his lap, overcome by a possessive urge to never let her go. She was like a jewel, precious piece of gold that he wanted to secure in a safe haven and guard, even sleeping with one eye open. He smiled as he drank in the sight of her face. She was even lovelier than he'd expected. The glimpse from the security camera photo hadn't done her justice.

"Why are you smiling?" Rurik demanded suspiciously. "You *never* smile."

Despite his frustration with his brother, Grigori didn't stop smiling. "I don't know, I can't seem to stop it. But she's mine. Do you understand? You're not to touch her. Are we clear?"

Rurik's brown eyes blazed to life. "Is that a challenge?" If he had been in his dragon form, the ruffled frill about his neck would have stood up in an opposing way to make him look bigger, fiercer. As a battle dragon, it would have been a deadly warning to anyone save close family.

"It's not a challenge." Grigori returned the warning

with a growl of his own. "She is mine, end of discussion. You have an entire city of women who worship you. You do not need this one."

Rurik huffed, the sound so similar to the disgruntled noise as he made in dragon form that Grigori laughed softly.

"It's not as though I know what to do with a virgin anyway," his brother muttered.

Grigori's smile only widened. Rurik may not know what to do with a virgin, but Grigori definitely did. It had been so long since he had the pleasure of making love to a woman and introducing her to the sensual world that awaited her, but it wasn't something a man forgot.

In that moment, he decided it didn't matter what Madelyn's plans were in regard to James Barrow's book. He would discover that soon enough, but he was going to seduce her and possess her. While he had the strength to force her, he'd never done that to any female. Any man could take a woman's body, but only a master could make them surrender to passion of their own free will. And he wanted Madelyn to surrender to him.

When they arrived at his penthouse, Grigori carried Madelyn to his bedroom and set Barrow's journal on the night stand beside the bed. She was still unconscious and would be for several hours. It would give him time to make arrangements. He was going to take her home, to his house in the country. It was a place he could be himself and not worry about the city or the restraints it placed on his dragon half.

Grigori removed Madelyn's coat and slipped her boots off before he placed a pillow beneath her head. Her hair was soft, like silk beneath his hands as he brushed it away from her face. Even just an innocent touch made his body tense with hunger. He had to regain control.

He retrieved a white mink fur blanket and draped it over Madelyn's sleeping form. Impulsively, he leaned over to brush his lips on hers before he turned off the lights and closed the bedroom door.

"You're acting very strange, brother," Rurik noted. He was leaning back the doorway to the bedroom.

Grigori bristled. "I am not acting any differently." He used the tone that Rurik would recognize as a warning to drop the subject. But Grigori knew he was acting differently. The little human was bringing out old instincts in him, ones he thought he'd mastered long ago.

As the eldest of their family, his duty was the preservation of their lands and its protection. It was also his duty to carry on their line by either finding his true mate or by breeding with an eligible dragoness. He couldn't afford to let himself become entangled with a mortal that would leave him open and vulnerable. The pressure of his duties had left him cool, aloof, and in many ways unchanged over the years. But he was willing to let that part of himself go in order to seduce Madelyn.

"Come into the kitchen with me," Grigori closed the bedroom door and they headed into his kitchen.

His brother trailed a fingertip along the onyx granite countertop. "You aren't considering starting a relationship with a mortal. You know that doesn't end well, at least not unless you promise to keep it to only one night. Let's not forget she was researching the Barrow journal, and the last time I checked, that made her a possible enemy. She could be working for the Brotherhood of the Blood Moon. Or worse . . ." His brother frowned. "She could be working for the Drakors. Better be careful with this one, Grigori. After losing Mikhail, we cannot take any chances."

"I know," Grigori replied, not admitting he was planning more than one night with Madelyn. The last thing he needed was his little brother lecturing him on relationships and not sleeping with the enemy.

Their middle brother, Mikhail . . . The mere thought of his name struck Grigori like a dagger to his heart. His brother was in exile. They didn't know if he was even still alive. The last time he'd seen Mikhail had been two hundred years ago, the year he had returned home and brought James Barrow with him.

We were the fools who spilled our secrets. Barrow had never intended his diary to be their potential downfall, but over the years it simply became a font of knowledge that no one expected to survive the ravages of time.

"Grigori, I know you. You hide in your office, running

the family business and playing the part of a mortal, but you are not. You are the eldest Barinov dragon. You cannot lose yourself to some human female. Even assuming she's not helping to bring us down and destroy our family, she will make you soft and when she's gone . . . It will weaken you. You're acting like she's a possible true mate. Father warned us about mortals," Rurik said.

The mention of their father brought back ancient memories. It was strange to think that their father had only died only two decades ago. It felt as though he'd been gone for a lifetime.

"I remember." He shut his eyes for a brief moment and almost saw his father's face, the stern but loving countenance as he told Grigori and his brothers the rules of dragons. *"Never mate a mortal. When dragons lose their mates, they grieve deeply and don't live much past the moment their mate dies."*

"She isn't my true mate, it's simply her scent that's caught me. But I do plan to seduce her."

Rurik chuckled. "Father said that about mother, you know. He only wanted to seduce her and thought he could resist her being his true mate. They ended up mated for three thousand years."

"But Mother was a Dragoness, not a mortal," Grigori reminded him. He walked over to his stainless steel wine fridge and retrieved a fifty-year-old bottle of Bordeaux and a glass. He reached for second one but his brother interrupted him.

"None for me. I have to head back. The club needs me. Call if the little mortal gives you any trouble."

"She won't." He listened to the sound of his brother's laughter, scowling until he heard the door to his penthouse close.

Then he poured himself a glass of wine, retrieved a book of German poetry by Rainer Maria Rilke, and sat in his favorite chair by the fire place in the center of the room. His fireplace was a circular stone structure two feet tall and was full of glass crystals with flames powered by gas. The sight was intoxicating, like diamonds on fire. Two of his *favorite* things. He tried to lose himself in the poetry and not think about Madelyn asleep in the other room. The scent of her filled his head and made his body throb with an almost violent need, but he kept control. *Barely . . .*

ABOUT THE AUTHOR

Lauren Smith is an Oklahoma attorney by day, author by night who pens adventurous and edgy romance stories by the light of her smart phone flashlight app. She knew she was destined to be a romance writer when she attempted to re-write the entire *Titanic* movie just to save Jack from drowning. Connecting with readers by writing emotionally moving, realistic and sexy romances no matter what time period is her passion. She's won multiple awards in several romance subgenres including: New England Reader's Choice Awards, Greater Detroit BookSeller's Best

Awards, and a Semi-Finalist award for the Mary Wollstonecraft Shelley Award.

To Connect with Lauren, visit her at:
www.laurensmithbooks.com
lauren@laurensmithbooks.com
Facebook Fan Group - Lauren Smith's League
Lauren Smith's Newsletter

Never miss a new release! Follow me in one or more of the ways below!

facebook.com/LaurenDianaSmith

twitter.com/LSmithAuthor

instagram.com/Laurensmithbooks

bookbub.com/authors/lauren-smith

amazon.com/Lauren-Smith/e/B009L54K-TC/ref=sr_tc_2_0?qid=1384012235&sr=1-2-ent